SOME
DAYS
ARE
DARK

SOME DAYS ARE DARK

MIRANDA SMITH

bookouture

Published by Bookouture in 2020

An imprint of Storyfire Ltd.
Carmelite House
50 Victoria Embankment
London EC4Y 0DZ

www.bookouture.com

ISBN: 978-1-83888-220-4
eBook ISBN: 978-1-83888-219-8

Mom—thank you for pushing me to read, encouraging me to write and showing me what it means to be a good mother.

CHAPTER 1

After

I was happy my husband died, but I couldn't admit it, otherwise people might resume saying I killed him. The world, especially the South, labels all types of women. Smart types and dumb types and nurturing types and cold types. For about any situation, there is a type of woman who does or doesn't fit. Some women lack the grit to swat a fly, while more hysterical types are fully capable of shooting their husbands. Apparently, I fall into the second group.

In the eighteen months following the murder, I sat down with three separate camera crews to forever document my life's most trying moments. The first aired on American News Channel, a cut-and-dried case depiction featuring forensic evidence and law enforcement input. No one had to ask me questions. I told producers what they needed to know via Skype. The second program aired on Crime Station, a network dedicated to broadcasting all things murder. It was more salacious due to the reenactments.

The third program was a formal interview with Vanessa Hardgrave, an in-your-face victims' rights advocate who speaks about murder investigations with an almost orgasmic lilt. Soon after the murder, she publicly vilified me, describing my provided timeline as *too convenient*. Until police made an arrest. I received a phone call a few weeks later from her producers requesting an appearance. They made it clear the segment would focus on the injustice of being wrongly accused.

All the episodes were recorded on my DVR. I spent most mornings wrestling my memories into submission, the good ones and the bad. But, as always, boredom crept in, and I decided to rewatch the interviews. Sometimes I needed a reminder that the hardest part of my life was almost over. The Hardgrave interview was my favorite; it provided the platform to tell Vanessa—and the world—my side of the story.

I prepared an omelet and poured a mimosa before returning to the living room and clicking on the television.

"Tonight, on *Vanessa Hardgrave Investigates*," the announcer beamed, "we venture to Whitaker, Tennessee for an exclusive interview with Olivia Miller. Her husband, Dane Miller, was found dead inside their home on July 14, 2018. Investigators initially considered her the prime suspect in her husband's brutal death. We will hear, for the first time, about the painful reality she has lived since the murder."

I fast-forwarded through the opening credits and the inessential introduction Vanessa gives before each show. Jumping out from the blur was my face, patient and calm. I wore a tan pantsuit; Eddy, my lawyer, said it conveyed literal and figurative neutrality. My hair was shorter then, a lighter shade of brunette than it is now. Even though I was in my thirties, the contouring around my features made it hard to tell. I appeared well bred and civilized, a stark contrast to the woman hiding in her living room and drinking alone.

On the screen, I sat across from the weathered interviewer. Vanessa wore a yellow turtleneck and a coral hue stained her lips. She was styled to appear vibrant and approachable. In person, she was neither. I pressed play.

"Let's discuss how life changed in the days after you found your husband dead," she said. Vanessa's voice was annoyingly northern. Vowels stretched thin and consonants overly emphasized. I remembered, when the cameras weren't rolling, her voice sounded much less unique. "When did you first realize the police viewed you as a suspect?"

The camera panned to me.

"Almost immediately. The spouse is always placed under suspicion. Finding the body made the target on my back larger." I appeared confident, my legs crossed and my posture upright. The camera returned to Vanessa, her pixie hairstyle sprayed stiff against her temples.

"Did you feel unfairly targeted?" she asked.

"Not right away. Police walked me through all the procedures. They kept my clothing for DNA analysis and brought me to the station for a formal interview. Of course, I was pretty shaken up. It was stressful, but I wanted to help with the investigation."

"When did the tables turn?"

"A few days after Dane was... after the event, questions took a more accusatory tone. The detectives had issues with my alibi." On screen, I flinched before calmly returning my hands to my lap.

"Where had you been earlier in the night?"

"I was with my ex-husband, Frank," I answered.

Vanessa had wanted a detailed timeline, but Eddy refused to let me speak further. Their tense argument lasted several minutes, but viewers would never know because the exchange was edited out.

"Frank Grier?" Vanessa asked, as though she wasn't already aware of the details.

"Yes." I stared back at her. My eyes lost their brightness as I realized the interview was turning into another interrogation.

"Other than your alibi, what issues posed a concern for police?" she asked.

"They were interested in the state of my marriage. Dane and I had been having problems."

Alone in my living room, I considered how bizarre it was to reveal such personal details to a stranger. Details I might not even share with a friend, if I had any.

"What types of problems?" The woman had no shame. With each question she kept the same, steady gaze.

"Typical disagreements. But we were on track to repairing our marriage." That was a lie.

"Did you have financial issues?" she asked, twirling a pen between her long fingers.

"There were financial stressors, yes."

For the first time on camera, she looked down at her notes. "Because you were married, you were entitled to his life insurance policy. Correct?"

"Yes, I received a substantial amount." I wiggled in my seat, both on camera and presently on my sofa. I got uncomfortable when people presented me with motives for why I must have wanted Dane dead. Like they were trying to convince me I did it.

"According to his policy, you received high six figures," Vanessa said.

"Yes. Substantial." My annoyance with this line of questioning showed.

I laughed watching the moment play back, chomped another morsel of melted cheese and egg.

"I assume this was another reason the police grew suspicious," she continued, adopting a condemnatory voice.

"Yes, Vanessa, it was."

We took a short break in the interview. Vanessa believed I was being too confrontational. She thought I needed to mellow my reactions, which meant a lot coming from her. As the interview progressed, I sensed Vanessa had a vendetta. She wanted to use her journalistic muscle to grill the former prime suspect, probably to spike ratings. She'd cornered me in front of a camera, but she got the narrative wrong. This was my opportunity to tell my story, my truth. Or at least the most flattering version of the truth. Again, what I recalled as several heated interruptions appeared as a seamless second on the screen.

"Life insurance and the imminent dissolution of your marriage weren't the only reasons police were interested in you. Let's talk about your other issues," she began with a hint of professional vengeance.

Let's not, I thought and pressed fast-forward. I didn't stop until I saw Rowe. A grainy mugshot floated closer into the camera's frame. Blond hair and blue eyes. Attractive, even, except his youth was visibly withering away. Editing made the picture look dangerous and worn.

I pressed play.

"Tell us when you first heard the name Marcus Rowe," Vanessa said.

"My lawyer and I were scheduled for yet another conversation with detectives when I received the phone call. I was told our meeting would be postponed because police had come across a new person of interest. Marcus Rowe. They already had him at the station."

On camera, I immediately appeared relieved. We had finally shifted the focus of the interview away from me and toward the person responsible.

"Must have been quite a surprise," Vanessa said, raising her eyebrows.

"It was a relief. After almost three months of being under suspicion, there was a new name in the mix." For the first time during the interview, I smiled sincerely.

"And you had never heard the name before?"

"Never."

Vanessa's voiceover kicked in, narrating a photo collage featuring Rowe:

"Marcus Rowe, a lifelong Whitaker resident, had multiple run-ins with law enforcement on his record. Crimes included trespassing and theft. At the time of Dane Miller's murder, Rowe was estranged from his family, addicted to opioids and homeless.

"In October 2018, Rowe was linked to several robberies across downtown Whitaker. During a routine search, police found suspicious items in Rowe's possession. He was carrying Mr. Miller's wallet and credit cards. This immediately piqued investigators' interests."

A middle-aged man entered the frame. Portly and bald, he wore an ill-fitting suit. The name on the bottom of the screen read Detective Lester Wooley. Someone I'd encountered far too many times in the past eighteen months. I could almost smell the stale coffee on his breath when he spoke.

"Even though he was in his early twenties, Marcus Rowe had a long criminal history. The items in Mr. Rowe's possession provided a direct link to the crime. We asked him where he found the wallet," Wooley said.

"What was his response?" asked Vanessa.

"First, he claimed to have found it in a dumpster by Blue Ridge Mall, a good twenty minutes away from the crime scene. Then he said he stole the wallet from another homeless man he met downtown. When we pressed him to provide a name, he could not."

"What did his change in stories tell you?"

"He was lying." Wooley stared straight ahead, as unamused by Vanessa as I was.

Rowe's mugshot flashed across the screen again. Vanessa's voice read, "Detectives questioned Rowe for hours and uncovered several other inconsistencies. Eventually, Rowe gave them what they needed."

The camera went back to Vanessa interviewing Wooley. Her expression was all shock and surprise. Fakery at its best. "He confessed?" she asked.

"He did," Wooley replied. "He admitted to breaking into Mr. Miller's condo, as he had several homes in the area. He was not expecting anyone to be there. Rowe panicked. Using Mr. Miller's own weapon, he fired two shots at the victim. Killing him."

"You must have been thrilled to get a confession?" Vanessa asked.

"It was important to find justice for Dane Miller," Wooley said, without much enthusiasm. "His family deserved it. He deserved it."

I rolled my eyes. Dane had no family. Only me.

"What about the gun?" she continued.

"Rowe admitted to tossing the gun in a nearby lake," Wooley said. "Dive teams were unable to recover the weapon."

A black screen broke in, words written in bold:

Marcus Rowe later recanted his confession. His court date is set for January 2020. All individuals are considered innocent until proven guilty.

I pressed pause, staring at the sentences. Like previous statements, the words revealed a partial truth. The trial date was accurate, and only a month away. It explained why Dane's memory had weighed heavily in recent weeks, disrupting my sleep and tempting me to drink earlier in the day. Vanessa Hardgrave was merely a dress rehearsal; Eddy and I had spent months practicing for my debut performance in court.

Until proven guilty bothered me the most. I desperately needed Rowe to be convicted if I ever wanted to close this chapter of my life. Staring at *innocent* too long quickened my pulse. I had no particular reason to consider Rowe blameless, but I couldn't ignore the public campaigns professing his innocence.

Your average Crime Station viewer might watch a program at night, forgetting the minutiae by morning. Some viewers become obsessed, creating alternate theories and sharing their findings online with the masses. Sherlock Holmes wannabes posting to Reddit boards and armchair detective websites. I'd even stumbled across a few blogs with threads specifically dedicated to Dane's case. Those contributors didn't say nice things about me. I used to devour every word, but eventually stopped. I could skip over television segments with the press of a button. Once I started reading, it became difficult to breeze past the parts I didn't like.

I pressed play and Vanessa reappeared inside the studio with me.

"How did it feel to learn police had made an arrest?" Vanessa asked.

"It was a big shock," I said, looking genuinely reassured. "After everything: losing Dane, finding the body, being named a suspect… it was all over. They found the guy."

"Of course," Vanessa started again, "this event had lasting repercussions. Losing your husband wasn't the end of your suffering. Tell us about the impact this crime had on your family."

My stomach churned. I turned off the television, practically ran to the kitchen for another drink. The clock read half past three. The combination of bad memories and my inability to work made day drinking a viable option during the week. While participating in the television interviews provided an opportunity to polish my tarnished image, there were also financial incentives. Between those paychecks and Dane's life insurance policy, I'd barely worked in the past eighteen months. At least Dane did something right when he was alive.

After the murder, I tried to continue my photography business. Freelance opportunities didn't arise nearly enough. A bored housewife would stumble upon my website and decide to book a session. Usually a maternity or couples shoot. Upon meeting, some clients recognized my face from the papers. Rowe's arrest didn't completely erase the hesitancy people felt around me; this produced awkward expressions in the photos I took and zero return customers. By following a moderate monthly budget, I could get by without actively working for the foreseeable future. After the trial, I hoped the scandal would quiet enough for me to restart my career.

My phone vibrated, interrupting my defeatist ponderings. I looked at the screen. Farrah. I needed to meet with her eventually, but watching the interview left me drained. I silenced the call. The phone buzzed again a few seconds later and I answered.

"I'm at your front door, buttercup," said the raspy voice on the other end.

I slumped to the door, drink in hand. Her shadow bobbed behind the curtained screen. I admired her persistence.

"Catching you off guard?" she asked when I opened the door.

"What do you mean?"

"Clearly you had no interest in answering my first call."

"I silenced it by mistake," I said, darting my eyes away from her.

She groaned. Her stare traveled from the pajamas on my body to the drink in my hand. "Early in the day for drinking, eh? And I'm guessing it's not your first." She smirked. "Aren't you going to offer me one?"

She wiggled past me, a large handbag in tow. Her naturally pale skin was made darker with bronzer. Her strands were black at the roots and painfully dry at the ends. Confidence blazed her trail. She was Dane's only friend who stayed in contact after what happened.

People wouldn't stay away in the days following Dane's murder. Everyone wanted a piece of the story, a piece of me. As suspicion around me increased, however, attitudes changed. The phone rarely rang, save the occasional anonymous caller shouting "Murderer" into the receiver. Former friends saw me outside the condo and looked on with disdain. No one wanted to be associated with the big, bad husband-killer. Farrah was never one of those friends. She continued to call, and when I wouldn't answer, she dropped by.

"How have things been? You know I get worried when we go too long without speaking." My kitchen was mostly white and gray, with a large island in the middle and four barstools surrounding it. She sprawled across two seats, kicking up her feet. Wherever Farrah went, she owned the place.

"Nothing new to report," I said, pouring her a drink. "And you? What stories do you have to tell?"

"I've got to share my latest predicament," she said, and started rambling about a patron who came into the bar last week.

Farrah worked at Fahrenheit's, one of those joints that had been around since the drinking age was still eighteen. I met her there through Dane. Her life was so colorful, I could never fully retain all her experiences. She never married, although she'd been close a few times. *Bullet dodged*, Farrah would say (before Dane died, of course). Even though she was approaching fifty, Farrah savored being single.

"I worry about you, chickadee. I hate picturing you cooped up in this place alone." Her eyes scanned the living area and stopped on the black sofa in the room's center. I read her mind. *That's where it happened. That's where she found him*. She tried not to look shaken, but it got to her every time. She tilted one chair until it stood on two legs. "You miss him, don't you?"

"Sometimes," I lied.

Farrah never knew how bad things had become between Dane and me. She never knew I was afraid of him. She preferred to envision the happy couple she first met. Despite her aversion to marriage, Farrah played a hopeless romantic when it came to the lives of others. She paused, considering what to say next.

"You never stop loving a person, no matter how long they're gone," she said.

I smiled back. I could never tell her how things really were. How I really felt. There were far more pure forms of love in this world. I had experienced them.

When she seemed satisfied I wasn't on the verge of losing my mind or offing myself, Farrah left. Once the sun set, I did, too. I was more comfortable interacting with the world at night, when there were fewer eyes on me and fewer whispers. Part of my self-induced punishment included staying indoors during the day, but eventually I needed to roam and shake off my loneliness. My night needed to start.

*

Whitaker isn't your typical Tennessee town. It's bigger than Knoxville, smaller than Nashville. The perfect mix of old and new, hip and country. Visitors come for the rock climbing, only a twenty-minute drive from the city center. Locals applaud that our diners offer more than biscuits and gravy to eat. I've never lived anywhere else, besides the outskirts where I grew up. People there are poor and bitter. Like your typical Tennessee town.

Each sector of Whitaker used to have its own style. The health nuts jogging by the river, college students dominating the center, the Old Money millionaires funding their passion projects from atop Tellit Mountain. Families remained in suburbia, unless a festival or holiday lured them to the city streets.

Within the past decade, two major corporations opened Whitaker branches. Hundreds of relocated workers followed, their own cultures and expectations in tow. Thank goodness, otherwise I'd be stuck looking at the same faces, eating the same fried food and listening to the same twangy music. Now when you walk the streets of downtown, the people are as diverse as the businesses. My favorite nail salon was replaced by a sushi restaurant. Across the street a tobacco store transitioned into yet another coffee shop.

Downtown remained in a state of constant change, but Chili's wasn't going anywhere. I pushed past the crowded entryway and sat at the bar. Drinking in the early evening seemed more acceptable when accompanied by dinner.

By the time my appetizer arrived, I'd already locked eyes with another lone diner a few seats over. My relationships had suffered since Dane's death, but not my sex life. My main reason for leaving the condo was to seek companionship, even better if that involved getting laid. It had been over a week since my last hookup, so when the stranger looked at me again, I smiled invitingly. He took the seat next to mine and introduced himself.

"I'm Brock," he said. He looked young, possibly younger than me. He was tall and slim with thick brown hair, which dangled just above his eyebrows. "What's your name?"

"Kelsey," I lied. Dead husbands are a buzzkill, so I preemptively limited any potential familiarity with the case. If someone took the chance to speak with me, it was likely because they didn't know my past, and I wanted to keep it that way.

"Can I get you another drink, Kelsey?" He was excited for an in. He motioned the bartender near and ordered two more bourbons. He scanned the packed dining area. My eyes followed his.

"Thanks for the booze," I said. I downed the shot, loving the burn as it hit my throat.

"Where else is there to go around here?" he asked.

"A few places. Depending on what you're after. Not from Tennessee, I take it?"

"Florida. I get sent this way for work on occasion. You from here?" Instead of throwing back his drink, he took a small sip.

"Born and raised just outside of Whitaker." I didn't care enough to ask about his occupation.

Brock shared his experiences in Whitaker to date, which only partially occupied my attention. His looks, on the other hand, held my full interest. Every few sentences, he'd brush the strands of his shaggy hair away from his face. I pictured how he might look in my bed, how he might feel pressed against my body. By the time I'd finished dinner and several more drinks, I'd decided to have a go with the garrulous stranger.

"Wanna head back to my place?" I asked, slowly raising the glass to my lips. "You can talk more there."

"Sure," he said, sounding both eager and hesitant. He was noticeably less drunk than I was. He grabbed his coat and a stack of notebooks that had been seated on the empty chair next to his.

We bumped into a family exiting the restaurant. The mother gave me a disapproving stare. She could probably smell the booze. I returned the dirty look. *A little late for a school night*, I thought. Brock stumbled close behind me, his hands nervously tucked inside his pockets as we waited for an Uber. I hoped to loosen him up by giving him a playful nudge and lost my balance.

Between the clumsiness and the laughter, I barely noticed the trio of onlookers closing in, trying to get my attention.

"Olivia," said the man.

It was Frank, standing beside me on the sidewalk. His face morphed into disappointment as he registered my public drunkenness. Julie, his new wife, was with him, her politeness cloaking embarrassment.

I saw Jake and my heart broke.

"Hi, Mamma," Jake said. "What are you doing here?"

Frank stood with his hands on our son's shoulders. Fuming.

CHAPTER 2

Before

Suburbia surrounded Whitaker like a pack of beasts inching closer to its life source. Pick a scenic view (lake or mountains) and a location (accessibility to the mall or golf course), and you had two dozen subdivisions jangling keys.

Frank and I bought our three-bedroom, three-bathroom home on Smithwood Avenue shortly after Jake's first birthday. We traded cramped, downtown cohabitation for residential, starter home bliss. Adulting at its finest. It should have taken years to afford the place. Frank's real estate connections helped, and we moved into an enviable Whitaker neighborhood far before our time.

The past year had ushered in many changes. Before we got married, Frank had worked as a real estate agent. His career had evolved from selling homes to improving them. Too many HGTV shows sparked his inspiration. At first, I thought he was being overly ambitious. Frank was right, though. Many Whitaker subdivisions had deteriorated in recent years. Downtown became the desired destination for the influx of worldly hipsters, pushing families and the less-entitled toward the outskirts. Affordable homes were needed. Frank bought his first foreclosure after Jake's birth and recruited his own construction crew to renovate. While his parents could always serve as a safety net should the business fail, Frank hungered for his own success.

My career had also changed. Before Jake was born, I worked as an assistant to Holland McGraw, a high-end wedding photographer in Whitaker. Landing a position with her was like hitting it big on a $5 scratch off. Holland loved hiring country bumpkins like me because she believed it justified her shrill attitude. I left her tyrannical agency during my second trimester, hoping I'd earned enough credentials to start my own photography business by the time Jake got out of diapers. Until then, I was a full-time wife and mother.

Being home with Jake was exactly as I'd imagined it would be, equal parts blissful and terrifying. I grew up in the era when *parent* evolved from a noun into a verb. Mamma had tried with me, but no one would say she excelled at childrearing. She modeled what life choices to avoid, ushering me from one toxic situation to the next.

Her cancer diagnosis was the most permanent aspect of my childhood. The doctors made it clear: there was no running away from this. I loved her, sure. But she was a miserable person. The most responsible thing she'd done was invest in a meager life insurance policy on my behalf. It provided the necessary expenses for my move to Whitaker, twenty minutes on the highway and a world away from the life I'd known. I married Frank, a Tellit Mountain boy with deep pockets and a good heart. And now it was my turn to give mothering a try. I just didn't want to mess it up.

As a family, we eased into our new routine. I wrestled with Jake during the day while Frank logged long shifts at the flip house. In the evenings, we'd stretch out the hours between dinner and bed by sitting on our front porch, admiring our new surroundings. Frank nursed a drink while Jake crawled in the grass. I enjoyed spying on our neighbors, glimpsing a preview of what our own future might hold.

The neighbors to our left were my favorite family to observe. The mother, with her bright eyes and red hair, was hard to miss. Only one kid had her coloring: a boy, who looked to be around six. The baby, a girl, had tight blonde curls like the father. Their evening walks were predictable; I presumed a final effort to release the children's energy before bedtime. They'd wave when they passed, both coming and going. They looked genuinely happy. Frank and I would spy, hypothesize about them and their lives, then we'd carry Jake back inside the house and put him to bed.

"This can't be true," I said, my soapy feet pointing toward Frank's chest at the opposite end of our tub. After a busy week unpacking boxes, we celebrated home ownership with a shared soak in our Jacuzzi bath while Jake slept in his new crib.

"What can't be true?" he asked.

"This house. Jake. You," I mused. "I'm afraid any day now I'm going to wake up."

"Wake up to find out the ugly truth about me? Yeah, I worry about that, too."

We both laughed because there could never be anything ugly about Frank. He supervised our world with meticulous calm. He made sure we never went too many days without a date night, even after the baby arrived. He protected me in a way I had been raised to believe could not exist, and he still took time to rub my sudsy feet.

"You know what I think you are missing?" he asked.

"Tell me," I said, concerned by what he might say next.

"You need friends."

Frank was raised in Whitaker, attended private schools, and came from a family with enough money to solidify any long-term friendships. The way I grew up, everyone fought to be on top. Be the best in the outskirts, you had a better chance of making it in Whitaker. Or anywhere else. Loyal relationships were as far-fetched as unicorns. I learned to worry about myself, not others. He didn't understand how I could be content without companions.

"Jake does a good job of keeping me busy," I said, encouraging him to keep massaging by wiggling my toes. "Besides, I have friends."

"My friends' girlfriends do not count." He lowered his voice and used his hand to spritz me with water.

"Sure they do." I smiled.

Frank's friends were lovely to me. As were their girlfriends, albeit a tad boring. No matter the event, they groomed to perfection, with their wand-created curls and their curler-created lashes. Matching serving dishes housed the chips and salsa. Always homemade, never bottled. I was amazed they received the label of girlfriend, while I had been promoted to wife and mother.

"I want you to be happy here," Frank said, his chestnut eyes staring back at me. "Set down roots."

The magic word. *Roots.* That word led to conversations I'd rather not engage in. Dread dribbled into my brain, fear I couldn't live up to the woman Frank wanted. The familiar sensation of not being enough.

"I am happy here," I said, inching toward him. "And here." I moved closer, until we occupied the same space. "And here." We kissed, and all our future and present thoughts melted away.

*

I struggled to sleep that first week inside the new house. Despite my physical exhaustion from unpacking boxes and chasing after Jake, my mind was too wired to turn off. While Frank slept, I'd sneak to the downstairs office area and paint. Creating art had always been my way of injecting color into an otherwise bland world. Growing up, I couldn't control my surroundings the way I could maneuver the paint on the canvas. Diving into my imagination helped me escape reality.

In another life, I would have attended a pricey art school. Such opportunities weren't awarded by birthright, and I never inherited the dig-deep gusto to create such opportunities. I shifted my focus toward photography, where learning technique was considerably more affordable. But I still enjoyed returning to the canvas, when I had the time.

One night, I stayed up painting well past midnight. Afterwards, I decided to enjoy a hot mug of tea on the front porch and bask in silence, something mothers rarely get to experience. Fireflies flickered above me, a friendly reminder that darkness doesn't always mean bad.

Suddenly, I wasn't alone. A tiny noise, which would have been unnoticeable during the daytime bustle, grabbed my attention like an intercom.

My redheaded neighbor stood at her door, her hair distinct underneath the entryway light. She wore a robe, laughed and nudged a man off the front porch. I expected her husband, all tall and blond and surfer. Instead, I observed his physical opposite. Shorter build, darker skin, no hair. My neighbor offered a farewell embrace, kissed the man in a way people do only when no one is watching. As she turned to re-enter the house, she saw me. She hadn't anticipated an audience. I slid inside, carrying with me the extra weight of a secret.

The next day, my neighbor and the baby appeared on my porch. I'd been feeding Jake in the kitchen and watched her walk up. Frank had yet to return home, and I was tempted to ignore the knock altogether, but her jutted hip and percussing foot suggested she had no intention of letting the incident go unaddressed. Begrudgingly, I opened the door.

"Hello. I'm your neighbor, Maura. And this is Samantha," she said, giving the infant a healthy shake. "We've seen you around the neighborhood. Probably should have come over days ago. I lose track of time with the kids." She smiled. Her beauty was more striking up close.

"I'm Olivia. My husband Frank is out." The awkwardness initiated a stutter. I considered saying we had seen her family around the neighborhood but reassessed. Seeing too much prompted her visit. Her petite frame struggled under the child's weight and my Southern manners kicked in. "Come on inside. Can I get you a drink?"

"Water, please."

I returned to the living room holding two water bottles. Samantha was already seated next to Jake on the carpet. The infants stumbled over each other in pursuit of random toys, their adorability postponing the inevitable discussion.

"I know you saw my visitor last night," Maura said without the slightest hesitation, her voice steady and shameless. She studied my reaction to her blunt segue. The hint of a smile dangled from her lips.

"I was half asleep myself," I said, thumbing the buttons of my cardigan.

She leaned forward, demanding my full attention. "His name is Jim. He's obviously not my husband. My husband is the goofy blond guy stumblin' around with me and the kids in the afternoon."

"Maura, I don't need an explanation—"

"We've lived here a while now," she continued. Maura had clearly rehearsed her response and wanted the opportunity to deliver it in full. "I thought I could predict the comings and goings of everyone on this curb. I was foolish. You have no reason to be loyal to me. But I would hate for gossip to reach my husband."

"What's his name? Your husband." I tried to normalize the scenario. I knew nothing about this woman, yet I also knew her biggest secret.

"Oh, Ronnie. We also have Stevie, the redhead. He's in kindergarten." She smiled again. Samantha let out a spontaneous cry, briefly distracting us both. "We were high school sweethearts, Ronnie and me. He has a fancy bank job I barely understand. Whatever it is keeps him gone half the month. I get lonely sometimes."

"Maura, I didn't see anything worth talking about." She pressed her hand over mine. It felt foreign, touching a person besides Frank. Especially considering the intimate subject matter of the conversation.

"Thank you." Maura did not appear to be a public crier, but tears formed. Her stiff demeanor softening.

"You know, you are the first neighbor to stop by and introduce yourself," I said, trying to ease the awkwardness.

She let out a laugh. "I hate to tell you, but you've moved into a neighborhood of snobs."

Random names and stories rolled off her tongue like a melody. Within minutes, her secret was almost forgotten. Even by me.

Over the months, Maura's plea for silence blossomed into a genuine friendship. She'd come over during Jake's afternoon naps and entertain me with neighborhood gossip. We'd strap the babies into strollers and take evening walks, usually when Ronnie traveled, which was often. We never discussed her late-night visitor.

One night, after Frank and Jake went to bed, I joined Maura on her front porch. Ronnie was out of town again, and I'd promised to keep her company. We sat outside for hours, and eventually too much wine gave me the courage to ask.

"The man at your house," I began, slurring my words just enough so if she took offense, she would interpret me a drunk and not a snoop. "Did he only visit once?"

Her wrist swirled, painting the glass with translucent red circles. "Would you judge me?"

I had never considered judging Maura. Maybe it was the unfamiliarity I had with her situation. It wasn't until we sparked a friendship I realized how often Ronnie was away. I had only been around him a few times, not enough to pity his predicament. Her moral obligation to remain faithful became an afterthought.

"I'm sorry. I shouldn't bring it up," I said.

"I figured it was a matter of time before you asked." She smiled, took a swig of her drink. "I guess now's that time."

"We don't have to talk if it makes you uncomfortable."

"I need to get this off my chest. Would you believe you are the only person who knows my secret?"

That *was* something I believed.

She continued, "He's an old friend. We went to school together." She waited. She was deciding how much to tell me. "It's a harmless fling. We've met up two or three times over the years."

"Does Ronnie know?" I asked.

"Sweet, dumb Ronnie know I'm banging his former baseball teammate?" She laughed. "He's clueless. Hasn't talked to Jimmy since graduation. I make sure not to get involved with his current friends." She had said too much.

"He's not the only one?"

She hesitated. "No, he's not the only one."

"Is there someone else?"

"Not a particular someone. Emotional affairs are complicated."

"So, you sleep around?" And that time it *was* the wine talking. I laughed self-consciously, reached for her hand. "I'm sorry. That sounded bitchy. I don't know anyone who's had an affair. I'm curious."

"I understand," she said, squeezing my hand. "We're not a club that broadcasts our conduct. Anyway, I don't have affairs. Just the casual hookup."

"Hookup? I've not heard that term since college."

"Not sure what else to call it," she said, flipping her hair. "I'm not looking for a boyfriend or romance or anything. Just, fun."

"Fun," I repeated, thrown by how effortlessly she approached the subject.

"I'm coming off cold-hearted. It's not that I don't love Ronnie. I've always loved him, since I was sixteen. Our relationship went through the annoying bullshit all young relationships do. We grew up. I wanted to be with him. And, oh boy, did he want to be with me.

"We've been married eleven years. The early years were as they are meant to be. All love and sex and new experiences. Then, life kept happening. His life did, anyway. Mine became… boring.

Ronnie's the sole provider. That was the plan. All I wanted was to be his wife and raise his family. I never considered how mundane my world would become." She strained for words that would make sense. "When I meet these men, I'm interesting again. I'm sexy. One fling makes the next six months a little less dull."

"Does Ronnie suspect anything?" I asked. I admired Maura's honesty, with me anyway.

"Doubt it. He's certainly never found the nerve to ask me. Best not to confront it. I don't want to hurt him, and I don't want to lose my family." She poured the last of the bottle into her glass, glided back and forth in her rocking chair. "I also don't want to stop."

*

I never told Frank about Maura's visitor because I knew he'd judge her. He wasn't used to the world not being perfect and wasn't as compassionate about people's shortcomings. It was the only detail in my life I never shared with him. Maura needed a friend as much as I did. Her approach to marriage was unorthodox. Cheating didn't tear her relationship apart but helped hold it together. It kept her resentment at bay.

At times, I sensed my own resentment growing. Frank's hours stretched longer in the summer months, making the mundanity my life had become more obvious. When we'd agreed to buy the Smithwood house, we knew the first year would be difficult. Frank's company was still new, and he needed to make enough money to support both the business and our mortgage. But I missed him, and I missed the freedom we'd forfeited in exchange for our suburban zip code.

When I needed a break from routine, Jake and I ventured to the splash pad across town. Jake enjoyed the change in scenery as much as I did. The rubberized turf cushioned his stumbles. He erupted in laughter when the water sprayed at inconsistent intervals, soaking his hair and skin. I walked behind, holding his hands until he grew brave enough to explore on his own. He'd attempt a run and patter through the puddles and streams.

Eighteen-month-olds aren't much for longevity. After playing an hour in the sweltering heat and munching a quick snack, I changed his clothes and loaded him into the car.

"I love you, Jakey," I said, smoothing out his damp hair.

"Ma," he mumbled back. Preliminary words starting to form. These were the moments that mattered. My bond with Jake grew strongest when away from an audience.

I called Frank to tell him we were on our way home.

"Should we meet for dinner?" he asked. We hadn't gone out much since we bought the new house.

"Sure." I gambled Jake wouldn't misbehave. I eyed him in the rearview mirror. The sun bleached his blond hair white and freckles constellated across his cheeks. He let out a mature laugh, reminding me the baby years were almost over. The demanding days behind us.

Crossing the intersection, I looked to my left and saw the truck. Large and industrial with unnecessary speed. Headed right toward us. Hitting us. Spinning us. Dangling us upside down.

After the initial jolt, there was calm. My senses refused to regulate, like waking from a deep sleep under the illusion the next day had arrived, only to realize it hadn't. Burning palms. Wrung neck. Glass—pieces two inches thick—jutted out from my leg. Blood spooled around the tiny daggers. The sun hovered over my face, mockingly.

"Jake," I whispered. A dry voice reanimated from sleep or death. "Jake." This time, a wet scream. My seat belt immobilized me, prevented me from seeing him. Glass pushed deeper into my flesh as I tried to reposition. "Jake!"

And nothing else made sense.

CHAPTER 3

After

It was unfortunate my public display of drunkenness took place the night before a scheduled visitation. I hugged Jake and slurred through a brief conversation with Frank and Julie before the three-some escaped down the street. The man from the bar witnessed the awkward exchange and quickly concocted a reason to return to his hotel. I arrived home alone, embarrassed and stung.

After the divorce, Frank and I shared custody equally, which worked best for Jake. He stayed with me four or five days one week, spent more time at Frank's place the next. Holidays and special events were always agreed upon in advance. We amicably attended preschool functions, Frank and Julie sitting on one side of the plastic bleachers, Dane and I positioned on the other.

After the initial shock, I accepted the transition. An occasional flash of pain surged upon realizing Jake's absence in the mornings, or when Frank would take him for a long weekend and I counted the days until his return. Mommy days and non-Mommy days. On Wednesday, we'd lounge around watching *Mickey Mouse* and eating pancakes, and on Thursday, I'd be dressed up and ready for a night out with Dane. I didn't fall victim to the tedium I experienced during my first marriage.

After the murder, there was the natural concern for Jake's safety. Even I questioned having him in the same home in which my husband—his stepfather—had been murdered. I feared Dane's death might stunt Jake's emotional development, too. Jake was nearly four at the time; he was old enough to realize the disruption to his life yet not fully appreciate the situation's gravity.

The investigation changed everything. I never flaunted the extent to which Dane and I partied before. On nights we didn't have Jake, we were a couple without kids, and behaved as such. We never indulged when Jake was in the house. I wanted to fully enjoy those days we had together. Mommy days.

What Jake—and Frank—didn't know couldn't hurt.

The damned cops. Police examined our finances, which were suspiciously secure given Dane's career in construction and my photography sessions. Despite our stable assets, after examining phone records, police discovered Dane was desperate for money in the days before his death. They also discovered I'd recently withdrawn a large sum from our joint account. I explained to police I was creating a fund for Jake, which was true. But the timing of the withdrawal heightened their doubts.

Attaching these facts to their victimology profile, investigators assumed Dane had earned income through illegal means. Probably selling drugs. They pressed me about Dane's extracurricular activities, and I told them, honestly, I knew little. They tracked down our former friends and assessed we ran with a wild crowd, although nothing concrete connected Dane to narcotics.

Detective Wooley was especially relentless. He had to uncover any and every detail that might lead him to a killer—or a motive. And it was clear, even in the early stages of the investigation, that he wanted the killer to be me. Recreational drug use wasn't his biggest concern, but it was a point of leverage concerning my involvement in the case. He was willing to use whatever he could to secure my cooperation or rattle me until I broke.

I returned to the condo two weeks after Dane died. Everything in my life had changed, and yet the place looked as horrible as it had the night of the murder. Probably worse considering the numerous searches police had conducted. The usually tidy space was disordered with overturned drawers, pieces of broken glass and dried blood smudges on the floor. Forensic teams don't clean up the mess left behind.

Frank showed up that first night unannounced. He had endured yet another conversation with Wooley in which too many specifics about my life with Dane were revealed. Details I had never wanted Frank to know. He confronted me in the living room.

"Police told me they believe you and Dane were using drugs. And they suspect Dane might have been selling," Frank said. The anger in his voice penetrated my soul. His light brown eyes were almost black, filled with contempt. "How could you allow Jake around this mess?"

"Police have no proof Dane sold drugs. And Jake was never around anything illegal," I said. What Dane and I did on the days Jake was away shouldn't have mattered. The police wanted to give Frank reasons to argue with me. They wanted us to turn on each other. "You mean to tell me you don't have a drink on the nights he's with me?"

"A drink is a drink. Drugs? Pills? I thought you weren't taking them anymore—"

"I'm not—"

"Apparently you were when Dane was alive. You associated with known drug dealers!" Frank clenched his jaw and turned away, paced the cluttered living room. Dealing with grimy issues was not a part of Frank's world. His world was either black or white, and he'd already labeled my lifestyle with Dane as wrong.

"Not *real* drug dealers," I tried to explain. It's not like I put Jake in direct danger. I would never do that. "Those were Dane's friends and some of them had pasts. They have nothing to do with my ability to parent."

"You brought drug users into your home, the same home where our son spends half his life. After everything you've put us through…" Tears prevented him from continuing. I hadn't seen him cry since the divorce. "I never imagined you'd do this. I can't believe you would endanger Jake by living this life."

"He wasn't around!" It wasn't fair that the police, and now Frank, were using my behavior away from Jake to label me. I wasn't getting high and passing out around my kid. I'd grown up with that type of parenting, and I'd never allow Jake to suffer the same treatment. Dane and I had fun, but never on the days Jake stayed with us. I was a good parent.

"It doesn't matter," Frank scolded. "This wasn't a single occurrence. You weren't celebrating your fucking birthday. Police told me you and Dane hosted frequent parties where drugs were likely present. For all we know, his drug connections got him killed."

"Dane was not some big-time drug dealer. The cops are exaggerating. You know it."

"Even if they are, you chose to hide a huge portion of your life from me because you knew I would react this way. You know it's not right for Jake."

I didn't want it to be true.

"I will never touch drugs again," I begged. Frank expected me to be perfect when we were married, and now that he knew my faults, he was going to use them as punishment. "Please work with me on this."

"Too late, Olivia. I've talked to a lawyer and we are making an official custody agreement. If you try to interfere, I will make sure all the allegations police presented are addressed in court. And I'll request random drug testing." He pointed his finger with every other word, letting me know this decision was final. "Julie is on board with this. She won't shut up about it, actually."

"Oh, fuck Julie!" I shouted. Jake wasn't her main concern. She had her own reasons to distrust me by then. She wanted me out of the picture. "You know why she doesn't like me. She is not Jake's mom."

"No, she's not. We are both fully aware. But Julie helped raise him while his *real* mom and stepdad were off getting high."

For once, I lacked a rebuttal. Our son deserved better than me—always had. Still, I'd never felt more robbed. Jake was the only good part of my life, and he was being ripped away. Frank left me a sobbing pile of human on my living room floor. Dane's dried bloodstain was so close I could touch it.

Fighting Frank for custody would have been useless. He was a good father with an honest income. And he had Julie. At least he allowed unsupervised visitation. Maybe the new agreement was best for Jake until the trial ended and Dane's case officially closed. But I still hated everyone who contributed in taking him away from me, Dane the most.

Even if Frank wanted to punish me for my behavior last night, he wouldn't push legal and cordial boundaries. Despite the last two years' chaos, Jake loved staying overnight with me, which only happened every other weekend—twelve day breaks in between. The next two days were Mommy days.

*

I was already sitting outside when Frank's truck eased against the curb. Jake skipped toward me moments later. My beautiful four-year-old. The ideal combination of Frank and myself. Olive skin and blue eyes: me. Sandy blond hair and long legs: Frank. His head met my hips when we hugged. I smelled his hair and rubbed his arms, trying to absorb him as much as possible.

"Mamma," he said, holding on tight. "Whatcha got planned this weekend?"

"Fun stuff. Wave goodbye to Dad."

Normally, Frank would walk to the door, indulge in small talk. Instead, he leaned against the car and waved. His disappointment from our chance meeting made known. He didn't stop watching until we walked inside.

"Want to help me make a pizza?" I asked. His favorite. He gave a pitchy squeal and wiggled his fingers in excitement.

I had all the ingredients on display: flour, dough, even a small apron for Jake to wear. In high school, my first job was at a local pizzeria called Brooklyn Bites, although I'm certain none of my co-workers had ever been to New York. We specialized in oversized, greasy pizzas. I enjoyed sprinkling the flour and twisting the doughy mound in the air. Now Jake loved it. The mess spread like wildfire. We damaged the first pizza beyond repair. Thankfully, I'd bought more ingredients to start anew.

We ate on paper plates in front of the TV. There was a new show he wanted to watch. Something about robotic doctors living under the sea. He cuddled me on the sofa and fell asleep too soon. His growing weight sank into my chest, flour fragments dirtied his hair. It looked like snow. I hoped it would snow during a winter visit. Our time together was never enough. Minutes later, I succumbed to sleep.

*

Giving Jake back was always the worst. As Sunday afternoon intruded upon us, the sense of separation returned. For the first time all weekend, no smile marked his face.

"What's wrong, Jake?" I asked. I smiled, transferring the batch of cookies we'd made from the cooling rack into a glass container.

"Nothing." He rolled a toy car along an invisible track. His eyes stayed low.

"You better not be lying to me."

"I miss you, Mamma." Jake put down the car, walked over and hugged me.

I emptied my hands, wrapped my arms around him and squeezed. I felt the sadness in his words, as if they had been snatched from within me. Out of my heart and body, into this sad world I created for him. He was getting older. Picking up on the fact his friends had Mommies and Daddies who lived together. Those families didn't have Julies or Dead Danes. He grieved the normal family he never had.

"I miss you, too," I told him. "But don't you miss Daddy?"

"Daddy is always working," he said. "And Julie cries a lot."

I wanted to know more. "Maybe she's sad."

"She tells Daddy it's just hair moans."

"Hair moans?" I repeated. *Hormones*. Julie is crying because of hormones.

Frank had let slip once Julie wanted to conceive as soon as they got married. That was over a year ago, and she still wasn't pregnant. Maybe she was undergoing treatments? I'd spoken with other women in the past about struggling to conceive. They'd track ovulation charts and plan intercourse. Making a baby is more about science than passion, these days. If she were anyone else, I'd feel sorry for her. Seeing as she was the woman inserting herself into my son's life, I was less sympathetic.

"Jake, you'll be back over here before you know it." I kissed the top of his head. "There is no reason to be sad."

"I know," he said, ambling back to where he'd been playing.

"Besides, we'll be together a ton with Christmas coming up." Frank and I had yet to discuss the holiday schedule. Another painfully long bridge we would soon cross.

"And my birthday?" His grin was wide.

"Especially your birthday. We're already making plans."

He rapped off a list of desired toys until interrupted by a knock at the door. My heavy heart sank further down. I finished putting the cookies in the container and carried them to the front door.

I knew Frank was still angry with me because he'd sent Julie in his place.

"Afternoon, Julie," I said. I welcomed her inside, suddenly aware of the dirty sweater and leggings I was wearing.

"Hello. I'm here to pick up Jake." As if there would be any freaking other reason for her to be here. Julie and I typically engaged in a predictable parent/stepparent repertoire. Except I found her more annoying and she found me trashier.

"Honey, Julie's here. Time to go," I called into the other room.

"Just a minute. Gotta find more stuff."

He had nothing else to pack. He was stalling, and I found it funny. Julie pivoted awkwardly in the entryway. She folded her hands in front.

"Would you like a seat? A drink?" I asked.

"I'm fine, thank you. We need to get going. Busy week ahead." She pursed her lips and avoided eye contact.

"Did you enjoy the weekend alone?" I pried. I imagined my days without Jake were lonelier than Frank and Julie's weekends. They probably took advantage of the time together, planning romantic outings and relaxing evenings.

"It was uneventful. Unlike the other night I'm assuming." Her eyes flickered mean. Highlighted blonde hair, a slender frame and unduly white teeth, Julie was the epitome of a grown-up beauty queen. Though her poise was intentional, a ray of superiority occasionally winked through the cracks. Especially when it came to me.

I ignored the bait and handed her the container of cookies I'd prepared for Jake to take home. "Well, we had an eventful weekend. Baked pizza, made crafts, watched... uh, what's the show called again?" I asked.

"*Aqua Rangers*," yelped Jake from the other room.

"Yes, *Aqua Rangers*. His latest obsession. He watches it constantly," Julie said. I hated the assumption she knew my son better than I did.

"Hopefully not *constantly*," I barked back. "I don't want him turning into some media zombie."

Her uneasiness grew. I'm not sure if it was me, being in the house where Dane died, or a combination. If being at a former crime scene made Farrah uneasy, Julie was about three minutes away from pissing her khaki pants.

Her eyes desperately searched the entryway for anything at which to stare. She didn't want to focus on me, acting unbothered when we both knew she was. Her eyes stopped at the large canvas hanging by the door. It had only been there a month.

"Isn't it nice?" I asked.

"Lovely," she said.

She didn't find it nice or lovely. The picture: Frank, Jake, and me. Back when Jake had recently learned to crawl. If I weren't watching, she'd rip the image off the wall. She didn't like being reminded our family once existed without her.

She smiled that pageant smile. "Jake, time to go," she called.

He finally met us at the door, holding a blanket and a backpack. He danced around my legs like a cat searching for warmth.

"I wish I could stay longer," he said.

"You'll be back here before you know it," I said. "Remember all the stuff we talked about?"

"I can't wait for my birthday." His pitiful eyes momentarily perked up.

"Let's go meet Dad," Julie comforted him, before switching over to a chipper, fake tone. "Thanks for the cookies, Olivia."

They left, and the loneliness returned. The regret. I waited until they were gone, made sure they wouldn't reappear for a forgotten toy, and cried until I no longer could.

*

Hours passed before a knock on the door interrupted my haze. The clock on my nightstand read 7:04 p.m. I'd had more visitors in the past few days than the past two weeks combined. It was annoying to be so socially available.

The pounding continued, this time louder. I pulled on a bathrobe, left my glass and empty wine bottle in the bedroom. Two shadows bobbed behind the front door screen.

"Who's there?" I shouted.

"This is Tina Anchorage from the Whitaker Police Department. I need to speak with Olivia Miller," a voice answered.

Tina. Victims Coordinator, her official title. She was the link between the police and me during Dane's murder investigation. Any new development filtered through her, an extra layer of secrecy attached. I opened the door.

"Olivia, I've been trying to reach you," she said. Elfin in stature and strong in voice, she stood at my door cradling a notebook to her chest. Her former pixie cut now edged past her chin, and her glasses sported thicker rims.

"I've been busy." I had nothing against Tina, but I didn't see the point in staying in contact after Rowe's arrest. I paid Eddy to keep me informed about the case.

"I'm sorry to drop by this late. It is important we speak," she said. "Tonight." A man stood behind her. The approaching night made it hard to see.

"Rowe goes to trial next month," I started. "Eddy and I have been preparing—"

"Olivia, please," she interrupted. "Could we come inside?"

She moved forward, exposing the man I'd only hoped to see on the other side of a Vanessa Hardgrave interview. Detective Wooley. He was round in the middle, with a bald head and wispy facial hair. He chomped on a toothpick, lifted one arm to lean against the doorframe.

"What is he doing here?" I asked.

"He's only here as an escort. Normally I don't visit homes at this hour on a Sunday. As I said, it is urgent."

My memory was fresh. "I won't answer any questions without my lawyer present," I said.

"No one is asking questions tonight," he mumbled.

Tina snapped her head toward him, spun it back to me. "There is news surrounding the trial we need to discuss. Detective Wooley can wait in the car if you'd be more comfortable. May I please come inside?"

I let them both in, pulling my robe sash tighter as if the plush were armor. My face flushed, and I hoped they couldn't smell the wine on my breath. They took the sofa while I sat opposite them on the stone fireplace.

"Thank you for—" said Tina.

"Please," I cut her off, "tell me what I need to know."

"Trust us, we don't want to be here, Olivia." Wooley sounded almost grief-stricken. Far different from the behavior I encountered last year.

"We have unsettling news," Tina said. "Being the next of kin—the only kin—of your late husband, you need to hear this from us. Not from the press."

"Press?" I asked. The local press mostly forgot about me after Rowe's arrest. I wished Whitaker residents would do the same.

"There have been developments in the Marcus Rowe case," Tina said. "The District Attorney's Office will be holding a press conference tomorrow. New evidence has been discovered and the office decided to drop charges."

"Drop charges?" I had followed the case enough to know there was considerable doubt when it came to Rowe's guilt. Not necessarily enough to acquit him, let alone before the trial started. "We're due in court next month."

"His legal team prepared a compelling case. Most recently, they obtained video recordings which feature Rowe, seemingly providing a concrete alibi," she said. "The footage is from a series of ATMs in Georgia on the night Dane was killed. Rowe is seen using multiple stolen cards, none of which belonged to Dane. Facial recognition technology confirms Rowe's on the tape, proving he was nowhere near Whitaker."

"I'm not understanding." So much had happened in the past year, I must be missing something. Why were they reviewing new evidence? And why would they drop charges? "He confessed."

"His confession was unreliable," she said. She pressed her hands against her thighs and straightened her posture.

"They arrested him," I reminded her. I stood and walked closer to the sofa. "He's been sitting in jail for a year."

"Dane's wallet was the only piece of physical evidence tying Rowe to the crime," Tina said. She raised her hands to calm me. "Police never tracked the activity of the other cards found at the time of his arrest, but Rowe's defense team did. He's represented by—"

"Yeah, I know," I interrupted. In recent months, Rowe's case had been taken on by Project Justice, a defense firm committed to exonerating the wrongly accused. They'd reversed nearly a dozen convictions in the past ten years. Their agreement to represent Rowe before his trial even started confirmed he had weighty supporters in his corner.

"The prosecutor's office deemed the evidence legitimate. It would be highly unlikely to gain a conviction," she continued. "The murder charge has been dropped. This means Marcus Rowe could be a free man within a matter of weeks."

"Do they not think he did it? Or is there not enough evidence to prosecute?" Those were two different situations. Turning to Wooley, I asked, "Do you think Rowe did it?"

"No, I don't." He cocked his head to the side and smiled. Of course he didn't. He always thought the killer was me. If Rowe's release led to the case being reopened, he'd have a second chance at proving he was right.

"You arrested Rowe," I reminded him, feeling personally attacked by Wooley. Again. "He confessed."

"Unfortunately, false confessions are a common occurrence in our justice system," Tina said, ending my bickering with Wooley. "There are several factors—look, more information will be revealed at the press conference tomorrow at nine a.m. You are welcome to attend."

The flood of new information blurred my focus. In a matter of weeks, Rowe was supposed to be sentenced. Without a conviction, suspicion would be shifted back toward me.

"This was all settled a year ago," I said.

"Not settled anymore, Olivia," said Wooley, the superior professor with the perfect answer. He didn't look at me when he spoke. His palms pressed together as if in prayer.

"It is rare for the prosecutor's office to drop charges this close to a murder trial," said Tina. She stood, as did Wooley. "This revelation will gain media attention. We wanted you to be warned."

"Then, why? Why are they doing this now?" I asked, my brain trying to find clarity amongst my clouded thoughts. Even though I knew the answer.

Wooley, staring at the floor, shook his head and laughed.

Tina said, "The man sitting in jail for your husband's murder is innocent. That's why."

CHAPTER 4

Before

Silence. The crunch of broken glass and subtle sway of the upended car had disappeared. When I opened my eyes, I was in the hospital. Machines and wires crowded the small space, and a floral curtain divided the room in half. Frank sat next to me, his head in his hands, so stiff I doubted his reality.

"Jake," I said. Frank moved instantly. A call to action.

"Olivia, baby." He never called me *baby*. His face was rubbed red from crying.

"Where is Jake?" I asked, sensing a wave of anxiety rising.

"They've got him in another room running tests. Precautionary stuff. He has a few scrapes, but he's okay." Frank leaned over the bed and kissed my forehead. The relief left my body in a flood of tears.

"What happened to us?" I asked.

"A truck ran a red light and struck your car."

It all came back. The slam, the spin, the roll. The sun above, mocking my uselessness. The glass in my hands. I looked at them, bandaged and flat. I rolled my fingers to make a fist. The pain summoned a domino effect into motion. The jolt in my neck, the burning in my hip. I tried to bend my legs and the left one stared back at me with the same refusal Jake displayed when I fed him mushed green beans.

"Take it easy," Frank said, his hands in front to caution me. I was too fragile to touch, so he didn't. "He's fine. You're fine. We're going to be okay."

My leg was not okay. It needed surgery and six weeks of physical therapy. Frank paused the current flip house renovation to be home as I healed. Maura helped with Jake so much Stevie and Samantha became his surrogate siblings. I lived in the downstairs living room for the duration of my recovery. Our blue sectional became my prison, and I relied on reality television and women's magazines to keep me entertained. I felt like a modern-day Jimmy Stewart waiting on something bad to happen. Much to my displeasure, nothing did.

The only thing worse than the boredom, than the inability to rock Jake to sleep or give him a bath, was the pain. Constant and unforgiving. In the hospital, I could banish away discomfort by pushing a button. Morphine rushed through my veins like a piss in a creek.

I went home with Percocet, which I hated. Lacking the energy to eat, they made me nauseous. At night, I had the most horrible, realistic dreams. The worst: I was back in my old bedroom and pregnant with Jake, my belly swollen. A nurse fiddled with wires and cords, monitoring his heart. A home birth, perhaps? I heard laughter in the next room. Frank and Maura. Mamma was there. Their anticipation was audible through the walls.

The nurse pulled out a needle, equal in length to the one used for my epidural, and started stabbing me. "Just checking the baby," she said, a polite smile plastered across her face. My loved ones ignored my screams. They kept laughing and she kept stabbing. I was still wailing when Frank woke me. He helped me into a sitting position, as I tried to control my breathing.

"What's wrong?" he asked, rubbing his exhausted eyes with his knuckle.

"I had the most awful dream." My eyes brimmed with tears.

Frank kneeled on the ground and leaned against the sofa. "You want me to stay with you?" he asked.

"No," I said, attempting to conceal my fear. When he turned to leave, I stopped him. "Maybe stay a little while."

He made room on the opposite end of the sofa and held me until I drifted back to sleep.

*

I didn't realize how important the pills were until my first day without them. The pain returned in full force. It originated in my leg and slithered up my spine, spreading and thickening like spilled ink. Time slowed. Twenty minutes felt three hours long.

Frank recognized the struggle and overcompensated by controlling my every activity. He attempted to lift me from the bathtub after my first soak in weeks. Water sloshed onto our beige bathroom tile as my healthy leg struggled to find balance. I snapped at him, my body rigid but my tongue sharp.

"I told you I could get out myself," I said. I shivered, still naked, waiting for Frank to hand me a towel. When he did, I covered myself and leaned against the wall, gearing up to move again.

"I can't stand seeing you like this," said Frank. He bent down and dried the floor. "You're hurting too much."

"Seeing it's got to be easier than feeling it," I whined.

He slid my pajamas over my legs, even though I told him to let me. He fluffed my pillows and made sure the remotes were within reach. I knew he was only trying to assist, but when you're in pain, sometimes the effortless helpfulness of another person is enough to make you spit with anger.

"Maybe we could try some more physical therapy," Frank suggested. He sat beside me on the bed. I was still adjusting to being back in the bedroom after my stint on the couch. "My dad might be able to recommend someone."

"Stretching and kneading won't make the pain go away," I said, turning away from him and trying to shift into a comfortable position.

"I'm not—" he started, before changing direction. "Look, the more you push yourself the more you risk setting back your recovery."

I rolled my eyes and sighed. I didn't appreciate a healthy person timing my recovery.

"I know you're trying to help. But I don't need you breaking down the process for me," I said.

"You're the one hurting, but this is hard for me too. I feel so helpless. All I'm trying to do is help." He flopped on the bed, his palms covering his face.

Frank was used to being in control. The accident had taken that control away from him, shifting the focus of our lives away from what he wanted and toward my healing. I know he didn't view it that way, not really. But I was undoubtedly more of an inconvenience to Frank now than I was a month earlier, back when I was spritely and ready to fulfill his every wish.

I struggled to return to normal. I attempted a new activity each day. Finger painting with Jake. Straightening my hair. Any behavior to make me feel more like my old self. I was already doing the activities I typically would throughout the day, just at a slower pace with an increased level of pain. Bed rest and recovery weren't much different from an average day in suburbia.

As the pain skulked away, emptiness returned to fill its place. It took being rammed by a truck to fully realize how much of my life I'd given up in the past year. Moments with Jake, his pudgy fingers rounding my frigid ones, were worth it. But as my recovery dragged, I noticed how mundane my life had become. The routine and predictability. The most important purpose in the world juxtaposed against having no purpose at all.

Originally, the pills aimed all their power at dispersing pain. When there was no longer any pain to fight, the pills filled me. Filled the dissatisfaction burning inside. I was more than pain-free. I was improved. The anxieties muddling my path were no longer obstacles; instead of pushing through them, I hovered above. Floating as if perched atop a cloud.

The euphoric feeling aside, I knew the day would come when I'd no longer have my medicinal backup. I spaced out the time between pills as much as possible. The morning I vowed to not indulge until after lunch was the same morning Jake cut his first molar. He'd been exquisitely irritable, flailing about in a fit and crying so hard his voice crackled. I placed him inside the living room playpen, desiring a break from the constant struggle. He picked up and threw down the same toys that had amused him only a day earlier.

"Damn it, Jake. Can you please stop?" I shouted. It was impractical to reason with a toddler. He couldn't understand my words, but my anger he absorbed in full. He wailed harder. The guilt that washed over me temporarily dominated the pain.

I immediately went to the kitchen and grabbed the orange bottle. Six pills left. I swallowed one and returned to Jake.

"Mommy's sorry," I said. He too had pain, and I was his fix. I calculated how long I could stretch out the last five pills while he slept on my chest.

By the end of the week, I'd made an appointment with my primary physician, Dr. Polar. He ran a long-established practice next to the Westside Country Club and spent his spare weekends swinging clubs with Frank's father. I only had to slightly exaggerate my pain levels to get another prescription, although I understood an unspoken warning that this would be his last order. No longer leaning on meds worried me, but I thought having another focus might smooth the transition.

I returned home and cooked dinner. When I mentioned my newest prescription to Frank, he wasn't pleased.

"I don't want pills to be your only source of relief," he said, shoving steak into his mouth.

"I need to live my life. Take care of Jake." I looked at the steak and salad before me. My knotted stomach couldn't finish the plate.

I topped off my glass of wine, instead. "Eventually, I want to start working again."

"This soon?" I wasn't sure if he meant *soon* after the baby or the accident.

"It's been a year." Over a year, actually. Mamma used to brag to reluctant listeners about waiting tables three weeks after she gave birth. Taking this much time away from work felt extremely privileged.

I had been willing to stop working for Jake's infant years. The thought of sending him to a stranger's house for daycare with a half dozen germy kids bothered me. It didn't upset me to leave Holland's agency. I'd thought when Jake got older I'd start my own business. That's what Frank had done, with my support. With Jake turning two in December, I thought re-entering the workforce might deliver the spark I needed to stop moping.

"Do you plan on applying with agencies?" Frank asked.

"No. I want to freelance and build my own list. I thought about creating a website."

"Okay." His pause spoke caution.

"I would work around your schedule, of course," I offered.

"The flip house will be ready for market next month. Until it sells, I won't be as available around here." His polite way of telling me to stay in my lane.

Frank was a fantastic father but valued his life outside of our household. My sole responsibility was Jake. I handled late-night upsets, permitting Frank to rest. While he met with potential buyers and contractors, I carried the parental slack. Frank could be both a father and provider. A new mother isn't allowed any other titles.

"Focus on healing for now." Frank smiled, but his eyes looked concerned. "Work should be the last thing on your mind."

"Why? Because it means something to me?" My tone was harsh, and Frank seemed caught off guard. The pills made me irritable, worse when the effects diminished. The smallest annoyance, an event that in the past might illicit an eye roll, now made me seethe.

"I wasn't saying that, Olivia. I thought work might cause more stress. If taking pictures makes you happy, do it." He took another bite of his food, defeated.

"I'm sorry. It's been a long day," I said, trying to salvage the conversation. I didn't like taking my frustrations out on Frank. "It's been a long few months."

"I know it has." He put down his fork and looked at Jake, who favored his hands as utensils and now had mashed potatoes between his fingers. Frank smiled, and his tone lightened. "I've actually been wanting to surprise you with something."

"Yeah?"

"What do you hate most about this house?"

Easy. The kitchen. I'm not sure why it is a recurring trend in the South to incorporate natural wood at every turn. There is enough nature outside. Even if you live downtown, forest is only a short drive away.

"The new house has updated appliances," Frank said. "Buyers want stainless steel, though. I considered bringing the old appliances over here. Why not do a whole remodel while we're at it?"

Frank had sold three houses since starting his remodel business. Money was always available from my in-laws, but it was important to Frank that he create a profitable business on his own terms. It was also nice that after years of self-imposed budgeting, we could finally afford nice things. With our own money. Or, at least, Frank's money.

We both also knew, although we wouldn't say, the odds of receiving a substantial settlement stemming from the accident were high. The truck that struck my car belonged to a well-known drink corporation willing to shell out money to avoid bad press. Turns out the driver had been texting. The payout would take a while, but it was coming. A lawyer was already working on the case.

"You're telling me I'm getting my white kitchen?" I beamed.

"I'll have a few guys stop by this week. You can pick out colors, materials. Whatever you want, we'll make it happen." He stood, walked to my side of the table and crouched to kiss my cheek. "And when you're ready to go back to work, I'll support you."

"I know."

That night we made love for the first time since the accident.

*

I wasn't intentionally lying to Frank about taking pills. I'm sure he knew I still took some, but I didn't want the frequency to raise alarm. I didn't expect him to understand: the pills hadn't just improved the person I was after the accident, but the person I was before, too.

I no longer feared being insufficient for Frank and Jake because the pills sharpened my focus. Upkeep wasn't a chore, rather a challenge I eagerly met. I anticipated Jake's needs and better handled his fits. No more feeling tired and bitter when Frank returned home. I was loose and free. The mornings I didn't take a pill were the mornings I snapped at Jake or cursed at Frank or cried for no reason. One pill, and a half hour later, I was back to being Supermom. Capable and happy.

One morning, I waited too long. Frank took extra time before leaving and Jake demanded my constant attention. It was two o'clock before I had the thirty seconds of solitude needed to sneak into the downstairs bathroom and take a pill.

Desperation provoked clumsiness. The lid stuck, and I yanked it so hard the pills pitter-pattered across the tile floor. I hunched to my knees, frantically, and retrieved every last one. Even the ones trying to hide behind the commode. I counted them three times. I envisioned one just beyond reach that Jake might stumble upon. Or that they had fallen into the toilet water, their potency weakening before my eyes. I pondered the possibility. What would I do in that situation? Call in another prescription. Explain. Accidents *do* happen.

I escorted truth into the realm of pretense. I called Dr. Polar's office, explained more than half my pills had fallen into the bath. And so soon after I'd refilled, too. The receptionist on the phone knew me, always commented on Jake's curly hair. She promised to see what she could do, although her voice stalled.

The next morning, the receptionist called to say my new prescription would be ready by noon, and while I begrudged my lie, I enjoyed the security in knowing it would be a month longer before I would run out of pills.

When I returned from the pharmacy, I noticed Maura rocking on her front porch. We hadn't talked as much in recent weeks, and I felt guilty considering how helpful she had been after the accident.

"Hey, stranger," she hollered, sipping from a mason jar of (likely spiked) tea. Her red hair was tied up in a bun, and she wore spandex leggings and a tight V-neck top. "There's been heavy foot traffic over there today."

"We renovate the kitchen next week," I said. I held several grocery bags in my hands, hoping Maura would take the hint I wasn't available for a lengthy discussion.

"I'm jealous," she said. I didn't think that was true. Maura was very much living her best life. She balanced her responsibilities and desires, and still had time to drink midday on the porch.

"Don't be," I said, smiling. "Your kitchen is gorgeous. Our new one probably won't compete."

"New is always nice," she said, taking another swig of tea. "Let's get together soon."

"Definitely," I said, hurrying into the house to hide my pills before Frank arrived home.

*

Our shit-brown cabinets' innards were strewn about the living room. We'd placed baby gates around everything to protect Jake and made peace with the clutter until the kitchen was complete.

Frank had assembled more than ten people to assist with his business. He spared two, sending them over to install the new cabinets. He was too busy overseeing the flip house remodel to participate in our own. Jake napped after a difficult morning. I held my breath, hoping he wouldn't wake up when I transferred him from my arms to his stiff mattress. He rolled over and slowly palmed the downy blanket beneath him. I smiled, reminded how in between the moments of sleeplessness and stress, parenting provided moments of overwhelming love and peace.

I crept out of his room and gently shut the door. He needed rest, and I did, too. I didn't even have time to brush my teeth between his demands and the workers' intrusiveness. In the living room, I rummaged through the box that housed the contents of the obligatory kitchen junk drawer. That's where I'd last put my pills. I'd counted them the night before. Eighteen pills remained, which gave me nine or ten days before I'd be out.

The pills were gone.

I looked on the floor, under the box. The box under the box. I ran to the guest bathroom and searched the medicine cabinet. Then our bathroom cabinets, in case Frank had moved them without telling me. Then back to the junk drawer box. Nothing.

My fingers hurried to type in Frank's cell number. "Did you move my pills?" I asked.

"What pills?" He sounded confused.

"You know what pills. My pain pills." My volume alerted the workers' attention, who promptly returned to measuring and sanding in an attempt not to pry. I exited our disorderly living room and moved to the backyard.

"I can't remember the last time I've seen them," Frank said.

"Are you lying to me?" In a house with two adults, one of them had to know where they were. And I definitely didn't know.

"Lying to you?" He sounded both confused and hurt. "Olivia, why would I lie about moving your stuff?"

"I don't know. Maybe it's your need to control my life." I knew what he would say next. He didn't control me. I was overreacting. The pills were too important if I was behaving this way.

"I'm at work," he said. "We'll talk tonight." He hung up.

I resented the conversation to come. Maybe I *was* being irrational and placing too much emphasis on the pills and their magic ability to calm me. My skin flushed, and I was on the verge of tears. The sun beat down on me as it did the day of the accident. Menacing.

"Excuse me." A voice from behind brought me back to the present. I turned like I'd been caught doing something bad.

"Yes?" A bitter tone attached to the word's end. It was one of Frank's workers. He was slim with a beard, a bulky bag slung over his right shoulder.

"We're packing up for the day," he said, pulling on the strap of his bag. "We won't fit the new cabinets until tomorrow."

"Wonderful." I averted my eyes to hide the tears. "Thank you."

"I think you'll be happy with the finished product. Frank's told us to make it perfect," he continued. "He's a good boss. A good guy."

"Yes. He is." Shame fell over me as I worried what the workers might have overheard.

"He told me about your accident. Said it's been a hard road for you."

"Things are getting easier," I lied. Life had never been easy, and it was only getting worse.

"One day at a time, they say," the man said, tapping the cement with his boot. "I hurt my back on the job once. Not working for Frank, though."

"Sorry to hear." I brushed by him to re-enter the house. He moved closer to block me.

"I've got an extra pill if you want one. I couldn't do this work without something." His voice was a whisper. "I know how hard it is to deal with chronic pain."

He reached in his front pocket, pulled out a yellow pill and placed it into my palm. His hands felt calloused and rough. I stared at him in bewilderment. Was this a trick? A godsend? All that mattered was he had what I needed and wanted desperately.

I didn't know what to say other than, "Thank you."

"Don't mention it. And *please* don't mention it to Frank," the man said. "I wouldn't want him to get the wrong idea. I felt sorry for you in there, is all."

The pill had already traveled from my tongue down into my throat.

"I won't. Thank you, again." I turned before opening the door. "My name is Olivia, by the way."

"I'm Dane," he said, his grimy hand forming into a delicate wave.

CHAPTER 5

After

"No one could have predicted this, Olivia," Eddy repeated, a whoosh of defeat in his voice. I called a mere three minutes after Wooley and Tina left to berate him for not reaching out sooner.

My transition from grieving wife to suspect to vindicated scapegoat single-handedly built Eddy Fetzer's defense firm. Despite only having argued a handful of cases before mine, he adequately minimized my interaction with investigators and developed strategies for keeping me out of prison should the situation worsen. After Rowe's arrest, every drug dealer and car thief within a sixty-mile radius wanted the lawyer who represented *that dead guy's wife*. The publicity padded his client list and allowed him to erect a billboard on Highway 129, a route I now avoided.

Our relationship had curdled ever since I agreed to partake in the television interviews. He insisted my participation was a bad idea, heresy coming from a first-class camera hog like himself. I knew I would need the money in the future and overruled his advice. Although he disapproved, he committed to attending all tapings. In recent months, he'd check in biweekly to prepare my upcoming testimony and provide updates about the case.

"I just don't understand how this is happening so close to trial," I said, gnawing the cuticles of my free hand. I stood in the kitchen, fighting the urge to pour another drink. "And how did you not know about this sooner? I pay you to keep me in the loop."

"I found out the same time you did, possibly after. Trust me, the prosecutor's office kept recent developments under wraps."

"They've been building a case against him for a year. Why would they drop charges now?"

"Come on, Olivia. We talked about this. No one buys Rowe's confession. He was a homeless drug addict put under extreme pressure and he cracked. He would have admitted to killing his own mother."

"Whatever." I never wanted to believe there was truth to what people said about Rowe. He confessed. Even people without stacks of evidence against them can commit crimes.

"Why not just go through with a trial? Allow a jury to decide whether he did it?" I asked.

"From what I've been told, the video evidence is compelling and facial recognition confirms Rowe's identity," Eddy said. "Prosecutors rarely backtrack, but they'd rather admit wrongdoing now than end up with a Netflix documentary devoted to their screw-up ten years after conviction."

"How honorable." I rolled my eyes, deciding the *justice* system needed a new name.

"There is honor in doing what's right, Olivia. But ego is also involved." Eddy chuckled. "I know the D.A. is grinding his teeth in preparation for tomorrow's announcement."

"Tina told me I should attend the press conference." I tasted blood from where I'd bit too deep into my thumb. I envisioned the courthouse, hounded by memories of Rowe's arraignment. I wasn't supposed to re-enter the facility until the trial securing his conviction. A day never to come. "I just don't think I can go, Eddy. The idea of being surrounded by the same people who suspected me is suffocating."

"Consider attending Rowe's defense team's press conference. They'll provide more information than the D.A."

"Project Justice will be speaking?" I yelped.

"Ah, you have been following the case. I assumed you only cared about your own small-screen close-ups," he sniggered. "Yeah, they've booked a conference room at one of the hotels downtown. I'll send you the details, if you want to come."

"Maybe." I hung up, trying to decide the best course of action. I knew what I needed to do, but a large part of me had already started celebrating the end of this chapter. Knowing it was reopening felt like receiving an invitation to my own funeral.

I never gave Rowe much thought after his arrest. He was the addict who broke into our condo and murdered my husband. I easily could have been his second victim had I been home. He possessed Dane's credit card. He confessed. If anything, I was thankful, and not only because he had eliminated Dane's threatening presence in my life. Until his name entered the arena, police targeted me.

I grabbed my computer to search possible information leaks. Wooley and Tina were right; news about the dropped charges did not yet exist online. Upon googling his name, I revisited multiple forums advocating that Rowe's arrest was a classic abuse of the criminal justice system. The mission statement behind one website read:

On November 5, 2018, Marcus Rowe was arrested for the second-degree murder of Dane Miller. Miller was killed in his home on July 14, 2018. Weak circumstantial evidence and a coerced confession were the only details tying Rowe to this heinous crime. Our website is dedicated to raising awareness about the faulty police practices used in this case in hopes of preventing an innocent man, Marcus Rowe, from being convicted.

I'd avoided these websites for months. I didn't need reminding that a portion of the public believed I was a likelier suspect than Rowe. But now I needed to see what people were saying, what ideas could have possibly contributed to his release. Further reading revealed online sleuths knew more about the case than I had ever been told by investigators.

SpyGirl0405: *Rowe was held for questioning for more than 16 hours. By the time he confessed, his withdrawal (heroin?) kicked in and he became reckless. Any detective with half a brain knows you can't retrieve an actual confession under those circumstances!*

GetEm: *Boys in blue don't want the truth. They want a closed case.*

CrimeFighta: *@SpyGirl0405 Don't forget the fact he was starving! Police approached him for stealing merchandise from an outdoor food vendor. He had been living on the streets! He was not provided food or allowed sleep while held for questioning. As soon as he fessed up, detectives brought him a fresh meal. No wonder he was willing to confess.*

NancyDo: *Rowe claimed to have found the wallet inside a dumpster in an area he was known to frequent. Police found this explanation "laughable". He was homeless! Homeless people tend to wander! And rummage through dumpsters!*

DetectiveStone: *Anyone seen the clips from the Vanessa Hardgrave special? Those cops did everything in their power to confuse him. And that's just in the clips the corrupt police department would allow on TV.*

I'd examined the interview multiple times. I scrolled my DVR and fast-forwarded to the interrogation clips. No color and unfocused, the camera captured routine questioning.

An investigator asked, "Where'd you get the wallet?"

"A dumpster by the mall," Rowe answered, his head low and his shoulders hunched.

Again, the same question: "Where'd you find the wallet?"

"I already told you. Near the dumpster," he slurred.

"Was it in the dumpster or near it?"

"In it," said Rowe, clenching his fists and thumping the aluminum table.

"I thought you said it was near the dumpster," said the investigator, tone elevated.

Watching Rowe, clearly agitated, repeatedly answer the same question made my head ache. I couldn't imagine enduring such anguish for sixteen hours. Occasionally, Rowe pulled his hair or slammed his arm against the wall. Before I'd labeled him deranged. Now, I saw a broken man longing for a conclusion to this invasive cycle.

I returned to the forums.

DaTruth: *We must accept we live in a society willing to point the finger at the underprivileged for public gain. Whitaker wanted the case solved so they could continue perpetuating the "safe community" mantra they desperately needed homebuyers and business owners to believe. If an underling like Marcus Rowe takes the fall, oh well. That's the world's take on it. #SoSad*

WhitakerGal: *I went to school with Marcus. I can't make excuses for where he ended up, but I will say the boy I knew would never grab a stranger's gun and shoot them. If anything, he'd run scared.*

DetectiveStone: *Criminal record does not = violent history. Rowe broke into homes to buy food and drugs. Never a violent offender. But all you see in the media: "Known Criminal Kills Whitaker Resident." #WarpedMedia*

A bizarre wave swarmed inside me. Anticipation? Curiosity? Fear? I poured a drink, forfeiting any notions of sleep.

*

Hotels sprouted up in downtown Whitaker like dandelions through cracks. A new one was always being built, each with larger square footage and a more recognizable name. Project Justice held their conference in the newest construction. Eddy waited at the entrance, fidgeting and squirming with the expectancy of a Roman before a Colosseum-style bloodbath. This was his realm, his entertainment.

Inside the conference room, the daisy-shaded walls reeked of paint and bleach. Most of the press had yet to arrive. Eddy and I found seats on the back row. Swaying in the far corner, nervously, stood Wooley. His eyes occasionally darted in my direction.

"How did the first press conference go?" I asked Eddy.

"As I predicted." He unrolled a cylinder of mints and popped one in his mouth. "The D.A. announced the felony charges have been dropped and showed the ATM video clips."

"Nothing else?"

"He didn't answer questions because he said Dane's murder is now considered an *open investigation*." His voice chirped mockingly at the last part.

"Great." My ass sunk lower into the stiff fabric.

"I want to warn you again," said Eddie. "Multiple issues involving the case will be addressed. If you feel upset—"

"I'm not going to get upset," I snapped. "If I get bored, I know where the exit is."

He closed his eyes and scowled. Regardless of my position as the poster child for his law firm, Eddie grew irritated when I refused to play along. He wanted to hold my hand, whisper reassurances, follow me from the room after an emotional outburst. All the customary things good lawyers do before mailing out that month's invoice.

The chairs closest to the front filled with various media representatives. Most people in my predicament resent their vulturine thirst for information. I equate the press to streetwalkers. Both traffic in the most intimate parts of a person to pay the bills. In that regard, Vanessa Hardgrave is a high-end escort, no better than Wanda McGee on Channel 6, just with improved packaging. I get it. That's why it didn't chip away at my soul to participate in the television interviews. I shy away from the press now, frankly, because I'm no longer in the mood.

"Here comes the Big Dog," Eddie said, nudging my ribs and nodding toward the entrance. A woman, tall with silver hair, walked to the podium. Her posse followed, carrying boxes and bags and laptops. They started assembling and plugging with the conditioned routine of a band's road crew.

"Who is she?" I asked.

"Eleanor Baker. She founded Project Justice."

Eleanor approached the table with much more purpose and grace than her minions. They wore cheap, lint-ridden pantsuits, while she modeled a tailored off-white jacket with black high-waisted pants. Gold necklaces in varying lengths draped around her neck, the longest strand nearing her belt. Her hair bounced from a fresh blowout. She oozed professionalism. She oozed money, too. And not in the flashy, porcelain veneer way Eddy did.

Eleanor exchanged words with her aides, finalizing her script before showtime. She turned to retrieve a compact from her bag and we locked eyes. A moment of recognition. She must have memorized my face during her research. In an instant she returned to her underlings. Before she broke eye contact, she smirked.

*

"Good morning," Eleanor addressed the audience. "My name is Eleanor Baker and I established Project Justice. Many of you already know the Whitaker District Attorney's Office have decided to drop the murder charge against my client. I have two statements to present."

She unfolded the paper in her hands with deferred delicacy, paused. "The first statement is from Marcus. It says, 'I prayed I would be released, but feared it would never actually happen. I thank Project Justice for finding the evidence needed to prove my innocence. I would also like to thank the many, many people who wrote letters or contacted my family. Knowing there were people who believed my story gave me hope. I will be home soon! God bless you all.'"

"Rowe's a real wordsmith, huh?" I whispered to Eddy.

"Shh," he hissed back. He was captivated by Eleanor's celebrity and poise.

She shifted papers and hummed her throat before speaking again. "Project Justice began representing Marcus Rowe six months ago. We agreed to work on his case pro bono, enjoying the rare opportunity to represent a client *before* they are wrongfully convicted."

I poked Eddy in the stomach. "Her fancy firm represented Rowe for free?"

"Guess so," he said, never taking his eyes away from the podium. "Publicity will pay her back in full. She'll be referencing Rowe for years to come."

"Marcus was arrested for stealing food from an outdoor vendor," Eleanor continued. "Upon searching his belongings, police discovered Dane Miller's wallet. This established the one and only piece of physical evidence connecting Marcus to the crime. While possessing a murdered man's wallet appears damning, the other numerous items found at the time of his arrest were never considered. This included twenty-six other ATM cards belonging to various cardholders, none of whom had any connection to Marcus, or Mr. Miller.

"In his original statement to police, Marcus admitted to stealing wallets and scavenging dumpsters. It is our belief whoever killed Mr. Miller discarded his belongings and Marcus Rowe discovered them days, possibly even a week after the crime."

She raised her water and sipped, rouge lipstick stamping the glass. As though cued, a nearby associate fiddled with wires and lowered a white projection screen.

"Yes, Marcus Rowe confessed to killing Mr. Miller," Eleanor continued. "He must have done it, right? People don't confess to crimes they did not commit." Her masterfully rehearsed monologue addressed all the minds and cameras in the room.

"Research conducted in the past two decades has completely refuted this claim," she said. "DNA has exonerated many wrongfully convicted individuals. Astoundingly, a large percentage of those convictions had been impacted by the person's own confession."

A dramatic pause interrupted her speech. She studied the floor as though searching for the appropriate words, although clearly her presentation had been strategized. Every word. Every pause. Every point.

"Police coercion," she continued. "Mental incapability on the defendant's behalf. Fear of a harsher punishment. These factors contribute to a false confession. And all these elements existed in Marcus Rowe's case."

Her slender hands, tipped by blood-red nails, clicked a controller. The screen displayed Rowe inside the interview room.

She hit another button and an unknown detective's voice took over: "When did you arrive at Mr. Miller's home?"

"I've never been there," answered Rowe.

"You broke into a place three blocks away last month," said the voice.

"Yeah. So?" challenged Rowe, unaware of how critical this exchange would be in determining his future.

"So, you have been there," the voice decided.

The video rolled at a faster pace as Eleanor spoke. "Viewing these tapes is what inspired my firm to support Marcus Rowe. The entire sixteen-hour interrogation is grueling to watch." She read from a legal pad, although each statistic must have been committed to memory by now. "In the first fourteen hours and thirty-two minutes, Marcus Rowe denied harming Mr. Miller fifty-seven times. He denied knowing him. He denied being in his home. And yet, detectives continue to harass him. They yell at him. Physically intimidate him. Remind him killers who don't cooperate are more often sentenced to lethal injection."

The tape froze on an image of a detective, not Wooley or anyone familiar, out of his seat and yelling in Rowe's face. Rowe cowered beneath him, attitude defeated. I imagined his fear, his desperation for the questioning to end, his desire for one more hit of a drug.

"Finally, after all this," she continued, "it took less than ninety minutes for my client to verbally confess, for another officer to write his confession and for Marcus to sign his name—his signature so shaky, it's impossible to know if he suffered pure exhaustion, opioid withdrawal or a combination.

"When Project Justice agreed to represent Marcus Rowe, our initial objective was to determine his whereabouts on the night Mr. Miller died. We decided to review evidence officers had overlooked in their initial investigation. We tracked the activity of the other twenty-six cards found alongside Mr. Miller's wallet at the time of Marcus' arrest."

Pixelated grays colored the projection screen, revealing a man's torso and two hands fidgeting with something beyond the camera's gaze. The left corner time-stamped the video: 7/14/18, 11:07 p.m. A second clip, much clearer, appeared. The person's face was not visible, although the gait was reminiscent of Rowe. Time stamped: 7/14/18, 11:35 p.m.

The third camera centered on the ATM user's face revealed, unmistakably, Rowe. Time stamped: 7/14/18, 11:52 p.m. The fourth recording shared its predecessor's clarity. Rowe trying, without luck, to access money. Time stamped: 7/15/18, 12:33 a.m.

"As you can see," she continued, "the last two tapes show a clear image of the individual at the ATM. Facial recognition technology confirmed the person is Marcus Rowe. All four ATMs are in Ruthers, GA. A, what might you say? A hop, skip and a jump away from here?"

She sliced the tension with a presumptuous giggle. A few charmed members of the press joined in apprehensively.

"According to the timeline, there is no possible way Marcus Rowe could be in Whitaker around midnight when Mr. Miller was killed," Eleanor said. "Now, Mr. Miller's card was not used in any of this footage. Marcus Rowe would not have yet had access to it. Because investigators were eager for an arrest, they did not properly evaluate the importance of the other cards found in Rowe's possession. While we considered withholding evidence until trial, we shared our findings with the prosecutor's office in hopes they would drop charges. Thankfully, they agreed."

She took another sip from her water glass while her assistants audibly celebrated.

"What do you think?" I asked Eddy.

"Solid investigating. I agree with the decision to drop charges," he said.

"There's no way it could be Rowe, huh?" I asked, still hopeful.

"The ATM compilation we watched serves as Rowe's get-out-of-jail-free card."

"I will answer a few questions from the press," Eleanor announced.

Cameras clicked, and hands filled the air, although not in the chaotic swarm portrayed on TV. A methodical calm fogged the room.

"When will Rowe be released?" asked a female reporter I recognized from the nightly news.

"Hopefully, later this week," Eleanor answered. "We have a few legal loopholes to jump through."

"Where will investigators go from here?" asked another voice.

"I don't want to speculate," Eleanor said, slowing her movements like a shark lunging for a final bite. "However, I will say, Marcus

Rowe had no reason to harm Mr. Miller. He did not know him. He did not enter his home. He was not even in the area when the murder occurred, as the ATM video has now confirmed. Yet people who knew the victim possessed numerous motives, including financial gain."

Oh, shit. Eddy's heaving shoulders signaled he too felt anxious. I appreciated the momentary satisfaction of watching him sweat, although at my expense.

Eleanor provided a list of possible culprits. She addressed Dane's alleged connections to the drug trade and the lowlife crowd we used to associate with. *Don't say it,* I thought. *Don't say it.*

"Also, his wife was considered the primary suspect before Marcus Rowe's arrest…" Eleanor started. Her voice echoed, but I no longer processed her words. I drifted away, detached as best I could from the situation around me. A situation I had already barely survived. A fight I was not ready to take on again.

Uniformed officers barricaded the conference room exit. Leaving spontaneously would only invite further attention, but I couldn't take being there anymore. Eleanor had mentioned me, and as soon as she left the platform, reporters would pounce.

"I'm going to head out before anyone sees me," I whispered to Eddy.

"They know you're here, Olivia," Eddy said, protectively eyeing reporters near the podium.

"All the more reason to leave," I said, slinging my purse across my body. "Interfere if they come after me, okay?"

"Will do." He gave a quick nod. "Expect a phone call in the next couple of days."

I anchored my head low and made my way toward the door. We were wise to sit on the back row. I wiggled past a pair of chatting cops and made it into the lobby before I heard my name. Glancing over my shoulder I saw a gang of reporters trailing my exit. Eddy soon appeared, offering a neutral comment in exchange for camera time. The interference bought me a few more minutes. The sooner I could get away from the police and the press, the better.

Once in the parking lot, I picked up pace. The weather had dipped severely into winter. Leaves rustled around my feet and I tightened my coat to brace the wind. I savored the renewing sensation of iced air entering my lungs.

A man wearing a leather coat leaned against the car parked next to mine. He pecked at his phone with such intent that he fumbled the device as I approached. It was impossible to open my car door without disturbing him.

"Excuse me," I said, without making eye contact.

"No problem, miss." He moved away from the car before circling back. "Say, you're Olivia Miller. I'm Jack Kingston from the *Whitaker Weekly Press*. How'd it go in there?"

"No comment," I said, plopping into the driver's seat and shutting the door.

In my attempts to avoid him, I dropped my keys. He reached inside his jacket to retrieve a notepad and pen.

"Hey, I get you want your privacy and all. But a guy's gotta work, you know? You think I could get one comment?"

My body contorted awkwardly to reach the keys just beyond the gas pedal. By the time I cranked the ignition, a miniature horde of press members had assembled in the parking lot.

Not wanting to draw the attention of other reporters, he bent down and spoke through the driver's side window. "Say, if you don't feel like talking now, I get it," he said. "Do you have the same phone number? How about email?"

I yanked the gear into reverse and sped out of the parking lot. My pulse pounded and didn't slow until I had departed downtown.

CHAPTER 6

Before

Frank returned home from work sooner than expected. In the early days of our relationship, I'd rejoice at the opportunity to spend more time with him. But given our argument about my misplaced pills, I prepared for war.

"Why would you accuse me of hiding your medicine?" he demanded. He took off his jacket and slung it on the bed. Jake was already asleep, and even though I'd climbed in bed early, I knew there was no avoiding the conversation Frank had been gearing up to have.

"I couldn't find them," I explained, casually. "It was the first place my mind went."

"Your first thought was that I must have hidden the pills? Something's wrong here, Olivia." He was exasperated, trying desperately to solve the puzzle of our weakening marriage. He sat down on the bed and steadied his elbows on his knees.

"It's my fault," I apologized. "I freaked out and I'm sorry." *Please just let this go away*, I thought.

"You say the pills are not a problem for you. And I want to believe you." He turned to look at me. His eyes were glossy and tired. "But losing a few pills shouldn't lead to a meltdown."

"I overreacted." I couldn't allow Frank to see how desperate I really was, so I scrambled alternative excuses to end our argument. "You don't know how draining it is to be here all day. Dealing with the pain. Dealing with Jake. Sometimes the tiniest problem makes me lose it."

"I get it. I really do." He paused to consider all the pieces and the best way to make them fit. His hand touched mine for the first time since he'd been home. "But I don't see why you're taking pills without telling me."

"I told you I'm still in pain." I shoved his hand. "Don't make it sound like I have something to hide." That wasn't necessarily true, and I resented that I was now lying to Frank. He left the room, and I heard the backyard door shut. I looked outside our window and could see Frank was lighting the fire pit. I crawled into bed but had too much on my mind to sleep. It wasn't like me to hide things from him.

I thought back to what life was like before we met. I had been struggling to make ends meet by working as a photography assistant to Holland McGraw. Six months into my employment, we booked the Hopkins/Straight nuptials. Holland and I had been onsite for hours by the time the reception started. I was tired of adjusting lighting and lenses, but I stifled my frustration. Holland demanded utmost professionalism on all job sites. The previous month she had fired an intern for complaining about the rain.

I hoped the night would end soon. We would stick around for the traditional lineup—first dance, bouquet toss—and hopefully leave before the bridal party got too tipsy. I lugged equipment into the venue and bumped into an entry table, nearly knocking over a gaudy centerpiece.

"Watch yourself," Holland reprimanded.

"Sorry," I said. Insecurity surged as I tried to place the decoration into its original position.

"That arrangement probably cost more than her dress," a bridesmaid remarked as she shimmied past, which I found incredibly offensive because I wore an expensive dress for those days.

"Don't worry about it," said a groomsman with spotty facial hair. He had light brown eyes, broad shoulders and was at least a foot taller than me. "Need any help?"

No one outside our team touched the equipment, under any circumstances. I said, "I'm fine, thank you."

I made my way around the crowded reception hall. Holland oversaw all the major pictures. I was assigned candids. As I waited for the dance floor to fill, the tall groomsman reappeared by my side. He smelled like oranges.

"I actually like your dress," he said.

"Excuse me?" I was wearing a black sleeveless shift. My goal when attending work events was to blend in, not stand out.

"I know you overheard the bridesmaid," he said, his voice low. "She's my cousin, I'm ashamed to say. It's a nice dress."

"Thank you." I still wasn't sure what he wanted. Was he trying to flirt, or wanting me to feel less embarrassed about the mishap?

"She's a drunk mess," he said. "Completely mad she hasn't found someone to marry her yet. With that attitude, I doubt she ever will."

I returned a half smile. From across the growing crowd Holland motioned toward me with such verve I thought her limb would detach at the elbow.

The groomsman noticed, too. "I never knew taking pictures was an urgent ordeal," he said.

"Shouldn't be," I said. "Apparently, I'm needed."

"Maybe we'll talk later." He smiled.

"My boss is strict about interacting with guests. My guess? She's probably waving me over to scold me." I wrapped the camera strap over my shoulder, preparing to walk across the crowded venue.

"Now I really feel like an ass," the man said, looking down at his feet. "This must be a rough wedding for you."

"Been the easiest this month." I smiled a tired smile and proceeded to Holland. She had misplaced a lens, which I found within minutes.

In between snapping pictures of the Cha Cha Slide and the Macarena, I locked eyes with the friendly groomsman from across the room. As we loaded up equipment to leave, he brushed by me again, close enough to make me blush, and slipped a note into my jacket pocket. I waited until we left the venue to read.

My name is Frank. I'd like to know yours. Call me. Please.

His number was written underneath.

I didn't know then how much Frank would change my life. Making it in Whitaker had been a success in itself, even though I still struggled month to month. After we got married and had Jake, people looked at my life and felt jealousy, not pity. No one knew me as the poor girl taking pictures of the special people. Because now I was special, too.

*

I ended up finding the pills in my car the next morning. A simple misplacement due to the chaos of a crying child and my living room in disarray. To prevent future dilemmas, I placed the bulk of my stash inside an old jewelry box. Given to me by my mother, it sat on the top shelf of our walk-in closet. For sentimental reasons, Frank knew not to touch it. A problem easily resolved.

I spent the weekend walking on eggshells. Frank, on the other hand, skated over them, gracefully pretending our argument never took place. His instinctual protection had been in overdrive since the accident. The poorly masked worry in his eyes said it all. He wanted the wife and mother I'd been before. I tried. I cleaned our home, cared for our son and limited myself to two pills a day.

The Monday following my argument with Frank was the first time I felt relieved to see him leave. The tension I'd bottled throughout the weekend dispersed like mist in the air. Three workers arrived around noon, and, as I'd hoped, Dane was one of them.

He gave a friendly wave, as did the others. I spent the afternoon playing with Jake and cleaning upstairs.

When Dane went outside, my heart jumped. I followed him. The fall weather had finally cooled, and there was a nice breeze quivering the branches of the backyard trees.

"I wanted to thank you for what you did last week," I said, walking up behind him as he lit a cigarette. I didn't want the other workers to notice our conversation.

Dane turned just as he exhaled, and a tendril of smoke left his lips. Long hours in the sun had darkened his face, but his eyes were strikingly blue.

"Happy to help," he said.

"I don't want you to get the wrong idea about me." I looked around, paranoid we were being watched.

"No judgement here," Dane said, smiling. "Frank mentioned your recovery has been rough."

"Did you tell Frank about—"

"I didn't say a word. It's not my place," he said, firmly.

"Good. I don't want to give him reason to worry." It felt wrong enlisting one of Frank's workers to keep my secrets. I peered into the house. The other men were busy assembling something in the kitchen. "Look, do you have any more I could have? I can pay you."

"Mrs. Grier, I don't know about—"

"Call me Olivia." I didn't want to sound desperate, but I was. What if I couldn't get more pills when I needed them? The pills had been a lifeline for me, they made me the person I was too weak to be on my own.

"Olivia," he said, his smile strained. "I need this job. I'm not trying to cause problems."

"I won't tell Frank." I lunged toward him, my hands beginning to tremor. "My doctor refuses to write another prescription. He's an old bastard."

Dane laughed. "Yep, some docs are stingier than others."

"I wouldn't even know where to get more." I needed to make him understand how important they were to me. To my recovery. "And I'm not ready to stop taking them."

"You seem like a nice lady." He looked down.

"And I want to stay nice. I want to get better." I moved closer. "Please."

He sighed heavily, dropped the cigarette and stomped the stub with his boot. "If you give me until tomorrow, I could get you at least ten."

"Perfect." I was happy to have found a reliable solution. "Just tell me how much."

"You have to promise to keep this between us," he whispered, looking over my shoulder at his coworkers in the house.

"I swear," I said.

When he arrived the following day, he gave me his number and promised to supply me whenever I came close to running out, under the condition I never told Frank my source. His ability to provide pills without a prescription became our launching pad. Over the course of the renovation, I valued the opportunity to talk with a new person. Communication with Frank had lessened. Maura provided entertainment and companionship, but our conversations revolved around kids and marital life, mainly *her* marital life. Dane had no interest in domesticity.

"You from Whitaker?" he asked me once, about a week after we'd first met. In that short amount of time, the leaves had turned from green to a myriad of autumnal hues. I'd followed him into the backyard during another cigarette break.

"Adams County," I answered. "About twenty minutes in the direction of nowhere."

"Oh yeah. I know where it is. I'm Whitaker, born and bred. I've known a couple o' guys from Adams County." He pulled hard on the cigarette and a tower of ash fell from the tip. "I pinned you as a Tellit Mountain girl."

I smiled and slanted my head to the left. "That would be Frank. He's Tellit Mountain, born and bred."

We snickered in unison. Frank's status in Whitaker was really nothing to laugh about. It meant he had money and education and possibility. But a Tellit Mountain zip code, to people like me and Dane, also meant a rank one received upon birth, not achievement. I never gave Frank a hard time about the stereotype, just as he generally ignored my childhood on the outskirts. *She's from Whitaker*, he'd say during casual introductions, before moving on to another subject.

"Adams County," Dane repeated. He undressed the layers of superiority he had built around me. Normally, I cringe when people dissect me in such a way. As though my value is immediately lowered. But Dane's gaze was different. I wasn't less than. I was equal.

"I grew up there, but I've lived in Whitaker since I was old enough to sign a lease." Whitaker had been my home for almost a decade, but I could never fully escape my childhood in the outskirts, no matter how hard I tried.

"When did you hook up with Frank?"

"After he graduated college." I normally dodged my college history in conversations because I never finished my degree. It was tuition or rent, and a girl had to live. I signed up for the eighteen-month photography program offered by the nearest community college, and the rest was anticlimactic history.

"Looks like you made it now." Dane smiled and looked around. I followed his eyes as he took in the grill on the back deck, the hammock swaying between two trees and Jake's playhouse in the shade.

"My own little Whitaker Happily Ever After," I mumbled under my breath.

Dane turned to walk inside. "I'll bring you more tomorrow when I work."

"Sounds great." I smiled, a little too enthusiastically.

"Try to only take what you need," he said, before entering the house. "You have to be careful with these things."

Dane's concerns differed from Frank's. Dane didn't want my addiction (*was I starting to call it that?*) to worsen. Frank failed to understand altogether.

"Your schedule is taking a toll on me," I admitted to Frank one night. It was nearing ten o'clock when he returned home. His stench caught my attention as he entered the room, and mud and paint smears dirtied his jeans. I noticed his skin felt slimy when he attempted a hug. Frank worked hard, no doubt. But at what cost?

"My hours won't always be this demanding," he insisted. "I'm just in overdrive trying to get this house on the market."

"Aren't you the boss? Can't you control your hours?" I was growing tired of Frank's helpless mentality. If he truly wanted to be around more, he could make it happen.

He took off his shirt and tossed it into the empty hamper. I moved my blanketed legs, making room for him to sit on the edge of the bed.

"I'm not asking for business advice." He sounded mean but corrected his tone. "The company has existed less than two years. I'm getting better, but I'm still at the stage where I can't trust anyone else to do what I know. I need to oversee the finishing touches because I know buyers' expectations."

"I need you here more," I said. Frank could provide all the excuses he wanted, but it didn't change my needs.

"Listen, when this house sells I will be here whenever you need me."

"Yeah, until you buy your next flip house." I pulled on the covers, attempting to turn.

"You know the business. Some seasons are busier than others. But I'll always make time for you and Jake." He leaned in for a kiss. "And when I can, I'll make up for lost time."

I envied Frank's ability to juggle tasks without feeling like a failure. Admitting I needed help felt wrong. Why couldn't I effortlessly handle my responsibilities in the same way Frank did? He monitored complicated renovations and a crew. I only had our son.

"You know I love Jake. He's a cute kid," I tried to explain. "But you are only around for the cute parts. Dealing with the hard stuff—day in and day out—is different."

"I see what you do for our family, Olivia. I might offer income, but you provide everything else. Don't think your work here goes unnoticed." He leaned in for another kiss. "I'm going to take a shower now. Stay awake, if you can."

By the time Frank exited the bathroom, a lemony scent trailing behind him, I was on the verge of sleep. When he jostled my arm, I didn't respond.

*

Maura came the closest to understanding my frustrations, although our challenges differed. Her children made her whole, and she never desired to work beyond raising them and tending house; her greatest weakness was her commitment to Ronnie, and she accepted those flaws as best she could.

She had a natural ability to curb oversharing but always sensed when I needed a good distraction. Most distractions came from her *indiscretions*, a term she never used correctly. An indiscretion implies poor judgement, a careless oversight. Her affairs were always planned and intentional. Shaming her husband and losing her family were consequences she did not want to face.

Her latest paramour was a man named Luca. She had met him through his wife whom she'd met through Pilates.

"Such a stuck-up bitch," she said, twirling a strawberry strand of hair. Samantha and Stevie worked in unison to bury Jake under a pile of fallen leaves, enjoying a rare spike in the fall temperatures. We hung back, gossiping by the fire pit and drinking wine. "I should know better than to screw around with someone I know socially."

She bumped into Luca at Publix. He explained he and his wife were separated. Financial troubles. A brief flirtation via text resulted in an overnight visit the next state over. She planned it when Ronnie and the kids were visiting her in-laws.

"How long has it been since you've seen his wife?" I asked.

"Years. But divorces are messy. I can't run the risk of Bitter Bettys lashing out."

"Well, your love life is certainly more eventful than mine," I said. Listening to Maura was the most action I'd had in weeks. After my body healed from the accident, I expected the anticipation to return. Instead, sex with Frank had become a chore. No more hair pulling, no more dirty talk. We wanted it to be over so we could say it had been done.

"Come on, now," Maura said. "All couples work out the kinks after a little one. By the time Jake is in school, the spice will be back."

I couldn't bring myself to tell her the spice in her marriage came from trysts with other men. I didn't want to end up like Maura and Ronnie. Couldn't imagine Frank finding excitement in another woman's arms. The love was there, and if it remained, I knew Frank and I would recover.

Frank called and warned it would be a late night. I invited Maura and the kids to stay for dinner. Frozen pizza for Stevie and Samantha, wine and gossip for us. Playing outdoors had zapped Jake's energy, and he fell asleep peacefully upstairs. It was near midnight when Maura and the kids left. I snuggled deeper into the sofa, expecting Frank any minute. The alcohol made me sleep hard. All-consuming and deep.

I'm not sure what woke me first. Jake's cries or Frank's voice.

"What the hell are you doing?" he yelled. He stood over me in the living room. Jake squirmed in Frank's arms, crying hysterically. "Couldn't you hear him?"

I jolted upward. "I didn't." The monitor had been at my side. Useless. The batteries dead. "I fell asleep. What's wrong?"

"He has a fever." Frank moved toward the kitchen. I sprinted after him to interfere. Help him.

"The damn monitor is dead. I didn't hear him." The kitchen was still in disarray because of the renovation, but I knew exactly where to find Jake's wellness box. I filled a syringe with medicine and handed it over to Frank.

"I heard him crying before I even walked in the house," said Frank.

"I was asleep. I'm sorry." He squeezed the syrup into Jake's mouth. I grabbed a teething toy from the freezer and handed it to him. Jake immediately latched, suddenly soothed. Within half an hour, he would be asleep again. "He's cutting another molar. Might explain the fever."

Frank didn't register a thing I said. He cradled our calmed son, holding him close against his body. "Have you been drinking?"

"Maura came over." I hadn't heard Jake cry, but I hadn't done anything wrong. Surely Frank understood that.

"And you decided to pass out on the couch? While our son screams?" His tone was condescending and cruel.

"I didn't drink much. The batteries—"

"Classy, Olivia." He went upstairs and slammed the nursery door.

When Frank made a lousy investment or failed to win over a buyer, those were bad days on the job. Everyone suffers them. Mess up as a mother? You're the worst human on the planet. It wasn't fair.

＊

By the end of the week, I finally got my white kitchen. Dark quartz countertops. A center island worthy of a design magazine, although unfortunately covered by half-empty sippy cups and amputated Cheerios. The perfect marriage of style and sensibility. Jake bounced in the jumping swing, which barricaded the entryway to the dining room.

"Is it all you ever wanted?" Frank asked, holding me from behind. He gave me a claustrophobic squeeze. Frank expected an answer. He wanted to know everything was all right. As usual after a fight, he floated a brief apology and then pretended the altercation never happened.

"This is officially my dream house," I said, looking around at the finished details.

I never imagined I'd live in a house this beautiful. I was happy. Partially. We kissed. When he went upstairs to take a shower, I took another pill. Within twenty minutes, I felt whole.

With the renovation complete, I started meeting Dane outside the house. We'd usually meet in grocery store parking lots. I felt rotten, inventing excuses to leave Jake at daycare and venture into town. But I reasoned with myself. Maura had been having affairs for years and her family remained intact. Stealing ten minutes to meet Dane was far from lecherous.

He drove a sleek two-seater, a purchase you can no longer justify after having kids. I pinned him a truck guy, but he kept on surprising me. I plopped into his passenger seat, which smelled like pine thanks to one of those scented oil clips. Dane was wearing ripped jeans, work boots and a tight black T-shirt.

"How much longer do you plan on taking these?" Dane asked. He counted them into my hand as if dealing out Skittles.

"You sound like Frank." I laughed. I was completely at ease, despite the illegality of our situation. I felt more pressure taking care of Jake or gearing up for a conversation with Frank than I did during a few stolen moments with Dane.

"He knows you take them?"

"Not exactly." Frank didn't understand my dependency, and he certainly wouldn't approve of me meeting with Dane in a grocery store parking lot to purchase more pills. I had no choice but to lie.

"Probably for the best." Dane pushed away the money in my hands. I always insisted he take it. "If he ever found out you got these from me—"

"I would never say I got them from you."

"I'm not going to give you the speech about how addictive these things can be. All I'm going to say is, there's a difference between a guy like me taking pills and—"

"And what, a girl like me?"

"Gender has nothing to do with it." He rolled his eyes. "You're just… better than me."

I fished out two pills from the container in which they'd been placed. I put one in his hand and one in mine. We swallowed them in unison, like two shots at the bar.

"I'm not much better," I said.

Dane smiled, his blue eyes creating a pleasant contrast against his tawny complexion. Darkness hid underneath the good-ole-boy charm. Mysterious to some, but not me. I knew his secret and he knew mine.

CHAPTER 7

After

I'd called Frank twice the morning of the press conference, but he still hadn't responded. I parked by the curb across from my old house, reassured by the sight of his lone truck in the driveway. Returning to Smithwood always made my stomach flip. Frank kept the house after the divorce, and Julie moved in after they married. This was supposed to be my happy place with Jake. Now she filled that role.

I knocked, not completely sure if he'd even answer. Frank had a variety of vehicles he used for business. Some days he'd haul appliances in vans or lumber in trucks, depending on the phase of the renovation. He could easily be at a worksite already. Seconds later, I heard steps and the door opened.

"Olivia. What are you doing here?" His face spoke confusion, then annoyance. I rarely dropped in without warning. He wore dark pants and a collared shirt. His hair looked longer than his usual cut, as he typically let it grow during the colder months.

"I tried calling. You got a minute?"

"Not a good time. I'm heading over to a rental property and Julie will be coming home for lunch soon." Julie in her scrubs eating a tuna fish sandwich in my kitchen. Nauseating. She did not approve of me being around Frank without supervision.

"We need to talk," I insisted. "I only need five minutes."

"If this is about the other night—"

"I'm guessing you haven't seen the news," I interrupted, hoping to bypass last week's run-in altogether.

"I have no idea what you're talking about. What is it?"

"Marcus Rowe is being released."

His grip on the door slackened and he ushered me inside to the foyer. He leaned against the staircase banister, emphasizing his height in comparison to mine. No seat or drink was offered. I was not welcome in his old/new home. The interior bones remained, but the place had changed. Walls wore different colors. Framed school photos replaced Jake's baby pictures. My pristine white kitchen looked the same.

"What's going on, Olivia?" He acted as though he had more important matters to deal with than me.

"Rowe's defense team uncovered ATM footage proving he was hours away from the crime scene. There's no way he could have killed Dane," I started. Simply telling Frank Rowe was being released wouldn't be enough. He would expect to know the circumstances.

"How sure are they?" For the first time, he seemed concerned.

"I just left the press conference. They announced the decision to drop charges this morning."

He pulled out his phone and started scrolling. "There's nothing online yet."

"The evening news will pick it up, surely. You think I'm lying?"

"Of course not," he said, his eyes glued to the screen. "I'm just trying to find out more information. Did they say anything about pressing charges again?"

"This isn't a clerical error. They released him because he's innocent."

"Do *you* believe he did it?" He stared at me.

I waited to answer. Two days ago, I desperately wanted to believe in Rowe's guilt. "No," I said. "Not anymore."

Frank's reaction wasn't dissimilar to mine. He sighed heavily, crouched on the bottom stair and covered his knees with his hands. I observed his platinum wedding band; ours had been gold.

"He confessed," he said, combing his blond hair with his fingers. "I don't understand."

"The confession was never credible," I said. We'd only been hoping it was. "There were a dozen reasons to throw it out."

"Rowe didn't kill Dane," he said. Repeating the words out loud made the idea believable. He rubbed his temples and the sides of his nose. "Everything is going to start up again, isn't it? The news crews. The police."

"It won't be as bad as before." It was an encouragement for my own nerves as much as for his.

"It'll be worse. An innocent man spent a year behind bars." He shook his head and looked at me. "Talk about a headline. They'll try even harder to find out who really did it."

Who really did it. Heavy words. I slumped down next to him, my knees brushing against his thigh. "I know the investigation was difficult on you. That's why I'm telling you. We need to be prepared. For Jake."

"Beyond difficult."

Police initially deemed Frank equally suspicious. He was my ex-husband, which provided an ugly motive. I'd recently transferred a large amount of money out of my joint account with Dane and into Frank's account, something investigators viewed as a red flag. I reiterated that I was creating a fund for Jake, but police weren't buying it.

Being each other's alibi didn't help. And it certainly didn't help circumstances with Julie. Marrying a man with a child and an ex-wife was complicated; adding a murder investigation to the mix was grueling. I predicted she'd forfeit and leave. Instead, when detectives disrupted my life, she became the rock Frank and Jake needed. He married her within months of Dane's death; I think I mourned the loss of Frank more than I did Dane.

"I don't want Jake dragged into this," he said, bringing me back to the present. I imagined the swirling thoughts in Frank's brain, trying to find a way to solve all our problems. "He's older now."

"We'll overcome this," I said, wanting to convey I felt the same. We could protect Jake. Together.

"There is no *we* in this. Julie and I will talk to him." He stood, spinning my knees in the opposite direction. "Just try to limit your bullshit the four days a month he's with you."

Frank rarely talked to me this way. I couldn't fault him for his anger. Frank deserved a life free from drama and suspicion. And Jake certainly did. I had brought these stressors into their lives. I supposed Frank's resentment was my price to pay.

"Frank—"

"Sorry. I didn't mean that," he corrected. He knew it wasn't right to take his frustrations out on me, but a part of him would always feel I was responsible for the pain we'd endured in recent years.

"I don't want Jake exposed to any of this either," I reminded him.

He stroked his neck and chin. Still thinking. "Jake staying with us might be best until this blows over."

"You can't be serious." *Less* time with Jake was not up for negotiation. "The police will be coming here, too."

"You don't think I know that?" He gave a resentful stare.

"Why am I the one being punished because Marcus Rowe is innocent?" I cried.

"I'm not punishing you, Olivia. My job is to shelter Jake."

"I've been wanting more time with him—"

Keys clinked at the front door. We stopped talking and froze as if we'd been caught doing something wrong.

"Home, honey." Julie would be the type of basic wife to announce her arrival in such an annoying way. The sunshine in

her voice vacated when she saw me. She looked at me, then Frank.
"Olivia, what are you doing here?"

"She's leaving," Frank said. "We had to talk about Jake. I'll fill you in later."

"Is everything okay?" she asked.

Frank gently tugged my elbow, cueing my exit. I jerked back, pulled tighter on the purse dangling from my shoulder. I didn't appreciate being promptly dismissed, especially after Frank's threat to limit time with Jake.

"Marcus Rowe is being released," I said. I walked past Julie, stared right into her widening brown eyes. She was always uncomfortable having me around Frank. It was worth the visit to watch her squirm. "Besides that, life's peachy."

Frank followed me, touching Julie's hand as he passed her. Once outside, I lingered on the porch hoping we might finish our conversation about Jake. I was more than capable of protecting our son, and I refused to not be given the chance.

"I'm sorry about Rowe, Olivia. We'll work something out with Jake," he said. I smiled. A peace offering? Frank still had a weakness for me, although deeply buried. He continued, "But don't drop by here again."

He shut the door.

*

I didn't have to deliver the news in person. I wanted an excuse to interact with Frank outside our awkward kid swaps. I missed him. And Jake. I never thought I would miss them this much, and all I did was blame myself for losing them. Frank blamed me, too. That's why he was harsher than he needed to be at times. He always apologized, but I knew he resented me for complicating the life he worked so hard to perfect. That's all I was now. A complication.

Back at the condo, I surfed the TV in case Rowe's release hit the national media circuits. The local channels were all over it by five o'clock. Focus firmly planted on Rowe, for now. Eventually they'd want to speak to cops and lawyers and friends and relatives. Anyone with a flimsy connection to the case. They'd want to speak with me.

Against my better judgement and at the insistence of a glass of wine, I returned to my computer. I wanted to gauge the public's reaction to Rowe's release, and the true crime websites lacked a filter. Sure enough, people online were having a field day.

Truth123: *Finally! Justice for the non-gentry in America!*

OnlyFacts: *I've maintained Rowe's innocence since the beginning. No DNA, no motive, false confession. I'm happy the police caught their mistake before putting an innocent man behind bars.*

Whistle72: *Project Justice is no bull. Seems they are the only people in the system you can trust.*

TruCrimeJunkie: *@Truth123. Right has finally been done by Rowe, but let's not forget justice has NOT been served. The person responsible for killing DM remains free. The cops railroading Rowe only gave the real killer more time to go unpunished.*

Another thread caught my eye: **Who killed DM? Killer theories.**

MPB0405: *Sorry to speak ill of the deceased… DM was no church deacon. He was a known drug user/dealer. A lot of people could have wanted him dead.*

RealWhitaker: *I personally knew Dane. He was the life of the party, but you couldn't trust him. Biggest con I ever met. Not surprised he ended up this way.*

Whistle72: *@RealWhitaker Agreed. I knew Dane, too. The suspect list on this investigation must be a mile long.*

LilSnoop: *Don't care what anyone says. The wife's ex did it.*

Truther89: *My vote is the wife. She found the body. Whoever smelt it, dealt it!*

FreeRowe: *Crazy bitch did it!*

ISpy: *The wife was loaded after he died. Money will always be the biggest motive.*

Dane's killer could have been anyone. As far as the world was concerned, it could have been me.

The next morning, clunking thuds woke me too early. I stumbled to the downstairs window. A few vans parked outside. Local news. They mostly filmed brief introductions and left. There wasn't much to say other than charges had been dismissed, Rowe was being released and the condo was the scene of the crime. When the phone rang I didn't answer. I didn't respond to knocks at the door. I had no comment.

Finally, my phone rang with a name I recognized. Farrah.

"Holy shit, there were a lot of people outside your place this morning," she said. Her words intertwined with chomping gum sounds.

"It's not bad now if you're thinking of stopping by." Frank hadn't been the best sounding board, and I wanted to discuss Rowe's release with someone I trusted.

"Sure thing, buttercup."

I kept Farrah on the line, considering what to say next. I stuttered out the words, "Can you bring me anything?"

Farrah's bohemian whimsy meant she always had good drugs on her. A major incentive for maintaining our friendship. I'd been craving a taste since the press conference. Typical behavior for when I'm stressed. The coming days were bound to be tense, and I wanted to be prepared.

"Does a bear shit in the woods?" she responded, her tone equal parts raspy and light.

I smiled at her answer. "Thanks, Farrah."

"You have to stop torturing yourself with the past," she continued.

"The past keeps torturing me," I said, lowering my head in shame before I put down the phone.

Her timing was impeccable. She banged on the door a mere three minutes after the final news van pulled away. I questioned how long she had waited to make a move. She gave me a bag full of pills and I handed her a wad of cash.

"You sure you want that many on you?" she asked.

"I bet you have more at your place," I said, trying to lighten the mood. Truthfully, I felt guilty about buying pills again, but I also knew how difficult the indefinite future could be. I couldn't revisit the trauma of Dane's death and Rowe's arrest sober. I just couldn't. Drinking caused me to check out. At least the pills actively improved my demeanor, helped me focus and heightened my mood.

"Yeah, I might have more, but I don't have the police and the press watching me. That I know of, at least." She lit a cigarette and laughed. We moved into the living area, her least favorite room in the condo. She sat on the couch apprehensively. "How you holding up?"

"Now that the shock is wearing away, I'm realizing there's not much I can do about it." I didn't mention the people online, what they were saying about the case and my suspected involvement. Or that Frank had threatened to limit my time with Jake. Or that I'd slept only a few hours since the news broke.

I took one pill and waited. I loved the tingling of the drugs entering my system. Bad thoughts soon gone, if only for the night. A few short hours without the pain of the past thrust upon me.

"There you go," Farrah soothed. "Don't take on more than you can handle. You talked to the press?"

"No. No plans on it, either. Not until we see how this plays out." It was one thing to speak with the press after Rowe's arrest. Cooperating with reporters amid a reopened investigation might set a trap.

"You could come down to the bar tonight if you want. Your tab is on me." Her rouge lips formed a smile. I appreciated the offer, although we both knew what my answer would be.

"You know why I don't want to go there."

"I've got ideas, but I want to hear your take." She arched her painted eyebrows and waited.

"Dane's friends love Fahrenheit's. I've not seen most of them since he died."

"I was also Dane's friend, remember. No one is gathering pitchforks and lanterns." She laughed. "It might do you some good to see familiar faces and talk about the good times."

"What good times, Farrah?" My tone was unnecessarily harsh. Dane's friends had always made me uneasy. Partying with someone wasn't the same as knowing them. Farrah wouldn't understand; she was the type of person who never met a stranger. "Sorry, but it's not like these people went out of their way to defend me, either."

"They were more afraid of the cops than you. That's why people kept their distance. No one wants to end up like Sturger."

"Gah, I've not heard that name in forever, and could go a bit longer." Steve Sturger was one of Dane's closest friends, although I'd not seen him since before the murder. He was someone I instinctively knew not to trust. I couldn't put into words why. Something about his constantly glazed eyes and mellow voice. "What happened to him?"

"You know, he was caught up in pills. Cops got involved." She took another hit of the cigarette. "You can guess the rest. It was his third strike, too. He'll be gone for a while."

What types of people had Dane introduced into my life? People being sent to prison? He made perilous choices, and the danger consumed him.

"Did they think he had something to do with Dane—"

"No, nothing like that," she interrupted before I could complete the thought. "He just had a lot to hide and wasn't very skilled in hiding it."

Both our eyes darted in the direction of my living room cabinet, the place where I'd stored the pills.

"With so much risk, why do you still come around?" I asked.

"Because that's what real friends do, lovebug." She dropped her cigarette into her wine glass. The blaze fizzed out and a final plume of smoke hovered above the rim. "Besides, I'm not scared of the cops. Or anyone else, for that matter."

We laughed as the pills took their full effect, like a protective hug from an old friend. I felt peace. In the coming days, I'd better adopt Farrah's confident defiance. I was going to need it.

*

When Farrah left, I followed her out. I needed a few necessities from the store but had been too paranoid to leave earlier in the day. Besides, it wasn't fair I stayed hidden in the condo simply because Dane's murder was back in the spotlight. I hadn't done anything. I deserved a walk at night and a whole hell of a lot more, to tell the truth. I had already started walking before I grasped how high I already was.

The store's fluorescent lights were sobering. The clerk behind the counter stared hard when I walked in. She bent over, whispered something to a customer at the front of the line. That morning's paper had contained a summary of Dane's murder and Rowe's release. Just when I thought people had forgotten about me, the press was giving them reasons to remember. I skipped over to the toiletries aisle and started filling my basket.

"Olivia Miller," said a voice at the end of the row.

I jumped, not expecting to encounter anyone I knew. Detective Wooley stared back at me. He wore a collared shirt tucked into a pair of stained khakis, different from his work wear. He was off the clock.

"Wooley," I said.

"Big news about Rowe. Didn't get to speak with you at the Project Justice conference." The familiar toothpick swirled in his mouth as he spoke.

"It's a new case, Wooley," I reminded. "You're no longer involved. Remember?"

I wanted to crush his ego, remind him his team's previous failures resulted in an innocent man's incarceration and required intervention from outside sources to resolve. He wasn't intimidated.

"New investigators run information by us. Already shortlisted some names." He moved closer as I clenched my teeth. "For the record, I never believed Rowe killed Dane."

Of course. Wooley always believed I did it. That's why he harassed our old friends. That's why he contacted Frank about my lifestyle, hoping by increasing the emotional stakes I'd confess. Instead, he provided the ammunition Frank needed to take Jake away from me. All a waste. I didn't know anything then and still didn't have any answers.

"Creep." I bumped him as I walked away.

"Good night, Olivia. I'll be seeing you around."

A threat to follow me? I dropped my basket on a shelf and left without making any purchases, careful not to look in Wooley's direction.

Passing cars splashed puddles onto the sidewalk from the afternoon's squall and the wind blew hard preparing for another. Normally I loved downtown at night, the streets buzzing with excitement. Cars and minivans scurried home to safe little nests, while undergrads and the unburdened came out to play. Just last week I had been one of those unburdened souls. Now I couldn't even visit the convenience store without running into the likes of Wooley.

When I was finally alone, I felt it completely.

Until I didn't.

Nearby footsteps alerted me. I lowered my head and kept walking. Three blocks remained until the condo. It was foolish to reason I could enjoy an evening without detection. I expected Wooley again, but he wasn't there when I glanced back. The person behind me was Wooley's opposite. Tall and lanky. Wearing a dark hoodie. The street lamp's angle prevented me from seeing a face.

Two blocks.

My breath hastened, as did my stride. Walking alone at night was more than foolish, it was hazardous. Hell, there had already been one murder inside my condo. The footsteps pounded louder.

One block.

I longed for a member of the press to be outside. I looked around for an unmarked police car. Perhaps Wooley lurked nearby after all. A hand crept over my shoulder, stealing a gasp from me in the process. All the anger and fear I'd suppressed bolstered together and gave me the will to fight. I used my fist to slam the stranger's mouth. A voice cried out.

"Damn it, Olivia." The hooded figure hunched over in pain. Now, under the light, I recognized his face. The man from Chili's last week. I remembered I'd considered taking him home.

And I hadn't given him my real name.

CHAPTER 8

Before

My favorite activity growing up was playing dress up. I didn't have proper clothes from a costume shop, but, over time, Mamma collected an assortment of random items that she stored in a trunk we found at a yard sale.

I'd suit up and imagine I was a doctor or a police officer or a princess. It was thrilling, pretending even for a few moments I had a different life. The mattress on the floor was actually a sailboat, and our kitchen table was a secret dungeon. Even then, I was looking for ways to escape. Occasionally, Mamma joined me by playing a sick patient or a flamboyant dragon. Those were my happiest memories, even if those moments were few and far between.

As an adult, I'm not sure my life really changed. I was still playing dress up in a house I hadn't bought, wearing clothes I couldn't afford on my own. Only this time I was pretending for Frank's enjoyment, moonlighting as the wife he expected me to be. I never felt like I was acting when I was around Jake, but I worried eventually he'd grow up to see what everyone else saw. A fraud. A mother who was only imitating the other moms in the neighborhood. Someone who wasn't enough.

I made the most of my time with Jake, especially since it seemed Frank was rarely around. In the weeks leading up to Christmas, we crafted decorations and baked seasonal cookies and cake. I wanted his childhood memories to be better than my own.

I was cleaning up the kitchen after baking sugar cookies when Frank came in, late as usual. I was on my knees scrubbing flour mounds off the tile. Cooking with a two-year-old was fun, but abundantly messy.

"I haven't made dinner," I said, concentrating on the tight grooves which seemed impossible to clean. "Jake and I ate a late lunch. Then we made cookies, if you want some."

"That's fine," he said. He unwrapped the scarf around his neck and pulled off his puffy coat. "I grabbed some takeout on the way here."

"Good," I said. Jake would be satisfied with a grilled cheese before bed. Knowing my appetite, I wouldn't be hungry again until morning.

"Mom and Dad are on their way over," Frank said, opening the hall closet and depositing his outerwear.

His parents rarely left their Tellit Mountain estate unless it involved charity work or recreational sports. Around the holidays, that changed. They saw more of Jake during the month of December than they did the rest of the year. It's like they remembered there was a grandson to spoil, and they wanted to take full advantage of the opportunity.

"I didn't know they were coming over," I said, irritated. I was still several minutes away from having the kitchen cleaned, and I wasn't much in the mood for guests. With Christmas days away, I'd wanted to meet Dane and re-up my supply. "I was hoping to go out. I have some last-minute shopping."

"They won't stay long. They want to visit with Jake and discuss the Christmas Eve menu with you," Frank said.

"I thought your parents were travelling this year?" The Griers owned a vacation home in Montana, and they sometimes preferred to spend the holidays there.

"I guess they've changed plans," he said, walking toward the stairs. "We're going to their house for Christmas Eve dinner."

"Frank." I threw down the dishtowel in my hands and looked up. "I've already planned a meal for Christmas Eve."

He stood at the steps but waited to climb. "I told you my parents had a change of plans. They want us to celebrate at their house. We did it last year. What's the problem?"

"I've organized an entire menu," I said. I pictured all the dishes that I'd no longer have the chance to make. Roasted duck and cranberry chutney and sweet potato soufflé. This would be my first holiday meal prepared in the new kitchen. At least that's what I'd intended. "It's not fair I have to cancel my plans because they've cancelled theirs."

"You *planned* a meal, you didn't cook it. You didn't even cook tonight." He chuckled, leaning against the banister. "That was a joke."

"I get it," I said, slowly standing and dusting leftover flour off my knees. Frank's parents had barely reached out since the accident, rarely asked about my recovery. But here they were, coming around to mess up the plans I'd made. "I'm just aggravated, is all."

"Talk it out with them tonight. I shouldn't be gone too long."

"Wait," I said, following him to the staircase. "Where will you be?"

He stopped his trek upstairs for a second time and sighed. "This is my last chance to finalize paperwork before the New Year. I told you I was meeting with Denise tonight."

Denise handled all the secretarial nonsense for his remodel company. He insisted he'd told me weeks ago, but I couldn't remember. The holiday chaos lumps time into two categories: Before Christmas and After.

"I forgot," I said, rubbing my head. I worried I wouldn't have the chance to meet Dane again. "It doesn't seem fair I have to stay when you aren't even going to be here."

"That's fine," Frank said. "Just review the menu with Mom and head out. I'm sure they won't mind watching Jake for a few hours."

I dreaded making conversation with Frank's parents, but at least I had an opportunity to leave the house. I waited until Frank went upstairs to text Dane.

You got any?

He responded with: *Yep. Meet me at the mall?*

Can't make it until after 8. Cool?

Fine by me, he wrote back.

It was nearing eight thirty when I entered the parking lot. My used SUV looked matronly parked next to his sleek coup.

"Sorry. I couldn't escape my in-laws. Around the holidays, each day is another family reunion." I was rambling. He listened attentively, as if he hadn't already been patient enough. "I hope I didn't inconvenience you."

"No worries. The holidays are jam-packed for families. We bachelors? This is the slow time of the year." I assumed Dane was single yet had never pried. He was handsome enough to have plenty of girls chase after him. I'd never asked about his family either.

"Any holiday plans?" I asked.

"I'll visit people here and there. My parents aren't around anymore. No brothers or sisters. I don't have to worry about the shindigs you do."

It was selfish complaining about being surrounded by people. I never considered the alternative. I remembered the orphan years Dane described all too well. And he believed I was better than him.

"At least you have a few days off work." I tried to lighten the mood.

"That's my favorite part about Christmas. I can sit around and do absolutely nothing. And the lights, of course." He put the pills in my hands. "I'm actually going to grab a drink. I'd invite you to join if you weren't so busy."

"Tonight I'm not. Frank is working, and Jake is being spoiled by my in-laws. I guess they're calling the shots between now and the New Year." Was I bumping for an invitation? Even I wasn't sure.

"You should join me, then." He smiled and opened his car door. "I'm sure you don't make it out much."

We went to Champions, a cheesy bar attached to the mall. Until we walked inside, I didn't appreciate how long it had been. The dim ceiling lamps. The loud music. Only adults, no children in sight. I'd missed this.

"I can't stay long," I said to Dane, and a warning to myself.

"I won't keep you," he promised. "What do you want to drink?"

I fumbled like a college kid drinking underage. Gah, it had been too long. I got a margarita and Dane drank bourbon. I asked Dane about his family; we had spent plenty of conversations talking about mine. He told me about his father, absent nearly all his life. His mother had died a few years back. Strangely like my background.

"How's the baby?" he asked, steering the talk into happier territory.

"He's practically a boy now. He just turned two." I drank. "Amazing how fast they grow."

"Frank talks about him constantly."

I smiled, imagining Frank bragging about our little family. "What else does Frank say?"

Dane's mouth opened, but words failed to come. He took another sip of his beer, instead.

"What is it?" I pushed.

"I sense a shift in him." He put down the glass and grabbed a bar napkin to wipe the condensation on his hands. "Used to be, he'd come to work ready to hit the ground running. He's as driven as ever. At times he seems… preoccupied."

Was our marriage that low? Even the outside world saw the crumbling pieces? I wondered if Frank was confiding in Denise now like I was with Dane. The idea made me uncomfortable.

"What do I know?" he continued. "I'm not the marrying type."

Sometimes I wondered if the same description applied to me.

A pool table emptied, and I suggested we play. I was tired of talking. *One more hour*, I told myself. Last minute shopping can take a while. If I smelled like alcohol, I'd say I met up with Maura. Frank wouldn't be home for a few more hours, so my excuses were only for his parents.

Dane mastered pool. Could look at the table and immediately know what angle to play. Predict the outcome of the next outcome. At one time I had been good, but my skills, like everything else from my previous life, had fallen into disuse. After three rounds, I knew it was time to leave.

"I'm heading out, too," Dane said. "Might get a full night's rest for a change."

Dane and I were both in our late twenties, but we were at completely different stages in life. He still enjoyed his youth, was allowed the space to be selfish and make mistakes. I never had those years. I went from taking care of Mamma, to taking care of myself, to taking care of Frank and Jake. *Jake*. I missed him.

Dane walked with me to the parking lot. There were more cars than usual for this hour. The meteorologist's promise for snow flurries had not been fulfilled. Instead, the air was cold and dry. Maybe if it were to rain we'd get a little bit of snow. The stuffy bar had made me forget about the miserable weather beyond the doors.

"I enjoyed this," I said.

"I'm happy you could blow off steam," he said. He held my car door open for me. "I'm sorry if I got too serious in there. I didn't mean to snoop into your marriage."

"You weren't snooping." I couldn't be mad at Dane for telling me what I already knew. Frank and I had not been in a good place since the accident. "Maybe I needed to hear an outsider's perspective."

"My opinion shouldn't count for much."

"No, I needed it. It's hard trying to balance everything. Keeping secrets from Frank doesn't help." The pills burned a hole inside my bag. What would Frank think if he really knew what I'd been up to tonight? He wouldn't be angry. He'd be disappointed. He expected better from me.

"No one's expecting you to be perfect, Olivia," Dane said, as though he could read my mind. He could tell I was beating myself up, as usual. "Not even Frank."

"I need more nights like this." I stretched my arms, watched my breath dance in the December air. "Nights when I feel fun and exciting again."

"You're still all those things. Now that I know you better, I can tell you aren't some Tellit Mountain girl." Dane moved closer, as though he could sense the chill creeping up my torso. "You've got too much bite."

My belongings sat in the driver's seat, the door open, the keys begging me to leave.

Instead, I leaned in until my lips found Dane's. They were smooth and sweet from the bourbon, another contradiction to this man I so badly wanted to understand. Because he understood the old me. The person I, at times, wanted to be again. Dane positioned his hands at the back of my neck, right where the hair meets skin, and lightly tugged.

✳

Maura and Ronnie had clearly not spared any expense on the kids' Christmas gifts. Usually, their house resembled a manufacturer's showroom; family portraits were scarce, replaced instead by over-priced canvases from Kirkland's and Bed Bath & Beyond. The holidays had left their house in disarray, like my house looked on a normal day. We sat on her white sofa and waited for the children to wander.

She was the only person I told about my kiss with Dane. I had never mentioned him before. A condensed backstory filled in the details. My voice hummed low and the children's howls from upstairs muffled our conversation.

"You little slut," Maura said. She went from sitting on her bottom, to perching on her knees, like an excited animal ready to pounce.

"Should I tell Frank?" My legs were crossed, and my arms folded. I felt dirty admitting to Maura what I had done.

"No, no, no. Do not tell Frank about this." She deemed the question more shocking than the betrayal.

"I feel horrible." I did. By the time I arrived home, guilt had burrowed into my gut. When Frank returned, tired as usual, I almost felt sick. He worked so hard to provide this life for us, and I had repaid him by kissing another man.

"Do you?" Maura asked. Her unconvinced eyes evaluated my reaction.

"I am sick with guilt. I could barely cope over the holidays." I felt like a fraud throughout the dinner at Frank's parents' house. Exchanging gifts with Frank and Jake felt like a chore, knowing I had this secret.

"You didn't enjoy the kiss at all?" she pushed.

I thought back to the parking lot and Dane's warm body against me, blocking the frigid air. His musky cologne mixed with smoke and liquor. "The kiss *was* nice. But it wasn't with my husband. Between the drinks and the pool table… the moment seduced me. I forgot I'm a wife. And a mother."

"You deserve fun now and then," Maura consoled me, our roles reversed.

"Not at Frank's expense."

"Look at it this way." She moved closer with the fervor of a SWAT team planning an attack. "If the kiss was a screw-up, do you want your marriage defined by one weak moment? You can't predict how Frank will react. Contemplate the bigger picture. Your family."

Her point of view was seedy but sensible. I knew what I'd done was wrong, but I'd made one mistake in the entirety of our relationship. "Not telling him will be hard," I said.

"I know." Her hand rubbed mine. I wiped my cheeks and tried to regain composure. "Have you talked to Dane?"

"No. I considered deleting his information altogether."

"There you have it. You've made the decision to keep your distance," she said, rubbing my back. "Telling Frank will only cause more problems."

Bickering cries interrupted our chatter. Stevie and Samantha argued over the same toy. Maura released an annoyed groan and marched up the steps to fix another dilemma. Most people wouldn't look to Maura for advice, but I admired her ability to take charge. She never felt flustered and insecure. If she wasn't happy, she did something about it. I was too complacent. I had been hoping for months my relationship with Frank would improve. Now I'd added one more secret to that already heavy load.

At home, the truth begged to leave my lips, but endless excuses stopped it. The dynamic with Frank was problematic enough without admitting the mistake. We fought over his late work hours and our increasingly unkempt house. We squabbled over Jake and which parent was best capable of fulfilling his needs.

I cut off communication with Dane. He backed off, not wanting to encroach upon my tenuous marriage, an act I viewed as admirable. Still, he clouded my mind. When I prepared meals in my new white kitchen. Or passed the mall en route to Jake's preschool. Or in the shower, touching my body in ways I imagined Dane might. I took fewer pills each day, stretching out my dwindling supply. Weaning off Dane and the meds was hard. I couldn't decide which vice I missed the most.

Swallowing my last pill felt like a death sentence. Day Two without a pill physically hurt. An icy sweat snaked my body and the air lacked healing. By morning, I had thrown up the previous night's meal. I hid my symptoms to avoid alerting Frank, causing him to misinterpret my mood.

I slumped downstairs to the kitchen. Frank looked as though he'd been awake for hours, probably sitting by the fire pit in the backyard, his new sanctuary for stressful times. He wore his typical uniform of cargo pants and a long-sleeve thermal. Jake was sitting in his chair watching cartoons and munching on the fruit Frank had sliced for breakfast. I groggily prepared a cup of coffee, trying to avoid eye contact with either.

"What is wrong now?" Frank asked, looked at my disheveled hair and robe. Usually I was dressed and ready for the day by this hour.

"Nothing." I couldn't tell him I was ill because then he'd want to know why. We didn't need an argument about pills on top of everything else.

"Don't do that." He placed his phone on the counter, giving me his full attention.

"Do what?"

"Don't say everything is fine," he barked. "If something is wrong, you need to tell me. I don't want to play mind reader."

"Then don't." I wanted him to grab his keys and wallet and go to work as he had many mornings when he knew something was wrong. *Just leave*, I thought. Instead, he rattled my cage.

"This isn't us, Olivia. I can't keep living like this. You must talk to me."

Frank was actually trying. For the first time, he wasn't just ignoring me. He wasn't pretending our problems didn't exist. He wanted to know what was wrong, but I couldn't find the right words to explain. "I don't know what to tell you. I'm just… sad."

"Sad about what?" A shout, not a question. His emotions, like mine, had been bubbling for weeks and the time for sympathy had passed. All he had now was frustration.

Just leave, my mind begged.

He continued, "You've been this way too long. I've tried looking the other way. I don't know what your problem is."

I wanted to tell him. About the kiss and the sadness and the deliciously wonderful pills. I almost did. Jake's fruit bowl fell from the tray, clattering to the ground. His cries interrupted us, prompting my tears to take over.

Frank twisted his head and spat out a defeated laugh. "You know what, Olivia? I'm at the point I don't care what's going on. I just want you to get your shit together." He slammed the door when he left, making Jake howl a little louder.

I'd never felt more like a failure. I didn't know how I was going to make it through the day—let alone the lifetime to follow—without medicine. Even in their absence, the pills had a hold on me. Trying to leave them in the past was premature. I wasn't strong enough, yet.

I need to meet. Do you have any? I texted Dane.

After twenty minutes, which seemed an eternity: *Yeah. All ok?*

I take Jake to daycare at 10. When can you meet?

Around 10.30. My place. I'll send the address.

My shaking limbs settled.

CHAPTER 9

After

When the man who had been following me removed his hand from his mouth, blood stained his fingers. Busted lips.

"Who are you?" I made sure an appropriate distance remained between us.

"My name is Brock Bowen. We met last week at the bar."

I barely remembered him. I'd had too much to drink that night, and our encounter took place before the news of Rowe's release. That seemed like a lifetime ago. He was tall, slim and wearing a black backpack. His hair was dark and chunky, as I remembered. I wondered if the added thickness was due to the extra humidity in the air.

"Still doesn't tell me who you are," I said, agitated. "Why are you following me?"

"I wasn't trying to alarm you." He had followed me to my house and attempted to touch my shoulder. I was still rattled from the Wooley encounter and feeling particularly vulnerable.

"Start talking," I ordered.

"I'm a writer studying your husband's case—"

"Okay, bye." I turned and continued walking toward the condo.

"Wait. Hear me out." The tapping of his footsteps followed.

"I've dealt with press. Usually they have the decency not to follow people home at night."

"Yeah, I'm rethinking my strategy here." He walked next to me, pulling tight on the straps of his backpack. "You're not an easy lady to track down. No social media. Ever-changing contact information."

"I purposefully make myself hard to find."

"Look, I run a true crime blog and I'm writing a book about Dane's murder. I've already talked to several people about the case. Now I want to hear your story."

If he wanted an opportunity to speak with me, he had that chance last week. He never mentioned being a writer. Hell, I gave him a fake name and he didn't call me on it. Our exchange had been flirtatious to the point I considered taking him home with me. Was I just that drunk at the time? Or was this all a manipulation on his part?

"I don't do interviews anymore," I said, hearing Eddy's warnings to avoid press in my head.

"A conversation, perhaps? I promise you, I'm in your corner." He stopped when we made it to my unit. He remained at the bottom of the steps and looked up. "For the record, I don't believe you killed Dane."

I stood outside my front door, blindsided by the idea of not walking inside. My pulse stabilized from the fear of being followed, as my mind weighed options. I looked over Brock one more time. Following me home was a tactical error, but something about his demeanor labeled him ditzy, not deceitful. Journalists are respected, or in my case distrusted, because of their objectivity, the latex gloves preventing any real grime from muddying their actual selves. Brock's vocalized support was appealing but could have easily been a constructed ploy to hook my involvement. Either way, the trick was working.

"The Copper Skillet is right down the street and stays open until midnight. Come talk with me and I'll answer any questions you still have," he said. Realizing I didn't have much left to lose, I agreed.

The restaurant buzzed around us. The booth, sticky from sanitation, pulled at my skin. A preoccupied waitress flurried past our table with oval plates covering both arms. I wanted to leave within minutes.

"I don't know why I agreed to this," I said.

"Sure you do." Brock sat across from me, rotating a pen between his thumb and pointer finger. He almost appeared intellectual and professional, minus the gash on his bottom lip. "No one can turn down a good mystery."

"I've had my fill."

"Ah, the story's not over yet." He smiled. I considered reinjuring him for the scare he'd provided earlier. "Let's start over. I'm Brock. You are Olivia, although you told me the night we met your name was Kelsey."

"If you knew who I was, why didn't you just say so?" I asked, annoyed by the mind games.

"I wanted to ease into a conversation and avoid an abrupt confrontation like we had a few minutes ago."

"You tried to take me home," I countered. He wiggled in his seat, started pulling notebooks from his backpack.

"I really wasn't trying to, Olivia. I apologize. I should have stated my intentions sooner." He paused again. "I was not going to take advantage of the situation. I planned on going back to your place and talking about the case. That's it."

A wave of embarrassment washed over me. Was I really that forward? I flipped through the mental Rolodex of random lovers I'd accumulated in the past year and a half. How many other encounters had been that messy?

"Clearly, I misread the situation." I shrugged.

"No worries." He looked away, doing his best to forever sidestep this conversation. "So, why'd you lie about your name?"

"It's just this thing I do. In case someone is familiar with my story." I stared at the tiny circles decorating my menu. They looked like happy, dancing meds.

"Interesting psychology." He rearranged the notebooks and papers piled to his left. "I was a psychology minor, journalism major. That's why I love exploring these cases. A blending of interests."

"Murder interests you?" My tone dulled.

"Doesn't it everyone? Murder is a billion-dollar business. The television specials and books. The movies and shows based on real-life tragedy. As an industry, it's right up there with weddings in terms of popularity."

"And you're wanting to contribute." The dig left him unfazed. "Written anything I'd be familiar with?"

"I spent a few years working for a local newspaper back in Florida. Shit pay. Our waitress probably makes more than I did. I wanted to write real stories and created a blog that gained an impressive following. *The Vindictive Type.* Dane's murder always drew me in."

I couldn't recall which websites I had visited during my internet searches. I usually typed either Dane's name or Rowe's and followed the most recent links. Perhaps I had stumbled upon his blog before without even knowing.

"Why Dane's case?" I asked.

"All the news outlets go after the big story. There are dozens of books covering Drew Peterson. Or the Menendez brothers. I like to aim for a smaller target. Pick a compelling crime. Study it. Bring it to people's attention. From the beginning, Marcus Rowe's guilt seemed unlikely, but they arrested him anyway. That's what hooked me."

He described the circumstances like a fanciful tale. Not real people. Not real blood. "What do you want from me?"

"Police reports and photographs are flat sources. I need input from the people involved. The people who lived this case. I've worked up theories on what happened to Dane." He ducked down, his bony shoulders bending upward. His voice lowered. "I might be able to solve this thing."

I laughed. "I get it now. You're not a writer. You're Nancy Drew."

He shook off my insult and straightened his posture. "I'd prefer Hardy Boy."

"Either way. Are you writing a book or trying to solve a murder?"

"Why can't I do both?"

I leaned in closer, my voice a whisper. "Here's a secret. I do not care who killed Dane."

"I predicted you'd react this way. My characterization must be pretty spot-on." He broke eye contact and scribbled onto a notepad.

"I'm not a character in your book. And Dane's murder isn't an urban legend you use to caution teenagers. This is all real."

"Which is why I actually care about the outcome." A sizzling plate being carried over our heads grabbed his attention. The smell made my mouth ache. "I can sell a book with or without a killer in custody. They got it wrong by going after you and Rowe. What if we could go after the real perpetrator?"

I stared blankly. "How do you know I didn't do it?"

"I thought you did, at first. Like everyone else, I made assumptions. There's a bigger case against you than Rowe, obviously. However, the way you've acted since Rowe's arrest—I don't think it's you."

"Elaborate."

"Despite what the media tells us, not many cold-blooded psychopaths exist. Normal people commit these crimes and struggle to cope. They *do* feel guilty. They let things slip. As—damaging—as your past might have been, your story never changed."

"What do you mean by *damaging*?"

He tilted his head. "From what I can tell… you aren't close to many people. No support system. Add in your substance abuse issues—"

"I don't have substance abuse issues—"

"Okay, okay. Poor word choice. What I'm saying is, you've got some unfortunate strings attaching you to the crime. Regardless, if you had killed Dane, you would have cracked by now."

I resented his accusations veiled as attempts to defend me. "Tell me, at what point in journalism school did they teach you to take your sources home?"

"Again, I made a mistake. I already apologized for my unprofessionalism." He waved his hands like tiny white flags. "Bottom line, and I could be wrong: I don't believe you killed Dane."

Eddy had never said those words. Neither had Frank. Or Farrah. Had anyone?

"The police do. Wooley, especially."

"Wooley wants the case solved. Rowe's release only made him more desperate."

Brock had a way of pulling me in. I imagined his persuasion would be as convincing on the page, and I was beginning to admire his blunt assessments. But defending my honor wasn't enough to make me stay. My involvement would only make matters worse, at least that had been my track record. I reached for my keys. "I appreciate your endorsement, but I think I need to avoid the media right now."

"Joshua Frederickson," he said. "Recognize the name?"

"No." I stood and zipped up my black hoodie.

"His parents were murdered in their California mansion. Police alleged he killed them in hopes of inheriting their estate. For years he was harassed by detectives, the press—until DNA proved a robber was responsible for committing the crime during a random break-in gone wrong. Took investigators fifteen years to realize their primary suspect was innocent."

Teenagers with full bellies huddled near our table, blocking my exit.

"Same circumstances involving a guy in Florida," he continued. "His girlfriend was found strangled on a hiking trail back in the eighties. He was the last person seen with her. Not enough evidence to arrest him, just enough for the police to railroad his life for the next ten years. It wasn't until DNA technology advanced that police were able to link his girlfriend's killer to a man already behind bars for committing similar assaults. I could tell you a dozen other stories."

"Please. Don't." My temple throbbed. Farrah's pills were wearing off. "How do any of those people connect to Dane's case?"

"How many years can you handle being a suspect? We both know DNA isn't coming to the rescue on this one. The only way to make the police stop looking at you is to find the person they should be investigating."

His logic conjured the image of Frank threatening to distance Jake. I had banked on the police never having enough evidence to arrest me. But could they really disrupt my life for the next ten years—or more? Intrude upon my relationship with Jake?

As usual, I wanted to numb my pain and forget. I didn't want to revisit Dane's murder and the many mistakes I'd made. But in the past, I'd relied too heavily on other people to solve my problems. Brock presented an opportunity to change that. He believed my story and was willing to help. If I wanted to reclaim the life that had been taken from me—Jake included—I needed to take control.

A tubby waitress with stringy curls finally acknowledged our table. I was still standing. "You know what you want yet?" she asked, pen and pad in hand to take notes.

I sat back down.

Brock and I designed an agreement: we'd provide each other with insight, on the condition he did not mention his interactions with me on the blog. I did not want unnecessary attention coming my way. If the case progressed and we found alternate suspects, I'd participate, exclusively, in a formal interview for his book.

One hour and two dissatisfying fried eggs later, I'd sobered up and we'd rehashed the case details. He shared specifics the police had hidden from me; I gave him an accurate understanding of timeline and setting. The biggest revelation: DNA had been found at the crime scene, after all. Aside from mine and Dane's.

"Female DNA. A minimal amount of blood," he said, taking a soggy bite of golden crust. "They will use the sample based on convenience. If the evidence helps their case, they'll lean on it. If it's a distraction, as it was when Rowe was their suspect, they'll explain the evidence as menial."

"How can they do that?" I asked.

"Again, the amount was small. Not from a laceration you might incur during a violent struggle. Could it belong to the killer? Or an accomplice to the killer? Sure. It could also have been left by a visitor or a friend days before the murder."

"Mystery on top of mystery." My head ached due to the overwhelming facts Brock spouted off.

"Do you know anything about his phone?" Brock asked.

"No," I said, rubbing my temples. "Police didn't find it at the condo. I assumed whoever shot him took it."

"That's possible," he said. "Dane's phone was never found with Rowe's belongings. So it likely wasn't dumped with the wallet. Maybe there was something on there the killer didn't want people to see."

"Police went through our phone records. I guess that's about the same as having the phone in hand." I never told the police Dane had a second phone, which I also never found. I wasn't ready to tell Brock, either. I didn't know yet if I could trust him.

"One detail never made sense to me," he said, flipping pages in a notebook. "Obviously, I know where you live."

"Because you followed me home…"

"Yeah, yeah. The condo is located on one of the busiest streets in downtown Whitaker. People crowd the area at all hours and the units in the complex are relatively close together. Despite this, the only 911 call came from you. How come no one heard the gunshot and called it in?"

"Our block has changed in the past year," I said. "Back then, the building was practically vacant. Also, Dane died shortly after July 4th. If anyone heard gunshots, they probably assumed fireworks."

"The murder took place ten days after the holiday and this is an upscale neighborhood. I can't imagine your neighbors shooting off fireworks in the middle of the night."

"It's Tennessee," I explained. "Rednecks exist in all tax brackets."

"See, this is what I need. The inside explanation I can't get anywhere else." He took another bite of his sandwich. A glob of mayonnaise dropped, staining his shirt. "Aw, shit."

"What else have police not been telling me?" I handed him my napkin. His had fallen on the floor earlier in the meal and he'd yet to retrieve it.

"Thanks," he said, mouth still full. He wiped his fingers. "Do you know about the witness?"

I almost spit out the tepid coffee in my mouth. "Witness? No."

"Calm down. We don't have eyes on a killer. All our lives would be easier if we did. A Lyft driver reported seeing a suspicious couple lurking around the condo."

"*A suspicious couple*. What time? Is the person credible?"

"Around midnight. The driver said he saw a man and a woman."

I slumped against the booth, my enthusiasm deflated. "Hell, the police probably think it's Frank and me."

"In this case, however, the information would exclude you. Witness described a short guy. Around 5'6. Frank's tall, isn't he?"

"Yeah." I sighed. "Were they coming from or leaving the condo?"

"No telling. The driver's eyesight must be as poor as your neighbors' hearing."

"How is it you have all this information? Eddy, my lawyer, never mentioned anything about female DNA or witnesses."

"Well, you're not charged. Police aren't obligated to provide him with details. Prosecutors weren't planning on divulging any of this information at trial, either. It would have helped Rowe, not hurt him. I've been speaking with sources long before I arrived in Whitaker. There's several disgruntled workers at the sheriff's office who will gladly snap a picture of police reports just to have a little more drama in their lives."

Our waitress circled occasionally, assessing whether it was time to leave our bill. She finally came over, floated the paper down and walked away. Brock grabbed the check before I could.

"You don't have to," I said.

"I'm thankful you accepted my invitation, Olivia. I'm hoping you'll agree to another meeting." He reached into his bag and pulled out a leather wallet.

"Are you staying in town?"

"Yep. I arrived a week before the press conference. I never imagined Rowe would be released. Now I plan on staying indefinitely, if funds allow. Some sources want more cash than others."

I debated whether to ask my next question. "You know more than I do about the case. Why are the police convinced I killed Dane?"

He whistled and leaned back. "The obvious reasons. You were the spouse. You found the body. You received a large financial sum after his death."

"Most spouses in my situation would fall into those categories. There must be more."

He rubbed his chin as he considered the facts. "I think the bruising piqued their interest."

"Bruising?"

"Dane's body had injuries beyond your typical defensive wounds, and there were bruises on his head. It appeared he had fought someone in the hours before his death." He paused. I already knew the rest. "When they brought you in for questioning, you had marks all over you."

Bluish legs and red arms. A swollen cheek. It had been a rough night. At the station, I stripped to a sports bra and shorts and they took pictures. Afterward, I asked for a lawyer.

"Fighting with Dane doesn't mean I killed him."

"I know." He left cash on the table. Seconds later, the waitress swooped by and picked it up.

"They did test my hands for gunpowder residue. Eddy said the results came back negative."

"I know that, too. There are ways to eliminate residue, though. Most people don't have time, but it has happened before. It's not enough to clear you on its own."

"If only I had facial recognition, like Rowe."

"Yeah, an ex-husband as an alibi isn't the most concrete excuse either."

"It's the truth."

"I believe you," he said, the words unintentionally reaching out and hugging my spirit. "Have you spoken with police since the press conference?"

"Eddy has. He scheduled a conversation with the new detectives for Thursday."

"You're willingly speaking with detectives about the case?" He seemed surprised.

"I'm apprehensive, too. They reached out to Eddy following the press conference. He says we should cooperate until given a reason not to."

"Could be enlightening. Make note of any unique questions they ask. Might suggest a turn in the investigation."

"Will do," I said. My finger saluting out from my forehead.

Our waitress clattered a plastic change tray on the table. "Have a nice night," she said, though her face read *get the hell out*.

CHAPTER 10

Before

Dane's building was located in an area I frequented during my early twenties. It was near the complex I had once shared with Frank. I missed those years.

"Thank you for meeting me," I said when Dane opened the door. Inside, his condo was new and bare, no amassed clutter. The walls were bright white, and the wooden floors were dark brown, no stained carpet. A thick leather sofa sat in front of the entertainment center, the perfect place for watching a movie or taking a nap. I was immediately jealous. "I've never noticed this complex before. It's nice."

"It's new. Have the place all to myself," he said, looking around the space. "The owner is an old buddy. He let me buy a place while they finish the other units."

"Lucky you," I said. I looked at Dane, having forgotten how handsome he was in our week apart. He wore a T-shirt and plush sweatpants, his boxers peeping at the waist. "Aren't you working today?"

He hesitated. "I stopped working with Frank last week."

"Why?" Frank hadn't mentioned anything, although he rarely discussed anything business-related.

"Taking his money didn't sit well." He looked down, put his hands inside his pockets.

"Please don't let this be about the other night." My mind immediately returned to the mall parking lot and Dane's kiss. I didn't want my poor judgement to impact him. I wanted our lives to remain unchanged.

"Don't beat yourself up, Olivia." He looked up and smiled. "Other work will come around. Always does."

Without invitation I took a seat on the sofa. "I don't know what I'm doing anymore. I feel like I'm losing my grip on everything."

Dane handed me a pill. Not several, only one. He knew I needed it. I hoped he didn't notice the tremor in my hands.

"You mentioned the other night after the bar—" he began, unsuccessfully.

"No—" I lifted my hand to stop him from saying anything I might not want to hear. Touching his skin made the temptation to touch more of him stronger. He moved closer. His long arm branched my shoulder.

I tilted my head toward his and our lips met. We moved slow, waiting for a flicker of morality to flare up and stop us. His mouth tickled my neck. I slid my hands under his shirt and felt his tight middle. For every wrench of guilt there was a pang of pleasure begging me to continue. I unhooked my bra and he pulled down my panties. I climbed on top and pumped out every morsel of vulnerability and anger I'd been burrowing inside, until there was nothing left. Afterward, we cradled one another, winded and satisfied.

I kept waiting to be pummeled with regret, as I had after the kiss in the parking lot. We dressed, avoiding eye contact and staring intensely at the floor. Pretending as though we hadn't just seen and tasted every bit of each other.

After several quiet minutes, Dane spoke.

"I'm sorry for putting you in this predicament, Olivia. I'm not in my right mind around you. I shouldn't—"

I stopped him, placed my hand against his chest. "No, I wanted this."

Saying the words out loud triggered something inside, a realization. Sleeping with Dane was the first time in years I'd wanted something, and I'd had the control to take it. I didn't ask anyone's permission. I didn't consider anyone else's needs or reaction. I'd deceived Frank while simultaneously liberating myself. It felt bad and good.

"Where do we go from here?" Dane made eye contact for the first time since the romp, his piercing blue eyes asking so many more questions than that simple one.

"I'm not sure," I said. I had no idea how I might feel after returning to Smithwood, carrying the weight of what I'd done. "I need to get Jake. I guess I'll call you."

I left the condo with a pocket full of pills, not yet knowing if I'd again reach out to Dane. My thoughts were too crowded to concoct a plan. I drove to the daycare center and picked up Jake. When I returned home, I began manically preparing dinner. Chopping and baking and boiling away the memories of my afternoon.

I put Jake to bed earlier than usual and poured a glass of wine. The delicious aromas of Italian seasonings and bread filled the dining space, but I didn't dig in. Not yet. I waited on Frank. An outsider looking in would see a happy family. They wouldn't see a dissatisfied husband or an unfaithful wife. With each sip, I combatted my conflicting thoughts. Did I need to be honest with Frank? Could I handle such an enormous secret for the remainder of our marriage? Would I see Dane again? Did I *want* to see him again?

By the time Frank arrived, it was dark, and the food was cold. I was about one glass away from being wholly drunk, and my desire to talk with Frank, about anything, dissipated. Before I stomped up the stairs, he apologized for his morning outburst. If only he knew how much had changed since then.

*

People assume change is something that happens in an instant. Blunt and jarring, like a thundering wave crashing into you and pulling you under. But change is usually much slower than that. It creeps up on you under the pretense that everything is normal, fine. And then suddenly you realize your life is in a completely different state than it was before.

In the days that followed, I tried to push Dane out of my mind. I wrote off our tryst as carnal retribution borne from marital dissatisfaction. A momentary lapse in judgement. But I needed more than that one moment with Dane. With him, I felt seen. Understood and accepted. Even if I could give up Dane, I wasn't ready to lose those newfound feelings.

The next week I returned to the condo. And the week after that. Eventually, I was dropping by Dane's place multiple times a week. Our rendezvous took place while Frank was at work and Jake was in daycare. After a few months, I started visiting on Wednesday nights, too. Frank thought I attended a neighborhood book club. He was happy to see me getting out of the house.

Secrets became my armor. I didn't even confide in Maura, fearing by telling her about the affair I'd risk exposure. I liked having something to protect, something to hide. My relationship with Dane was like riding a continuous roller coaster. We enjoyed obvious highs together, then I'd dip back to my normal life, fabricating excuses and acting as though I hadn't just swallowed a pill and been screwed silly.

My bond with Frank remained strained, although I acknowledged the affair was not the catalyst for our problems. It seemed Frank finally accepted his inability to fix me. He worked longer hours, asked fewer questions. We didn't fight or trade slurs. We didn't raise voices. We had obligatory sex once a week.

Our marriage morphed into a cohabitation for Jake. Sweet Jake, who spoke in nonsensical circles, unaware of his parents' torment. Eventually, he would realize we only smiled for him, not for each other. Finally, I stood at peace with our ordinary marriage; when I needed an escape, I had Dane. And the pills.

My need for both became a tickle beyond reach of scratching. The tickle sank beneath the skin. It grew into a blister, raw and poisoned underneath. It overtook my entire being. You can't explain such longing to a person who hasn't experienced it themselves. But Dane understood. He had that tickle, too.

Four months into our affair, Dane told me he loved me.

We were in bed. I'd started to favor his olive-green sheets over my own, regardless of the lower thread count. He pulled me close, his pubic hair prickling my thigh, and said, "I love you, Olivia."

"It's easy to love me this way," I said, resting my head on his rising chest.

Loving or not loving—it didn't matter. I certainly had grown accustomed to, even preferred, my time with him over Frank. Dane and his bachelor swag never criticized my parenting. He never gave me the side-eye when I popped another pill. He handed me a glass of wine to make it go down easier. I valued our time together for what it was, a distraction from my problems back home.

"I don't follow," Dane said. He sat up and leaned his back against the headboard.

"Anyone can fall in love when the relationship consists of sex and fun," I joked. I wanted to make light of the conversation.

"Is that all this is?" His expression was serious. He wanted to know.

"I don't know how to answer." Dane's declaration had caught me off guard. I'd tried to downplay his developing feelings in recent weeks. I hadn't predicted he'd propel something as catastrophic as *love* into the universe.

He repositioned again, shifting away from me. "Well, all right," he said.

"Stop." I could sense a familiar disappointment with my inability to provide the right answer. "You're acting like Frank."

"At least Frank doesn't know he's sharing you," he said, those beautiful blue eyes haunting me. "Me? I'm forced to pretend my feelings don't exist."

"It's hard for me, too." I reached for him. I wasn't trying to turn him against me. Dane was the only person in my life who appreciated me for who I was.

"Is it?" he asked, unconvinced.

"Yes." I floundered, not knowing if what followed made the situation worse or better. "I love you, too."

Just like that, his demeanor thawed and the happy, understanding man I'd spent months getting to know returned. He held me close, pressing my head against his bare chest and stroked my hair. I smiled, too, at the idea a person could see all sides of me and want to stick around. We shared a glass of wine before I left. My head and heart in the cloud, migrating across life.

When I arrived home, the entire downstairs was dark. I aimed to sneak a shower before suffering an interaction with Frank. I noticed the door leading into the backyard was open. When I walked closer, I saw Frank sitting outside by the fire pit. He looked at me, a world of sadness in his eyes.

"We need to talk," he said.

"Is Jake all right?" I asked, stepping outside. For weeks our only conversations centered around him. I couldn't think of another reason for a discussion, for Frank's somber stare.

Then I saw the jewelry box on his lap and the assorted pills inside.

"This isn't about Jake," he said.

The heat originated in my torso and climbed upward, sprawling down my arms and pounding into my skull. Even my earlobes burned. How long had Frank been rehearsing this?

"Why are you still taking the pills?" he asked.

"You shouldn't go through my things." I tried to walk back inside. This wasn't a big deal. He would see. But Frank stood, grabbing my arm.

"Olivia, we both know you've changed since the accident."

"I'm fine," I said.

Frank, who usually accepted the opportunity to avoid difficult discussions, continued. "We hardly speak. I knew you were hiding something. This is it, isn't it?"

"*Hiding something.* You are overreacting, as always." I expected the familiar repudiation, an eye roll or gesture. But his expression remained focused.

"Overreacting is breaking down in tears when Jake spills his juice on the sofa. Or throwing your phone when you misplace the keys. Finding hidden pills in my wife's jewelry box warrants a reaction."

"*Hidden*," I mocked. "I'm not hiding anything."

"You didn't tell me you were still taking them. The accident was over a year ago."

"Must I run everything by you? Is that what constitutes a good wife?" Because that's what this was about. I was a problem, always was. And Frank thought he'd finally found his answer.

"Be honest, Olivia. Did Dr. Polar prescribe these?" he asked.

I was silent.

"No. He didn't," Frank continued. "You are getting them illegally."

"You don't understand. They make life easier. They make me happy." A moment of truth trudged past my many deceptions. Why couldn't he understand? Why couldn't he see the pills made me better?

"Doesn't Jake make you happy? Don't I?"

"Obviously, Jake makes me happy—"

"Life isn't always easy," he soothed in a patronizing tone. As if life had ever been anything but easy for him. "You can't use pills as an excuse."

"Well, it works, doesn't it? I don't freak out about spilled juice when I take the pills. When I'm not taking them? I'm angry. And irrational."

"Which only proves the pills aren't good for you. The woman I married wasn't easily rattled. These pills… you think you need them when you don't."

As though he knew what I needed. Frank, who'd only ever been successful and fortunate in life. His sole screw-up was ending up with a piece of Adams County trash who just couldn't handle the perfect life he'd provided. He wasn't allowed to highlight my faults while simultaneously rejecting my only means of curing them.

"And it's taken you all this time to pause your own routine long enough to diagnose me?" I asked, tears in my eyes.

"Diagnose—" he interrupted his own rant before it started. His jaw tightened, his hands in fists. "Olivia, I will love you and support you. We can get you treatment. Find a counselor. Hell, hire a nanny for Jake. Whatever will help. But you must tell the truth. Do you have a problem?"

I wished he hadn't found my stash or the confidence to confront me. I wasn't ready to sacrifice the pills, so I confessed my other life-altering secret instead.

"I'm having an affair," I said.

Within seconds, Frank forgot about the pills.

CHAPTER 11

After

Police stations are claustrophobic by design. People rushing around. Abandoned papers and files. Voices forever murmuring on a telephone. Must be the reason why people such as Rowe confess to killing people they did not kill, anything to escape the suffocation.

Eddy sat to my left. Cool, calm, collected. Lawyers are at ease in police stations, firmly perched on the wheel of justice.

"Remember," he hummed, "keep your answers straightforward. No wiggle room. If they ask any bizarre questions, I'll take over. We should be gone in under an hour."

"I trust you, Eddy." My sarcasm prompted an eye roll. Silly for Eddy to play professional around me.

"Olivia." Wooley's familiar voice barked above the cacophony of the waiting area. "It's nice seeing you here. Again."

"Good morning, Detective," answered Eddy. He placed his hand on my shoulder to steady my reaction. I shrugged it away.

"I saw you the other day." He held a mug, stirred it with a plastic spoon. "Was it the pharmacy by your place? Or the liquor store?"

All places I'd visited in the past week.

"Can we issue a restraining order against this asshole?" I asked Eddy.

"He's attempting to get inside your head. Don't let it work," Eddy griped through his teeth.

"Olivia Miller?" A female receptionist interrupted.

"Yes," I responded, thankful for a distraction.

"Follow me. A detective will be with you shortly."

"Hear that, Wooley? I'm speaking with real investigators this time around." I tried not to brush against him as I stood.

"Good for you," he said. "He's a good buddy of mine."

Eddy put his hand on my arm again, and I allowed it to stay until the closed hallway door separated me from Wooley.

Contrary to the lobby, interrogation rooms are never rushed. Eddy said it's all strategy. Cops give you time to think and rethink your responses, ensuring you're wholly psyched by the time the first question arrives. I had no problem with this ruse. I was used to waiting.

A man walked in the room with a name tag which identified him as Detective Crumb. He was a seasoned detective from bigger places. A trimmed beard littered with gray streaks covered his chin. Eddy initiated introductions.

"Ms. Miller, thank you for agreeing to speak with me," said Detective Crumb. "I want to look at this case with fresh eyes. Your involvement is appreciated."

Involvement. A subtle jab, already? I acknowledged his prelude by nodding.

"How long were you and Dane married?" he asked.

"Only three months." We had been together much longer, but that's not the question he asked. I provided a brief and accurate response, as Eddy had coached.

"When you arrived home on July 14th, you found your husband deceased?" he continued.

"Yes," I said.

"Where was he exactly?"

"In the living room. His body was slumped over the sofa." I flinched as the memory of finding him flashed in my mind. No matter how many times I retold my story, certain parts still bothered me and finding the body was one of them.

"What did you do?" he asked.

"At first, I thought he had passed out. I shook him. He didn't respond. I turned him over and I saw the blood." I imagined Eddy miming the words beside me. I recited them as we had rehearsed.

"When you arrived home, did you unlock the door?" he asked.

"No. The door was unlocked."

He bounced from discovery of a body to the triviality of the locked door. Trying to jumble my thoughts.

"Did you try to revive Dane? Perform CPR?" Crumb asked.

"He looked too far gone." Dane's open eyes still haunted me, like he was searching for answers. That's the one thing we both had in common.

"Where had you been that night?" Crumb asked.

I remembered a quartz corner jolting my back as we stumbled for stability. Felt Frank's hands on my thighs as he lifted me on the island. Anticipation as I readied into position.

"I stayed at my ex-husband's house," I answered.

"Frank Grier?" Crumb asked.

"Yes."

I remembered Frank's lips, thin and soft, on mine. Hurried, but familiar. I couldn't believe how long it had been since we'd last kissed. We ached for each other, as if physical contact was the only communication left. Too much lost time. His mouth moved to my neck, lingered a while, before travelling lower.

"Why were you there?" asked Crumb.

"I was visiting our son."

Jake was already fast asleep. And yet I stayed to talk things out. We talked until words were no longer adequate in expressing what we held inside. We went at it in the kitchen, lacking the foresight to move upstairs. Passing headlights beamed through the breakfast nook window in sporadic intervals. Our own little spotlight for our passionate reunion.

None of this was new information. Police knew Frank and I were intimate the night Dane died. I never denied it, nor did he.

Our tryst implicated us both, and yet alibied us at the same time. A lecherous paradox. Either we lied to protect one another, or there was no feasible possibility we killed Dane.

Our encounter, understandably, forever altered my relationship with Julie. Discovering her fiancé's infidelity during a murder investigation did not go over well, especially considering she thought we were becoming friends. She distrusted me and closely monitored my interactions with Frank from that point on. I couldn't blame her. She felt betrayed, by both of us.

Frank admitted the night had been a mistake. A moment of weakness. Sometimes I wonder if Dane hadn't been found dead the next morning, if the outcome would have been different. Maybe he would have called things off with Julie; instead, he married her four months later and distanced me.

Crumb wasn't looking for new details. He wanted to analyze my reaction as I retold the story. Test if his Detective Radar picked up an inconsistency Wooley and the others missed. Eddy and I were too good.

"And Frank was there the entire night?" Crumb asked.

"Yes." My answer quick and concrete.

Eddy was right. We were dismissed within the hour.

*

Ridgeway Inn brought me closer to the outskirts. I could almost smell the manure piles in the cow fields. Only a few weeks ago, the lush mountains wore a combination of orange and brown and gold. Now the trees looked empty and jagged and dangerous. The forest backdrop and a gas station across the street were the only landmarks in sight.

"Snazzy place," I said when Brock opened the door.

"I'm staying in Whitaker indefinitely, and funds are running out."

"Blog not doing well?" I joked.

"No, it's booming in popularity. I've been writing articles in real time. Readers enjoy following an active investigation."

I visited *The Vindictive Type* after our first meeting, although I didn't tell Brock for fear he might prematurely ejaculate. I was curious to know if he had mentioned our previous encounters. It read more professionally than the online forums I usually visited. His latest post detailed the ways in which Whitaker had developed over the past eighteen months, avoiding his connection to me. Maybe I could trust him, after all.

The room was poorly decorated and had two double beds. I kneeled on the one with fewer papers. Brock sat on the other bed, surrounded by folders and photographs.

"Let's get to work," I said. "I won't be able to meet again until Sunday."

"I thought you liked to keep your social calendar sparse. What's going on?"

"Not that it's any of your business, but it's Jake's birthday party this weekend."

"Nice," Brock said, rummaging through a stack of papers. "I probably knew that if I looked in one of these folders."

The idea of Brock knowing anything about Jake was odd. I rarely discussed him with anyone. He was my little secret and the restricted time we had together was sacred. I didn't like the idea of him being a footnote in someone's true crime book.

"What's the theme?" Brock asked.

"I'm not really sure there is one," I said, a tinge embarrassed. "We're having it at this downtown art studio."

"My niece's birthday party always has an extravagant theme. Unicorns or mermaids or farm animals."

"How old is your niece?"

"Ten. Which makes me feel old. She lives in Florida with the rest of the fam. I'm the de facto babysitter when my sister needs a night out." He leaned back on the bed.

"Are you good with kids?" In the short time we'd spent together, I couldn't picture him having the patience for them.

"Well, I'm kinda still a kid myself. We play dress up and eat junk food and stay up late, and then my sister blesses us both out when she gets back."

I understood that role, being more like a friend than a parent. Brock laughed spontaneously, and I understood that, too. Thinking of some quirky thing the kid did or said that produces a smile for no reason.

"What does your family think about you being here?" I asked. I imagined most parents would find it odd their son was taking off to another state to solve a murder.

"They thought I was crazy for blowing my wad to stick around. But they respect my reasons. Rowe's release was a fortunate sign I'm on the right track here."

I rolled my eyes. "You're dramatic, you know."

"I prefer driven." He rolled onto his side. "I'm staying busy enough. Got several interviews lined up in the next week."

"Care to drop any names?" I asked, arching my eyebrows.

"Not yet. You can always visit *The Vindictive Type* for updates." He smirked before his demeanor grew serious. He jabbed his phone and laid it flat on the dresser. "Tell me about your conversation this morning with the police."

"Are you recording this?" I wasn't expecting our conversations to be immortalized, at least until I committed to a formal interview for the book.

"It's easier than writing everything down," he said. He tapped the screen.

I reviewed the uneventful discussion. He absorbed my words. The questions. The new investigators. My interaction with Wooley.

"Please tell me you have dirt on that asshole," I interjected.

"Wooley is a sorry stereotype. Divorced. Probably an alcoholic. I'm pretty sure his wife left him for another guy." He paused, trying to figure out if he'd offended me. "According to my source at the police department, few people respect him. Rowe's arrest fractured his ego."

"Who is this source?" I felt suddenly territorial; Brock should be sharing his information about the case with me, not outsiders.

"I have many sources," he bragged. "I am an investigative journalist, remember."

"You're a blogger," I said, popping his balloon and bringing him down to earth.

"Call me what you want. I know about this case because I've studied it. I'm not required to share everything I've learned."

Blah, blah, blah. Brock the Bully.

"Whatever. You said you wanted to review Dane's background." I grabbed a liquor bottle from my purse and poured it into the paper cups beside the generic coffee maker. I couldn't continue dealing with this case sober.

Brock divulged a random assortment of information he'd dug up on Dane. Some things I knew and others I didn't. He'd been dishonorably discharged from the military after numerous physical altercations with his superiors. Dane told me he'd left when his contract ended. Brock revealed Dane's mother died under suspicious circumstances in a house fire. I knew she was deceased but wasn't aware of the conditions. Dane benefitted from two separate insurance policies after the tragedy.

"Are you suggesting matricide?" I asked.

"You were married to him. Was he capable?"

"Who knows," I said, twirling a wavy strand of hair. I hoped not, but after all this time, my confidence wavered. "It would explain why he was so pushy for us to take out life insurance policies when we got married. Police thought it was suspicious we had large payouts given he died a few months later. I told them it was Dane's idea, but I doubt they believe me."

He read off some quotes he'd pulled from numerous interviews, many of them negative. An old classmate disliked Dane for stealing his girlfriend, an old hunting buddy accused him of borrowing money for a business that never came to fruition.

All stories shared the same underlying theme: Dane was not a good person.

"Okay, we get it. Dane had enemies." I picked at a miniature popcorn bag bought at the vending machine. "Which one killed him?"

"I've got three solid theories." Brock sat on the bed and folded his legs. "I'd rather tackle them one by one."

"Give 'em up."

"First, I need more information. What do you know about Dane's drug dealing?"

I rolled my eyes and popped a kernel in my mouth. "Do we have to call it that?"

"What would you prefer? I mean, he obtained drugs illegally and sold them to people without prescriptions."

"When I think of drug dealers, I envision extravagant spending and weapons and henchmen."

"To a lesser extent, all those applied to Dane." I tried not to view my life with Dane through the same lens Frank and the police used. There was no doubt Dane, and I at times, liked to party. Sure, Dane wasn't completely on the right side of the law, but he wasn't in *consistent* danger. I didn't see any danger at all, until the end.

"I don't know much. Only what he told me. He wasn't exactly an honest person." I don't like reopening this chapter of our history for multiple reasons. "Police already went down this route and couldn't get anything to stick. If one of his secret drug buddies offed him, I'm screwed because we'll never be able to prove it."

Brock reached into his backpack to retrieve a picture. "Have you met this man?"

It was a mugshot. Though only taken from the shoulders up, the person appeared rotund and rough. No hair on his scalp and the hair from his chin swiped his chest.

"No," I said.

"His name is Max Eastwood. He's a big drug guy around here. Word is he and Dane had a falling out shortly before the murder. This is not a fella you want to cross."

"Didn't the police look into him?"

"That's the thing. It wasn't until I really started pressing my street sources that his name even came up. There's no record of police questioning him about Dane."

Without knowing Brock's sources, I couldn't determine how legitimate this lead might be. "You heard his name from a couple of gossips. Why are you so convinced he could be connected?"

"Testimony is a dressed-up form of gossip, equal parts juicy and insightful. Eastwood's rap sheet is long, but his reputation is worse. He's got a bad habit of making his problems disappear. Does the name Steve Sturger sound familiar?"

"Yeah. I knew Sturger." I stretched my arms and walked around the room. "He's already locked up."

"Well, rumor has it the same drug deal that took Sturger down was orchestrated by Eastwood," Brock explained, his tone eager.

"Then why is Eastwood not in jail?"

"He is, actually. But they got him on lesser charges. He probably cooperated with investigators in exchange for a short sentence. His release date is approaching."

"What is this? The year of second chances?" I couldn't help but be bitter. Rowe, Eastwood, even Dane all had been graced with the opportunity to show they weren't as bad as they seemed. Meanwhile, I felt eternally punished for the mistakes I had made. "If Dane and Eastwood were so close, wouldn't I have met him?"

"Maybe Dane had good reason to distance you. How did Dane act in the days and weeks before the murder?"

"Agitated. Angry." I remembered his demeanor changing, morphing so quickly I contemplated if I ever knew the man I married at all. I remembered the sudden struggle to breathe and the burning embarrassment of being tricked by the man I thought I loved.

"Did he say what was bothering him?" Brock asked.

"It involved money." That's all I knew for sure. "He wouldn't say exactly."

"Was he usually forthcoming with you, you know, about how he made money?"

"I never knew about major criminal activity until after…" My words trickled away as memories bled into the present. Dane pacing the room, raging and stammering.

"Olivia, you with us?" Brock asked.

"Dane was maddening on that last night. Irrational." I missed my mouth, and drink spilled on my sweater. "Damn it."

"We can take a break, you know," Brock offered. "If discussing the case is too much."

"I lived it. Talking about it doesn't bother me." I went to the connected bathroom, patted wet napkins on the stain. "I feel light-headed, is all. I need more than shitty popcorn to eat."

"Let's grab dinner," Brock said, picking up his phone and stopping the recording.

"I need to leave, anyway. My eyes turn bad after dark." My head dizzied and ached. No longer gliding with the clouds, I had slipped and was falling through them. Too much too soon, or not enough? "Maybe we should tell the police about Eastwood. Force them to consider other possibilities."

"No, no. Not yet. We'll involve the police when we're convinced we found the right person. Give them too much, and it will muddy the waters." All this *we* talk. Like together we formed a team. "You have contacts from Dane's life. Ask questions. Find out what you can about Eastwood's trouble with Dane."

"You're the reporter. Why can't you look into it?" I spat back.

"I've hit a wall when it comes to Eastwood. You're Dane's widow. People will be open with you in a way they won't me. Likewise, people reluctant to speak with you will chatter away at the idea of their name in print. Together we're an unstoppable team."

He was officially using the word *team*. It didn't hurt having someone on my side, I decided. Brock's information gave me hope there were other people to investigate. I could suffer being haunted by the past if it meant building a brighter future for myself. And for Jake.

I gathered my things, stumbled over the stacked heel of my boot.

"You okay to drive?" Brock asked.

"Fine, fine. I'll get food on the way home."

I left the motel, an annoying homework assignment weighing on my mind and Dane's memory weighing on my soul.

CHAPTER 12

Before

There's nothing worse than watching another person shatter, knowing you caused the fracture. Before my lips whispered their hateful truth, I made my choice. Dane. My confession had slipped out so quickly I didn't consider the devastation Frank would endure. I was only trying to protect myself.

We left the backyard and continued our conversation in the bedroom, not wanting any neighbors to overhear our heated argument. First, came the questions. The Whos and Wheres and Whens. The answers were as difficult to provide as they were to hear. Frank had hired Dane, brought him into our home. I tried to gravitate the discussion away from the affair and toward the marital tension Frank and I had brewed over the past several months.

Anger ensued. He yelled and cursed, while I cautioned him to keep quiet. Jake didn't need to hear his father's reaction to his mother's affair. Forced to lower his voice, Frank released his anger by breaking the jewelry box that housed my pills. Next, he cried, which was the hardest part to watch. Frank rarely showed emotion in the years we'd been together: our wedding, Jake's birth, the car accident. After a parade of frightening reactions, his nerves settled enough for a conversation.

"Is this something we can move past?" he asked, and I wasn't sure if the question was intended for me or himself. His desperate stare never left my face, urging me to speak.

"Frank, I'm the one who messed up. Can *you* move past this?"

Frank, conquering the bed, heaved a wrecked sigh and sat silent. I was sitting in the armchair by our window, cradling my knees like a child who had awoken from a bad dream. I replayed the horrible hours since I'd been home. Imagining the peacefulness of the evening had Frank not found the box, and I had simply showered and succumbed to sleep. I could have started a new day, Frank unaware of the secret hurt I'd generated.

"It will take time," he finally said. He stood and walked closer to me, although he was careful not to touch. "Trust has been broken. I'm going to be bothered for a long time. But I do love you, Olivia. I want to keep our family together."

His response blindsided me. How many husbands in the early stages of an adulterous revelation would be so hopeful? Frank, despite his upset, had more opportunity than most to pick up the pieces and leave my cheating ass in the dust. That's what I had been waiting for. Orders for me to pack my bag and get out. My days of pretending over.

"Okay," I said, hesitantly.

"You can't see… *Dane* anymore." He stammered out the name and looked away from me. "And you must stop lying to me…"

He continued talking, but my mind had already checked out. The last leg of this marathon argument left me exhausted. The only thing I'd been craving more than sleep was a pill, and even though I still wasn't registering the words Frank's flapping mouth delivered, I knew the likelihood of me quitting cold turkey was insurmountable. Impossible.

"Maybe some time apart would be a good thing," I said, realizing only after the fact that I'd interrupted him. Frank was already scheming how to gloss over my failures, like always. "You aren't going to be getting over this anytime soon."

He stared for a beat with his mouth open before speaking. "No, Olivia. I don't think more space between us is the answer."

I remembered Frank's obsessiveness following Jake's birth and the accident. His concern in those early days turned into complete refusal that there were any problems. Frank couldn't foresee it now in his optimistic frenzy, but within weeks he'd be back to gliding over the uncomfortable truth, only this time he'd be bogged down with resentment.

"Frank, we can't just pretend nothing happened," I said.

"I'm not suggesting that's what we do!" His brown eyes bulged, and the yelling returned. "But what do you want from me? You want me to give you your space? So you can go running back to Dane and whatever else you're hiding?"

I couldn't just change myself overnight, and I couldn't change my relationship with Frank in a matter of weeks. As pain-inducing as the affair had been, at least I felt a slice of acceptance when I was with Dane. There were no impossible standards or ultimatums. I didn't deserve someone like Frank, and he certainly deserved better than me.

Frank, still ogling me in silence, recognized my conflict.

"That is what you want, isn't it?" His voice cracked as he asked.

"I didn't say that," I said, and I realized, again, I was crying. It's not like I didn't want Frank. By anyone else's standards, life with him was easy. But I wasn't used to easy. That was the problem. "I'm only saying, maybe I need some time."

"Time." He moved away from me again. "You've had time. You've had *fun*. And all at my expense."

"I'm sorry, Frank." I was. I was truly sorry for the pain I'd caused. Even when Frank ignored my needs, he wasn't intentionally trying to hurt me.

"Apologize later." The rattle in his words was gone. Now his voice was loud and firm. "I need to know right *fucking* now if you want to work on this."

"I… I don't know." I didn't know what I wanted, but I knew I couldn't return to the way things were.

I should have counted my blessings that Frank would even consider giving me another chance. But recommitting to Frank meant forever feeling inadequate, not to mention wilting under the pressure of life without pills. Could I really spend the rest of my life not being good enough? All the while knowing every sad moment, every silent evening between us stemmed from my affair? Frank's version of our family no longer existed and never would.

Dane accepted the real me. The person who needed more than a picket fence and Happily Ever After. The person who craved edge and excitement. My faults were not able to be wished away.

"I think you do know what you want," Frank said, interrupting my thoughts and solidifying our future. He left the house and didn't return until morning, at which point I had already started packing.

*

Jake shone a light into the overtaking darkness. Focusing on him is what carried me through those early days of our separation. I didn't realize how few people I had left in my life to care about. The only other person I needed to share the news with was Maura, and at least she would understand my choices. I'd refrained from telling her how serious my affair with Dane had become, but there was no use in keeping secrets now that Frank knew.

"Frank knows about Dane," I told her. We were in her living room. No kids this time. We'd dropped the kids at Mother's Day Out, weekend childcare aimed at allowing parents to recharge and refuel. I spent our child-free hour explaining what happened.

"Knows what?" Her face strained. "Wait—about the kiss?"

"We've done more than kiss since then. We've been sleeping together for the last four months." I hadn't expected telling Maura to feel so painful, but I supposed that was a shame I'd carry every time I revisited the topic.

She covered her perfectly painted mouth with a perfectly manicured hand. "And you didn't tell me?"

"Admitting it to another person made it real and I wasn't sure I was ready for that." I looked down at my own nubby cuticles. I hadn't properly dressed in days, barely taken the time to shower.

"I understand." Maura had the presence of mind not to make the situation about her. I was going through it, and she could tell. She lurched off the couch and paced. Affairs, she knew well. Being caught was new territory. "Are you okay?"

"Things are understandably horrible." I sobbed. I'd thought, after three days, I'd be able to discuss the ordeal without breaking. My emotions were still raw.

She stopped walking, the tip of one thumb pressed against her teeth. She asked, "How did he find out?"

"I told him," I said, dryly.

"You did?" She appeared shocked for the first time during our conversation.

"He confronted me." I didn't want to tell her what his initial concerns were about. Maura knew even less about the pills. "I couldn't hold in the lies anymore. I told him the truth."

She nodded in understanding. If anyone knew about living with lies, it was Maura, although she arguably handled it better. "How did he take it?"

"Angry. Threatened to kill the guy. Hurt I could do this to him and Jake. He said some nasty things." I looked down again, recalling the worst comments and their sting.

She sat beside me on the couch and stroked my hair. "Honey, that's his anger talking."

"He has every right to feel the way he does. I betrayed him."

"What's happening now?" she asked, a pragmatic demeanor taking over.

"The next week will be dicey. I've decided to move my stuff—"

"He's kicking you out?"

"Given the circumstances, I should be the one to go." I used the long sleeve of my oversized top to wipe a falling tear. "Jake will come with me, for now. Custody will be a whole other mess."

"You and Frank… are divorcing?" She wore a befuddled look on her face, waiting for correction. She clearly hadn't understood the magnitude of my confession and how it would shape our lives moving forward. "I can't believe it."

Another cry bleated out. "I never planned on divorcing, let alone under these circumstances."

She gave me a moment and rubbed my back. "It won't be much distance, but you and Jake are welcome to stay here until you sort things out."

"I'm staying with Dane," I informed her, clearing my throat.

"Dane?" She spat out his name like a curse.

"Yeah."

"How long?"

"Indefinitely, I guess. Dane hates the pain I'm experiencing, but he's thrilled Frank finally knows." I smiled, focusing, for the first time in our conversation, on Dane. I'd hurt Frank and myself with what I'd done, but the decisions I'd made in recent days were deliberate. A necessary Band-Aid-ripping so I could properly heal and start a more authentic life.

Maura didn't say anything. She meandered into the kitchen and poured wine for herself. Not me.

"So, you didn't only admit to an affair," she said, finally. "You are *leaving* Frank for Dane. And taking Jake away?"

"I'm not *taking* Jake." I didn't appreciate her delivery, as though Jake was some object for his parents to fight over.

"Did you even consider breaking it off with Dane?" The question sounded like an accusation.

"Frank and I aren't going to work, Maura," I explained. "And I love Dane."

"You're not supposed to fall in love with the guy you're sleeping with." She recited this as though I'd broken a rule. She shook her head. "Don't you love Frank?"

"I'll always love him. He's Jake's father. But our marriage was unhappy before Dane came along. Since the accident, really."

"All relationships ebb and flow." She brought back the same, soothing tone she always used when counseling me.

"You always say that," I snapped. "If we were happy, I would have never had the affair."

"You said he's not throwing you out. Maybe there's a chance of reconciliation." She shrugged and took another sip of wine.

"I *want* to be with Dane."

"It's been four months! You don't even know the guy." Her glass clinked hard against the counter.

"Look, I came here for support—"

"I don't support your decision to tear your family apart," she shouted, emphasizing each word with the wobble of her hand.

Maura. My friend. The woman who kept secrets and told me hers. No judgement. No cattiness. Where had she gone?

"You are the only person I thought might understand." My voice cracked.

"Don't compare our situations. What I do is wrong, but it's fun. It breaks up the monotony. My *heart* will always belong to Ronnie." My old friend momentarily reemerged. The one who hated her actions yet resisted change. "I would never break up my family."

"What you do is just as bad. Don't you realize?"

"Maybe it is." She gulped more wine. "But I still have a husband coming home in a few hours."

I arrived late to Mother's Day Out because I cried in my car for twenty minutes. Already beginning to question what I had done.

*

Nothing mattered when I was with Dane. I spent the first night at the condo, crying in his arms. Mascara rivers streaked his white shirt.

"She is a bitch to treat you that way," Dane said when I told him Maura's reaction. He cuddled behind me in bed, fully clothed, trying to diminish the pain of recent days.

"What I'm doing isn't admirable."

"She's your friend." He combed strands of hair away from my face, though some stuck to my wet cheeks. "She shouldn't kick you when you're down."

"I'm a fool. As if ending my marriage would be easy."

"Babe, the hardest part is over." He pulled me in, kissed my forehead. "And I love you for doing it. Now I get to have you all the time."

Dane was right about the hardest part being over. The divorce itself was amicable. We didn't fight over assets or money. He kept the house and gave me a moderate lump sum to avoid ongoing alimony, enough to hold me over until I could start earning an income of my own. I didn't touch his Tellit trust fund, his parents' only real concern. We agreed to 50/50 custody of Jake. Child support wasn't an issue; I knew Frank would always provide.

The absent drama almost made the situation more hurtful. Like Frank didn't have it in him to fight, and I certainly wasn't going to further complicate things. At each mediation, he sat motionless, his eyes glued to the table. Our hired help did the talking. I broke his heart by cheating, crushed his spirit by refusing to stay. Within three months, our family legally and emotionally dissolved.

Jake was only two. He would never grow up with his parents under a shared roof, but he would forever have our shared love and commitment to him. Better than dragging out my unhappiness until he was old enough to resent us both.

Frank's demeanor improved with each custody exchange. He eventually accepted that the marriage he'd envisioned was not attainable for us. I knew he would rebuild. Frank had mastered taking something broken and making it anew.

I also wanted this to be a new chapter for me, and not just with Dane. Part of the reason I felt so stifled in my marriage is because I was wholly reliant upon Frank. I might have rushed into another romantic relationship, but this was my chance to recapture some of the independence I'd forfeited during my first marriage.

I created a website to display some of my old photographs and allotted the rest of my budget for new equipment. I reached out to some of Holland's former clients, who at this point were getting pregnant and having children, and offered my services. Within a few months, I'd already lined up an impressive appointment list of birthday and maternity shoots.

Adjusting to life at the condo was easy. Dane was thrilled to have me there and told me I could redecorate however I liked. Dane's guest bedroom became Jake's new room. I wanted Jake to feel welcome at the condo on his days with me. This wasn't Mamma's new house. It was his, too.

I spent weeks painting an automobile-themed mural. A thin rug displaying roadways covered the floor and various industrial signs dressed the walls. Dane nailed the decorations up the same day I bought them. Chaotic work hours prevented Frank from completing such tasks. Dane had unlimited energy.

Jake was in awe when we revealed the new room. I'd bought him a freight of new toys, not wanting to disturb his familiar ones back at Smithwood. He loved playing with cars and tractors and trucks. Anything with wheels. Dane got down on the floor with him.

"This one is an excavator," Dane said, lifting the toy. "It moves dirt. And this one is a garbage truck. It takes away all the stinky stuff." He scrunched his nose and rolled back his eyes. Made a *shoo* sound. Jake gurgled with laughter.

For the first time since leaving Smithwood, I felt peace. Jake would survive. I would, too. Floating happily in the cloud without judgement or discovery. This is what had been missing, what my words could never express.

When Jake fell asleep, Dane pulled the new comforter over Jake's shoulders. He left the door ajar and a stream of hallway light soaked the room. I had two wine glasses waiting in the living room. A full night's rest had evaded me for weeks. Even though my days had gotten easier, at night my mind stirred. I halved a sleeping pill; Dane and I split it like two apostles breaking bread.

"He's warming up to you," I said. Dane's only hesitancy in combining our lives was his connection to Jake. Not because he didn't want him, but because he wasn't used to kids. He understood my role as a mother and was intimidated by the responsibility. I wanted to reassure him.

"Kids have never been my specialty," Dane admitted. "Not sure how to act around them."

"Not everyone takes to it right away. I didn't. Now it's second nature. I couldn't imagine life without him." I leaned my head on his shoulder.

"It's hard to picture you struggling with him. He's clearly devoted to you."

"Some days, I fear he's raising me more than I'm raising him." I took a hefty sip.

"You're a good mom, Olivia. Don't let the other stuff get you down." *The other stuff.* The accident and the affair and my increasing need to self-medicate. For months—maybe even years—my life had been shrouded in darkness. Dane ushered in brighter possibilities.

"I love you, Dane. I love our life together." His hand squeezed my fingers.

He kissed me hard and pressed his body against mine.

"Jake's here," I reminded.

We snuck to the bedroom and had tingly sex, only quieter than normal.

*

I soon realized Dane loved to socialize. So much of our relationship had taken place in secrecy. I never had the opportunity to watch him in his natural environment.

When Frank and I were married, we'd attend the occasional dinner party at another couple's house, usually a prospective client or an old co-worker from his real estate days. Yet another viable opportunity for my insecurities to gush. There would be mahogany tables and linen napkins. Diverse wine and polite conversations. Wives or girlfriends, depending on said friend's commitment, prepared well-seasoned meats and a plethora of delicious accompaniments.

On the nights Jake was with Frank, Dane preferred hosting parties on his *turf*. We ordered pizza. During warmer weekends, we grilled. Guests brought sides: slaw, beans, corn, and okra. No set menu. Just bring what sounded tasty and dig in.

This mantra included party favors. Frank and I had welcomed our guests with wine. Maybe bourbon if Frank aimed to impress. People came to the condo with a menagerie of intoxicants. Adderall if you needed speed and weed if you needed relaxation. It was like a college free-for-all except the participants were in their late twenties through early forties and there was no more than an Associate's Degree amongst the group.

"Olivia," Dane said, coming up behind me on the balcony. It was one of the first big gatherings we'd hosted since I'd moved in. I'd stepped outside to temporarily avoid the blasting music and breathe in the muggy air. "There's someone I'd like you to meet."

I turned around to see a scrawny man wearing a dark coat. He had hair that went past his shoulders and a newly-lit cigarette between his fingers. "Hello," I said, offering my best smile.

"This is Steve Sturger," Dane said. "He's one of my oldest friends."

"Howdy there," Sturger said, extending his empty hand to shake mine. "So, you're the one Dane's been raving about?"

"I would hope," I said, smiling. I'd met many people in my initial weeks at the condo; it would take time for each person to be committed to memory.

"You sure are a looker," Sturger said, taking a drag of the cigarette.

"Easy, buddy," Dane said, clapping his shoulder. Sturger stumbled under his grasp. He clutched the balcony banister.

"You all right?" I asked, instinctively putting out my hands.

"He's fine," Dane said, turning to go back inside.

"Had a little bit to drink, is all," Sturger said.

Most people arrived at the condo tipsy and left fully inebriated. It was an entertaining break from the routine that had dominated my life back at Smithwood. Dane warned me about his parties and insisted we could stop them if I became uncomfortable.

On the contrary, I craved the riotous atmosphere. My college experience was short-lived. And I always hated those damn dinner parties. Dane's crowd partied every weekend. More, if their schedules allowed. Behavior I'd felt the need to hide with Frank suddenly normalized.

"Do your friends have families?" I asked. It was the morning after another gathering. We lounged in our dirty living area, still hungover, and not yet motivated to do anything productive.

"Everyone has a family, Olivia."

"You know what I mean. Are they married?" I wasn't used to people behaving like this, with such abandon and free will.

"Some. Most of the guys are bachelors. Like I was."

"What about kids?" I asked, spraying the coffee table and wiping the surface.

"Some. Sturger had a daughter in high school. Doesn't see her much. A few others have kids, but they're still single. Pretty messy world once you move beyond the suburbs." My face soured. "Don't get all sore."

My assigned role among Dane's friends was reformed housewife. I spent my years in suburbia not feeling good enough, then transitioned into a new life which categorized me too good. It didn't matter that I grew up dirt poor. It didn't matter I had been so dissatisfied I chose to leave Smithwood behind. I was an outsider. I overlooked the occasional digs—the homemaker banter and Barbie jabs—because I enjoyed the lack of judgement. I'd rather be labeled a princess than a bad wife or mother.

CHAPTER 13

After

The morning after I met Brock at the hotel, I woke up early to do some investigating of my own. I started by typing the name Max Eastwood into my computer's search engine, but nothing useful appeared. After thirty minutes, I slammed my laptop shut.

I knew my most productive option for tracking down Max Eastwood would be contacting Dane's old friends. However, I was reluctant to reach out. Despite Farrah's reassurances, I wasn't convinced Dane's friends believed I was innocent. I wasn't sure they ever liked me, really. I knew they wouldn't help if they thought I killed Dane. And I only wanted to speak with people I could trust.

Brock was convinced Eastwood had motive, but there could easily have been more familiar suspects. I tried to remember anyone Dane might have wronged. Steve Sturger was the first to come to mind; he was one of the few people I saw Dane directly harm. Farrah insisted Sturger was locked away now, but that didn't prove his whereabouts around the time of the murder. I struggled to remember other names; Dane's friends left a minimal imprint on my life and memory.

Even I had to admit, at times, I had more motive than anyone to want Dane out of the picture. In theory, Dane's death improved my life. He was gone. I was single again. I had a purchased condo and hefty insurance policy for future expenses. But the peace brought on by Dane's absence was short-lived.

When Frank decided to take custody of Jake, I lost everything. The condo and the insurance money didn't matter at that point. Nothing did. Entering a new phase of my life was meaningless without Jake along for the journey. Jake was my biggest loss, but he wasn't the only one. The photography business I'd waited so long to start wasn't much, but it paid the bills and gave me a sense of professional purpose. That was gone, too.

The familiar mixture of self-loathing and regret tempted me to pour a drink, ingest something that could displace my memories. I was on the verge of grabbing a glass when my phone rang. The screen read: Julie. I slung back my head and looked at the ceiling. I was already depressed enough, speaking to Julie would certainly worsen my mood.

"Morning, Olivia," she said, when I answered.

"Hi, Julie," I said, slathering a piece of toast with butter. I'd decided eating rather than drinking was a healthier way to wrangle my emotions.

"I'm sure you're gearing up for the party this weekend," she said.

"I am." Frank and Julie had reserved The Painter's Lounge party room for Jake's fifth birthday. Birthday parties used to be fun for me, back when I was the one in charge of planning them. This would make the second year in a row I wasn't given say. I was told where to go and what to do. "Do you need help with anything?"

"That's actually why I called," she said. "Do you think you could make gift bags to give the guests as they leave?"

"Sure," I chirped. I hadn't intended to sound so eager. "I was wanting to make something. How many kids will be there?"

"We invited his entire preschool class this year," she said. "We wanted him to have a big party."

Last year, Jake's birthday party took place only a month after Rowe's arrest. While the arrest was a relief, Frank and Julie didn't feel comfortable hosting a large gathering that might draw more attention. They kept their wedding small for the same reasons. Jake deserved a lavish party this year; Rowe wouldn't get the opportunity to ruin it a second time.

"I'll run to the store this afternoon," I said. "I can help with other stuff, too." I'd hoped the purpose of Julie's phone call was to collaborate, not just assign menial tasks.

"I think everything else is covered—" She sounded bored now, like I was delaying her pre-established plans. I didn't care. This was my opportunity to be involved, and I wanted to know all the details.

"What are we doing about cake?" I asked. "Are you making one?"

"I ordered one," she said.

"What about decorations?" I chewed a bite of toast as I spoke. "I wouldn't mind making centerpieces for the tables. Or a banner."

"Kids will be painting most of the time, so I don't think we need to go overboard," she said, as kindly as she could.

"I understand." I shifted my weight from one foot to the next. "Well, if there's anything I can do, Julie, let me know. I'd really love to help."

"I appreciate it," she said, sounding a tad too smug. She recovered by shifting the focus back to Jake. "I know it means a lot to Jake when we're all together."

As much as it bothered me, Jake loved Julie. And she loved him. She treated him like her own; I just wished she'd remember he wasn't hers. He was mine and sharing him with her was the biggest punishment of all.

"Thanks, Julie," I said, clicking off the phone.

*

I rushed to the craft supplies store. Now that I had a designated responsibility for the party, I needed to perfect my contribution. I gathered knick-knacks for the bags' contents, colorful ribbons and stickers. While I was out, Farrah called to ask when we could meet. I told her to come over, on the condition she stayed around and helped.

Cellophane crackled as I tried to morph the material into an appropriate shape. The belly was stuffed with silly string and miniature mazes and plastic whistles. I wrung the paper at the top while Farrah handed me ribbon in eight-inch cuts to secure the contents.

"The Painter's Lounge? I've never been to this place," said Farrah, meticulously clipping string.

"It's big with the ten and under crowd. Jake and I went once for Mother's Day. You pick out pottery or wood, paint it, and they finish it up for you. He made me that." Her eyes followed mine to a ceramic mug on the counter. Primary colors spurted unevenly on one side of it. I used it to hold candy and mints.

"Cute." Farrah's true feelings about children remained a mystery. She never mentioned wanting them, and I guessed she was past the age of exploring options. Were kids this fun adventure she never experienced, or a burden narrowly avoided?

"I appreciate the help." I sat on the floor by the fireplace with my legs folded. Usually when Farrah visited, I wore pajamas; I'd either just left my bed or was about to enter it. Because of my spontaneous run to the craft store, I was wearing leggings, a hoodie, and small traces of makeup. I felt, remotely, like a productive member of society. "My mind has been in the gutter lately, and I need a happy distraction."

"I know whatcha mean, buttercup." She sat next to me, her hair piled atop her head in a thick bun. "Everywhere I look there's another story about the Marcus Rowe fiasco."

Rowe's release was approaching, although an exact date had not yet been determined. Each edition of the local newspaper devoted more space to the story. Even the indie biweeklies in Whitaker covered the case. They focused on an innocent man wrongly accused. For now. No telling when articles would march toward a new target, and if that new target would be me.

"It's a mess," I said, thinking back to some of the awkward looks I received while at the store. Perhaps my strategy of staying indoors until dark would draw less attention.

"Any updates with the case?" Farrah asked.

"Eddy convinced me to meet with the new investigators yesterday. Give them a formal interview."

"I thought his job was to steer you away from the police." She squinted her eyes and tilted her head.

"Instead of being chased down, I'm coming to them."

She made a *hmph* sound and yanked the string. "How'd it go?"

"It's unsettling when half the department thinks you killed your husband." I remembered Wooley's smug smile and the arrogance of the new investigator. I'd told the horrific story repeatedly and still wasn't convinced anyone believed me. "I'd do about anything for this ordeal to end."

"Hopefully they'll solve the mystery a second time around," she said.

This was supposed to be the final stretch before trial. I should have been polishing off my testimony with Eddy and counting down the days until Rowe's conviction. Instead, I was worrying about being named a suspect. Again. I fluffed the tops of the complete goodie bags, convinced they didn't appear quite right.

"That reminds me, do you know a Max Eastwood?" I asked.

"Doesn't ring a bell." She cut another string with the scissors, handed it over.

"He's bald. Heavy facial hair."

"I see a handful of guys fitting that description every week at Fahrenheit's." There was no telling what types of people she encountered there. "Think I'd remember the name, though. Why do you ask?"

"He's an old friend of Dane's I want to know more about."

"Last time we talked I invited you to hang with the crew and you turned me down. Now you're hunting down old friends. What gives?"

"I met this writer, Brock. We've been reworking Dane's case."

"Ah. You're an investigator now?" She laughed.

"Far from it. I tried looking this Eastwood guy up online. I guess potential killers don't spend time on social media." I wasn't one to talk; I didn't have Facebook either. I tied up the final party bag. "You're the only person from Dane's group who keeps in contact. Let me know if the name gets brought up."

"I'll ask around. Fill you in on who knows him." As usual when Dane was mentioned, her eyes drifted to the sofa. She seemed unsettled by the fact we were stuffing Jake's favors mere feet from where Dane died. "Be careful out there."

"Always," I said.

"So, Brock. Is he cute?"

*

After Farrah left, I noticed I had two missed phone calls from Brock. I'd been so distracted by Jake's party, I'd almost forgotten my intended investigations for the day. I turned back to the computer and logged onto *The Vindictive Type*. Brock had supported me since we met, but I didn't wholly trust him. Not yet. I scrolled through his blog. He still hadn't mentioned my name, opting to write about his interview with an unnamed member of the police department.

The post outlined investigators' most recent understanding of what might have happened to Dane. The source claimed detectives were reviewing "former persons-of-interest in hopes of establishing a motive". Not a good sign for me. I scrolled through the comments; Brock avoided mentioning my name, but his readers weren't as discreet. I clicked through some older posts and discovered bashing me in the comments section was a growing trend. I called Brock immediately.

"Well, I visited your semi-interesting blog," I admitted, reluctantly. I knew this would only boost Brock's inflated ego.

"Wow, semi-interesting," he scoffed. "Tell me how you really feel."

"Do you actually read the comments people leave on your posts?" I asked.

"Every last one."

"So, you are aware of what people write about me?"

He exhaled, sounding suddenly less lively. "Unfortunately, yes."

"I just read a comment which claimed Dane *'pimped me out'* and that one of my *'disgruntled customers'* must have killed him. I'm not sure which part is the most offensive, but it's definitely untrue."

"I know, I know," he said. I knew he was expecting praise for his passion project, not backlash. "Some people read the blog without considering the facts. They're trying so hard to outdo each other with bizarre theories, they end up in left field."

"Well, it's ridiculous. Not to mention slanderous. Can't you turn the comments off?"

"I choose not to—"

"Brock!" He might believe in my innocence, but there were still several details Brock hid from me. He wouldn't tell me his sources, and now he was allowing people to further soil my name. "I thought you wanted to help me."

"Hear me out. Part of what *The Vindictive Type* offers readers is an interactive experience. Now that I'm in Whitaker, I'm providing updates in real time. The comments allow readers to react. The site has been blowing up since Rowe's charges were dropped."

"Well, I'm happy my tarnished reputation is improving your readership." My ally had abandoned me, and there was nothing I could do about it. Brock wouldn't do anything to demean the legitimacy of his blog.

"There's more. I've actually been able to find some good sources through the website. A lot of my readers are Whitaker-based. They're looking for a place to analyze the case on a neutral platform."

"I thought the comments were anonymous."

"They are, kind of. My site requires commenters to create a username and provide an email. When the same username pops up multiple times, I take notice. Then I try tracking them down online. Sure, some leads are bogus, but some become relevant sources."

"Like who?" Maybe he'd finally give me an idea of where he was getting all his information.

"People contributing context to the case. People who knew Dane. One commenter ended up working at the sheriff's office and consistently leaks details off record. That's how I knew a big revelation was coming before they even announced the press conference."

"How do you know these people aren't bullshitting you?" Brock might be persistent, but I predicted he was also gullible.

"I vet everyone I speak with. The average person has so much available online, all you need is a name and you can find out a lot about them. Where they live. Where they work. Hell, what types of people they date. Social media has basically eradicated anonymity, and most commenters aren't clever enough to prevent a trail from leading back to them."

"What about the people that call me a prostitute and a killer? They're not offering insight. They're writing lies! Lies the police could see." Surely he saw this was more than protecting my image; the police didn't need any more reasons to believe I was the one who killed Dane.

"The people writing those comments are trolls you'll find on any website. It's part of the game." He waited, but I didn't respond. We were playing two very different games. "If it makes you feel better, I'll delete the prostitution comment."

"And the others?"

"I can't just scroll through and delete every anti-Olivia post. It would take away the objectivity. And it would scare off readers who might deliver relevant input down the line."

"All right," I said. I was annoyed Brock wielded the control to clean up my image but refused to budge. "You're the professional."

"Can I quote you on that?" He followed his question with a smug laugh.

"Look, I told you I can't meet until after the weekend." I'd allowed Brock's blog and my anxieties surrounding the case to cloud my optimism. I needed to refocus on the party and the parts of my life I *could* control. "Tell me why you called."

"I didn't announce it in on the website yet, but I got word Rowe will be released late tonight. I thought you'd like to know."

"Great," I said. It didn't really matter whether he sat in jail or returned to society. Dane's case was already reopened. Rowe's release only meant another media storm was accumulating. "Thanks for the heads-up."

CHAPTER 14

Before

I met Frank and Jake in the Chicken Dinner parking lot. Custody exchanges since the divorce had been civil, but I considered it best to limit Frank's interactions with Dane. It bothered Frank I had established a new life so quickly, but he knew there wasn't anything to be done about it.

"Mamma." Jake reached his arms out toward me as I unbuckled his car seat.

"Hey, baby boy," I said. Although, no longer a baby. He seemed to grow a little bit taller between visits.

"I want to play," he squealed. Brightly colored slides branching out from the play center captured his attention.

"He's been talking about those slides since we pulled into the place," Frank said.

"I guess we could grab food while we're here." I lifted Jake from his car seat and grabbed his bag.

"Care if I join?" asked Frank.

"Sure." I couldn't remember the last time we'd shared a meal.

Jake took off running before we completed our order. I waited at the counter while Frank monitored the playground. I carried the food over on a tray.

"Thanks for letting me crash lunch," Frank said. He towered over the tiny table. I could tell he'd recently had a haircut.

"He should see us together," I said. Jake needed to know we would always be family, even if we lived separate lives. I tried to grab his attention, but he was immersed inside a ball pit.

"Let him play," Frank said. He squeezed mayo on his sandwich and took a bite. "It won't hurt you to spend a few minutes with me."

Frank's role in my life, outside of being Jake's father, was difficult to define. Bitterness from the divorce had dissipated, but I couldn't quite classify him as a friend. Being around him reminded me of the hurt I'd caused.

"How's life?" I asked, initiating a friendly chat.

"Fine. Working nonstop." He wiped his fingers with his napkin. "We broke ground on our twelfth flip house this month."

"Congratulations." I was happy Frank found professional success. I imagined his income had increased in the months since the divorce, although it wasn't my business and I didn't ask.

"How are you and Dane?" The wince accompanying the name was not as prominent as in the past. He was healing.

"Fine. I think Jake is adjusting." Our cordiality hovered into an awkward silence.

"Dane worked with me. Beyond that, I don't know the guy," Frank said, stewing over his words. "He's clearly able to provide. The condo alone is worth a fortune—"

"I don't need you to worry about us," I interrupted.

"I do worry," he insisted. "You and Jake will always be my family. You appear happy. I just need to hear you say it."

Our conversation now felt like an accusation. An attack. I shouldn't have had to prove my contentedness, justify the decision I'd made. Frank stared back at me, displaying more concern than he did during our marriage. Then, he'd simply expected me to be happy. Now, he actually wanted to know.

"I'm happy, Frank," I said. We ate our meal in silence and watched Jake play.

Typical Frank. Believing it was his place to protect, even when it wasn't. The comment about the condo bothered me, though. It was a nice place, sure. Not necessarily a *fortune*. Curiosity got the best of me, and I decided to search for our building on

Zillow. Some of the completed units were already posted for a staggering price.

While Jake napped, I confronted Dane. He was in the living room tackling a load of laundry.

"How much did you pay for this place?" I asked. I sat on the sofa with my arms crossed. Dane had recently shaved his beard, which made him look youthful and clean. But I suspected he had something to hide.

"My buddy owns the complex. He cut me a deal," he said.

"Do you know how much the other units cost?"

"I have an idea." He avoided eye contact, focusing intently on the laundry in front of him.

"High six figures," I said.

He nodded, folded a dish towel.

"You owned it before I moved in, so I never thought to ask," I continued. "It seems higher than what the average construction worker makes."

He flinched playfully. "Ouch. How much is that?"

"Well, you worked for Frank. His workers' wages are far less."

He put down the bed sheet he was holding in his hands and looked at me. "Frank wasn't my only income. I had money before I began working with him."

"I'm sure. But there's the condo. Your car."

I never worried about expenses with Frank, and moving in with Dane had happened so quickly, I didn't take the time to consider these financial details. I'd asked him once what he needed me to contribute, and he told me not to worry. The condo was already paid off, and he'd rather me put my money toward photography than the same bills he'd been managing for years.

"What are you getting at Olivia?" Dane asked.

"You have a great deal of money at your disposal," I said, choosing my words carefully. "My photography sessions are pocket change in comparison. I'm wondering, how?"

"How much did Frank spoil you?" He played it off like he was joking, but there was a mean edge in his tone. "You didn't have a realistic idea of what it cost to provide then, and now four months after you've moved in, you're asking me how I pay the bills?"

"It's a bit cart before the horse," I said, shifting the weight in my hips and brushing the hairs away from my face. "But I am living here now. I sense you're not telling me something."

He sighed and returned his attention to the laundry-covered sofa, but he kept talking. "I received some money when Mom died. That's what paid for the big things. Our condo. The car—which I've had six years, mind you. The construction company I'm at now compensates well. Better than Frank did."

"Okay." I needed more.

He abandoned the pile and sat beside me on the sofa. "Do you realize how much the pills you take cost?"

"They can't be much." I hadn't filled a prescription in my name in over a year. Dane supplied me with what I needed.

"Yeah, when insurance provides them. On the street, they cost more. And people are willing to pay."

"How much?"

He huffed like a dragon out of burn. "I make several hundred a month selling my prescriptions."

"So you're, like, actively selling them?" I always looked the other way about the amounts of medicine Dane was able to access. He told me he'd hurt his back on the job several years back and that's why he had a prescription. But I never imagined Dane was purposefully seeking pills as some sort of enterprise. "What about the ones you take? The ones you give me?"

He wore the same expression as my math tutor in high school. "It's called doctor shopping," he said. "I have five prescriptions coming in. I keep some for us, sell the rest."

"How can you obtain multiple prescriptions?" I asked, struggling to keep up. "My doctor cut me off a few months after the accident."

"Yeah, well I don't go to some golf course physician. Plenty of doctors will write a prescription for the right price."

"Don't they regulate medications?" I knew a person couldn't get their hands on multiple prescriptions without some level of duplicity.

"There are always ways around the system," he said. "I fill some prescriptions the next state over."

"Dane, that's illegal."

"Taking my pills is illegal, Olivia. You gonna stop? I could use an extra couple of hundred." He laughed and squeezed my shoulder. "You really don't know what your lifestyle costs, do you?"

"You win. I'm clueless." I shifted my body away from him. I didn't like him pretending as though I was some immature bunny who didn't know how the world operates.

He wrapped me in his arms, put his lips to my neck. "I'm sorry. I'm beating up on you."

"You can't blame me for asking."

"You're right. I blame myself for not telling you sooner. You deserved full disclosure before you moved in."

"Then why didn't you tell me?" I asked, not yet convinced this activity was as minor as he made it out to be.

"Because I still wanted you to move in. And I want to be with you." His charm returned, washing away my caution, though not completely. "A lot of people make extra cash the way I do. My salary funds our lifestyle. The pill money covers the fun stuff."

"How serious is this, Dane? Could you get hurt? Arrested?"

"No need to worry about me." He sounded like I did when coaxing Frank.

"It's more than you." My eyes darted in the direction of the bedroom. "I have Jake to worry about."

"I would never put Jake in danger," he said. "You know me better than that."

"I learn something new every day," I whispered when he walked away.

*

Explaining to Dane how I felt about his admission was difficult, especially when I couldn't even make sense of it myself. A part of me felt foolish because I'd lived with the man for months and never suspected he sold drugs.

He'd sold to me back when he worked for Frank, but I'd stupidly thought he'd done it to help me during my time of need. Like I was special, in a sense. I didn't realize I was one of multiple people with whom he shared his plenty. That I was no different from Sturger or one of the other nameless visitors who entered our home on the weekends. He must have charged me a cheaper rate, at least, if he was making as much as he said.

I understood why Dane was reluctant to tell me. For people like Frank, drugs were an absolute nonnegotiable, taking them or selling them. Partying with Dane's friends, on occasion, didn't bother me; he couldn't understand why selling pills to those same friends, on occasion, would.

As a teenager, I never partied. I already had too much on my plate with Mamma. By that time, we had done the relentless tango of diagnosis and treatment for so long I was almost relieved to know it would be over soon.

I had been without a mother for years before she got sick. But now her adult brain was as mushy as my teenage one, so I kept my teenage rebellion at bay. I didn't cheat on tests. I didn't get high. Once I told Mamma I was spending the night at a friend's house only to sneak off to a concert an hour away. I consumed two and half beers that night and felt so guilty, I cried off and on for a week straight. What kind of person lies to their dying mother?

I wanted to provide Mamma with the appearance of stability. Allow her to leave her only daughter in peace. I think that's why I justified my need to let loose, at times; I never had the opportunity when I was younger. But Dane selling drugs actively invited trouble. It was a risk I wanted to avoid, both for Jake and myself.

I didn't know how to communicate those concerns to Dane. With Frank, I learned to bury my problems. Vocalizing them always left me shot down. I didn't want the same dynamic with Dane. Besides, he had a better understanding of his situation than I did. His supply couldn't be that large, otherwise I would have suspected something sooner. I chose to trust him, which meant carrying on as I had before finding out. Instead of considering the negative implications of our lives together, I focused on the good parts. On the fun parts.

The next weekend, after Jake had returned to Smithwood, I ended up getting high in my bedroom with Dane and Steve Sturger. The guys were reluctant to share with the others outside. I normally turned down the weed people brought over; I hadn't smoked since before I married Frank. But with my worries accumulating, I decided I'd earned the release.

"Don't hit it too hard," Dane said, passing the bowl.

As I inhaled, the stuffy smoke burned my throat. I coughed hard, and Sturger laughed.

"Cut it out," Dane told him, turning his attention back to me. "Breathe. You'll feel great in a minute."

It's funny how the most random moment can trigger a memory locked up deep inside. I remembered Mamma on some holiday, maybe Labor Day. We'd spent the long weekend camping with some of her friends I barely knew. Mamma always had a way of making new friends.

Noises from outside woke me, and I snuck out of the tent to see what caused them. Even then, maybe aged ten, I was curious. Strangers sat in foldable chairs by the water's edge, blaring 90s music from speakers. It was dark, the only light streamed from the moon and stretched out over the lake. Mamma dipped her feet in the water, laughing and smiling like always.

Suddenly, she stood up, marched away from the dusty riverbank and into the grass. Barefoot, she danced. Not to a specific rhythm. She just danced. It wasn't a human movement; she mirrored strands of seagrass or cornstalks in the wind, something organic and of the earth. She looked happy. Away from the crowd, away from me. Complete with herself. I quietly watched her, wishing one day I'd be as beautiful as she was in that moment.

I knew now she looked how I felt. My body tingled, but my mind relaxed. Sturger's rookie jokes be damned. My confidence swelled. I'd finally found a way to unleash my pent-up anguish. I laughed and danced. Later that night, when everyone had left, Dane wrestled me into bed and slid inside me; I felt each pulse and sensation. And I knew immediately I wanted to experience this carnival of fabulous emotions again.

By morning, I felt guilty. Pot wasn't like pills. The pills helped me, made me a better parent. I would have never considered smoking weed back when I lived at Smithwood, but I also had my son every day back then. If I was forced to split my kid with Frank during the week, then I deserved a reward when they weren't around.

My non-Mommy days.

CHAPTER 15

After

Jake was a toddler the last time we went to The Painter's Lounge together. Old enough to participate, still too young to create artwork with any precision. There was more paint on the table and apron than on the mug. Overpriced pottery worth all the fun with no clean-up.

Now he was turning five. So much had happened in the years between visits. One would never infer by looking at him his parents were divorced, or his stepfather had been murdered. Jake beamed, all smiles and glee as a dozen of his young friends crowded the studio aisles.

"Not a bad turnout," said Frank. We resumed our affable repertoire come birthday season, whether we were on good terms or not.

The advantage of renting a venue meant no additional work. Order pizzas, pick a cake and write a check to compensate for doing nothing else. At least, that's what Julie had led me to believe during our phone conversation.

Apparently, Julie had taken time to come in early on a Saturday morning and decorate. Canvas seat covers with paintbrushes blanketed the tiny metal chairs. Each craft area bedecked with a different colored tablecloth, following a ROY G. BIV sequence. A personalized birthday banner drooped over the food table.

Jake's happiness was our main priority, but I was also bitter Julie hadn't told me the amount of effort she had really put into the party. She assigned gift bag duty, so I couldn't say she completely iced me out, but she also distanced me to maintain control. In many ways, Julie provided for Jake what I couldn't, but sometimes I wish she'd give me the space to try.

"I would have helped with decorations," I said to Frank. He was standing by the gift table reorganizing presents. "Julie assured me she wasn't going overboard when she called me."

"You know Julie," Frank said, with a dewy smile on his face. "She lives for parties and crafting."

"Maybe I don't paint as much as I used to, but Jake and I make crafts on every visit. It's our thing." Julie wasn't some party-planning mastermind. Surely Frank hadn't forgotten my hobbies, too. "If she was putting in this much effort, the least she could have done was give me more than goodie bags."

Across the room, Julie stood at the glass doors greeting guests as they arrived. Other than our similar interest in crafts, we differed tremendously. I was her physical opposite with a petite frame and wavy brown hair that dangled past my breasts. Long overdue for a cut. I wore black leggings, a V-neck and combat boots. My idea of dressing up meant wearing a blue shirt.

Julie, on the other hand, looked like she stepped out of a J. Crew ad. Pleated khakis and a robin's egg sweater over her navy blouse. Simple jewelry, not flashy. A blonde bob tickled her clavicle. Her smile emanated kindness, an aura I could not match. Even on my happiest days I didn't look that pulled together. I may have been naturally prettier than Julie, but she put in enough effort to come out on top.

Was she what Frank had wanted in our marriage? A stereotype of the American soccer mom? Even before the drama and the divorce and the heartache, I always had an edge. Hard to imagine the same man could love two opposites.

"Cute gift bags, Olivia," said Julie when she approached.

"Thank you," I responded, gritting my teeth. Her kindness didn't always seem as genuine when directed at me. "I told Frank how great the place looks."

"Appreciate it." She stretched out *it* long enough to annoy me. "I really wanted to make Jake proud."

As if a preschooler gives a damn about seat covers. The additional effort had nothing to do with Jake, and I might respect her more if she would admit it. Parties used to be about dropping your kids off in exchange for a few hours of solitude and sanity. Even better if you scored an invitation to an overnight. The philosophy has changed. Now the parents stick around, their expectations looming. Guests would leave this party impressed, Julie had made sure.

"Mamma, which should I paint?" Jake left a huddle of friends and extracted me from the co-parenting trio. *Thank goodness*. My attendance was solely about him.

We ended up choosing a Christmas decoration. "You can hang it on our tree," I told him. He liked that idea.

"You need to make something," he said. I looked at all the other adults, casually standing around the tables and observing their little artists at work.

"I think the painting is for kids, hun," I said.

"Come on, Mamma. You're a great painter."

Once, Jake found a stack of my old canvases I'd painted before college. He pulled each out, oohing and aahing at the different colors and images. A sketch of a girl eating a sandwich in the park. A painting of the Whitaker Bridge over the river. A watercolor of two hands, their fingers connecting at the tips. That was the first time I pulled out my old supplies, watered down the stiffened brush fibers and peeled off the hardened globs of paint around the tubes. We spent the rest of the afternoon creating an artistic mess, one of my happiest memories.

Screw it, I thought. "All right. Only if you help me."

I chose a tile on which to place his palm print. He laughed as I tickled the underside of his hand cobalt. His friends saw, decided they too wanted to paint their appendages, greatly annoying the staff. I valued the moment. My baby boy was growing up but still wanted me around.

It was clean-up time and then pizza and then presents. Jake already had more toys than one child could need, but when your belongings are split between two homes, it never hurts to have more. He tore green wrapping paper off another box and celebrated the plastic dinosaur set inside. Julie moved the scraps away, creating a path for each new gift.

"Where does the time go?" I asked Frank. He stood back from the crowd, avoiding the chaos.

"No idea. He's had a blast today." He leaned against an exposed brick wall, staring at our happy son.

"I hope so." I smiled, watching Jake's unfiltered reaction to another toy.

"He's so taken by you, Olivia," Frank said, turning his head so a passerby wouldn't hear us. "He doesn't share the same connection with me or anyone else. You're his mom."

Words I needed to hear. I may not be the image of what a mother should be, but I still was one. Frank always managed to remind me.

"I'd love to spend more time with him, Frank." He lowered his head. Custody talks were never easy. And he had already suggested his stance on the matter. Rowe's release and the unknown direction of the investigation created another obstacle. "I mean, now I'm the fun parent. He's going to be a teenager before we know it. We need to make sure he has equal opportunity to resent us both."

Frank laughed, stared at me a few seconds. Uncrossing his arms, he said, "I know you want more time with him, but I don't want him caught up in a new investigation. Have you heard from the police?"

"I met with them last week." I clenched my teeth, knowing Frank wouldn't be impressed.

"As in an interview? Olivia, surely not—"

"Eddy suggested it."

He shook his head. "Eddy is a hack. You shouldn't listen to the guy. I'm sure you have enough money to hire a better lawyer."

I had enough money to justify not working and keep Dane's roof over my head. I couldn't exactly afford the Dream Team. "He's kept me out of jail this long."

"I'm just saying, keep your distance from the police. You can't trust them." He looked down and tapped his foot. "What did they ask you?"

"It was a standard conversation. They asked all the typical questions." His stare told me he wanted more. Reassurance. "I gave them all the typical answers. Nothing new was said. By either of us."

"Good." His forehead smoothed.

Julie noticed us talking and crept closer. Her discussion with friends continued, although her neck craned in our direction. After all this time, even in a public setting, she didn't trust us together.

"Have you talked with police?" I asked.

"They've contacted me. I won't be volunteering to any interviews, though."

"Things might run smoother if you cooperate." I twiddled my fingers and looked at the concrete floor. "I've been reviewing the case with this guy. Brock."

"The blogger?" He looked bewildered.

"You're familiar?"

"He sent some emails. Wanted to sit down and talk. Obviously, I turned him down. Why are you getting involved with him?"

"Dane's murder already stole a year and a half of my life. Not to mention Jake. It was all a waste because they arrested the wrong guy." I sensed my volume increasing and moved closer to him. My chest tapped his shoulder. "I want more visitation with Jake, eventually. If talking to the police or Brock expedites things… I'll do whatever it takes to solve this case."

"You should allow the police to handle it, not willingly insert yourself into the drama," Frank scolded. Despite our strained relationship, he still mistakenly thought he had a right to control me. "There's danger in it for Jake, and you. You do realize this is a murder investigation, right?"

"I know better than anyone." Jake, wearing a cone hat and frosting on his face, headed in our direction. I squeezed Frank's shoulder as a warning. "Besides, it's not your place to protect me anymore."

*

Frank's trunk and backseat filled with presents and deconstructed decorations, so we put the remaining items in my car.

"Now you'll have new toys to play with when you visit," I told Jake, running my fingers through his hair.

"Sounds good, Mamma." He went inside and joined the last of the partygoers.

Walking back through the parking lot, I noticed Julie perfecting her role as hostess amid the other moms. Paranoia piqued me, as I thought I heard my name. I ducked behind a tall SUV and listened.

"How often does she take him?" asked the mom wearing plaid. I didn't know her name or any of the others. They were Julie's friends, not mine.

"Not much," said Julie's voice, a whisper. "Every other weekend."

"Did you see her painting with all the children? Pathetic," said the short woman stuffed into a pair of Hunter rain boots.

"Like I said, we don't interact with her often," Julie said. "Only big events, like this."

"Well, that's how those types of parents are. They show up for the fun stuff," said the wannabe lumberjack. "Jake's lucky to have you."

Tears welled, and my cheeks burned. Julie and her cronies vocalized all the fears I had about my own parenting, were judging me at my son's party. I never claimed to be the best mother, but in my defense, no one ever showed me how to be one. I'd tried to atone for the pain I'd caused. No one understood the gravity of my faults more than I did, and I'd been punished in the worst way possible: by having my son taken away from me. *My son*. Not hers. Never hers.

Pity morphed into anger; there was no stopping me. Julie needed to suffer the same pain I was experiencing, and I knew how to hurt her most.

"You're so right," I said, coming around the corner. After all the subtle jabs made between us over the years, I finally felt justified in hurting her back. The release felt good. "Jake is lucky to have you, Julie."

Shock painted Julie's face. Her friends stood mortified.

"Olivia. I—" Julie tried to recover, but I blocked her input.

"And even more, you are lucky to have him." My voice low, my tone mean, I said, "It's not like you have children of your own."

The woman in plaid audibly gasped. The boot-wearer looked down in shame. Julie's mouth slung agape, her mind processing what I had said in front of her friends. If my biggest fear was losing Jake, hers was being publicly humiliated. I waited for the tears to fall. Instead, she raised her delicate hand and slapped me across the face hard enough to make my teeth ache.

CHAPTER 16

Before

As the months passed, my worries about Dane increased. His rowdy parties. His disreputable acquaintances. Ignoring his lifestyle was easy when I was reaping the benefits, getting high and letting loose. Under the light of day, his misdeeds became harder to ignore.

Dane maintained I had nothing to worry about when it came to his *side business*. He'd been selling pills long before he met me, and he didn't push enough product to draw anyone's attention. But he had my attention. Behaviors I overlooked in the past now rang loud alarms inside my head. I was aware Dane had two cell phones, one for personal use and one for work. It took me several weeks to realize his *work* phone had nothing to do with construction. As he explained, the second phone was a pay-as-you-go cell, easy to ditch and incapable of tracking interactions.

Now with every ping and buzz, I wondered. Who was reaching out? Dane had always been popular, of course. Most of his friends wanted a good time, like me. Some, I feared, wanted more. Those friends concerned me.

I mustered the confidence to confront him over brunch, hoping he'd willingly consider more legitimate ways of earning income. We sampled a new venue a block away from the condo, and I raised the subject over fluffy pancakes and syrupy fried chicken.

"I've been thinking about your hobby," I said, sounding like an idiot, but not ready to use words like *dealing* and *drugs*. "Maybe you should stop while you're ahead. We're not hurting for money."

"We're not hurting for money because of what I do," he replied, straining to hide his irritation. "I've already told you. There is nothing to worry about."

"I do worry, Dane. I can't help it. I'm not used to this lifestyle."

Dane was right about one thing: Frank had spoiled me, but not purely in the financial sense. I never worried about Frank making risky decisions which could jeopardize our future. Even if he did, we always had his parents as a safety net. There was no safety net with Dane.

"Your outlook is black and white," he said. "You see good and bad, legal and illegal. There's a whole lot of people that live successful lives by living in the gray. You think the folks living on Tellit Mountain came by every dime honestly?"

"I'm sure some didn't," I admitted. "But some did. Besides, I don't care about the rich people living on Tellit. My life is with you. That's what I'm worried about."

"Lots of people sell stuff on the side. They maintain normal jobs and provide for their families. That's all I'm trying to do." He leaned back, pressed his hands against his chest. "Hell, the doc who writes my prescriptions doesn't care about looking the other way. And I bet *his* wife doesn't give him a hard time about it."

"I realize you're not the only person taking risks." I looked down. He painted a vivid picture of his operation, but Dane's mansplaining failed to erase all my concerns. "Nothing is worth you getting arrested or hurt."

"You're taking too many ideas from TV. Police couldn't care less about one guy pushing a couple of extra prescriptions and selling them to his friends. There's far bigger fish to catch than me."

He sounded confident and sure of himself. He also sounded like I did when reasoning with Frank about pills. If he could only see we didn't need the extra income, maybe he wouldn't feel the pressure to provide.

"My photography business has picked up a lot in the past six months. I've got three maternity shoots booked for next week."

Successful maternity shoots were a gateway to return customers. Down the line there'd be milestone pictures and birthday parties and holiday cards. I'd finally found stability in my career and was able to contribute to our future.

"Olivia, I'm proud of your accomplishments." He slid his hand across the table and held mine.

"We're already making more money. Legally." For the first time in our discussion, I thought I was making positive gains. "Even if we cut back on spending, we'd be doing all right."

He shook his head and looked down at the table. "I wish I could make you understand."

"Try." I squeezed his hand, encouraging him to share.

"Downtown Whitaker wasn't always packed with hip places to eat brunch. As a kid, you avoided the streets at night. Now people loan their life away to live here. Funny how life comes full circle, huh?" He looked around the room, which now appeared vapid and flimsy. He slugged his beer. "I remember being broke. I worked my ass off to grow beyond my roots. I've not struggled since I was a teenager, and I never will again."

"You said it yourself. You've outgrown your past." Dane wasn't some poor kid anymore. The man sitting in front of me, wearing distressed denim and a crisp button-up shirt cuffed at the elbow, appeared accomplished. No one would ever guess he came from so little, or that he sold drugs now. I wished he could see the same person I saw.

"No one escapes their past." Our eyes locked in a duel of wills. "Besides, money isn't the only reason I do what I do. I enjoy the thrill."

"Dane, that's ridiculous." I pushed a fake laugh.

He shook his head, frustrated by his inability to better explain. "How did you feel when you started sleeping with me?"

"Horrible, because I cheated on Frank." I was surprised Dane brought up the early days of our relationship. They'd mostly been a taboo topic since we moved in together.

"You didn't like having a secret?"

I recalled sneaking around during those surreptitious months. Having all that control. The type of dominance Maura used to rave about. It felt gratifying. Powerful. I couldn't fault Dane for wanting to inject adventure into his life. That's what I'd done when I'd feared my own life had become too predictable and constricted.

"On some level," I said. "But I prefer being with you and not having to hide anything."

"I love our life together," he said, lifting my hand and kissing it. "Occasionally, I need excitement. Each time I'm able to make a deal—doesn't matter if I'm making a quick profit or just helping a friend—it wakes me up inside. The adventure. The risk. I don't need it constantly. But I can't let it completely go either."

I hated to admit I understood.

*

I was happy to leave my Dane frustrations behind and focus on Jake. It amazed me how much he seemed to grow up after only a few short days with Frank. People were right about enjoying the little moments before they were gone.

Frank and I agreed to meet at the aquarium for our next kid swap. The floor-to-ceiling tanks mesmerized Jake as we raced from the colorful Caribbean exhibits to the local freshwater fish.

"Mamma, did you know there were fish that big in Whitaker Lake?" Jake asked.

"I was happier not knowing," I answered, prompting a laugh.

"When you get older, we'll try catching a gar that big," Frank said.

"Come on," I said, nudging Frank's shoulder. "You're not a fisherman."

"No, but I could be," Frank said. "Especially if I have a helper." He swooshed Jake's hair before the boy skipped off to an exhibit of otters. Frank and I stood back, smiling. I was happy Dane didn't invade our family time. It was good for the three of us to create memories together, and I hoped it would stay that way.

Then Frank brought up dating.

"I've been seeing someone," he told me.

"Great," I said, my voice chipper and artificial. We'd been separated seven months. Frank was still the handsome and dedicated man I married, although damaged from what I put him through. Plenty of girls were willing to settle down with a guy like Frank, even with Jake as a tag-a-long. "I am happy for you."

"Don't worry. She's not met Jake, yet." He looked in Jake's direction, making sure he was too engaged with the exhibit to hear us. "I'm telling you because it's headed in that direction. I thought maybe you'd like to meet her first."

I had never asked Frank's permission to introduce Jake to Dane. Or to sleep with Dane. Frank wanted to do right by me. Regardless, I wasn't sure how I felt about another woman being around.

"Um, I don't know." I was curious where this was headed. "Where?"

"I thought we could go to dinner. You know, the four of us."

Me and Frank and the new girl and Dane. I knew then she must be serious. "We'll talk it over."

"Great. Maybe we can get together sometime next week?"

"Sounds good, Frank. I'll let you know what we decide." I touched his arm. It pained us, trying to navigate Jake's future in between our separate lives.

Dane understood why we had to attend the dinner. This was Frank's first serious girlfriend. He wouldn't have arranged a meeting with some floozy. And I had to see her. Not because I was jealous. Not because it bothered me Frank was moving on. I just had to see her.

I tried on four different outfits before going with the second option: a black dress that made me look slim without appearing sickly. In recent weeks, Dane had made comments about the lack of *meat on my bones*. I couldn't control my diminishing appetite.

"You look good, babe," Dane said. My hair lingered past my shoulder blades in bedhead waves. I wore a purple-hued stain on my lips. Dane kissed me, transferring the excess color.

"You think?" I asked, pushing for confirmation.

"There's no way Frank found a prettier girl than you."

My palms were covered in a nervous film and I failed to keep the jitters at bay. "I need to take something before we go."

"Let's drink, too." He walked into the kitchen to retrieve two rocks glasses and ice. He poured an amber liquid over the cubes and handed me my drink. He fished inside his pocket and handed a pill to me, too. I swallowed it, couldn't remember how long it had been since the last one. The nerves made it hard to tell.

Frank had made reservations at Alejandro's, an upscale restaurant near the mall. We went there often during the early years of our marriage, before Jake came along. Dane and I were the first couple to arrive. The place was stuffy, with hurried servers carrying steaming plates past the cluttered booths.

"Should we wait at the bar?" asked Dane.

"Yeah. Let's." We perched on two barstools, although the bartender was too busy to notice.

"You all right?" Dane asked.

"Fine."

"You seem uptight."

"It's stressful. And awkward. This is the first time we're really getting together since the divorce." My dress fabric inched up, and I couldn't tug it into submission. "I should have worn a different dress."

"You look fine," Dane reassured me. "Since when do you care what people think?"

Looking around the room, I recognized the different facades of people I used to be. Everyone appeared composed and poised and fake. I didn't belong seven months ago, and I certainly didn't belong now.

"I do care, Dane. Only for tonight, I care what people think."

"Get it out of your head," Dane said, surveying the room. "These people aren't better than us, Olivia. They have their secrets, too. I might not know what they are, but I know they got 'em."

Dane always managed to give my dwindling confidence a boost. I leaned in and kissed him. "I'm going to the bathroom," I said.

"Need anything to drink?" he asked.

"Water, for now."

The last thing I needed was alcohol. My head already spun, and I burned hot all over. Surely this was more than nerves. In the bathroom, I folded a damp towel and held it to the back of my neck. I wanted to splash my face with water until my temperature cooled, but I couldn't risk streaking my makeup. I took a few deep breaths, staring at my reflection. Dane was right, I had lost weight, but I still looked good. Frank's girlfriend was the one needing to prove herself, I reminded myself.

When I returned, Dane had three drinks in front of him: two tequila shots and a water.

"The water is for now. And I went ahead and got you a drink for later." He slid the glass over. Minutes later, Dane nodded toward the dining room. "Showtime."

Frank and his date ambled by the hostess stand. From a distance, they had a newly established couple's fidgety body language. His hand clasped hers as she wiggled the bracelet on her wrist. He refrained from touching her below the waist, which told me they had not yet had sex. Perhaps they weren't as serious as he claimed.

Dane stumbled when we stood, finding balance by grabbing my hip.

"What's wrong with you?" I whispered.

"Missed my step, is all," he puffed.

I immediately recognized the cutting scent on his breath. "Are you messed up already?"

"Aren't you?"

"Hold it together," I ordered.

Frank spotted us, and they walked closer. The woman's blonde hair brushed her shoulders. She stood slim and tall, her heels almost elevating her to Frank's height. She wore an emerald wrap dress and nude shoes. Frank wore a navy suit and burgundy tie.

"Olivia." His hand braced my shoulder, Dane's remained on my waist.

"Hello, Frank," I said. Dane nodded.

"This is Julie," he said. "And this is Olivia and Dane." We dove our palms into the pit of handshakes. Julie had perfect posture, delicate gestures, and a firm grip. Dane's body weight leaned into mine. I felt the blood creeping up my neck to my head as we walked to our table.

There was a lot of chatter exchanged before appetizers were ordered, but by the time entrées arrived, conversation began to stall.

"Julie, what do you do?" I asked, pushing lettuce around the plate with my fork. I'd entered a bizarre limbo where each bite of food sobered me, while simultaneously making me feel sick.

"I'm a nurse in the pediatric ward at Whitaker General," she answered.

"Impressive," I said. "Must be a taxing job."

"Shifts are long and often sporadic, but I love the opportunity to work with children."

"I bet that's fun," Dane said. "Working with kids all day."

"Unfortunately, I'm with them during their lowest moments," she said. "Being able to brighten their day is a true blessing."

Ah, Julie was the type of person to describe common life occurrences, like going to work, as a blessing. This told me a lot about her.

"Frank tells me you are a photographer." She smiled.

"Yes. Mostly couples and family shoots," I said.

"And what do you do, Dane?" she asked.

"Construction." Perhaps Frank hadn't fully divulged the circumstances of the divorce. The waiter came around and Dane ordered two more drinks. "You sure I can't buy you anything, Frank? Julie?"

"I'm fine," said Frank. For the first time all evening, I noticed Frank seemed particularly antsy. He pulled on his shirtsleeve and periodically looked down. Perhaps he too had relied on liquid courage before arriving.

"Not a big drinker," said Julie. Miss Perfect was officially dancing on my nerves.

By the end of dinner, I'd learned more than I cared to know about the new woman in Frank's life. She'd grown up in rural Tennessee and earned her degree from Whitaker University. She'd even dabbled in local beauty pageants, perfectly sensible given her thoughtful responses and careful body language.

"Frank talks about Jake all the time," Julie said to me. "I can't wait to meet the little guy. You must be so proud."

I tried not to focus on the image of this beautiful woman hugging my son, and, instead, continued the conversation. "He's very sweet. So smart. I'd like to think he's the perfect mix of myself and Frank."

Dane and Frank took heavy gulps of their drinks, almost in unison. "He is a good kid," Dane said, wiping his wet chin.

"Frank says he's artistic," Julie said.

"Yeah." I smiled. Talking about Jake made the evening easier, but I was growing impatient of entertaining Frank's date. "I think he gets that from me. We're always painting or drawing something together."

"That's wonderful," Julie said.

"Dessert?" Frank interjected. His tone suggested he was as ready to leave as I was.

"We should probably get going," I said, turning to Dane.

"We promised to catch up with friends downtown. You know, enjoying our weekend without the kid," Dane said. I'd lost count of how many drinks we'd had during the meal, and I worried his drunkenness was about to show.

Frank wasn't sure how to take the comment. "Jake's with my parents, by the way," he said to me.

"Great." I'd entered the phase in which I was unsure if I came off friendly or sloppy, so I kept my responses to a minimum and smiled.

"Olivia, it was lovely to meet you," Julie said.

"And you." We all stood. She moved closer and I dodged her attempted hug by extending my arm for another handshake. Frank noticed my intervention and snickered.

"Frank Grier, is that you?" called an approaching voice.

To my horror, the voice was coming from Jackie Winnipeg, the wife of Marty Winnipeg, an associate at Frank's old real estate agency. Jackie, an epic people pleaser, had hosted numerous dinner parties in the years Frank worked at the company. I'd attended several. She moved in and gave him a half embrace.

"Hello, Jackie," Frank said. "Where's Marty?"

"Oh, we're seated in the back. He's still talking with the guys," she said. She nodded at Julie, then looked at Dane, then me. She did a brief double take upon recognition, undoubtedly trying to piece together when we divorced and why we were all together. "Olivia, what a surprise. I almost didn't recognize you. How are you?"

Her cheek mushed soft and sagging next to my chiseled one as we hugged. "Fine, fine. And you?"

"Wonderful." She paused, silently awaiting introductions from the other two in our party.

"Jackie, this is Julie," said Frank. The two women smiled and shook hands, and I pictured Jackie as an older version of Julie in the years to come. Jackie's eyes washed over Dane.

"This is Dane. Honey, this is Jackie. She throws *the* most amazing parties." I was being too chatty. Was it my nerves, or the miscalculated drinks? I pinched my forearm to sober up.

"Now, that's an exaggeration," Jackie said. Her appreciation was apparent. What I remembered most about Jackie was how much effort she put into every event on Marty's behalf. "Pleasure to meet you, Dane."

I wondered how much she and Marty and all of Frank's friends really knew about the divorce. I needed them to know I wasn't the monster who ran off with the contractor. If anything, this bizarre dinner should have proved everyone was moving forward unscathed.

"Well, I guess we're going to head out," I said, nudging Dane forward.

"Frank, if you have a minute, you should visit Marty. I'm sure he and the guys would love to see you," said Jackie.

"Sure, we've got time," Frank said. He gave us one last nod. "Goodnight, Olivia. Dane."

Just like that, we were dismissed. Julie and Jackie, almost in unison, waved. As they walked away, I noticed Frank's hand dancing across Julie's lower back. *Shit*, I thought.

Dane sauntered off to the bathroom, and as I waited, I watched Frank and Julie waltz the room. Frank oozed confidence as he spaced introductions between his new girlfriend and our old friends. Julie beamed at the compliments she received from perfect strangers, didn't dare turn her head to look at me, inadvertently sending the message: I was old news. She was Frank's future.

When the resentment settles, you want your former spouse to find happiness, but you never want them to be happier than you. After meeting Julie, I had never been more convinced of my own failure. She exuded grace amid an awkward assembly with the ex-wife and her drunk boyfriend. Frank had won the Happy Contest and he knew and our old friends knew and now I knew, too.

*

I was hungover the next morning, and not just from the drinks. I was emotionally drained. It was one thing to embark on a new life with Dane. There had been hard adjustments since the divorce, sure. But I was at least partially happy with my new life. Meeting Julie, I finally saw the person Frank had wanted all along. The woman I could never be, and that hurt so much more than I wanted to admit.

"You okay?" Dane asked. I was on the couch watching reality television. I'd barely left my post all day.

"Fine," I said, grabbing the remote and switching from one dull program to the next.

"What do you say we invite some people over?" Dane asked. He sat beside me, although he wasn't his normal, touchy self. He kept his distance because he sensed I was on the verge of something hostile.

"Not tonight, Dane." I sunk deeper into the couch and pulled the blanket over my shoulders.

"Come on," he said, daring to play with my hair. "You need some social interaction."

"I had plenty of interaction last night," I said, staring blankly at the television.

"A whole lot of good that did you."

"I told you I'm fine." I waited for him to say something else, push again for a gathering. But he remained silent, when I turned to see what he was doing, he was staring at his phone. I asked, "Everything okay?"

"Yeah," he answered, unconvincingly. "I need to head out for a bit."

"Where are you going?" I asked, suddenly invested in what he was doing.

"Just need to meet someone." He walked to the closet and started gathering his belongings. "I'll be back soon."

I'd been waiting for an excuse to let my anger puddle over, and Dane's sudden departure gave me that opportunity. "Does this have to do with your side business?" I asked.

"Olivia—"

"Answer me," I said, sitting up straighter on the couch. "We have a life together. I deserve to know."

He shrugged. "If you'll feel better knowing, I'm meeting someone, giving them a few pills and coming back home." He appeared both irritated and ashamed, but at least he was honest. "Is that better?"

"No, Dane. It's not better," I answered. There was no denying I'd been on edge since last night. The dinner put a lot into perspective, mainly how unorthodox my life had become since the divorce. Dane's drug dealing never sat well with me, but it irked me even more when compared to the domestic normalcy of Frank and Julie. "I told you how I feel."

"And I told you not to worry." He wasn't expecting our conversation to turn. He'd given me space since last night, even tried distracting me today. Now he was facing the full wrath of my paranoia and insecurity.

"You can't control how I feel, Dane." The urge to cry overwhelmed me. "I know it might not make sense to you. I enjoy partying, every now and then. I take pills to get through the day. But selling them? It's different. I want you to stop."

"I told you I can't do that," Dane said, frustrated. He clenched his fists but kept his arms at his sides. I imagined he wanted desperately to leave the house, the way I'd felt when I failed to make Frank see circumstances through my eyes.

"What you do is a choice." I ripped the blanket away and stood. I wanted Dane to see both my concern and sincerity. "And now I'm asking you to stop."

"It's not that simple, Olivia." Dane flinched when I touched him.

"Well, make it simple," I whispered, tears rolling down my cheek. I hadn't displayed this level of emotion in front of him since the divorce. "Stop selling. Or I can't do this anymore."

"Do what?" He was so not getting the picture.

"When I'm with you, I'm happy. We have fun together, and you accept me for who I am. I accept you, too. But I can't support this." It might have sounded hypocritical, telling him I accepted him alongside asking him to change. It wasn't about Dane as much as it was me. "I can't be with someone who sells drugs."

Dane sat on the sofa, the severity of my ultimatum finally sinking in. "I didn't know it bothered you this much."

"I didn't know either." Until last night, I'd been trying to keep the peace. Ignore the parts of Dane's life I didn't like, stealing a move from Frank's relationship playbook. But now I was looking past this moment and toward my future. My future and Jake's. I couldn't attach myself to someone who took such risks.

"You've been here seven months," he said, trying to crack my logic.

"I'm not making excuses for anything I've done up until this point," I said. "All I know is I won't be sticking around if you don't stop selling pills."

I went into our bedroom and locked the door. A few minutes later, I heard Dane leave. I had no idea where he was going, but at least I knew where I stood.

CHAPTER 17

After

Julie and I were both in shock.

My face adjusted to the burn. Her friends, heads low in humiliation, mumbled excuses and promptly left. Frank sensed the tension from across the parking lot.

"She just hit me," I told him as he marched toward us.

"Julie, what's going on?" he asked. She was his primary concern.

"She was talking about our family," Julie answered. She covered her face with quivering hands. "I'm sorry."

I couldn't decide if she was apologizing to me or Frank or both. Her voice reverberated in a queer octave as she tramped away.

"You need to go, now," he said, jerking my elbow.

"This isn't my fault, Frank. Her friends—"

"I will get the story from her later. We are not doing this now. You need to leave."

He wrangled me to my car and maintained his post until I merged on the highway.

The interaction was my fault—and wasn't. I earned the hit and didn't. Julie was right and wrong. Per usual, my decisions lacked distinction, clouded by too much gray.

Julie didn't deserve what I said to her. I did what I always did, let my resentment build until when the inevitable release came, I spewed. That's how I ended up with Dane in the first place. It was easier to act out with an affair than it was to address the real issues in my marriage.

Instead of telling Julie the truth, that she intimidated me, that she represented everything I could never be as a wife and mother, I found her Achilles heel and sliced. Because that's what we do when we're weak and hurt, we refuel by undermining the strength of others.

Normally, I camouflaged my desperation for pills when reaching out to Farrah, but I was too rattled. She answered my third phone call in a half hour and promised to stop by the condo when her shift at Fahrenheit's ended. Still, that was hours away, and I didn't want to be stuck at the condo alone and sober.

Since the case reopened, Eddy had warned me to discontinue my nighttime tradition of going out and getting blitzed. Brock said the same thing. I knew the police and media would jump at the opportunity to target me, but the last eighteen months also taught me regular people tend to only focus on what's in front of them. People read about a murdered man and his suspicious wife, experience a few seconds of outrage or fear, then they read the sports section. Besides, Rowe was the celebrity of the hour. Not me. After what happened with Julie, I deserved a taste and dared someone to stop me.

The Tavern was the perfect place for a strong drink with a small audience. The patrons there were always alone. They came to stretch out the minutes before returning to their starched blouses and patterned ties and nagging wives.

I dibbed a booth in the back, hoping I wouldn't be seen. The bartender came over and took my drink order, returned a few minutes later with chilled tequila.

"Ay, turn that up," shouted a voice from the bar, disturbing my calm. I'm a quiet drunk. Always have been, even before I resented so much attention. Loud drinkers irk me, and I hated for my attempted wallowing to be interrupted by theatrics.

"Chill out, Les." The responding voice was calm and sober, probably the bartender.

"I wanna hear the damn news," the drunk shouted back.

"It's loud enough, bud. Thought you'd tire of hearing the news in your line of work," soothed the bartender.

"Damn it, Bill." A glass clacked against the counter. "I said I want to hear the damn news."

"Well, we don't," hollered a third voice.

If my relaxation had to be interrupted, a bar fight was a good enough excuse. I turned to see what might go down and couldn't believe the loud guy with the news fetish was someone all too familiar. Detective Wooley.

"Don't you go yelling at me," Wooley shouted at the other man. He stood up from his barstool and tripped, just in time for the bartender to catch his shoulder.

"All right, guys. Let's calm down," said the bartender. "Not even dinner time yet. Les, you wanna burger or something?"

"Aww, forget it. Bring my check," he replied.

The bartender obliged all too quickly, happy to put out one of the endless fires the night might bring.

Anger bubbled at the assumption Wooley had followed me again. But then I considered his drunken demeanor. He was acting like an absolute fool. Even he wouldn't stoop so low knowing I was nearby. If we were both emotional drinkers, as preceding behavior suggested, it was only a matter of time before we stumbled upon the same watering hole. How can people not believe in fate at a moment like this?

As he walked past me, I couldn't help but gloat.

"If this is another sting, you might want to work on the low-key factor," I said.

His eyes flickered recognition and fear, the reaction I have when I bump into someone I wish I hadn't. He recovered quickly, and I wondered if it was a tried habit for cops to switch mode, even from the depths of inebriation.

"Seen you come here a couple of times," he said, tucking the exposed ends of his shirt into his waistband. "Thought I'd give the place a try."

"When are you going to let up?" I asked.

"I'll keep my strategy to myself."

"Yeah, seems like you're doing a good job of that." I nodded in the direction from which he'd just stumbled. The mean spirit I'd conjured at the party hadn't been fully exorcised, so I took out my frustrations on Wooley. "Say, why are you so convinced I murdered my husband?"

"I can't talk to you, Olivia," he said, moving away from the table.

"I'd say we're about as off record as it gets." I paused, eyed his flushed face and wrinkled attire. "I want to tell you this, again. I did not kill Dane."

"This discussion is not taking place." He wagged his finger at me as spittle exited his lips. "My superiors wouldn't approve, and neither would that lawyer of yours."

"Look, I don't plan on telling anyone I ran into you. We're all allowed our secrets. Or do your superiors already know about your recreational exploits?" I laughed and took another sip. "At least tell me why you are so convinced it was me."

"Do I really need to explain motive to you?"

"I get the angry spouse going off the rails and shooting their partner is about as overdone as the alcoholic cop—"

"I'm not an alcoholic," he interrupted.

"I don't care if you are," I said, locking him into a stare. "I understand shit looks bad for me. But there are other possibilities, other people—"

"Who, like Rowe? Every case presents a dozen different possibilities, but there is always one that fits. The truth." He smacked his fist against my table. His face beamed abnormally red under the booth's glaring lamp. "Not to mention, I just don't like you very much."

"Keep looking for the truth, because I did not kill Dane."

"Look, I showed my ass a few minutes ago. But don't tell me how to do my job. I know you're hiding something, and one day I'll find out what it is."

"I'm not hiding anything about Dane's murder." I refused to break eye contact. He'd already helped destroy my relationship with Jake, the only person I'd loved more than myself. He wasn't going to intimidate me now.

"I know you are. You think being on my radar for the past year and a half is bad?" He hunched his shoulders and lowered his voice. "It's a drop in the bucket."

We kept staring, two people desperate to push, knowing the other would never budge.

"Everything all right here?" asked the bartender. I hadn't even heard him walk up. He looked at Wooley. "Les, I thought you were heading out."

"Yeah, yeah. I am." Without further suggestion, he left.

"I'm leaving, too," I said.

Even getting wasted wasn't the same anymore.

*

Farrah showed up at the condo nearing eleven. My balance wavered as I trekked to the front door. My time at The Tavern had me approaching drunkenness.

"Rough night, buttercup?" she asked, lifting a paper bag. "I got us a bottle from the liquor store on the way here."

I didn't tell her about my encounter with Wooley, but I was fully ready to vent about Julie. I unraveled the day's events: the party and the decorations and the merciless comments and the slap. Frank's familiar disappointment in me. Farrah nodded along, doled out medicine, one by one. I swallowed two pills and valued the immediate comfort of knowing relief would come soon.

"She had no right discussing you with her friends," she said, waving her hand. "Had no right hitting you, either."

"If I'm being honest, Julie didn't say anything. Her friends did the talking." I'd rehashed the incident enough to already adopt a different perception of events. I'd aimed my rash cruelty at the wrong target.

"Clearly she has disrespected you to them before. They'd never bash you unless she gave them permission." She pulled the tequila bottle from her bag and retrieved two shot glasses from the cupboard, started pouring. "Were things always this difficult with Julie?"

"I've never liked her, truthfully. Hard to like your replacement. But there was a time, before Dane died, when the four of us got along." She handed me the shot and I drank. The unexpected warmth burned my stomach, made me gag. "I suppose I've given Julie reason to hate me since then."

"You slept with your ex. Big whoop." She lit a cigarette before pouring another shot. "She's been aware for how long?"

"Frank told her straight away. We had to tell police we were together the night Dane died. He wouldn't allow Julie to receive the truth from strangers." I twirled a strand of hair, watching memories play back in my mind like a silent film.

"She's had over a year to get over it. She could have left if she wanted," Farrah said.

"At the time, I predicted she would. No use fooling with Frank once his shine dulled."

"Why d'you reckon she stayed?"

"I think she always sensed there were unresolved feelings between Frank and me. She probably wasn't even that surprised when he told her we slept together. The investigation into Dane's murder gave her the opportunity to ice me out. She could finally have Frank all to herself." I swigged my drink. "Now she has Jake, too."

If the first half of today's party proved anything, it was that Julie would be a fantastic mother. It must be painful, having that desire blockaded. And I'd used that pain against her. I interpreted Julie's anger in a new light. Perhaps she was equally angry with Frank for revealing her fertility struggles. Yet another intimate bond between them he'd broken for me.

"How is she with the kid?" Farrah asked as she took another drag.

As much as I hated admitting it, I had to be honest. "She really does love him. Jake's another reason I think she stayed after finding out Frank cheated. He provided an immediate family."

"Do you think Frank loves her?"

"Frank is good to her. If I hadn't pushed him…" It all came rushing back. The passion and sting and betrayal. The intoxicants soaked my brain, making my opinions airy and smooth. I leaned my neck back. "Sometimes it's like I infect people, you know? Make them worse than they are. Frank would never have cheated on Julie if I hadn't tempted him."

"You talk about him as though you never stopped loving him."

"Maybe I still do." I rolled my eyes, trying to play off my feelings. Truthfully, I wasn't sure what I felt for Frank. I knew my decision to divorce him was rash. When we reconnected on the night Dane died, I loved him. Now, with everything that had happened, love remained, but I was unsure to what extent.

Farrah ruminated on what had been said. She took another shot before speaking again.

"You can't beat yourself up for not knowing how life would unfold. You made the best decision in the moment based on the feelings you were having at the time. Second-guessing what's been done will get you nowhere."

"How come you don't judge me?" The words slurred. My mind wrestled with sleep.

"Those picket fence princesses got you all wrong. I've encountered bad people in my day. You ain't one of 'em."

"Some days I am the bad guy," I whispered.

Her chewy palm smoothed my forehead. She stood, rummaged across the room until she found a blanket and pillow.

"I'll let myself out, buttercup." She covered me with the blanket, propped a pillow at my back to prevent aspirating. "Trust me, you ain't bad."

*

I woke up scrunched and sore. Too much damage done. I hadn't had a night that bad in a while. I tried to be better for Jake, but every day was a challenge. The stress about Rowe and my own foolish mistakes only contributed to my hopelessness.

As usual the morning after a binge, I vowed to change, avenge last night's despair with productivity and purpose. I could vindicate a lifetime of blunders in one glorious day. Two cups of coffee later, I opened my front door and shivered, caught off guard by the afternoon wind. Mail nested in the letterbox; it had been over a week since I last checked it.

I sifted through envelopes of varying thickness and importance. The thinnest, with only my name, was an outlier. Inside, a single paper: the vibrant randomness of the letters clipped and glued together, at first glance, was engaging. Cable crime dramas, however, conditioned me to know this was not mere artistic ability on display.

The words read STOP SEARCHING.

I surveyed the street for a familiar sight, as if the sender would be lurking behind a trashcan or streetlamp. No one.

Back inside, possibilities swarmed like sharks to blood. Who would send such a letter? The case-obsessed true crimers thirsting for involvement? The boundary-crossing media angling for my contribution? Perhaps a junior officer, provoked by Wooley, sneaking to my mailbox at night, the two taking turns monitoring my reaction through binocular lenses?

There could be others out there, though. Whoever killed Dane was bound to get nervous, Brock had said. Maybe the person was watching me. Knew I was trying to find them. Knew I was getting closer to the truth. Maybe they missed the taste of blood.

CHAPTER 18

Before

While Frank pretended our arguments never happened and hoped our friction would disappear, Dane confronted issues directly. We took the rest of the night to evaluate our feelings independently; by morning, he was ready for a conversation.

"I don't want to lose you," he said. He was dressed for work. His real work. The bags carrying his construction gear sat beside the front door. Dane said he'd been unable to sleep most of the night. I wore pajamas, cupping my morning dose of coffee. The only tasks I had on the agenda were editing pictures and trying to keep from thinking about Dane and Frank and Julie.

"It's not that I want to break up," I said. "I'm not trying to be a hypocrite. It's one thing if we have people over when Jake isn't around. But I'm not comfortable with you selling drugs. Period."

"You realize I've been doing this since before we even met," he reminded.

"I do," I said, hoping he wouldn't try convincing me to change my decision. Because I wouldn't. "It's only a matter of time before all the risks catch up with you."

He looked down and nodded. "You're right."

"I care about you, Dane. I can't sit around and watch you get in trouble. Not with Jake in my life. I know I rely on pills more than I should." I lowered my head in shame. I wasn't saying he couldn't *take* pills. Even I wasn't ready to stop them completely. "We have to draw the line somewhere."

Dane stared at the floor and waited several minutes to speak. "I think I'm scared of giving it up because life might turn boring." He looked at me, and there were tears in his eyes. "I've never had much to lose. But now I have you. And I don't want you going anywhere."

"I don't want to leave. But I can't skirt around the hard issues with you like I did with Frank." I reached for his hand and squeezed. "I also don't want to change you. If this is the life you choose, then choose it. Frank tried to change me, and all it did was cause me to make decisions that hurt us both. I don't want to give you this ultimatum and then you regret it."

"Olivia, I'll never regret being a better person. For you." He picked a piece of fallen hair from my face and tucked it behind my ear. "Hell, I'd be an idiot to let you go over something so stupid. I want to stop. I want to focus on our future."

"You promise?" I asked, searching his eyes for truth. Dane had never lied to me before, but this was undoubtedly the biggest thing I'd ever asked of him. He was changing a fundamental part of who he was; it would be difficult for anyone to handle.

"Yes." He leaned forward, held my face with both hands and kissed me. When he pulled back, his eyes were alight with promise. "But I also want more than what we have now. We love each other, right?"

"Of course."

"We live together. Jake has his own room." He glanced around the condo. Our home. "Does the buck stop here?"

"I'm not following." I said, leaning deeper into him.

"I guess this is my shoddy way of asking if you'll ever consider marrying me."

My eyes bulged. Only last night, I'd considered leaving him. "Dane, the ink on my divorce is barely dry. The last thing on my mind is marriage." A dry laugh trailed my words.

"I see." He stepped away from the couch and walked toward the door.

"Don't take it the wrong way." I followed him.

"I'm not." He turned and forced a smile. "It's just—you know I'm not a relationship guy. Never lived with someone before. Never even thought about getting married. Never loved a person the way I do you."

I leaned in to kiss him. The last thing I wanted to do was burn him after he'd acquiesced to my demands. "Dane—"

"With me, it's either all in, or nothing. Explains why most of my life has been nothing. Now?" His eyes gazed out the large window near the balcony. His face turned empty, as though what he was seeing wasn't enough. "What we have is real. It was enough for you to leave Frank. I don't want to be the guy you left him for. I want to be your husband."

I'd spent the past year reviewing each day—each decision—singularly, not factoring a bigger picture. *Marriage*. The word weighed heavy on my soul.

"Dane. I love you." My hands touched his face and pulled him closer. "What we have works. What I had with Frank worked, for a while."

"What you and Frank had didn't work because he wasn't the right person for you. He didn't see in you what I do." He bent down and lifted his work bags. "You weren't bad at marriage. You went into it with the wrong guy."

"The past year has been a whirlwind." My eyes darted down the hallway leading to our bedrooms. "And I'm bringing Jake along for the ride."

"Take the time you need." He opened the front door and walked down the concrete steps.

I wasn't sure how to feel about our conversation. Dane's decision to stop selling pills moved us forward, but he'd raised the stakes by bringing up marriage. It was certainly the first time we'd ever discussed it. Maybe the threat of losing me had put Dane's feelings into perspective.

I still wasn't sure, but at least I could be honest with Dane about my uncertainty. That's what I loved about Dane. I could tell him exactly how I felt. No expectations. No bullshit.

*

Dane stopped selling pills that week. He contacted his suppliers and told them he no longer wanted their prescriptions. Now he only had access to enough pills to get us through the month. Although technically still illegal, I rested easier knowing Dane was being discreet.

But with change came some growing pains. Financially, we were used to spending what we wanted, within reason. We took advantage of nearby eateries multiple nights a week, and I rarely cooked. After he stopped selling, I budgeted weekly groceries and prepared meals at home, opting to go out only one night a week. We hadn't turned from princes to paupers overnight, but I didn't want Dane to sense our reduced income was affecting our livelihood. I wanted him to see we could make it.

I booked at least four or five photography sessions each week, mostly family portraits. I felt an occasional pang of sadness when snapping my clients' happy faces. Watching the mothers and fathers pose with their children reminded me of my life with Frank then, or his life with Julie now. Dane and I were far less traditional, which worked for us. But I worried I'd robbed Jake of the opportunity to have unity in his life. I hoped one day Dane and I would be able to provide the normalcy I'd stolen from Jake the first time around.

Dane's behavior wasn't the only change; I sensed a shift in his personality, too. He was noticeably somber. Selling had provided an authority he couldn't obtain in the other areas of his life. As much as I tried to shake my upbringing on the outskirts, Dane tried to shake his past, too. Being the man doling out pills and making fast cash had a certain sheen to it that being an ordinary construction worker lacked.

I sensed his newfound desperation, but he never directed his upset at me. If anything, he dove deeper into our relationship after he quit selling. He took turns preparing meals and initiated date nights. He even suggested we take Jake to local festivals and make decorations over the holidays. In his mind, he could give up one aspect of his life if it meant gaining something more meaningful in the process.

We certainly took advantage of downtown living and all the inexpensive opportunities for entertainment. Food fairs and Christmas bazaars and music jamborees kept us busy, and Jake loved the opportunity to tag along. When I had a two-car garage in Smithwood, it seemed a hassle to drive twenty minutes and attend such events. Living with Dane, I experienced Whitaker as I had before, the girl from the outskirts relishing the city for a second time.

That February, we went to a lantern release in Calhoun Park. Whisper a wish, and biodegradable paper and bamboo escorted dreams into the sky. The winter weather was unforgiving. We spread a blanket atop stiff grass and used each other's bodies for warmth.

"It's too cold," I said, burrowing deeper into him.

"We'll leave as soon as the lights go up," Dane promised.

A child on the other side of the dark field laughed. "I wish we could have brought Jake to this," I said. I wondered what he and Frank were doing, what they always did on their nights together.

"We will bring him next time," Dane said, pulling me close. He reached inside his backpack and pulled out an extra blanket, a bottle and two glasses.

"Are we celebrating something?" I asked, unaware our impromptu night in the park warranted champagne.

"Yes, actually. We are," he replied, filling my glass, then his.

I searched my mind to find what occasion I must have missed. We'd been together over a year, but we didn't have an official date with which to celebrate our union.

"We're alive, isn't that enough?" He clinked his glass against mine.

I laughed and sipped my drink. "All right, I guess that's plenty."

Cheers from the knoll signaled the show would start soon. We turned and looked at the hordes of people.

"I've also been really happy the past few months," he said. He sat and pulled my body to lean atop his.

"That's good to hear." I wasn't sure I truly believed him. I'd picked up on the tension, but I knew he was trying to be happy. He was trying to be a better person, which is the hardest job of all.

"To being alive and being happy." He raised his glass again and emptied the flute in one gulp.

"You're being weird," I said, nudging his side.

"Those aren't reasons enough to celebrate?" he asked.

"They are, I guess." Not sure what point he was trying to make.

The lanterns took flight. Each orb began its slow ascension alone, before joining the others. They mingled against the starless, black backdrop. Beacons carrying hopes and dreams into the clouds. I soared with them, buzzing and floating.

"All right," he said, reaching into his pocket. "If those reasons aren't enough, how about this?"

He presented the box and lifted the lid. Despite the night, a miniature light inside the box illuminated its contents: a diamond ring, with two different jewels on either side. I gasped, straightening my posture to gain a better look.

"You see, I looked it up," he said, using his other finger to point at the different stones. "I've added your birthstone, which is conveniently a diamond, alongside mine and Jake's. We're already a family, Olivia. I just want to make it official."

"It's beautiful, Dane," I said, tears filling my eyes.

The ring was different from my old one, which was so generic I'm not sure I'd be able to pluck it out of a lineup. I tried not to compare every aspect of my new life with Dane to my old life with Frank. Dane didn't deserve that, especially when he put effort into making a difference. He put effort into being what I needed.

"Olivia, will you marry me?" he asked, an audible crack in his voice. "Please?"

"Yes," I said, leaning forward and kissing him with such force, the illuminated box fell out of his hands and onto the grass.

After the mistakes I'd made, I didn't know if I deserved happy endings anymore. But this wasn't a fairy tale. This was my reality, and it was so much better.

*

We didn't need much time to plan. Our lives were already blended. Dane added my name to the condo and insisted we take out life insurance policies. *You never know what might happen*, he said. By April, we were ready both on paper and in spirit. Dane wanted a destination wedding, but I couldn't remarry in Jake's absence. We settled on City Hall and flew to Cancun the following week.

The ceremony blinked by, but the honeymoon lingered. We went the all-inclusive route. Everything was covered: food and entertainment and alcohol. If only there had been a pill dispenser to dish out all our favorites. Dane made sure we flew with his prescribed meds, the only hiccup I feared we might face.

The entire week was a blackout blur. All drink and sex and sea. Dane did more than fawn over me; he hungered for my love. Built me up in a way Frank, nor any other man, ever had. When he whispered I was the most beautiful woman in the world, I believed him. We sobered up enough to take professional photos on the beach, the ocean thundering in the background. Our glazed eyes spoke possibility. Dane was my second chance.

By the last night, indulging got the best of me. I couldn't stand, let alone sit through, another meal.

"Are you gonna make it?" Dane asked.

"I binged on alcohol and sun. I'm fine." I fell on the mattress and covered my face with a cool rag.

"Let me stay in with you," he said.

"Please. I feel guilty enough sleeping it off. Go grab dinner. Take advantage of the free drinks. I'll be here when you get back."

"Are you sure?" he asked, unsure.

"Positive. I don't want to spoil this for you." I rolled over, sinking into the plush pillows.

"You're not spoiling anything." He kissed the top of my head. Before he disappeared into the night, he hollered, "And nothing here is free."

Sleep wouldn't come. Like when Jake was a baby, it was impossible to turn off my brain. A hot shower woke me up and improved my senses. It was after nine o'clock, too early to retire on my honeymoon. I threw on a maxi dress and slicked my wet hair into a low bun.

I walked beside the various pools, breathing in the salty wind sprayed by the nearby sea. We'd made plans to eat at the outdoor Italian restaurant on our last night. The crowded deck was lively, filled with diners enjoying a late meal after a day of lazy splendor. Dane was nowhere in sight. I asked the host if he'd seated any single men, but a language barrier prevented an answer. I left the restaurant to revisit some of the other locations we'd frequented during our trip.

Blaring music at the poolside bar caused my headache to return. I spotted Dane near the back, a bottled beer in hand. He bent down and talked to the petite waitress we'd spoken with earlier in the week. His mouth nearly touched her ear. He smiled. It made me uncomfortable. His hand wandered to her waist and met a sliver of bare skin.

That's just Dane, I told myself. Life of the party. Friend to all. I waited another beat, as the waitress meandered around the crowded room before returning to Dane. The conversation reignited. Their faces moved closer and closer. A harmless exchange to anyone watching, worrisome to me. Familiar.

Part of me wanted to approach. A bigger part did not want to disrupt what had been an amazing week. I returned to the room, slid back in bed. Confronting Dane about being flirtatious a week into our marriage was too embarrassing. I seized another pill to help me rest.

When he returned, he thudded in the bed and surrendered to sleep within minutes. The clock read 2:26 a.m.

CHAPTER 19

After

I knew the mysterious letter I received would intrigue Brock. I called him immediately, and he agreed to meet me at The Copper Skillet.

When I arrived, I ordered a cup of coffee from a waitress at the front before taking my seat. She had a sour look when she brought the drink. I wondered if she recognized me from my last visit, or from the papers. I couldn't decipher whether people avoided me because of my history or because I'm just naturally unlikeable anymore.

Brock looked as though he had been in position for hours, his booth a mess and his hair shaggier than usual. "We've got thirty minutes," he said.

"What's the rush today?" I was looking forward to discussing the case with Brock. I thought investigating the past would be a good distraction from my memories of Jake's party. I'd given Frank and Julie several reasons to dislike me over the years, but I wasn't sure we'd ever fully rebound from this.

"I'm trying to fit in as much work as I can before Christmas. I've got a big interview later in the day," Brock said. He moved some papers to better clear my side of the table. "By the way, what did you find out about Max Eastwood?"

"Nothing. No social media."

"You don't think I looked online? I wanted you to speak with people who might know him." He combed his hair with his hand, leaving some strands awkwardly suspended in air.

"What do you want from me?" I asked. "I don't hang around with the same crowd."

"Whatever." His frustration mimicked a toddler being told *No*. Sure, I could further investigate by reaching out to Dane's friends, but that didn't mean I would discover anything new or helpful about Eastwood.

"I brought this," I said, wanting to perk him up. His interest in the paper scraps did not disappoint. He scanned the document repeatedly, as if the page presented more than two damn words.

"This is interesting," he said at last. "And you found this at your house?"

"In my mailbox. Anyone involved in killing Dane would pose a risk by coming near my place. Do you think it could just be some psycho obsessed with the case?"

"Possibly." He thumbed his chin, staring at the letter. "This could also support the second theory I've been tinkering. Aside from the Max Eastwood connection."

"What?" I asked. It still bugged me Brock chose to withhold information. I'd have a better understanding of the case as a whole if he'd simply tell me all his theories upfront.

"Crime can be gender predictable. Reviewing the case, certain details suggest a woman might be responsible."

"Nothing new there, Brock." I tore open a sugar packet and added it to my coffee. "The police have been focusing on me for a long time."

"Hear me out. Dane was shot. He wasn't bludgeoned. He wasn't stabbed. It would be easy for Dane to overpower a woman, not a gun."

"The gun was used because it was there. He had it out." I remembered well. "It has nothing to do with the killer's gender."

"Sure, a man could be responsible for the crime. I'm only saying the manner of death would give a woman an advantage. And this letter supports my theory."

"How so?" I leaned back, cupping my mug with both hands.

"Some experts suggest these notes are usually—not always—written by women." He held up the letter again, analyzing it a second time. "Women have easy access to gossip mags and watch soap operas which feature such amateur tactics."

"This is your perception of the everyday woman? Reading glossies and collaging intimidation letters?" Brock could be so basic sometimes. "You really should get laid."

He flung the paper down. "I'm not trying to spark a debate. I'm not talking about *all* women. I'm only saying when it comes to crime—race, gender, age—they typically fall into certain parameters. It's called profiling."

"Angry drug dealer seems like a probable profile." I pressed my lips.

"Look at it from this angle. Women are more methodical when it comes to ensuring they don't get caught. Men are arrogant, more likely to write a threatening note by hand without considering future implications."

"I just can't imagine a woman murdering Dane." I looked out the window to my left. The Copper Skillet parking lot was almost deserted this time of day. I supposed early mornings and late nights were prime dining times, unless you were like Brock and preferred setting up camp for hours on end.

"I'm only making suggestions. Remember, drops of female blood were found inside the condo. Dane's killer could have been a woman. Maybe from his past. He was popular with the ladies. No offense."

"None taken." Dane had been gone only eighteen months, but it felt longer. His multiple deceptions erased the happy moments we'd once shared.

"This is a bit awkward," he said, clearing his throat. "Do you know if Dane was faithful during your marriage?"

I had my suspicions about Dane's fidelity. The police never uncovered an affair (to my knowledge), but clearly Dane possessed many secrets and he certainly chose risky lovers. His absence during the honeymoon rang an alarm that was never fully silenced.

"I never caught him doing anything, but it wouldn't surprise me. If Dane was sleeping around, someone's husband could have come after him."

"Possibly." He sipped from his mug. "If only we had a log of Dane's confirmed lovers, we could map out a suspect list."

"I can't tell you much. I didn't know any women he dated before me." I knew almost nothing about Dane's life before me.

"What about Maura Murphy? She was married. When was the last time you spoke with her?"

"My old neighbor, Maura?"

"Yeah."

"Gah, it's been years." My face scrunched. "Why would I need to speak with her? Maura didn't even know Dane."

Brock leaned back, laced his fingers behind his head. "Philosophically, no one *really* knew Dane. Biblically, she did." He snorted at his own pun. Brock frequently spoke in goofy circles, making it difficult to separate important data from nonsense.

"Wait. What are you saying?" I asked.

"Maura slept with Dane."

"Dane and Maura never slept together," I corrected. Their faces floated through my memory, overlapping to create an image which didn't fit.

"Olivia, yes they did. She told me about it when I interviewed her." Realization caught up with his words. "Did you not know about this?"

My stomach tightened and I leaned hard against the booth. I pictured beautiful and secretive Maura. I thought I knew everything about her life then, but we hadn't spoken in years. Not since the conversation where I confessed my affair, prompting her distorted sense of moral appropriateness to end our friendship. She was as dead to me as Dane. She couldn't have slept with him, could she? And still judged me the way she did?

I rocketed out of the restaurant, bag and keys in hand. Brock cursed in confusion as I left.

*

When I turned into Smithwood, I almost parked in my old driveway. In my previous visits to the neighborhood, I had greeted Maura's brick house with indifference. Frank mentioned a while back Maura and Ronnie separated; he moved out and left her the house and kids. Frank was perturbed by the sudden departure. He still didn't know about her consistent infidelities. I figured the truth had eventually revealed itself, as it does for us all.

I was surprised when my loud, midday rapping brought Ronnie to the door.

"Olivia?" His face, no doubt puzzled by my presence, twitched as if calculating which year we were in. It had been even longer since I last interacted with him. "What are you doing here?"

"I need to speak with Maura. Now. Do you know where to find her?" I was half-tempted to reveal his wife's, or ex-wife's, lewdness. Not only had she slept with Dane, she ended our friendship in my time of need. She made me feel guilty for the exact thing she had done.

"She's inside. What's going on?" Ronnie, whose blond curls were frizzier than I remembered, twisted his head to inspect the rest of the porch.

Before I could answer, I saw Maura's familiar carmine tresses poking around the corner of the door frame. She pushed Ronnie back.

"Olivia. What the—"

"We need to talk, now." I wasn't interested in exchanging greetings. I wanted to know what she'd been hiding and how long she'd been hiding it.

"You seem a little worked up. Maybe you should leave," said Ronnie. Pretty boy had finally found his spine.

"Honey, just give us a minute," said Maura. She placed a hand on his chest before walking outside.

He gave us both a look of uncertainty before backing away. She walked to the end of the porch and lifted herself a few inches so that half her bum was nestled on the railing. She looked plumper than before.

"When I first saw you, I thought I'd seen a ghost," she said. Her arms wrapped around her body, and her face had the beginnings of a smile.

"You and Dane?" I gave an accusatory stare.

"You heard about that, huh?" She looked away, scanning the familiar view we once shared. "I knew one day you'd call me out on it."

"Tell me everything. I think you owe me that."

She sighed. She'd clearly been waiting to tell this story for a long time, but that didn't make it any easier. "It happened once. And before he was involved with you."

"You knew him?"

"He caught my eye when he was doing work around your house. He was quite the looker, if you remember. We sparked up a conversation. He came over one night when Ronnie was gone."

I tried to remember an interaction between Maura and Dane but couldn't. I'd pulled away from everyone in the months following the accident. My mind flurried in those days, always scrambling for a way to find my next pill. Of course, that was when Dane entered my life. I never had trouble tracking down pills after that.

"Why wouldn't you tell me?" I asked.

"He worked for Frank refurbishing your kitchen. I had no way of knowing you'd start sleeping with the guy. It was just a random hookup. Next thing I know, you're telling me you kissed him. Then you're dating him. Then you're leaving your family—"

"You're ridiculous." After all this time, Maura's outlook hadn't budged. "It's acceptable for you to sleep around on Ronnie. I never judged you for that. But I fall for a person, think I might have a chance at a happier life, and you turn on me?"

"Are you happier, Olivia?" Her eyes narrowed on me, cold and searching. We both knew the answer.

"Frank told me Ronnie moved out." My eyes darted back to the front door where Ronnie had just stood. "I guess you're not above breaking up families now either."

"Yeah, we separated for a while. Do you know why that was?" She didn't give me an opportunity to respond. "Because when Dane, *your new husband*, got murdered, the police questioned me."

"You said it only happened once. How did the police get involved?"

"Dane reached out a few days before he died. We hadn't spoken in years. He had… pictures. Of us. Said he was in bad shape financially and needed some fast cash. He knew we were good for it. He threatened to show Ronnie and anyone else it might offend if I didn't pay up. Police had transcripts of our texts."

This solved the mystery of how police knew Dane needed money. He'd clearly made the mistake of contacting Maura on his personal phone, leaving a revealing trail behind. I wondered what other people he might have intimidated during his time of desperation.

"Did you give him any money?" I asked.

"He died before we had the chance to meet. Whatever you two were into, it must have been some shady shit."

"I didn't—it doesn't matter." I didn't owe Maura an explanation for anything. Not after she had held onto this for so many years. "So, what did the police say?"

"They asked me about you, of course. Figured we were friends, being old neighbors and all. Then they brought up Dane's pictures of me. Apparently, he'd backed them up to his computer. I freaked.

Admitted it to the cops. To Ronnie. And then for good measure, I told him about all the others." She bit her lip, clung tighter to her beige sweater. "You know, I always thought I was tough. I'm just chickenshit like everyone else."

Her eyes fixed on her front lawn, which was littered with leaves. When I lived on Smithwood, Maura's yard was completely immaculate. Everything on the outside looked perfect. Maybe Maura had finally decided to prioritize the emotional needs of her family over the material ones.

"And that's why Ronnie left."

I understood. Dane's death had fractured more relationships than my own.

"Packed his bags and leased an apartment that same week. I was wrong about him not having the guts to leave. I was wrong about so many things." Her eyes teared up again.

"How is this the first I'm hearing of this?" I asked.

"The police aren't required to tell you anything."

"I'm sensing there is a lot they're holding back." I looked to the left and could see into my old backyard. Maura likely saw Jake more than I did these days. The thought made me jealous.

"How did you find out?"

"Brock Bowen, a writer covering the case. His blog is *The Vindictive Type*. He said he interviewed you."

"Oh, him." Maura rolled her eyes. "I wouldn't really call it an interview. He called me, asking questions about you. Which I answered. He brought up the affair with Dane, I cut off the conversation."

Poor Brock and his shitty investigative skills. He probably received a tip from his police station leak but couldn't hold Maura's interest enough to pluck a decent quote.

"You could have told me. Countless times," I said, still embarrassed by how little I knew about Dane and the past.

"The whole scenario unfolded too fast. There was never an appropriate time to bring it up. Nothing happened after you got with him. I swear."

I wouldn't be surprised if it did. Neither Dane nor Maura had a strong moral compass, although Maura seemed to be changing direction. "Dane turned out to be a real ass."

"I don't keep up with the case much." A passing breeze tangled her hair. She caught the strands around her face and secured them behind her ear. "All too weird. I did hear they let the guy who did it go."

"He didn't do it," I said.

"Is that why you're here? To ask if I did?" That hadn't been my main priority, but it was a possibility. She turned, faced me completely. "Go ahead, ask me."

"Did you kill Dane?"

"No." Her gaze was steady. She came off the railing and stood firmly on both feet.

"And Ronnie—"

"Ronnie was devastated when I told him about Dane. About everyone. But he didn't know Dane existed until… well, he didn't. You can't blame a dead guy for screwing your wife. I guess that's why I got his full wrath."

"Where were you the night Dane died?"

"You need an alibi now?" She shook her head and smiled. "Police haven't reached out to Ronnie or me in ages. I don't think we're even on their radar. They just came around long enough to ruin my marriage."

Maura didn't provide a clear answer, but that was typical. She was a good liar. I found it hard to believe Ronnie was calm when he discovered their affair. If he found out before Dane died, he might have confronted him. Dane's phone, which according to Maura held scandalous pictures, *was* missing. Still, even though Maura had a lot of nerve, I wasn't convinced she had enough to commit murder.

"Ronnie's back now?" I asked.

"Been home six months. It took a lot of work. A lot of healing. He's forgiven me. Seems to, anyway. I hate to use this word, but I've… *changed*."

"I'm happy you're in a better place." If remnants of the Maura I knew remained, she was likely still struggling under the surface.

"My family always meant the world to me." As she spoke, I pictured Stevie and Samantha. They were older now, old enough to be disturbed by their parents' fickle behavior. "I was selfish back then."

"Are *you* happier now?" I asked.

"I am. Still bored as hell. But boring is safer."

A conclusion I wish I'd reached much sooner. I sighed. Had it really been years since Maura and I had last talked?

"What do you think of Frank's wife 2.0?" My eyes glanced next door. The house and yard looked very much the same, and yet emptier, because I no longer had a place there.

"Perfectly polite. We keep our distance from everyone on the block these days. You and I might have had our differences, but I can't stand to be friends with a perky bitch likc that." We laughed, genuinely, like we used to.

"I'm constantly reminded Frank started a new little family."

"If it makes you feel better, I have overheard a handful of arguments. Happens sometimes when you live so close. Nothing compared to what they've witnessed with Ronnie and me, I'm sure."

"That does make me feel slightly better." I smiled, lying.

"Funny thing. I never remember hearing you and Frank fight."

Her words weren't funny at all. They grabbed at my insides and pulled tight. Reminded me of what I lost. What I gave up.

CHAPTER 20

Before

We arrived home from Cancun sunburnt and queasy. The hangover lasted days. During that time, Dane's friends surprised us with a wedding reception at the condo. Food and drink were provided. Some people brought gifts. Farrah was there, although I'd only met her a few times then.

She wrapped her leathery arms around me as though she'd loved me all her life. "Welcome to the family, kid," she said. Her openness didn't feel fake. Farrah treated everyone with warm acceptance until they were unfortunate enough to be iced out.

The riotous environment was like an extension of our all-inclusive trip. All fun and no worries. I welcomed the celebration. I needed to take my mind off Dane and what might have happened our last night in Mexico. The courage to ask him about the incident never came. We had enjoyed an idyllic week and I couldn't bear the thought of ruining the memory by exposing my insecurities.

I also did not want to fall into the unfortunate stereotype I so often read about before deciding to make my union with Dane official. *If they do it with you, they'll do it to you.* The overwhelming majority of relationships originating while one partner is already committed end in divorce or ruin. The statistic prickled at the back of my mind during our ceremony, pounded harder after the honeymoon.

Still, I refused to believe this was the case with Dane. I knew his heart. It belonged to me. Any distasteful interactions didn't originate from spite, rather ignorance. I was his first true commitment, in love or otherwise. It would take time to learn how to navigate marriage. And I was willing to wait without being a nag.

Dane helped prepare the condo to the standard I expected before Jake visited. He finished unloading the dishes, and I suffered an unusual twinge of guilt.

"I'm sorry you didn't get the wedding you wanted," I said, lifting and tying off a heavy garbage bag.

"What are you talking about?" he asked.

"I know you wanted more than a courthouse ceremony. You have so many friends. You deserved to be the man of the hour for one night."

"In case you haven't noticed, I'm the man of the hour every night." That was true. People were drawn to Dane in a fascinating way. I understood the pull.

"I just hope you don't have any regrets."

"I married the girl of my dreams. That means more to me than some classy event with a girl I can only tolerate." He walked over to me and kissed the top of my head. I grinned.

"I'm the girl of your dreams, eh?"

"Better."

"Even though my toddler is about to be with us the next four days?" You don't find many dream girls with car seats in their vehicles and baby wipes in their bags.

"Olivia, I love having Jake here. I love watching you with him." He gripped my shoulder and pulled me close.

"You have a lot to handle by being with me," I said, flattening my cheek against his firm chest.

"Doesn't matter who you date, there's always a lot to handle. Being with you is a choice. Sure, the past year was messy. But that's why I wanted to marry you when I did. I don't need to tinker it back and forth for the next year or two. I want you. I knew six months ago, I wanted you. From the first time we really talked, I knew you were a woman worth loving. And now I get to do it all the time. I'm the luckiest guy in the world."

In that moment, I knew Dane was a man I could trust. He would never do anything to hurt me.

*

Frank asked if he could take Jake out of town for a weekend in May. Between his work schedule and my photography, which usually dominated my weekends, we rarely made plans outside of Whitaker.

"Where are you wanting to take him?" I asked, curious. We spoke over the phone, having only seen each other in person twice since the wedding.

"I was thinking of taking Jake to his first baseball game in Atlanta. I think he's old enough to get a kick out of it."

"That'd be nice," I said. I never worried about Jake in Frank's care. He was always more than responsible.

"Thanks," he said.

"Is Julie going?" I asked. I'm not sure her attendance would have changed my mind, but I wanted to know. I knew she was becoming a serious part of Frank's life. Even Jake had mentioned her once or twice.

"No, she's staying here. She works this weekend." There was a hint of annoyance in his voice. Being recently remarried, I didn't deserve much say about his romantic life. He turned the tables. "You and Dane have any plans this weekend?"

"Not yet," I said before creating an excuse to get off the phone.

With Jake gone for the weekend, Dane and I decided to host another party. I sensed he needed the distraction. The honeymoon had been amazing, minus his brief disappearance on the final night. But since we'd been back, his demeanor had started slipping again.

Dane seemed unnecessarily frustrated. He wouldn't admit it, but I knew his empty feelings stemmed from his decision to stop selling pills. Saying he'd stop had been easy; doing it was much harder. Six months since the switch, he still wasn't totally adjusted.

"I can run by the liquor store," I said. Dane was spreading raw meat onto a platter, preparing to take it outside to the grill. "We could make a punch for everyone."

"Don't worry," he said, sprinkling spices over the plate. "They can take care of themselves. Bring their own shit."

I was used to his sharp replies. "All right, I just thought if we were preparing food—"

"They'll be fine bringing their own drinks. Stop trying to impress people," he snapped.

"Dane." My cheeks felt hot. "I'm not trying to impress anyone. I'm only trying to have a good night, something your attitude right now is making impossible."

Dane put down his utensils and stood behind me, putting his hands on my shoulders. "I'm sorry," he said, kissing my neck. I flinched. "I'm on edge about having people over."

I'd never heard Dane say that before. "Honey, we can cancel. Let's—"

"No, no." He stopped me, used my shoulders to spin my body so I could face him. "I want people to come over. I'm just on edge about seeing some of the guys."

"Why?" Dane didn't get on edge, and if he did, he didn't admit to it. "Is something going on?"

"Nothing's going on. I've just been… I don't know… sensitive lately. I'm letting them get under my skin and I shouldn't." He kissed my forehead, then returned to the meat platter.

"What are they doing?" I asked. Again, Dane wasn't the type to be bothered by others. He did what he wanted to do.

"Just giving me a hard time about growing up, is all." He lifted the platter and walked toward the balcony. I followed him, sliding back the glass so he could walk outside. "Maybe they should give it a try."

"Give what a try?" I asked.

"Growing up," he said, sliding the door shut. I watched him through the translucent pane as he lifted the grill lid and transferred the meat. I wondered what was really going on in that handsome head of his. I wondered what he was really thinking.

A few hours in, I'd forgotten there was anything wrong with Dane. He spent most of the party walking around by himself, solo cup in hand. He'd stop and talk to one huddle of people, wander out to the balcony, then repeat the process. But each time I caught a glimpse of him, he was smiling, and the mischievous shine glossing his blue eyes was familiar enough.

I sat on the couch with Farrah, discussing the fabulous beaches we'd visited in Mexico, when a crashing sound interrupted our chatter. I stood, walked to the back of the living room and saw a picture frame had fallen to the floor and crashed into a dozen pieces. Sturger swayed awkwardly beside the bookcase from which the picture of Jake had fallen.

"Damn it," I said under my breath. Sturger hadn't done it intentionally, but there was an added sting that he was the one who'd broken the frame. I already didn't like him very much.

"Sorry about the picture," he said, an uneven twang in his voice. Then he laughed.

Dane darted across the room and lifted Sturger by his shirt collar. "What's your problem, man? Can't you handle your drink better than that?" he yelled.

"I said I was sorry," Sturger slurred. His apology didn't appear genuine; he was finding humor in everything the way drunk people do.

"What's funny about you breaking Olivia's stuff?" Dane continued clutching the collar, waiting for a response. Sturger, whose mind was too liquified to provide a compelling answer, didn't. He shrugged, tried to smooth the whole altercation over by laughing again.

Dane shoved Sturger to the floor, pushing his face into the broken glass shards. "Is this funny?" he asked.

"Dane," I said, the upset over the broken frame replaced with embarrassment. And worry. Everyone stopped what they were doing, staring at Dane as he held Sturger's face against the glass-riddled floor.

Dane ignored me. "I don't see anything funny about this, Sturger. Do you?" he taunted.

"No, nothing funny," Sturger said. He was trying to sound tough but was noticeably weak under Dane's grasp.

Dane didn't let up. Instead, he pushed Sturger's head down harder.

"We take pride in what we have here," Dane whispered into Sturger's ear. "You need some respect."

"I said I was sorry," Sturger yelled, trying to stand, which only made Dane push him more.

"Dane," I yelled. I wasn't even sure what I was watching. I'd never seen Dane's anger escalate so quickly, especially over something insignificant. I was upset about the broken picture frame, but it was nothing compared to Dane's violent reaction. "That's enough. Stop."

Dane removed his hand from the back of Sturger's head but remained low. "Want to try this again?" he asked.

Sturger remained motionless on the floor. "Sorry," he murmured, after several seconds.

"Not to me," Dane said, tilting his head in my direction.

Sturger stood up, eased slowly into a comfortable position. He brushed off his knees. "I'm sorry, Olivia," he said. There were tiny drops of blood on his cheek left by the fragments on the floor.

"It's all right," I said, still in shock.

"Thank you," Dane said. He walked to the closet and grabbed a broom and dustpan. I took them from him.

"Let me," I said. I was embarrassed and angry. Dane could have defended my honor in a more humane way.

The remaining party guests stopped staring and returned to whatever it was they were doing before. Even Dane reverted to normal.

"Come on, Sturger," Dane said, draping his arm around his rattled friend's shoulder. "Let's have a shot."

I dusted glass off the picture of Jake and placed it on the counter. I swept the broken pieces of the frame, blinking back tears. I'd never seen Dane act that way before, even toward someone he didn't like. Sturger was supposed to be his friend. Maybe there was something going on between them I didn't know about. Or maybe whatever was going on with Dane was worse than I thought. I needed to try to correct the problem.

The next morning, I woke up earlier than Dane. I allowed him to sleep, while I sat in bed thinking about his behavior. When he did roll over, awake, I went in immediately.

"We need to talk about last night," I said. "Don't you think that was a bit extreme?"

"What, the party?" Dane asked, rubbing his eyes with his knuckles.

"No, although it could have been toned down a bit," I said, recalling how late people stayed and how inebriated they seemed upon leaving. "I'm talking about Sturger. The way you pushed him to the ground like that."

"Oh." Dane laughed, remembering the incident. "Sturger can never handle his liquor."

"I really think what he did was an accident," I said, concerned Dane wasn't picking up on the bigger problem at hand. I'd never liked Sturger, but even I had felt sorry for him, watching him writhe under Dane's clutch. "You didn't have to be so rough."

"Aw, he'll be fine." Dane rolled away from me, fluffing the pillow under his head.

"You were the one who concerned me," I said. "I've never seen you lash out like that."

"Well, I'd had a lot to drink, too. Don't get worked up. We're guys. We can punch each other in the face, share a drink and forget anything ever happened. We don't hold grudges like women."

"Are you sure about that?" I said.

"Sturger's not going anywhere. He's like a cockroach. Nowhere to go. He probably doesn't even remember what happened. Until he sees that scarred up cheek, that is." He laughed.

"Dane." He was displaying cruelty instead of remorse.

"I get it. I embarrassed you. I won't get so carried away next time." He rolled back, tried to pull me down so that I would lay in the bed with him. "I just saw red when I saw what he'd done. I knew it was important to you."

"Just don't lose your cool like that again," I said, surrendering under his pull. "At least not around me."

"I'm so lucky to have you," Dane said, kissing my neck and rubbing my legs.

"There's something else I wanted to tell you," I said, postponing the romp he was primed to have. "I have news."

"Pregnant?"

My hand smacked hard against his chest. "Don't joke," I said.

"What is it?" Dane pulled me against him, impatient.

"We've finally reached a settlement from the car accident," I said, knowing if anything was going to stall sex, it would be this. The relationship with my accident claims lawyer was longer than my relationship with Dane. When he told me the amount, I was floored.

"Really?" he asked, sitting up a little taller in bed. "How much will you get?"

I told him the number, and he coughed to catch his breath.

"Are you serious?" he asked.

"Lawyer says the money should be in my account by the end of next month."

"Holy shit, Olivia." He kissed me, pulling me down again.

The months following the accident had been trying. Nurturing a child while cradling a failing marriage. All the pain. The insurance money proved good could come from bad. Maybe the dark days were over.

CHAPTER 21

After

Every new revelation altered my understanding of the present, changed the lens I used to survey the past. How long had my head been in the clouds, ignoring the truth around me?

My conversation with Maura revealed Dane was more desperate for money than I thought. I knew he wanted it from me but didn't realize he had been reaching out to other people. If the police knew Dane attempted to blackmail Maura, I wondered if there were other people he had threatened as well.

Brock was the best person to help me sort potential targets. Also, I wanted to apologize for my abrupt departure from the diner that morning. I called him, but he didn't answer. His car was parked outside his room at Ridgeway Inn. I knocked, and after several seconds, he opened the door a sliver.

"What are you doing here?" He lacked his usual star-struck enthusiasm. He seemed annoyed.

"I wanted to apologize about leaving the way I did earlier. I tried calling you."

A shadow swooshed behind him.

"Give me five minutes," he said.

"What's going on? You got a girl in there?"

"I told you I had a big interview. Hold on." He closed the door and I recognized the muffled hum of a conversation taking place on the other side. I looked at the desolate surroundings; Ridgeway Inn looked so poor compared to the manicured lawns of Smithwood.

When Brock opened the door again, his expression wore a mix of nausea and excitement.

"Okay, I'm going to let you in. There's someone who wants to talk with you," he said.

"Is it the police?" My anxiety spiked, my body conditioned to expect something bad.

"No. It's Rowe."

My lone memory of seeing Rowe in person climbed to the forefront of my mind. His prison garb hung from his scrawny body as he sat in the courtroom, barely listening to the charges against him. That was a year ago. A picture taken on that day had decorated papers in recent days, celebrating the dropped charges.

"Rowe? Brock, what the hell?" I knew he conducted various interviews, but I was stunned he'd let a conversation with Rowe slide under the radar.

"He wants to speak with you," Brock said, hopefully.

"No, no way. I have nothing to say to him." I took a few steps back.

"Please. He only needs a minute."

"I don't care."

"Olivia, the man spent a year in jail being accused of killing Dane—"

"Not my fault. He's the one who confessed—"

"Look, I'm done interviewing him." He stepped outside to speak with me in the breezeway, clutching the doorknob behind him. "He was loading up to go when you knocked. Three minutes, at most."

I let out a heavy breath. "Will you tell me your last theory?"

"Promise." He smiled big. "Give me a second before you say anything. I need to turn my recorder back on."

I rolled my eyes and followed him into the room. Rowe sat on the bed, the one I usually occupied during my visits. He stood when I walked in.

Gone was the wide-eyed youth I remembered from the court-room. His face was notably rounder and covered in stumpy blond hairs. The rest of his body had filled out, as well, making him appear shorter, I decided. He wore khakis and a gray hoodie, and an aura of misfortune lingered about him.

"Ms. Miller. I've wanted to meet you for a long time," he said.

"My name is Olivia," I said. Brock signaled the recording device was in use. "Brock said you wanted to talk."

Rowe looked down at his hands, which rolled and laced about one another in a nervous twist. He searched his palms for the confidence he lacked. "You know, I tried writin' you when I was locked up. Not sure if you got anythin'."

"I did not." Anything I received about the case was reviewed by Eddy first. I didn't need more reminders of what had happened.

"I wanted you to know I did not kill your husband. I confessed, and all. You've probably hated me for the past year. I'm a different person today." His stammered speech presented an audible delay as his thoughts caught up to his words.

"I don't hate you. I don't care about—"

"Olivia, stop," Brock interjected, against his journalistic aspirations. "Listen to what he has to say."

"I never hated you," I said to Rowe, biting my tongue not to say more. My arms crossed my body and hugged tight.

"At some point everyone thought I killed him. Hell, even I thought I had after speakin' with them guys so long. They mixed up my words and made me…" He rolled one hand inside the other, appearing agitated.

"It's all right, Rowe. You don't owe me anything," I urged.

He walked closer to me, staring at Brock for permission. Interactions were regulated, where he had been.

"I'm sorry for what you've been through," Rowe said. "I didn't cause it, and I got no clue who did. I hope you can find peace."

"Thank you," I said.

"My defense talked you up a lot, you know, preparin' for the trial. Said you was the most likely suspect." I nodded, never again wanting to discuss my probability of committing this crime. "I don't know if you did it. Sometimes there's things linkin' you to a case… might look bad. Doesn't necessarily mean you did it."

"Thank you, Rowe." I shot Brock a *help me* glance.

Brock sensed my unease and finally intervened. He walked over to Rowe, grabbed his shoulders. "Thank you, Marcus. It's nice seeing you on the outside," he said. "I believe your ride is waiting."

"Oh, yes. Thank you, Mr. Bowen. You've believed me from the start." Finally, his attention was directed to a person other than me. He patted Brock's hand, bent down to retrieve his bag. He returned his gaze to me. "You know, this whole mess saved me. Jail kept me off drugs. Gave me a new outlook on life. I found Jesus again. I grew up Christian, you know. Although my actions back then didn't show it—"

A horn beeped in the parking lot.

"I'll be in touch, Marcus," Brock said.

"Thank you." The open door chilled us all with December wind. He hugged Brock before he left. "Speaking with you has been a true blessin'. I didn't think it would ever happen. I didn't think any of this would ever happen." He took one more look around the room as if it were Main Street USA.

"I wish you well," I said.

"I'll be prayin' for you, Ms. Miller," he said.

Finally, he left.

"Gah, I thought he'd never leave," I said, crashing down on the bed where Rowe had sat. "Why on earth would you meet him here?"

"He's trying to keep a low profile," Brock said. "One car dropped him off, another picked him up. The media frenzy won't die down for a while."

"That was the first time I've heard him speak. He's a little loopy, no?"

"Can you imagine what he's been through in the past year? Drug addiction, incarceration, vilification. You treated the guy like an absolute freak." He jerked his head and assembled papers on the bed.

"He is an absolute freak."

"Why? Your track records aren't dissimilar, and if you aren't careful, your future could end up looking very much like the fate he avoided."

"When I am in prison, I'll be a freak, too." Brock's eyes narrowed in on me, then darted in another direction. Clearly, my comments irritated him. "Why are you so touchy about Rowe? You barely know the guy."

"This was our first meeting, but we've exchanged letters for almost a year."

"I didn't realize—"

"I'm trying to help you, Olivia." He turned toward me again. "But you make it really hard when you treat people that way. Like you're better than them."

"I wasn't trying to come off as better, Brock. What can I say? Rowe makes me uncomfortable." That's what I do under pressure. I react. That's why I'd been so cruel to Julie, because I felt threatened. She didn't deserve my cruelty, and Rowe didn't deserve my superiority.

"Rowe makes you uncomfortable because of what he represents," Brock continued.

"Which is?"

"Possibility. You were the number one suspect until he came along. Suddenly, you could go back to your life—what you had left, anyway. Now Rowe is no longer guilty, all the bullshit you've kept buried is getting drudged back up and you resent him for it."

"Geez, here comes the psychology minor again." I rolled my eyes.

"Manners, Olivia. You didn't exactly display Southern Belle behavior back there."

"Well, I'm not a Southern-fucking-Belle. Will you stop trying to typecast people? How many times do I have to tell you my life is not fiction?"

"You should take your own advice. You dismissed Rowe as though he were nothing more than the scary man from the news.

He is an actual person who spent a year behind bars for a crime he did not commit. And it's by God's grace he's not there longer." He threw the folder in his hands against the wall; index cards showered the ground like oversized confetti. "I thought apologizing for your behavior was the whole reason you showed up here."

I didn't know what to say. Brock had been the only person in my corner, and now even he was fed up with me. I longed for an escape. The room's bathroom, dingy and poorly lit, provided the sanctuary I needed. A few moments away from the escalating panic. This damned week—Julie at Jake's party and Wooley at The Tavern and Maura at Smithwood.

Brock was right: I resented Rowe for no longer being the scapegoat I needed. I also resented our similarities. Rowe, plagued by addiction and inaction, allowed others to write his story. Fill his head with their versions of what happened, ignoring the truth. That's why I'd devoted time to helping Brock. I couldn't simply tell people I was innocent anymore. I had to prove it. I didn't want to end up like Rowe, a prisoner to other people's lies.

Brock stood on the other side of the door, rustling papers and breathing heavily. At least it wasn't only me overreacting this time.

"Why do you care so much about this case?" I asked when I re-entered the room, wanting to lighten the mood. "Surely you can find something better to write about."

He revved up another quip, but, instead, released a heavy sigh.

"Remember the night we met at the diner? I told you how an unfair accusation can ruin your entire life."

"Yeah."

"I brought up the Florida guy accused of killing his girlfriend." He danced his fingers along the dusty nightstand. "Well, the Florida guy is my dad. He met my mother a year or so after the murder. My childhood provided a front row seat into how people are treated once suspected of a crime."

Almost all my interactions with Brock centered around Dane's murder. He'd mentioned his family, briefly. For the first time, I viewed him as a real person, with people he loved who loved him back. It was strange to hear him discuss his family in this way, revealing their secrets.

"Why were the police convinced it was him?" I asked.

"He dated the girl, and he was the last person she was with before she died. He had an alibi, no real motive. But police believed he did it, because it's always the significant other, right?" He let out a somber laugh. "Nowhere near enough evidence to arrest him, thank God. But they wouldn't leave him alone, either."

"They?"

"The cops. Neighbors. Dad would get excited about a new job. A month or so in, an investigator would drop by to speak with his new boss. Few days later, he'd come home defeated and we knew why. Must have happened a dozen times." He paused, looked out the hotel window at the frosty landscape. "Mom knew what she was getting into when she married him. Always believed him. But the rumors and stress took a toll on her. They divorced after I turned twelve."

"I'm sorry, Brock." I was accustomed to my emotional baggage on display. Experiencing another person's anguish left me raw. "What ended up happening?"

"I told you. They got a DNA hit on the guy responsible. He'd assaulted three women during the years they chased after Dad. So his wasn't the only life ruined."

"He's why you write about true crimes?"

"I knew what the words *alibi* and *circumstantial evidence* meant at a scarily young age."

I could tell, regardless of the outcome, it was still difficult for Brock. He sat on his bed and slumped forward, elbows on his knees. Admitting the truth about his past exhausted him. He knew more about being placed under suspicion than I realized. I imagined, would this be Jake in the future? Retelling the childhood complications of having a murder suspect as a parent? I didn't want that for him.

"Your heart is in the right place, Brock," I said, trying to sound sympathetic. "I'm sorry for the way I reacted to Rowe. It's just hard having to confront a new issue every day, realizing I didn't know the people in my life the way I thought I did."

"You say you want to know the truth. It may not be easy." He stared at me, making sure I understood the seriousness of this claim.

"I need you to tell me everything about this case," I said. "I'm not going to be blindsided anymore."

"There are reasons for holding back information." He looked at me, concern in his eyes.

"The police are tightlipped because they believe I'm guilty. Is that why you won't be honest with me?"

"No. I told you I don't think you killed Dane. I'm hesitant to share information with you because I'm afraid of your reaction. Case in point, the way you stormed out when you found out about Maura."

"I never knew they slept together. I was upset she never told me."

"You should understand by now new discoveries will be upsetting." He stammered, unsure of how to phrase what he wanted to say next. "Especially if the person responsible is close to you."

"What are you getting at?" I asked, confused.

He twirled one thumb over the other. "I've wanted to address this theory with you since we met, but—"

"Brock." I shoved his shoulder. "Stop stalling and tell me already."

He looked toward the ceiling and released another heavy breath. "You are the most frustrating woman. Anyone ever told you that?"

"If you don't tell me what you're getting at, I'm leaving and will refuse to participate in anything you do." I stood, hoping he'd realize my threat had weight.

"It is probable Max Eastwood hurt Dane. Or he could have easily been killed by a jilted lover from the past—"

"But?"

"I need more information about Frank." He scooted back, nervous for my reaction.

I'd always understood the police and their interest in Frank. But Brock? He should know by now, through me, that Frank was not involved with Dane's death. He knew we were together the night Dane died.

"There is no way it could be him," I said, firmly. "I know for a fact."

"Do you?" He stared at me, unconvinced.

"We were each other's alibis!" I shouted, stomping my foot. "If you trust my whereabouts, you must believe he was there, too."

He smoothed hairs away from his face. "I read over your statement. What time did you fall asleep?"

"Close to eleven, I think." I shrugged. "It's been nearly eighteen months."

"And when did you wake up?" he continued.

"Not until the morning. After six."

"Are you a heavy sleeper?"

In college, I signed up for afternoon classes because anything earlier guaranteed I would sleep through my alarm. I remembered the night with the broken baby monitor, wholly asleep as Jake cried.

"Not particularly," I said.

"What about when you drink… or more?"

"What are you getting at?"

"Did you drink with Frank that night?" he asked. "Take any pills?"

"Cause I'm a junkie, right?" I was tired of the entire world trying to label my behavior. It's not like I drove around drunk or got high around my son. We all make mistakes, but mine were constantly being used against me.

"Stop deflecting." His tone, sterner than usual, for a moment, replaced the clumsy blogger with a studied investigator. "I don't care if you were inebriated the night Dane died. But I think you were messed up and probably have no idea what happened between the hours of eleven p.m. and six a.m."

I shook my head, recalling memories of Frank and Dane. Brock's persistence in uncovering Frank's whereabouts that night bothered me. He knew more about the case than I did. Did he really think Frank was a likely culprit? I turned my eyes to the ugly carpet, palms starting to sweat. "Frank was there when I went to sleep," I said. "And he was there the next morning when I woke up. What makes you think he killed Dane?"

"Besides you, no one else would have more reason to want Dane dead. You said it yourself. An angry husband—"

"I wasn't talking about Frank," I said, defensively.

"Subconsciously, maybe you were." He shrugged cautiously, wanting to make sure his allegations wouldn't fracture our friendship. Then he smirked. "There goes the psychology minor popping up again. I'm curious if you're remembering things as clearly as you want."

"Frank was with me," I insisted.

"Okay." He held up his hands. "Only a theory."

Brock had wormed his way inside my head. I was already reexamining my memories, analyzing them through a different lens. I stopped. If Frank did it, I didn't want to know. It would mean I was responsible for both Dane's death and ruining Frank's life. I didn't want it to be him.

"The theory Frank killed Dane would create a juicy revelation in your book," I pointed out.

"I suppose it would." He stood, stretched his arms high over his head. "We'll continue looking at other suspects. You know Frank better than I do. I only wanted to run the theory by you."

"Right," I said, hoping what he said was true.

CHAPTER 22

Before

Frank was also made aware of the payout stemming from the car accident. Dane worried Frank might expect a cut. I knew better. For the same reason I never tapped into Frank's Tellit trust fund during the divorce, Frank never mentioned profiting from the accident. Jake was his only concern.

We swapped Jake shortly before the money was deposited. The June heat had stretched from inviting to sweltering. We met at a restaurant more inclined to adults than children so we could discuss the situation. Jake nuzzled up to me in the booth, headphones plugged into the iPad my in-laws had bought him, against my wishes, for his most recent Christmas.

"I'm happy you are finally receiving the money. I thought maybe the drink company was opting out," Frank said.

"We probably could have accessed it sooner if I'd been more proactive." Truthfully, the past two years had been so hectic with the divorce and Dane, the insurance payout had been the last thing on my mind.

"I know technically it is none of my business, but what are your plans?" He sipped through his straw, never taking his eyes off me.

"We'll use some for us. Dane might start a business." I waited, fearing this would be a sore spot. Frank couldn't care less about Dane's professional successes and likely resented his getting ahead as a result of my suffering. After all, our own marital problems intensified after the horrendous accident. "But I'm going to set up a fund for Jake, too. It's important a big chunk of the money goes to him."

"Good to hear." He nodded, then fiddled with his napkin.

Frank didn't push the situation. He understood he was no longer my husband and far from my financial advisor. However, the one constant connection we shared was Jake. His best interests were always at the forefront.

"Any idea what kind of business Dane plans on starting?" he asked. Frank casually pried when it came to Jake and me, but he rarely asked questions about Dane.

"Something in construction, I guess." Truthfully, concrete plans had yet to be made with Dane. We'd floated around a few ideas. I didn't really care what he decided to do, as long as it was legal. I knew receiving this amount of money was a way to change our lives for the better, allow him to still be his own boss, on the right side of the law. "Don't worry, he won't intrude on your territory."

Awkwardness set in. I hadn't intended for the comment to sound the way it did. Clearly Dane had already taken from Frank's territory before. Frank gulped his water glass.

"I wish you both luck," he said, forcing a smile.

"How are things with Julie?" I asked, giving him a turn to gloat. Jake was still tapping at the tablet screen, unaware of our conversation. "Does she get along with Jake?"

"Yeah. They get along fine."

"Good." I should have left it at that, but I just couldn't. Besides, he started it by asking questions about Dane. "Do you see a future with her? With Julie?"

"Maybe." Frank took another sip of water. "Yes, actually. I do."

I nodded. Even if I hadn't asked, I think I knew the answer. Jake had been dropping Julie's name more and more. Frank tagged 'and Julie' onto almost everything he said. They had dated for a while, several months at least. And yet I still wasn't ready to watch this woman, nice and wholesome as she was, waltz into my life and replace me.

"Sorry if that's hard to hear," he said.

"I'm fine, Frank. You need to move on with your life." It wasn't right for me to address unresolved feelings at the precise moment Frank found happiness. I needed to work on nurturing my relationship with Dane, not him. Besides, Frank's practicality meant he'd likely moved on from me months ago.

Our entrées arrived, breaking the tension. Jake devoured a bowl of macaroni and cheese. Frank and I had ordered club sandwiches, but my appetite was gone.

*

"How did it go?" Dane asked. He awoke from a snooze on the couch when I returned, alone, from my lunch.

"Fine." I hung my purse and keys on the rack beside the front door and walked into the living room.

"Did he bring up the money?" he asked, propping himself up with a pillow.

From the time I told him about the windfall, Dane pestered me about discussing terms with Frank. I tried explaining why Frank would not turn greedy, but he wasn't convinced. Dane, after all, had encouraged me to take as much money as I could during the divorce. Sometimes, self-consciously, I wondered if Dane would have rushed to marry me if Frank and I had made other arrangements. I predicted he would have adjusted just fine to living-in-sin if monthly alimony checks arrived, but I opted not to go that route.

"We talked about creating an account for Jake," I said. "That was it."

"You don't think he'll want any money?" Dane refused to let the topic rest. "Frank, I mean."

"No, I don't," I answered, bitterly. I'd already told him Frank wouldn't have a say. I don't know why he felt the need to pester me.

"Even if he did, he wouldn't be entitled to any of it. He was never involved in the crash and we haven't been together for over a year."

"I'm just looking out for you," he said, clearing a space for me to sit on the couch.

I wasn't so convinced.

"What about you? Have you thought any more about starting a business?" I wanted Dane to seize the opportunity we'd been given, find something legitimate to boost his confidence. If he was tired of being the man taking orders, this was his chance to advance.

"I've talked to some guys. Floating a few ideas around," he said.

"Like what?" Broad statements weren't good enough. I wanted to hear a plan.

"I'm thinking of starting my own construction crew. Not like what Frank does. We'd have our own team that could be hired out for different jobs."

"Like, commercial construction?" I was surprised Dane wanted to remain in the field. All he talked about was change. Wanting to be a boss. This was more like shifting positions.

"Nah, we'd complete weekend projects for people in need of an extra set of hands." He pulled out his phone and showed me an abbreviated business plan he'd typed out on his notepad app. He even included some marketing companies he could contact to get his name out there. Maybe he'd taken the opportunity more seriously than I'd thought.

"Would this make you happy?" I asked.

That's what I needed to hear. Income wouldn't be a problem for the immediate future. His long-term satisfaction was my main concern. Dane needed to find personal fulfillment to avoid the temptation of immoral thrills. Otherwise, he'd get an itch and start scratching.

"I think it will." He hooked my neck with his forearm and pulled me in for a kiss. "I enjoy being my own boss."

"This could be a new start for you." I leaned into him, placed my cheek against his chest. "For both of us."

"I'll need some money to start things up," he said.

"Makes sense." We actually had the money to start something and needed to spend it wisely. "How much?"

"What do you think about fifty thousand dollars?" He lifted a strand of hair and twisted it between his fingers.

"Whoa." I exaggerated my reaction by bulging my eyes. I had planned on contributing, but the cost for starting a business of that scale surprised me. When I started my photography business after the divorce, I didn't spend anywhere near that amount. "Don't you think that's a lot?"

"Well, I'll need to get a team together and do some marketing to get our name out there. Plus, I'll need equipment."

"I see," I said, calculating figures in my mind.

"I'll make a quick profit. As soon as we start completing jobs, I'll be able to give you the money back." He rubbed my arms and kissed my forehead. "You plan on investing in your photography business, right?"

"My equipment is fine. The website could use an overhaul. I thought about hiring someone who knows what they're doing to create a new one. It might attract more clients."

"Sounds good, babe." He turned and kissed the crevice of my neck. "We're going to have a happy life together."

*

That summer, we agreed to interact more often with Frank and Julie. As couples, we weren't close, but we made ourselves available for Jake's benefit.

Acclimating to our new normal was difficult for me, especially tolerating Julie. Her overwhelming friendliness worked on Frank and Jake and, after a while, even Dane. *Don't be so sour*, Dane would scoff. *She's not that bad.* I wasn't jealous, merely territorial.

Frank invited us to the Smithwood house for a weekend barbecue. His family and my family, which together made one. Like it or not, Dane was a forever part of our life. And Julie was quickly defining her place.

"Thanks for coming, you guys," Julie said. She opened the front door and ushered us toward the back. I found her welcoming us into Frank's home presumptuous. She still lived in an apartment somewhere downtown, although I suspected she spent most of the week sleeping over at the Smithwood house. She wore white shorts that could have used another inch of material and a red tank top. Girlish pins pulled the hair away from her face.

"Happy to be here," I said. I stopped in the kitchen to deposit potato salad into the refrigerator. "Head on outside. I need to use the restroom."

I closed the door and stared in the mirror. Wearing black again, hindsight suggested I could have added a splash of color. It was a party, after all. I admired my slim figure, but next to Julie, her soft curves made more seductive by the sun, I just looked boney. My hair grabbed attention but could benefit from a good conditioning treatment. *Get it together*, I told my reflection. I slipped a pill from my wristlet and swallowed.

When I made it outside, Dane and Julie walked over to the swing set, debating over who would get to push Jake first. Frank stood by the grill, a slab of meat already sweltering above flames.

"Smells great, Frank. You've outdone yourself," I said. I didn't remember him putting in this amount of effort when we were together. Of course, he was always at work in those days. Smart business transactions had provided Frank time to be more available, which is all I ever wanted.

"No big deal. I want to create memories like this. For Jake." He lifted the slab with tongs and flipped it.

"He's only three, Frank. I don't think he will remember this meal." I nudged him with my elbow.

"No, but he is getting older. It's important he interacts with the four of us. Eventually, we can celebrate other holidays together, too. He needs tradition in his life."

The four of us. I looked over at Julie. It was her turn to push Jake, who was soaring inches above the ground. Dane stood on the opposite end of the swing, pretending to grab Jake's legs whenever he swung in that direction. Was this *really* a permanent match? Frank and Julie?

I didn't talk much during dinner. Instead, I observed. Frank and Julie were certainly more comfortable around one another than they'd ever been. In earlier interactions, Julie seemed intimidated by Dane. I assumed she rarely encountered his type of rough. Like everyone, she eventually succumbed to his charms. Even Frank and Dane got along better than they had in previous visits. Looking at this addled version of a family, everyone smiling and eating and drinking, I wasn't sure where I fit.

*

I walked inside and started unloading our dirty dishware into the sink, trying to be a considerate house guest. Julie followed me.

"Enjoying yourself?" she asked. The harsh kitchen lights shone down exposing what appeared to be a glare in her eyes. I had seen the look in my own plenty of times. But I always thought Julie wasn't a big drinker.

"Julie, are you drunk?" I asked.

"Oh gosh, is it obvious?" She touched her palms to her cheeks trying to erase the flush. "I never do this sort of thing."

"Don't worry about it. It's a party."

"He talked me into it."

I wasn't sure which *he* she was talking about and I didn't care. I continued washing off the plates and, out of instinct, started loading the dishwasher. We could hear the guys laughing beyond the sliding glass door.

"You know, Olivia, I've been wanting to talk with you," Julie said.

"Okay." I nodded.

"We've spent more time together lately, but we still don't really know each other. There's no way to say this without sounding corny," she continued, whittling her fingers. "But I want you to know, I have no intention of taking your place. I know Jake is your son. Even though I love him, I respect your role as his mother."

The knife I was washing fell from my hands and clattered into the sink. The sound startled her, and she jumped back. The water kept running, as the soap on my hands slowly slid downward.

I wanted to tell her to shut up. The words shouldn't have been spoken, rather, understood. Of course I was his mom. Of course she had no place in comparison to me. And yet her role had become increasingly more important. With each visit and every gathering, her connection with Jake and Frank grew. Mine diminished.

And I shouldn't have had to admit this either, but it bothered me. She bothered me. It didn't matter if I was the one who created our predicament. Sharing Jake and Frank with this woman hurt, and I wasn't sure how long it would take for that hurt to dissipate. Her poise and maturity only made it worse. The fact she cared enough to make sure I was okay. Respecting my role. It only made my resentment grow.

Several seconds later, I realized the water was still running and Julie was staring at me, waiting for a reply. I turned it off and looked at her.

"Thank you, Julie. Thank you for saying that." The only appropriate response.

Her features thawed, and she seemed back at ease, the alcohol in her blood warming the chill I'd sent her way.

"And I hope I'm not overstepping by saying this," she said. Her soft hand reached out to mine, which was still soapy and wet. "But I do hope, one day, you'll consider me a friend."

I couldn't say anything back. I returned to the bathroom and swallowed another pill.

CHAPTER 23

After

On Monday, Frank called and offered to let Jake stay the night. It was rare for Frank to suggest a weekday visit. He claimed he and Julie had some holiday errands to run, but I believed he wanted to atone for cutting my time short at the party. Thankfully, Jake remained unaware of my argument with Julie. Hiding my behavior was bound to get harder as he got older.

Jake and I spent our evening watching a 3D cartoon at the IMAX cinema. Afterward, we walked the streets of downtown, admiring the Christmas lights that speckled the lampposts and street signs. We ordered takeout and returned home to eat in the living room like pigs. We both fell asleep there, and when I woke up close to 3 a.m., Jake's body had slumped to the floor. I lifted him up and gave him the sofa.

Our entire visit, I succeeded in keeping the cloud at bay, but I'd earned a taste. I poured a glass of wine and drank in the kitchen watching the subtle lift and fall of Jake's chest as he slept.

Saying goodbye on Tuesday afternoon was harder than usual. Although grateful for the time I had with him, I knew Christmas would be a new chain of missed events.

"Will you come for Christmas?" Jake asked. He sat on a barstool, his duffel already by his side.

"Not this year." We had tried blending celebrations in the past, before Frank's infidelity. Since then, the line in the sand had been drawn. I'd deepened the divide with my behavior at the birthday party, which still hadn't been formerly addressed.

"Everyone came to my party," he argued. My face blushed, remembering Julie's hand striking my cheek. Jake knew little about the relationship dynamics of those around him.

"Of course, we did, honey." I leaned over the counter and kissed his forehead. "No one would miss it."

I heard a knock at the door and sighed, not wanting our visit to end. Frank waited on the front steps. I looked toward the curb where his truck was parked. Julie remained buckled into the passenger seat, watching me from afar.

"Come inside," I told Frank when I opened the door.

Jake leapt off the seat and nearly tackled Frank with a hug. "Hey, Daddy."

"I've missed you, buddy," Frank said.

"Can Mamma come to Christmas this year?" asked Jake. Frank shot a disapproving glance my way.

"I've told him that can't happen," I responded. Given my altercation with Julie, we were several months away from being able to enjoy a blended holiday. Turning to Jake, "We will do our own special celebration, I promise."

His lips wrinkled into a scowl. Bribery was an antiquated parenting ploy. He wanted his family together, a simple desire the adults in his life had made impossible.

"Hug Mamma and get in the car," Frank said. He hated the awkwardness as much as I did. Jake wrapped his arms around me and I buried my mouth into his thick hair.

"Love you, bud," I said.

He grabbed his bag and walked outside, the front door closing behind him.

"How's Julie?" I asked Frank.

"Still embarrassed. You two need to talk." He plucked his hands in his pockets and shifted his weight.

"None of this would have happened if Julie wasn't gossiping about me. At our son's party, mind you."

"Julie resents her friends' comments. And she regrets slapping you. You need to take it up with her when she's ready."

When she's ready. Why was Julie calling the shots?

"I bet she didn't tell you what I overheard."

"She told me, Olivia. Julie tells me everything. Her friends had no right to talk about you. You are Jake's mother. But as a mother, can you blame Julie for reacting?"

I'd intended to hurt her in the moment, but ever since then all the comment had done was bring more difficulties my way. I needed to get along with my son's stepmother, even if it meant swallowing the insecurities she highlighted.

"Are you and Julie trying to get pregnant?" I blurted out. I'd been wondering ever since Jake mentioned Julie's hormones during our last visit. I had to know.

He didn't answer. "Olivia, I'm leaving. My life is none of your business."

When Frank opened the door, Brock blocked his exit. He stood in the doorway, lanky and loose like a noodle, his hand in position to knock. Frank jumped back, unnerved by the unexpected appearance.

"Sorry, I didn't mean to scare you," Brock said. His eyes grew when he registered the face in front of him. He raised his hand to shake Frank's. "Name's Brock Bowen."

Frank reflexively shook back and looked over his shoulder to me. "Seems there are things you don't tell me either." Frank probably recognized Brock from when we bumped into each other outside of Chili's, so his presence at the condo sent an ambiguous message.

"There's nothing going on here." I moved closer. "Brock is a writer. I told you, we've been looking into Dane's case."

Before I could stop him, Brock pulled out a business card and tried to hand it over. Frank shook his head. "You're chasing after nonsense and trying to tell me how to live my life? Olivia, stay in your lane." He eyed Brock as he passed. "Both of you."

My teeth ground in embarrassment over Frank's behavior. Brock gawked after him, dissed by his celebrity. "So, that's husband number one, huh?" he asked.

"Charming, isn't he? Sorry he blew you off."

"Wasn't the first time. He's just as aloof via email. Got to talk to Julie, though." He arched his eyebrows and smiled. As annoyingly acute as Brock was when it came to relationship dynamics, he must have gathered I didn't really like her much.

"Oh yeah?"

"I introduced myself on the way in. Hoped I could change her mind about an interview."

"How'd it go?" Imagining Eager Brock trying to wriggle the stick out of Julie's tight ass produced a genuine smile.

"Not well, either." He laughed and swiped his shaggy hair away from his face. "Met Jake. Cute kid."

"I hope you weren't harassing him," I said, defensively.

"Olivia, I'd never. He's a child." He twisted his face at my ignorance before saying, "Even younger when the murder occurred. He'd lack relevant insight." I sensed sarcasm, but with Brock I couldn't always be sure.

"Maybe Frank refuses to speak with you because he's guilty," I said, cocked my head to the side.

I was joking, but I hated to admit that ever since Brock shared his suspicions, Frank had been on my mind. On paper, Frank had motive. But I did, too. And I knew I didn't shoot Dane. Brock didn't know Frank or the person he was before I'd turned him bitter. Frank had plenty of reasons to dislike Dane and want him gone, but he wouldn't act on rash feelings. And he wouldn't be so upset with me over the past year and a half if he'd contributed to events.

"It was only a theory," Brock said. "You wanted me to be open with you."

"I appreciate your honesty." All this time Brock stood by the entryway like a vampire awaiting invitation. I'd postponed the condo tour long enough. Jake's visit kept us from meeting yesterday, so I invited him over to see the place in person. Plus, I was tired of spending long afternoons inside Brock's musky room at Ridgeway Inn. "Come inside."

"This is where it happened?" Brock walked through the kitchen into the living room, hands in his front pockets.

"Yep. Not the same as looking at pictures," I said. "Of course, the couch is new. But it's in the same spot."

"It's strange. You spend months reading about a case, studying the images. One day, you're in the thick of it. Standing in the room where someone died."

"Imagine living your normal life. Ex-husband, son, new husband. Overnight, your boring, messy life interests the masses. Neighbors, police. Bloggers."

"Easy." He laughed off my diss. "I propose we attempt real investigating today."

"Oh yeah?"

"Max Eastwood is back in Whitaker. I thought we might patrol a few locations. See if we can get eyes on him."

"Are you sure you're not asking for trouble? Hunting people down? Stalking them? Diane Sawyer didn't put herself in such risky situations."

"Don't be so dramatic. We're only scoping out a scene. You never know what we might find. We might even get the chance to talk to someone." He grabbed my coat off the nearby rack and handed it to me.

We drove beyond revitalized downtown, through the university blocks, and toward the unimproved streets of city center. Tanning salons turned frozen yogurt parlors and thrift shops turned farm-to-table bistros blurred together as we passed. Each mile marker made the clash of old vs. new, rich vs. poor more apparent.

Brock parked his car near the only apartment complex on Washington Avenue.

"My source said he was visiting here." In front of us stood a painted brick building. It was four stories high and looked utterly desolate.

"Visiting for what?" It was hard to imagine someone like Eastwood catching up with old buddies after his stint behind bars.

"Probably drugs. Maybe a gun." He popped a stick of gum in his mouth, offered me a piece, but I declined.

"You said he was just released from prison."

"That isn't going to change a guy like Eastwood." He adjusted the heat, wiggled uncomfortably in his seat. "You ever been here before?"

"No, definitely not."

A rectangular light glowed over the concrete steps that lead to a lone glass door. Entry required a swipe card. Left of the steps, huddled by the bushes, silver garbage cans overflowed with junk. A broken toy truck, the kind Jake used to own, balanced at the top.

"So are you and Frank still close?"

"He's still on your mind, huh?" I wasn't convinced talking about Frank to Brock was a good idea, especially given his suspicions.

"Just curious. What's it like co-parenting with Frank and Julie?"

Interpreting casual conversation with Brock was difficult. I never knew if he was genuinely interested or digging for something deeper. "It was better before Dane died," I said.

"From what I've heard, Dane doesn't strike me as the kid type."

"He wasn't. But he tried. I will give him that." I thought back to the times Dane and Jake played together, some of the few happy memories of Dane I had left. I hoped those moments didn't stick with Jake the way they did me.

"What about Frank? How's he as a father?" Brock asked.

"Great. Dependable. I just wish he was a little more forgiving." I hadn't taken many pills in the past few days, and I was starting to feel a little shaky. I wiggled my neck and looked toward the felt ceiling. "Julie makes it hard. If you've researched her, I'm sure you know she's a Supermom in the making."

"Yeah, well. She might come off as the perfect replacement, but you're Jake's mother. Nothing can substitute that bond."

"Thanks." I spent the better half of my days hoping what he said was true.

We sat inside the car for almost two hours. Brock wanted to kill the engine, but I pestered him to start it for periodic bouts of warmth.

"This is a lost cause," I said. There had hardly been any activity. A male duo, probably in their teens, had exited the building more than an hour before. An older woman, round and slow, entered thirty minutes later.

"Give it more time. My source says he's been spotted at this address."

"Who is your source?" I asked, fully aware his unprovided answer would start a spat.

"I'm not going to tell you."

Irritated, I swallowed a gulp of whiskey. "I've been completely transparent with you, Brock. And you are still hiding things from me."

"Concealing a source is not the same as keeping secrets."

"Ah, yes. It's part of being a journalist." I waved my hands in the air at that last, important word.

"You know, if this book ever gets finished, maybe you will take me seriously. My online readers do."

"Your readers are virgins obsessing over dead people."

"We've been here a while, I get it. You don't have to start acting bitchy." He grabbed the warm whisky bottle from my hands and took a sip.

"What a nice thing to say," I said. Brock was right. Anxiety had turned my fingernails into nubs. He wasn't any better, impatiently tapping his thumbs on the steering wheel.

"Besides, don't you have a hobby?" he continued. "Some people enjoy reading about true crime. It doesn't make them freaks."

I liked giving Brock a hard time. But I kept coming back to the fact that he believed me. He supported me. I needed to break the habit of distancing those who actually cared about me.

"You're right. I don't enjoy reading about crimes. After all, I did find my husband dead. But you have grown a loyal following, and that's admirable."

"My following of virgins?" he asked.

"That was a catty comment. I'm sure your readers have had sex. It's just been a while."

Within seconds, Brock reverted to detective mode. "What do we have here?"

A blob of people clustered near the glass door, pushing their way outside. The two leading the charge looked mildly familiar. There were so many people in and out of the condo when Dane was alive, I'd never know if we'd once met. Had this been where Dane's friends lived? Getting high at the condo before returning to their own desolation? No wonder Dane, the street kid who raised himself atop the shoulders of others, had enemies.

Eastwood exited the building next. His torso and arms were more swollen than in the picture, but all his other characteristics were the same. Bald head. Scruffy beard. Inked neck.

"There's our guy. You recognize these other people?" Brock asked.

"Hard to say," I said, repositioning for a better look.

A fourth person came out. A hand clawed Eastwood for support. A woman. She shimmied closer to him and they kissed. Her blonde hair shone white under the streetlamp, and, as she bucked up for air, I could almost hear her throaty laugh.

"What about her?" asked Brock.

"Her name is Farrah."

"Who?"

"My friend." Or so I thought. "The one who denied knowing Eastwood."

CHAPTER 24

Before

The first time I met Farrah, she was behind the bar at Fahrenheit's. I assumed she owned the place based on the similarity in names and her comfortable rapport with the patrons.

"I'm a lifer, not a leader," she said in her unforgettable squawk. Part of Farrah's lovability. She accepted her place in this world and carried the same demeanor from the first day you met her.

Defining her presence in the group proved difficult; she had a miniature connection to everyone. Her sister once dated Sturger. Dane had known her much longer, though the origin story never got told.

"Never used to picture Dane as the marrying type," she said once. It was another weekend without Jake and we were hosting a gathering at the condo. "You two seem happy together. Gives hope to the rest of us, I guess." She clinked her bottle against my wine glass. I didn't quite believe Farrah needed hope. If she wanted love, she'd go out and get it.

"He's far from boring," I said. True. I never knew what to expect with Dane. With the arrival of the insurance money, I hoped he was finally heading in the right direction.

I took another sip and scanned the room. A half dozen people occupied the living area, a few more huddled close on the patio. Dane had invited more people than usual, and there were always tag-a-longs who showed up. Our HOA had informed us the remaining condos in our row had sold. I wasn't much excited about having neighbors again. I'd miss living as if we owned the block.

"We'll still have people over," he had insisted. "But we can't be as loud."

We could never be too loud. People might hear. And if people heard, they might become annoyed, which could turn into anger. And if they got angry enough, they might call in a noise complaint to the police. And if the police arrived, odds favored several people in our home possessing items of an illegal nature. The fight between Sturger and Dane contributed to my reluctance toward having people over. I wondered what types of people were in my home, and what type of person Dane was when he was around them.

I couldn't express such emotions to Farrah. As she said, she was a lifer. She chose her path years ago, and it didn't revolve around tradition. Maybe that was my biggest downfall. I couldn't choose.

"How often you get 'im?" Farrah asked.

"Sorry?" I'd drifted away in thought.

"Your son. How often you get 'im?"

"Our agreement is fluid. We keep him every four days. Switch off. Try to be fair around holidays." Farrah was the only one of Dane's friends who even acknowledged I had a son. She understood everyone had a story, people only limited how much they chose to tell.

"It's healthy for kids to have both parents around," she said, bringing the bottle to her dry lips.

"Yes." I took another gulp. Spilt wine wormed down my cheek. "Things might become tougher once he's in school."

Laughter erupted on our narrow balcony. A loud *Woo* followed. This was the boisterous energy I wanted to tame.

"Excuse me." I left Farrah in the kitchen to investigate the commotion. A few guys ambled about, clinking together glasses and rummaging through shirt pockets for a working lighter.

"You guys seen Dane?" I asked.

The group ignored me, blinded by revelry. A tall man I'd only met once shrugged. The condo was only so big. I walked past the vacant bathroom, even opened Jake's bedroom door. No sign of him. I went to our bedroom and recognized his voice behind the closed door. Something told me not to enter just yet.

"… you good for it?" The voice wasn't Dane's. The remaining people in the living area and the loud stereo made it difficult to focus on what the people in the room were saying.

"All I know… give me time… he has my word." This time, Dane's voice. There was quiet, and then, "When?"

"… a week," the jumbled voice responded. "Have patience… might say… a big deal."

"… what I'm hoping… how much?"

A clatter came from inside the living room. One of the gatherers on the balcony had stumbled on his way inside, crashing to the floor. I stood halfway down the hall when the bedroom door opened, and Dane came out.

"What's going on out there?" Dane asked, standing behind me.

"A rowdy guest, is all." I dreaded his reaction, given his violent outburst on the night Sturger broke the picture frame.

"You fools." Dane laughed. He placed an arm over my shoulder. I looked back toward the hallway. Sturger exited our bedroom, his phone in hand. "This ruckus better quit once our neighbors move in."

The laughing continued as Dane leaned in closer to kiss my cheek.

*

My headache arrived before I even fully woke up, and I took medicine to ease the pounding away. I knew something was discussed in that room, something Dane didn't want me to know about. Plans impeded my ability to find out Dane's secret. Earlier in the week, we'd agreed to meet Frank, Julie, and Jake at the county fair. I postponed my confrontation, hoping to enjoy the afternoon.

The crowded fairground made the July heat almost unbearable. I couldn't help bumping into strangers as we walked from one corny booth to the next, feeling their sweat mix with mine. The environment made my hangover worse, and I wanted nothing more than to retreat to somewhere with air conditioning. Jake, however, was having fun. And I wasn't going to verbalize my complaints, especially with Frank and Julie there.

Dane and Julie offered to ride a kid coaster with Jake. They stood in line talking and laughing. The two developed this ridiculous banter whenever around each other. The oddball stepparents smoothing the rigidity of our damaged relationship. Some blended family bullshit they'd adopted from watching too much primetime TV. *We're so adjusted and mature. Just look at us!* I sensed the act annoyed Frank as much as it did me.

"You all right?" Frank asked as I gobbed a handful of cotton candy.

"Yeah. Why?"

"You seem tense. Haven't said much today."

"I'm a little hungover." The truth spilled out readily, catching us both by surprise.

"Oh." Frank was as surprised by my blunt response as I was about delivering it. There had always been a wall between us when it came to what we thought the other wanted to hear. But I could tell Frank was concerned about me.

"Actually, there's more. Trouble with Dane, I guess." At the front of the line, Dane tickled Jake. Julie laughed obnoxiously. "How long have you been with Julie now? Five, six months?"

"Nine."

"Damn." Where had the time gone? "Does she enjoy Jake this much when I'm not around?"

"She loves him. As a nurse, she's used to seeing kids at their worst. With Jake she gets all the good stuff."

Aside from his concerns about me, Frank appeared happy. "We've come a long way, huh?" I asked.

"We have. Most importantly, Jake is happy."

The ride rolled into action, our trio sitting on the back row. Dane and Julie exaggerated their excitement at each little dip. Jake blinked hard, dared to raise one hand above his head.

"All will work out, Olivia. Cheer up and enjoy the day," Frank said. He gave me a hug, didn't move his hand from my back until our family rejoined us.

*

The previous night's party had left the condo in disarray. We immediately began cleaning when we returned from the fair. I barely spoke to Dane during our outing. I was afraid if I did, an unstoppable stream of questions would follow. He didn't pick up on my stiffness the way Frank had. After a few minutes of silence, I couldn't contain my curiosity anymore.

"I need to ask you something. And I need you to be honest," I said.

"Uh oh." Dane held a half empty trash bag in his hands. "That's not a promising start."

I was losing my subtlety by the day. I said, "I heard you at the party. Talking to Sturger."

"Okay." He stopped stuffing the bag for a moment. He took a seat on the sofa, scooted upward toward the cushion's edge. "Well, what did you hear?"

"Bits and pieces. You were talking about money."

"Sturger pulled me to the side for a reason. I wish you wouldn't eavesdrop, Olivia."

"I didn't intend to." I put the bleach spray on the coffee table and sat beside him. "I was looking for you. You were already talking with Sturger. I want to know what you were talking about."

"It's not important," he said as he stood.

"If it involves money, it is."

He let out a heavy breath. The bag crinkled as he collapsed his arms to his sides. "Sturger knows a guy. Said there'd be a quick way for me to make cash in the next few weeks."

"A job?" I asked, optimistically.

"Sure."

"Do I want to know?" I asked, dryly.

"Probably not," he said, defeated.

"Dane, you told me you'd stopped selling." I was outraged, infuriated he'd tried to hide this from me. "Have you been doing this all along?

"No, it's a new opportunity," he said, waving his hands. "I could set us straight with this one."

"No. You're supposed to be starting a business. I don't want you involved with anything illegal."

"It's too late." He turned and started walking away.

"What do you mean?" I couldn't understand his reasoning. Dane hadn't sold pills for almost nine months. Now this?

"I committed to Sturger last night," he answered over his shoulder. "All I'm doing is giving them money. Other people will handle the selling."

I couldn't believe it. I knew it had been difficult for him to change, but he had. Why backslide now? "Call him today and tell him you can't," I said.

"It doesn't work that way." He laughed, but clearly didn't find this discussion funny.

"I'm not interested in the etiquettes of your criminal activities." I walked to him and tapped his shoulder. "If it's illegal, I don't want you doing it."

"It's illegal for me to give you my pain medicine. You want me to stop?" His tone heightened.

"Dane—"

"I'm sorry, Olivia. But you don't decide what's wrong and what's right." He knocked my shoulder when he rushed by me, like a moody teenager who'd broken curfew and been caught.

"I know my faults, Dane. You are making decisions that could jeopardize our future. Jake's future." My arms crossed over my body. Maybe I didn't have a moral high ground on which to stand, but I had to draw the line somewhere.

"I already gave him money," he yelled, turning to face me. His blue eyes had a meanness in them I'd never seen before, at least not directed at me.

"How much?"

"More than what I want to throw away. He'll need the rest soon." He opened his mouth and closed it, unable to decide how much to tell me. "I didn't want to worry you, but I've been behind on some payments. This deal is worth a lot of money. Big enough that I can pay off debts and I won't need to make money illegally anymore."

"Behind on what payments? You told me the condo and your car were paid off."

"They are. Everything on paper looks fine, I make sure of that. I'm behind on different types of payments. To people."

Scary people? Drug dealer people? He was hiding more than his conversation with Sturger. What else was he not telling me? Maybe he wasn't in trouble with anyone and only wanted to scare me into submission.

"You said you wanted to start a legitimate business. Why are you doing this now?" His pupils flickered down. And then I realized. "The insurance money. You think you can use those funds to buy drugs, or whatever it is you're doing?"

"I'll be able to triple my investment." He lowered his voice, trying to sound calm. "Then I can walk away."

"Dane." I almost laughed. I couldn't even look at him, so I started wandering. "You can't use that money. It belongs to Jake. It belongs to me."

"And what about me, huh?" He followed me across the room. "You don't care about me breaking the law when you need a fix. You wanted the bad boy to steal you away from your boring marriage. Now it's *your* money? *Your* life?"

I was hurt he'd describe our relationship this way. "The accident took place before I even met you."

"And now we're married. I'm entitled to what's yours. Didn't you say it would help *our* future? We can choose how to spend it. Together."

"We already decided you would use that money to start a business." I gave him a hateful look, my anger building. "We aren't spending it illegally."

"Fine. You can decide what to do with the rest. I'll take my part. The amount I promised Sturger."

"You made a deal without talking to me. You'll find a way to pay him back." I moved toward the balcony. I needed to leave the room. Leave this situation. My lungs needed fresh air and my mind needed a new perspective.

"Olivia—" He grabbed my arm.

"Stop. Just stop this, Dane. You are being irrational."

"Irrational?" He shoved me backwards, guiding me until I slammed into the wall. His hand moved from my arm to my face, as the other hand, the one holding the trash bag, came up. Together, his hands pulled the plastic tight across my nose and mouth.

I lost my breath when Dane pushed me. The material blocking my airways made it impossible to find. I stamped my feet, helplessly tried to move the bag away. Dane remained in position.

"Irrational," he repeated. I continued to squirm. When I clawed his wrists, he let go.

I slumped forward and inhaled a few breaths in rapid succession. I looked up at Dane, my husband. I had upended my entire life to be with this person, and he rewarded me with lies and deception. And now this. Was he really trying to hurt me? Scare me? I began crying.

"What the hell is wrong with you?" I shouted, my hands covering my chest.

Dane laughed nervously.

"Babe, you okay?" he asked. I didn't answer, still wheezing in as much air as I could. "I need a drink."

He walked to the kitchen, grabbed his keys and left. Like nothing happened. Like he hadn't tried to smother me. When the footsteps and banging disappeared, I scrambled to the balcony. He strolled away, leisurely. I waited until I could no longer see him before returning inside.

There had always been a sense of mystery surrounding Dane. It's what drew people in, daring them to take a closer look. It's what drew me in. I'd witnessed Dane's violence in the past, but he never directed those emotions toward me. The scene flashed through my mind repetitively. His firm clutch on the bag. His intent stare. He found amusement in my fear, in my weakness. I never knew he was capable of such cruelty, and the threat of experiencing it again terrified me.

Dane had never acted violently toward me. I'd also never told him No. I'd told him Probably Not and Not Sure and Maybe. Never a concrete No. His reaction didn't stem from his transition into marriage or his shady peer group. I couldn't explain the outburst away. All I could do was protect what I had left and prepare for an unknown future.

I swallowed down tears and reached for my phone. I had to sound calm. I had to keep it together.

"Frank—" My voice shook. I stopped and took a deep breath, trying once more to normalize my speech. "I need to ask you a favor."

"Olivia, is everything all right?"

"I'm fine." My words were not convincing but telling Frank what had just happened would accomplish nothing. I knew what Dane wanted, and it wasn't me. It was my money. "I'm going to move some money into our old joint account. It's still open, right?"

"Sure. I didn't bother resolving an account we hardly use."

"Expect a large deposit on Monday. It's mostly money to put away for Jake. I'm going to leave it there until I set up a new account."

"No problem. Are you sure you're okay?" The background noise on the line mellowed. He had stopped whatever he was doing because he knew I needed his attention. He knew something was wrong.

"Thanks, Frank." I hung up.

My emotions tangled with memories, trying to pinpoint exactly which mistakes had brought me to this point. Leaving Frank. Trusting Dane. My childhood. I was nine the first time I saw Mamma with a black eye.

"Why do they call it a black eye when it looks blue?" I had asked.

Her smile spoke relief, but her crackling voice gave way to struggle. "Pain comes in all sorts o' shades, honey," Mamma answered. She played with my hair while I unpacked a box. We were in a new apartment. Left our old place and Mamma's old man behind.

"Why do we always gotta leave?" In those days, I structured my syntax after what I always heard instead of what I'd been taught.

"We're always after better." She moved her hands from my hair to my chin and held my face. "Listen to me. When you leave, you don't owe it to anybody to tell 'em. You just do it, okay? Talking about leaving will only bring you trouble. You're brave enough to talk it, you're brave enough to do it."

I settled into Jake's bedroom for the night. For a few seconds, I leaned against the closed door. His hanging shoe rack nudged at my back. Leaving wasn't hard. Starting over was. And I would need time. At least a week. I could get through one more week.

CHAPTER 25

After

Calhoun Park is sandwiched between the revitalized and under-developed parts of Whitaker. One of the few places in downtown unbothered by metal and sheen. No promise of new, no reminder of old. Just a happy place to enjoy the present. This was a location to visit with Jake, not Farrah.

Suggesting a meeting outside the condo already appeared strange; she knew I was a lazy hermit. However, Brock and I agreed questioning Farrah about Max Eastwood in a public place encouraged protection. I couldn't imagine Farrah instigating harm, but she had also lied about knowing a dangerous person possibly connected to Dane's death.

Farrah was brusquely and unapologetically honest. I searched my memory to find a lie—even a white lie—she had told in the two years I'd known her. I came up blank.

I met Brock at The Copper Skillet on Wednesday afternoon. He downloaded a recording app on my phone and placed it in my bag. No mic or secret code would extract me from the conversation, should I feel threatened.

"Keep the recorder rolling," he said. He took a deep breath and leaned against his car. We didn't even waste time going inside the restaurant. "Start by asking about Max Eastwood. See if she denies knowing him a second time."

"She might have good reason to lie. Maybe she is embarrassed." I was still reaching for logical excuses. Although, Farrah seldom expressed embarrassment.

"Maybe there is a better reason to guard the truth," he countered.

"I'll call you as soon as I leave the park." I zipped up my jacket and opened my car door.

"You better. I'll be keeping myself busy going over interviews. We should have loads to discuss when you get back."

I parked on the street and paid the meter. The area where I was supposed to meet Farrah was in sight. I didn't take any pills before arriving. I needed to conduct a clear analysis of Farrah with fresh eyes, evaluate what I had missed. I felt the sudden urge for a cigarette, something that usually only happened after my third or fourth drink. I crossed the street to buy a pack at a convenience store, anything to keep my jitters at bay.

The cashier threw my products in a plastic bag, skirted it toward me across the counter. When I turned to leave, I bumped into Wooley. The last person I expected to see. He was an immovable obstacle blocking my path.

"Afternoon, Olivia," he said, exposing his sickening grin. "I haven't seen you around much."

The last time I saw him, he was drunk at The Tavern. I'd hoped that interaction would be enough to keep him away from me. But seeing him outside Calhoun Park couldn't be a coincidence. For whatever reason, he was continuing to follow me.

"Pretty far from the old watering hole, aren't you?" I asked, prodding him with our last encounter.

"I'm exactly where I need to be." He didn't move an inch in any direction. He wasn't holding anything to buy. He stared solely at me.

"You know what, Wooley?" I said, pushing past him, harder than I had in the past. "Eat me."

I left the store and didn't dare look back to catch Wooley's reaction. Knowing he was still following me only heightened my existing anxiety. I called Brock and suggested we call the whole thing off.

"Don't drag this out any longer," he ordered over the phone.

"I can always confront Farrah another time," I said. I kept staring at the park in the distance, not wanting to walk any closer. "I need to give my emotions time to settle."

"Don't worry about Wooley," Brock soothed. "Who cares if he follows you? It's not like he'll see much."

I got off the phone and took a final drag of my cigarette before entering the park.

The air was cold, like the night when Dane proposed. Early December weather did not deter college students from setting up a flag football game across the green. The temporarily resurrected skating rink, a Whitaker tradition, covered the field's larger half. I stood nearby, waiting nervously.

Farrah clopped down the steps on the opposite side. I waved my arms as my stomach dropped. Addressing Maura had been easy; knowledge powered the conversation. With Farrah, I feared what I might learn.

"Glad to see you out of the house, although I could settle for a warmer location," she said. She hugged me, felt bulkier than usual against my narrow frame. We waited in line to purchase cider from an outdoor vendor. Afterwards, we settled on a bench under a heat lamp at the Calhoun Park visitor's center.

"You know, this weather becomes more erratic by the year," she said, bringing the steaming liquid to her lips. "No use in being this cold without snow."

"Dane loved snow. Winter was his favorite season." I wanted to appear conversational, afraid Farrah would pick up on my edginess.

"I don't hear you talk about Dane much anymore." Farrah was always eager to talk about the good 'ole days.

"He's been on my mind lately. Between Rowe's release and the police investigating—"

"I wanted to ask about that. So, they're searching your place?"

I had told Farrah the police were conducting a search of the condo. The lie provided an excuse to meet elsewhere. Brock's idea.

"Yep," I said.

"Can't the bastards let the poor man rest in peace?" *Bastards* being the police.

"Apparently they're following a new lead," I said.

"Oh yeah?"

"An acquaintance of Dane's. Max Eastwood. I asked you about him before." My eyes zoned into Farrah's, gauging her reaction.

"Sure. You said your writer friend had mentioned the name."

"Police uncovered evidence linking him to the crime. An arrest could be forthcoming."

The lie, another invention of Brock's. *Make her think it's already too late*, he said. *See if she squirms.*

"Hmm. New evidence after all this time?" she asked, a rhetorical offering to the skaters in the distance or God or the sky. Not me.

I answered anyway. "I'm not sure what they found. Cops don't tell me much. Now maybe Dane can find justice."

"I hope so." She sat in silence, her decreased movements giving way to the voracious activity taking place inside her head. Her white fingers pecked a phone, manically texting… who? Eastwood?

My discretion ran thin. Knowing she had lied. Knowing she knew something. Brock might play cat and mouse with interviewees, but this involved my life and the people in it. I couldn't sum up a relationship with an index card. I stifled all logic and attacked the truth.

"You know Eastwood," I said.

"Excuse me?" For the first time her exterior softened and she stared, eyes bulging.

"When I asked you about Eastwood, you said you didn't know him. But you do."

"Okay." She wiggled, trying to put distance between us on the narrow bench. Literally squirming.

"Why would you lie to me?" The adrenaline pumping through my body overpowered the frigid environment. Underneath my layers of clothes, I started to sweat.

She didn't answer and returned her gaze to the rink. "Max didn't kill Dane, Olivia."

"Why didn't you admit you knew him?"

"This case has been a cancer to everyone involved. Somehow we avoided suspicion and I wanted to keep it that way." Her words were sharp, her good country temper beginning to boil.

"Dane spent the last week of his life scrambling for money. I knew he was in trouble with someone. Was that person Eastwood?"

A puff of frustrated breath vapored her face. I wasn't the only one tired from holding in secrets.

"Dane bit off more than he could chew. No surprise there," she said. "He told Max he wanted in on a *real* drug deal. Said he was tired of being some pill pusher. He gave him part of the money upfront. Max agreed to cover him until the rest of the money came in."

"The insurance money?" I asked.

"I didn't ask. All I know is this operation could set all parties up for a while. No more shitty jobs for Dane. No more hitting the pavement for Max."

"What was it?" I asked.

She released another defeated snuffle. "Heroin, I think."

Heroin? Dane's recklessness had intensified beyond what I realized. No wonder he refused to tell me the trouble he was in. He knew I'd never understand or approve. "What happened?"

"Max gave Dane multiple opportunities to pay up. On the day Dane died, he was supposed to meet Max with the money. They planned on going together to buy the product. He never showed, which left Max paying for everything." She spoke as if describing Frank's latest flip house, not a drug deal. "Dane bailed, disrespecting

Max in the process. You can't do that sort of thing without expecting some form of punishment."

"Sounds like motive to me."

"You had motive. Did you do it?" Her head snapped in my direction. "Motive can hurt a person. Which is why I didn't want Max's name dragged in this mess. Sturger was the only person who knew Dane owed Max. That's how the cops never found out."

"You knew. Why are you involved?" I asked.

"Max and I go way back." She stared down at her cider. "People are familiar with his reputation, make assumptions based on his looks. I remember the kid who used to get pushed around by his stepdad."

"He deals hard drugs, Farrah. He might have murdered Dane." I knew Farrah had a wild streak, but I didn't know she associated with someone so rough.

"I see people for who they are. You've learned more about Dane since he died than you did before you married him." She turned toward me again, upset spewing. "That's on you."

"Don't get mean, Farrah."

"Max is dangerous. Sometimes I think I'm the only one able to level with him. Dane kept you away for a reason."

"*Right*. His attempt to protect me amid a drug deal."

"Maybe he *was* protecting you. People aren't all bad or all good. When are you going to understand that?" She leaned back to get a better look at me. I wondered, through her eyes, what she saw.

"What makes you certain Eastwood isn't capable of killing Dane?"

"I didn't say he wasn't capable." She lowered her voice, remembering our public location. "I know he didn't kill Dane because I was with him."

I struggled to differentiate all the lies from the truths. Suddenly, Brock's voice echoed through my brain, reminding me of unexplained clues. A couple was seen in the neighborhood around the time of the murder. A woman and a shorter man, the exact silhouette I'd witnessed strolling from the apartment complex the night before. *Somehow, we avoided suspicion*, Farrah had said. I pictured her reaction each time she studied the living room. She wasn't staring in fear at the place where Dane died. She remembered.

"You were at the condo the night Dane died," I said.

"Bullshit," she replied, reverting to stone.

"A man and woman were seen leaving the area around the time of the murder," I told her. I had to make my information more convincing, so I fibbed. "The witness chose Eastwood out of a photo lineup."

Farrah folded frontward, hands pressing her face. "Max didn't do this, Olivia." She spoke between her fingers.

"You're covering for him."

"No." She returned upright. "Max had to buy the drugs on his own, which is risky. You tell someone you're showing up with a partner, and then you arrive alone? That put him in a real dangerous position. By the time I met up with Max, he was heated. I'd rarely seen him so worked up. The money was irrelevant by then. Dane hurt Max's ego. Dane in his *pretty* condo with his *pretty* wife, while Max took all the risks. He decided Dane needed a visit."

Out of the darkening night, holiday lights flickered on. Farrah continued her story, undisturbed by the merry surroundings. The carefree person I'd known over the years had been replaced by a desperate woman, trying to get her story straight.

"I always liked Dane. And I like you. Max worried me with the mood he was in. I thought maybe if I was there—there's no stopping Max when he's mad, but I wanted to try." She shook her lowered head. "When we got there, the door was unlocked, and the music was blaring. We let ourselves in and found Dane on the couch."

"Farrah—"

"He was already dead." Tears spilled as she looked around, trying fruitlessly to remain calm. "I'd never seen a dead body before. I was scared. Max was too, but he was smart. He was carrying an unregistered gun and had a record. We couldn't call it in, so we left."

"You just left him there?" I asked.

"He was beyond help. All we would do is incriminate ourselves. Max grabbed Dane's phones so that when the cops arrived they wouldn't be able to trace anything back to him. He pushed me out the door in such a rush I bumped into the counter and broke a wine glass. Cut my hand in the process." She searched her palm, the wound reappearing in her mind. "Max really lost his wits when that happened."

The unknown female DNA belonged to Farrah. Not a potential girl Dane was screwing. Not the killer. Unless, of course, she wasn't telling the whole truth.

"Max ditched all the phones—his included—and we waited the whole thing out. We were together the entire night. We didn't kill him." She wiped her face and heaved, her confession complete.

Eastwood got rid of the phones. He must have been as paranoid as Dane. He eliminated any record of communication with Dane, which is likely how police never knew to question him. But what if Eastwood was hiding something worse?

"You waited," I said. "You waited for me to find his body. You waited as the police tore apart my life. You waited as Frank took custody of my son. And never once did you think your information might be helpful?"

"No one would believe us. Max had motive. My blood was at the scene. Nothing we knew would help the investigation. We had no choice." Her eyes were wild and searching for forgiveness.

"You could have told me."

"Why? Would it make you feel better to know we found him first? I had to protect myself. When Rowe got arrested, I assumed the mess would all go away."

The crucial mistake we had all made. We hoped all our secrets and all our lies would evaporate into nothingness upon Marcus

Rowe's conviction. It wasn't about justice or truth. It was about blame and trying to shift it in any direction other than our own.

"I'm leaving," I said. I no longer trusted anything Farrah had to say.

"We didn't kill him, Olivia," Farrah said.

I was already gone, racing down the green and toward my car. I reached into my bag for the keys and touched my phone. The recording app continued running. I scrolled back and listened to a snippet of Farrah's voice. This could be what I needed to convince investigators I wasn't in the wrong. Other people wanted Dane dead, and the police needed to know about them.

I called Brock, but he didn't answer.

"Damn it, Brock," I said to no one. "I need you."

A plethora of possibilities played in my mind. Had Farrah maintained her friendship with me to stay close to the case? If anything, I thought I had been using her for pills. Maybe she had been using me. Our friendship over the past year and a half was a ruse allowing her to keep tabs on me. The list of people I could trust shrunk by the day.

Two more unanswered calls later, I parked beside Brock's car outside Ridgeway Inn. As usual, the lot was practically empty. The sun was nearly gone, but the frigid air made the hour seem later than it was. I thwacked the motel room door. Still no response. I twisted the knob and pushed inside.

Past and present welded together and I wasn't sure where I was or what I was seeing. I wasn't at the condo, and yet Dane's dead body sprawled out before me. This time face up, blood spooling out from beneath his back.

I blinked the image away. The body remained, but it wasn't Dane. It was Brock. I scampered to him.

"Brock," I shouted out, tears blurring my eyes. "Brock, are you still with me?"

His chest swelled, causing more blood to exit the stain. His eyes suddenly clenched tighter. He was still alive.

"Brock." I bent down to grab his hand. "Hold on, hold on. Help is coming."

I lunged for the bedside phone and dialed 911.

"I'm at the Ridgeway Inn off Bluff Highway. My friend is hurt—" Before I could finish, the door swung open and two police officers entered the room, their weapons drawn.

"Drop the phone and raise your hands," said one, his gun aimed at my head. The other one moved behind and forced me forward on the bed. Steel buckled my wrists, my worst fears coming to fruition. The muffled voice of the 911 operator drifted upward from the floor. Brock's labored breaths reassured me things weren't as bad as they seemed.

"Stay with me, Brock," I whispered, as the room filled with strangers attempting to make that happen.

CHAPTER 26

Before

Memories of my altercation with Dane kept me awake for hours. When he returned home after midnight, clatters and clanks echoing from the kitchen warned me he had been drinking heavily. He called out once, but I remained quietly locked away inside Jake's bedroom. The door to my right, our bedroom door, eventually slammed shut.

The next morning, the tempting scents of buttermilk and bacon woke me. The hunger in my belly rumbled. As I pictured the meal, yesterday's events flashed through my mind, and the fear returned. Sweat seeped from my underarms. My head hurt, too. I needed a shower. And pills. *No*, I lectured myself. *Think clearly*. I took a deep breath and walked into the kitchen.

"Morning," said Dane. He turned to greet me, the hissing skillet in his hand. "You hungry?"

"Not really." I didn't make eye contact. Dane placed the pan back on the stove. And walked toward me.

"I'm a fuck up," he said. I stayed silent. "There's no excuse for the way I acted toward you. I could think up several. I was hungover, angry… none would be good enough. And I'm sorry."

He put his hands on my shoulders, centering me in front of him. I wanted to wriggle away, but I couldn't yet reveal how disgusted by him I really was. Reigniting yesterday's feud wouldn't help matters.

"You hurt me, Dane." I don't know if he even realized, in his angered state, what he'd done.

"I know. Lashing out at you like that scared me." His hands slid from my shoulders to my elbows and I wanted to cry. "That's why I left. I needed a long hard look at myself."

"And?"

"And you are right. Messing around with criminals… all it does is hold us back. There's no point in it. I'm finally at a place in life where I can stop. I owe you that."

"You mean it?" I forced a smile.

"I do, babe."

"You're backing out of the deal?" I asked, seeking clarity.

He kissed me. "You won't have to worry about me anymore."

Dane had either truly rejected his lifestyle or avoided a direct answer to prevent a lie. It wouldn't matter. As soon as he left for work, I went to the bank and moved the money into my joint account with Frank. By the time I made it home, I was damp from perspiration. My fingers trembled as I dialed Frank's number. I was supposed to pick up Jake for the next four days, but he was better off away from me, and Dane, until I had a plan.

"Tell me what is going on," Frank said. He knew there must be a reason I'd forfeit a visit with Jake.

"Do you have any rentals open? A place I could stay?" I asked.

I knew Frank had acquired three properties in the last year. Depending on the area, he made more money from renting than selling outright.

"I can come up with something," he stammered. "It wouldn't be right away."

"How long until I could move in?"

"Five days. The lease has already been signed, though." He sounded nervous about upsetting me further. "You'd have to leave by September."

"Plenty of time. I'll get something worked out by then."

"You okay, Olivia?"

I couldn't bear to tell one more lie, so I hung up.

*

I stopped taking the pills.

They prevented me from seeing Dane for who he really was. And I needed to see. I needed to understand exactly what type of man I married, and what acts he was capable of committing. Dane had always been dangerous in a predictable sense; it's what attracted me to him. His reaction to the insurance money—slamming me into the wall, cutting off my airways—was far from predictable. A person doesn't villainize overnight, even in desperation. I had to know what signs I'd missed while my mind was lost in the clouds.

It had almost been twenty-four hours without a pill. I hoped a sandwich would sop up the sickness in my gut, but I couldn't finish the meal. The curtains pulled tight, I lolled on the sofa in the darkened room. My world was spinning. Out of Dane's system and into a new one, brand new. Change couldn't come fast enough.

My outlook had shifted, but my body struggled to keep up. One second I was deep breathing in the dark, the next I treaded toward the kitchen—the bathroom too far away. I flung my head into the sink and retched. The cycle of sickness and sleep and more sickness continued for I don't know how long.

"Damn it," I cried to the empty apartment.

You're brave enough to talk it, you're brave enough to do it. Mamma's voice sang to me. I tried to picture a life on my own, away from Dane and from all the disappointed opinions I'd allowed to control my life. My whole head rang now. Spinning me out of orbit again.

The answer to my problem was in one of the cabinets. I thumbed out a pill and bisected it. The smaller half on the counter, I used a wooden spatula to crush it on the countertop. I kept pressing and pressing, careless of the bits being lost in the frenzy. I couldn't wean pills and leave Dane in the same week. I rolled a dollar bill in my hand and snorted the powdery mound. I slid down the cabinet until my ass hit the floor and cried.

For the next four days, anytime Dane was around, I stayed in the bedroom. I told him I was coming down with a cold. I had all the symptoms: sneezing, drainage, sore throat. A Google search on my phone said it could be connected to withdrawals. I rested, but when Dane would leave for work, I'd snort a tiny pile of powder and pack my belongings.

I didn't need much. Jake's possessions in the condo meant more than my own. I shuffled our things out during Dane's work hours to ensure nothing was noticeable. I stuffed my car full. If he were to look inside, I'd tell him I was donating old clothes. Everything else got placed in the trunk.

A few items couldn't fit into the car. There was a good chance anything I failed to pack would be gone. Dane had a temper, and while only directed at me once, I imagined the realization I was leaving him would result in a few broken belongings. I drove to the rental house to unload, declining Frank's offered assistance. He had done enough by providing a place to stay. If I hurried, I could make another trip to the condo before Dane came home from work.

In the past five days, I'd only taken three pills. And they were crushed, making the effect come much faster, although the impact was not as potent. I looked forward to finally being settled. Dane wouldn't know where to find me. Might not bother to look. And I would have time to stop taking medicine altogether. Until then, I would need strength to finish what I'd started. I stretched out on my new bed and closed my eyes.

I woke up two hours later than planned. *Shit*, I growled.

My cell phone showed two missed calls. Both from Dane. He normally called around lunch.

Sorry. Took a nap, I responded via text and slid the phone into my pocket.

I rushed to get back to the condo. In the car, on the highway, three exits south, and finally, downtown. The destinations blurred past, mixing with my thoughts and calculation of time. I only needed a few more things, then I would be gone forever. I could start over and make things right.

I speedily shoved my key in the lock and creaked open the door.

Dane sat on the sofa. Waiting.

I sucked in a deep breath. I had timed my arrival. How could he be here? He twirled one thumb over the other, staring down at the floor.

"Dane. I wasn't expecting you home this early," I said, sweeping hair wisps from my face. I wanted to appear calm, not flustered. Not afraid.

"I decided to take a half day," he said.

"You feeling all right?" I stayed close to the door, too nervous to walk closer.

"I thought you were napping." He jerked his head towards me, his eyes narrowed.

"Excuse me?"

"You texted me thirty minutes ago saying you woke up from a nap." His quiet anger scared me. I knew he was upset but holding back. Allowing his fury to build.

"I did." I was too caught off guard to provide a lie or reasonable explanation.

"Where have you been, Olivia?" His voice was deliberate and clear.

"I—I had to run to the store," I stammered, slowly taking in a breath.

"To buy what?" he asked, curious and calm.

"Gah, Dane what does it matter?" I wrestled my temper into submission. "I needed stuff."

His eyes danced around me, purposefully. First, my empty hands. Then, my crossbody bag.

"You're lying." Dane stared at me, cataloging my every movement. My pulse quickened. It took all the control I had not to react.

"Why are you here, Dane?" My voice cracked. I had to put an end to this perverse charade he was pulling.

"Decided to stop by the bank." Sweat blanketed my body in simultaneous heat and chill. "There's hardly any money in our account."

"Not true," I said. My gaze fixed on the granite pattern of the island. "There's still money in there."

"Where's the insurance money, Olivia?"

I looked at him now. I had to. Even if he saw my tears. "It's not your money. And I'm not letting you have it."

"I noticed some of your stuff is missing. Do you plan on leaving me?"

His eerily calm voice made my stomach flip. I lowered my eyes.

"Okay," he said. I waited for him to lunge forward, as he had the other day with the trash bag. Instead, he walked down the hall and turned into our bedroom.

That was my moment. I should have left.

I didn't. There were things I needed to get. I was too stubborn to make the sensible choice, too curious to see what might happen next.

He returned to the kitchen, holding something. I didn't register what it was until he reached the island. By then, he was an arm's length away. With his free hand, he pulled me inside and slammed our door. His other hand wrapped firmly around the gun.

"Dane—"

He squeezed tighter on my arm and raised the weapon.

"Olivia, I don't have time to play games with you."

I nodded. Finally, I understood what was happening, my foolishness in refusing to leave when I had the chance. My head grew hot, like I'd been holding my breath. Maybe I had. The big bad wolf, huffing and puffing at my problems to no avail.

"I was already supposed to hand over my part of the money. I didn't, and now people are angry with me. I don't need all the money. Just some. Today," he said. For the first time, I saw more than anger in his eyes. He was afraid. Despite his fear, I couldn't give in.

"No." The tears made my cheeks much hotter.

"Olivia—"

"I'm not going to stand by while you do this. I'm not your accomplice."

"It's already been done," he roared. His useless anger escaping his body through his voice. "I'm supposed to meet someone today. The longer I go without paying my half, the more danger there is for me. For both of us. Don't you get it? They're not going to understand me backing out because my *bitch* wife wants me to change my ways."

His fingers gripped tighter around my arm, leaving white indentations when he finally let go. He gave me a shove. I lost my balance and fell to the floor.

"This does not involve me," I said, still on the ground. I felt safer there.

"These men might hurt me, Olivia. Does that bother you at all?" he said. He raised his arm, then dropped it. Dane didn't want to deliberately punish me, but I was blocking his access to what he needed.

"Aren't you friends with them?" I propped up on my hands, scooting away from him. "There must be a way to handle the situation without you getting hurt."

"Friendships change quickly when you owe money." He raked his scalp with his fingers and stomped the floor. "The only way out is to pay them. Today."

"Tell me exactly what you owe and where it is going." I was sick of being kept in the dark, as though I wasn't capable of understanding. Dane wasn't in a position to make decisions about my life anymore.

"The less you know, the better," he said.

"You can't hide things from me and expect my money and—and my support."

Dane lowered the gun, slumped over like he'd received a punch. He moved closer, standing over me. "Do you hear yourself?" He laughed. "You do nothing but hide things from people. Hide things from yourself."

"I don't hide anything from you." Until recently, that was true. Maybe I bit my tongue when I needed to confront his behavior, but I was always honest with Dane. He allowed me to be. With him, I was confident. The past few days had me reevaluating everything I thought I knew about our relationship.

"How about Frank? And Jake? Your old friends, my new friends? You're always playing a part. I'm supposed to believe who you are with me is the real you?" He grabbed my hair and yanked me to a standing position, pushing me against the wall. "Who you are with me, is a girl on the hunt for her next high. It's fine to bend the rules when you're after a buzz, but here you go, trying to change up your role again."

"Is this what you think of me?" I had forfeited my entire life for this person, and his opinion of me was lower than Frank's and his friends I never felt good enough for.

He blurted out his game plan like a worn sports coach. No remorse. All strategy. "It doesn't matter what I think. If you don't approve of my behavior, well, I'll find a way to hide it from you. That's what I've always done. What I will not take is an upscale junkie stepping in and messing around with my livelihood."

"Dane, I'm your wife—"

"My wife's about to leave me," he said, lifting his arms and the gun to showcase the living space. He shoved me again, violently ramming my shoulder into the back wall. "Now you're just a problem creating bigger problems."

"You're crazy." I pushed him forward and dashed toward the island. I grabbed my keys and turned toward the door. Dane took my ponytail in his palm and yanked. I cried out in pain.

"You aren't going anywhere, Olivia. Not until you tell me where you put the money." He turned me toward him and used his forearm to trap me against the door. He buried the gun into my gut.

"Just let me leave," I said, knowing my pleas were hopeless. His grip was too tight. I pounded his forearms and chest, anything to make him release me.

"Don't be tough, baby," he said. He removed his arm from my clavicle and started stroking the hair he had just pulled. I swatted his hand away. "You weren't a hard girl to love. Beautiful, smart, weak. So desperate for excitement in your life. So desperate for a little buzz. A load of cash coming your way. A couple of misplaced pills and you were wrapped around my finger. It wasn't hard."

How long had he planned this? From our first kiss? From the first time he gave me a pill? When Frank first told him about his broken-limbed wife struggling to cope? All those moments became mysteries. The man before me was a con, a stranger.

"Shoot me. If that's what you're threatening, shoot me." I leaned closer. Fighting anger with anger, fear with fear. The confidence Dane helped build over the years backfired against him. The last thing I was going to do was cower.

He pulled me by my arm into the living room and slammed me onto the couch.

"Two possibilities." He pointed the gun at my head. "I'm going to keep you here until the withdrawals kick in. I don't care how long it takes, you'll eventually hurt bad enough to tell me how to get that money. I know you've stopped taking pills and that's why you've been sick the past few days."

He returned to the kitchen, lifted a decanter, and poured bourbon into a glass. He placed the gun on the counter, pointed in my direction.

"Or you will stay here with me until my buddy and his friends show up," he said. "You think I'm tough, but these are real bad guys. People who trusted me. I broke their trust by depending on you. Depending on you to support me, as you fucking vowed to do." He drained his drink in one gulp, poured another.

"I don't even know you." The truth sank in, and it stung.

"You knew me enough to leave your husband. Your son."

If the gun were closer, I could have shot him then. Ended him. He recognized the hatred in my eyes. "You and I can share in the same fate," he said. "If they off me, they won't spare you."

He carried the decanter into the living room, settled in for a long night. He watched me, tear-stained and sore. We waited in silence. Dane poured a third drink, then a fourth. My lips longed for a taste, but Dane wouldn't allow it.

Anyway, I needed to stay present. I could take advantage of my sobriety in comparison to Dane's emerging drunkenness. I monitored my surroundings. My keys now hung from a hook by the door. The gun, no longer in Dane's hand, was on the end table near the sofa. A grim warning of how careful I needed to be.

"I gotta piss," Dane said after a long while. He came toward me, jerked my body to a standing position. "Come with me."

He walked me down the narrow hallway. When we reached the bathroom, he left the door open and instructed me not to move.

"This isn't necessary," I said.

"Stop talking, cunt." His words tottered from all the drinks. His stream thundered down. I waited, obediently as he fixed himself up and turned around. "Let's go."

I walked ahead, his hands on my lower back guiding me. His grip was inconsistent, and he stumbled at times into the wall. He kept looking down, occasionally raising his hand to wipe his brow.

I scanned the room, searching for the heaviest item within reach. The decanter, its long neck like the handle of a club. I palmed it without him noticing, his hand partially obscuring his own vision. I turned, both hands on the glass now, and swung hard at Dane's head. The glass caught his temple, sending him a few steps back.

"Bitch," he screamed, but my arms were already in position, over my head, to strike again. I came down hard on his head, this time shattering the glass. The impact was enough to force him to his knees. The neck of the bottle was still whole in my hands. I raised my arms to strike. I wanted to give him a third hit. A fourth, a tenth. But I didn't. He was down, if only for a few seconds.

I tripped as I hurried past him, falling hard against the broken glass on the floor. I scrambled to my feet and hurried to the kitchen. I grabbed my keys with such urgency the entire hook clattered to the floor. No time for my bag. Dane's laugh chased me out the door. I sprinted past the concrete steps, and into my car. Each second passed too quickly, as I fumbled to get the keys in the ignition and the gear into drive. I sped away, eyeing my rearview to see if he followed. He did not.

CHAPTER 27

After

The interrogation room looked sloshed in coffee stains. No pristine lobbies and viewing windows funded by tax money. This was the room in which you were sequestered if unfortunate enough to commit a crime past business hours.

"How many men in your life gonna end up dead, Olivia?" Wooley dropped a folder on the linoleum table, chewed a toothpick like popcorn. Brock's shooting was separate from Dane's murder, and Wooley was happily investigating the former, the known link between the two cases being me.

I wasn't placed under arrest. The handcuffs were protocol until officers secured the scene. Once they took Brock away in an ambulance, they released my hands and offered me a ride to the station. They said I'd have to provide a thorough explanation for why I was in that hotel room.

"Betcha can't guess what caliber gun was used?" Wooley prodded.

My eyes widened. Dane's gun had never been recovered. It would take time to determine if it was the same weapon. Perhaps Brock had finally found Dane's killer. All I could think about was Farrah tapping away at her phone. Had she contacted Eastwood and told him police were getting suspicious? Told him Brock had been digging into the past?

"You need to start talking," Wooley said.

"Eddy Fetzer," I said with a defiant smirk. Eddy had drilled repeatedly: *Do not speak to police in my absence.* I needed to heed his warning, the recent memory of steel around my wrists a grave reminder as to why. "I'm not talking until my lawyer is here."

Wooley bowed his head. "All right, have it your way. We'll drag this thing out a bit longer." He left the room, leaving me alone to ponder everything that had taken place in the past few hours. I tried to block out the image of Brock, blood-covered and struggling to breathe.

Instead, I replayed the conversation with Farrah in my mind. I'd made the mistake of telling her about Brock and his suspicions about Eastwood last week. Maybe she was the person who sent the letter telling me to *STOP SEARCHING*, afraid we'd uncovered they were at the condo. She was texting nonstop during our conversation at Calhoun Park. She couldn't have shot Brock, but she could have easily given Eastwood orders.

Eddy busted through the door wearing gray sweats and dirty sneakers. My misfortune had clearly interrupted something important.

"How much did you tell them before I got here?" he asked, already cross.

"I didn't say anything," I answered. "But we need to talk about what happened before police showed up."

"Wait." He took off his bag and slumped down beside me. "Right now, tell me about Brock Bowen. Explain everything that happened at that motel."

I told him everything of relevance. My willingness to help Brock investigate an open case clearly annoyed Eddy. Based on what I said, he concluded the police wouldn't have enough to arrest me immediately. The mishandling of Rowe's case benefitted me; police wouldn't make any moves without concrete proof of my guilt. He counseled me to keep my answers with Wooley concise.

"Tell me about your friend," Wooley started when he re-entered the room. "Who is he and why is he in Whitaker?"

"Brock is a writer from Florida. He blogs about true crimes and contacted me a few weeks back, right after Rowe's charges were dropped. Together, we were reexamining everything," I explained. "Brock accessed case files. He also conducted interviews. Tried to uncover anything overlooked last time."

"You mean, when Dane was murdered?" Wooley asked.

"Yeah. I helped him. We thought if we could reinvestigate certain aspects, maybe—"

"People would stop looking in your direction?" His smile turned my stomach.

"Brock believes I am innocent." I tapped the table with my nails. Wooley wasn't apt to believe anything I said. I couldn't make him understand Brock was helping me, trying to prove someone else was at fault. "He had his own theories about what happened."

"Care to share what those might be?" He lazily picked up a pen and circled it over his notepad.

Eddy shook his head, cautioning me to ignore the bait. But Eddy didn't know everything yet. There were other people to investigate, and every moment wasted on me gave the culprit more time to cover his tracks.

"You saw his room. His wallpaper is nothing but photos and newspaper clippings and index cards," I said. "He knows the case better than you do, I'm sure."

"I'll take the challenge." Wooley laughed. "Did he tell you about his plans to meet with anyone?"

"No." I wanted to slap the table, but muffled my reaction.

Brock's secrecy bugged me more than anything. Eastwood might have chased him down, but the possibility remained that Brock invited someone else into that hotel room. His eagerness for a lead outweighed his discretion. Brock should have taken more precautions. He sent me to meet Farrah with procedural hesitancy, then had no defenses himself.

"We are currently reviewing video surveillance. Desk guy already told us you were a frequent visitor." His eyebrows lurched upward at the word *frequent*. I rejoiced there were cameras. If we knew who shot Brock, we'd be well on our way to knowing who killed Dane.

"Good," I said. "I already told you Brock interviewed several people. Even spoke to Rowe. Although he wasn't always professional, or cautious."

I answered more routine questions. Wooley let slip that Brock's phone was missing from the hotel room. He also revealed the initial 911 call came from a Ridgway Inn resident who reported hearing gunshots, explaining why the police arrived so quickly. He didn't say how many minutes there were between the first phone call and my own, but I hoped it might further distance me from the crime. As time dragged, I realized I didn't even know where Brock was. If he was dead or alive.

"Is Brock okay?" I asked finally. Wooley cocked his head in a funny way.

"We're the ones asking questions, Olivia." He sensed my desperation for an answer and couldn't resist toying with me.

"I'm sure you love this. But I've been here long enough. I just want to know." I leaned my chair forward on two legs. "Is he okay?"

His eyes darted to Eddy. "They're still working on him. Touch and go," said Wooley.

I rocked back. "Shit."

Wooley catalogued my reaction, tried to decipher genuine worry from false. Was I hoping Brock would pull through because I was innocent, or hoping he'd succumb to his wounds to mask my identity as the shooter?

"For the record, where were you before arriving at the motel?" Wooley asked.

"Calhoun Park."

"Can anyone confirm that?"

Now would be an opportune moment to inform investigators about Farrah and Eastwood, but I needed to talk with Eddy first. I reached into my bag to grab my phone and felt the cigarette pack. *Thank goodness*. If I ever needed a sober smoke, this was the moment. Then I remembered, Farrah wasn't the only person who could prove my whereabouts.

"You can, Wooley," I said, clenching my newfound power card.

"Excuse me?" he asked.

"You saw me right outside the park. Remember?"

Wooley repositioned himself. I had forgotten about our previous encounter—so much had happened since then. Between inspecting a new shooting, his keenness to interview me and his frequent drinking habit, I banked Wooley had also forgotten the brief run-in.

His smugness from earlier disappeared. "Yes, I saw you at the park. Doesn't mean you couldn't have made it to the hotel before Brock was shot."

"How long did you watch me? *Did* I have time to make it to the hotel?" I asked.

"What's going on here?" a confused Eddy interjected.

"Wooley's habit of following me around town might have worked in my favor. He saw me at Calhoun Park."

Wooley's face burned red with embarrassment. I imagined he worried I might next reveal our chance meeting at The Tavern; his public drunkenness in the presence of a murder suspect would surely detract from his professional credibility.

"Is that true? Were you following my client before the shooting?" Eddy asked.

"Yes, but I—" Wooley stammered.

"Look, this is bordering on harassment. Your questioning her at all in connection to this case is a conflict of interest. Unless you have anything new to discuss, we are leaving."

There was no reason for me to stay any longer. I glanced at Wooley as we stood to leave; he appeared more determined than ever. Not only did he believe I was guilty, but I had just embarrassed him in front of his co-workers on the other side of the interrogation wall.

"Don't leave Whitaker anytime soon." Wooley clenched his fists as he spoke. "We'll be in touch."

*

I couldn't remember my last pill. Long before I met with Farrah. Leaving them behind was a blessing in disguise; if police had found my stash when they searched my belongings, odds are they'd lock me up for possession. I needed to return to the condo and take the edge off. Adrenaline had kept the shakes at bay, but now they rumbled to the surface. Eddy didn't sympathize with my noticeable flimsiness.

"Why are you so damn stubborn?" he asked once we were alone.

We stood under a flickering streetlamp. Eddy pinched tobacco and crumpled the wad inside his lip, visibly exasperated by both my behavior and the intrusion into his personal time.

"Listen—" I started.

"No. You should be distancing yourself from the case, not willingly interrogating people with some wannabe cop." Eddy spit on the wet concrete and readjusted his coat.

"I'm trying to help him," I explained. My jacket was still draped over my bag. The adrenaline pumping through my body made me immune to the dropping temperatures.

"Help yourself!" he shouted, mockingly. "You are the one who appears most suspicious. Tell me everything you know."

I provided a rundown of my interactions with Brock. He didn't appreciate the frequency of my visits—"damn timeline"—or that together we had been chasing down people connected to Dane's murder—"leaving breadcrumbs for the cops"—but his manner changed when I brought out the recording.

He bent down, his slick hair close to tickling my chin as he listened to my conversation with Farrah.

"When was this recorded?" he asked. Curiosity replaced his annoyance. I could tell he was considering a way we could use this to our advantage.

"A few hours ago," I said, my hands on my hips. "I visited Brock as soon as I left Calhoun Park."

"You two should not be poking around a murder investigation." He pointed his finger, still holding my phone in his other hand.

"We want answers, Eddy."

"Leave answers to the police. A badge scares people into submission. You and Brock are nothing more than obstacles, and if you aren't careful, you'll be picked off next," he warned me.

I didn't welcome the lecture, regardless if parts were true. "Is the recording helpful or not?"

He scrolled back a few minutes and hit play, relistening to specific parts of our conversation. "It could be. Do you believe her?"

"I don't know," I said.

"Either way, police need to know. I'll make sure it gets to them." He handed the phone back to me.

"I almost wanted to hand it over while we were in there."

"And that would have been yet another stupid mistake," he said. "Send it to me now. I'll make a copy of the file first. Possibly two."

"Do I need to go with you?" I asked, cautious about returning to the condo alone.

"No. I will present the recording to detectives in the morning. There's nothing else that can be done tonight. Techs are clearing up the crime scene. Brock is probably still in surgery."

Talking about the case made it easy for me to forget about Brock. When I pictured him at the hospital, fighting to stay alive, I felt sick. Someone did this to him. We needed to know who.

"He better make it," I said.

"That would be great for us," Eddy said.

I shot a glare in his direction. "I'm worried about Brock, not just myself."

"I know. I'm only pointing out that if he survives, he can tell us who pulled the trigger and why. Barring acute memory loss, of course." He rolled his eyes. "Nothing would surprise me in this case."

"What do you want me to do?" I asked.

"Stay away from the investigation. Spend time with your family. If Farrah calls you, you call me. I'll give you updates on Brock."

"Okay." He made it sound like I should be saying goodbyes. After all the suspicions, could this really be the end?

"I'm serious, Olivia. Police told you to keep close," Eddy said. "Depending on how the Brock situation plays out, they could be coming for you."

CHAPTER 28

Before

The retiring sun stabbed at my vision as I pulled into the Smithwood subdivision. The rental house was unknown to Dane, but I couldn't be alone. I banged on my old front door, looking over my shoulder in fear Dane would appear. The thumping of Frank's footsteps gave me comfort.

"Olivia. What's wrong?" he asked, his expression melting into a frown.

"Can I come in?" I rocked from side to side. My pulse was still pounding.

"Of course." He opened the door wider, allowing me in.

"Is Julie here?" I asked, remembering I'd interrupted Frank's new life.

"No, she's at her place."

"I see." Julie had been a persistent presence for so long, I sometimes forgot they didn't live together. I walked toward the living room. He stopped me.

"Wait," he paused, grabbing my forearm. "Clean up first. Jake is awake."

I snuck into the guest bathroom and looked in the mirror. I didn't recognize myself. Red streaks surrounded the blue in my eyes and rosy splotches colored my face. My hair stuck out in Medusa-like madness. My collar bent loose. Blood—mine or Dane's?—speckled my skin and shorts.

I couldn't remember my last meal or the last time I drank water. I knew it had been hours since my last pill, and I hurriedly took two. I could relax now, because I was safe. I was away from Dane. I knew within twenty minutes the pills would calm my rattled being, quiet the horror pulsating within me. I washed off my ruin in the shower. Crying the whole time. So much repair needed. If only I could be presentable tonight for my son, the rest would come in time.

After drying off, I brushed through my hair with a comb I found under the sink and rolled my dirty shorts up my legs. A knuckle tapped the door.

"Olivia, I've got clothes," Frank said. I opened the door to find pants and an old college shirt folded neatly on the floor. Frank's kindness was enough to make me cry again, but I resisted. I needed to gain composure, at least for the next hour when Jake would be awake.

I exited the bathroom, Frank's clothes hanging from my broken body. Jake sat in the living room rolling trucks along the fireplace. He looked at me like I was Christmas morning. "Mamma!" He dropped the toys and toddled in my direction, arms wide.

"Hey, baby." I embraced him longer than usual, taking him in, his softness, his smell.

"Wanna play trucks?" he asked, and I longed for the days when all problems could be solved with imagination and fun. I followed him to the hearth where Frank sat, his long legs folded. We played and laughed and didn't talk about anything important. Everything that mattered was in the room with us.

Frank and I allowed Jake to stay up later than usual, a silent attempt to delay our inevitable discussion. Jake fell asleep before I finished reading his favorite story, *The Little Blue Digger*. When I found Frank in the kitchen, he was doling out leftover Chinese food.

"Hungry?" he asked. He was being polite, making sure I was comfortable. He must have changed while I was in Jake's bedroom. His work clothes were gone and he now wore a familiar T-shirt and plaid pajama bottoms.

"Famished," I said.

"It's not much," he said, pushing the plate in front of me.

I would have gladly devoured the whole meal cold and clumped together. I shoved about seven bites in my mouth before he said anything. He stood watching as if I was the most bizarre thing he'd ever seen.

"So what's going on?" he finally asked.

I told him I moved the money because I couldn't trust how Dane might spend it, but I didn't mention drugs. I told him about Dane and the trash bag. About Dane and the gun. Halfway into my testament, he poured two glasses of wine. The alcohol made the truth come out easier. A cry would surface, and he rubbed it out, his hand on my back.

"Do you think Dane might come here?" he asked.

"He's too worried about whatever is going on," I said. "Plus, he was already royally drunk when I left."

"You did the right thing by leaving," he reassured me. "You should have told me things turned bad."

"Dane was bad from the start, but I didn't want to admit it." I swirled my drink, wiped falling tears with the back of my hand. "This is all my fault, Frank."

"You don't deserve this. He—"

"This is my punishment for bringing Dane into our lives. For choosing him—I don't know why I let him ruin us."

Frank took a long sip, suddenly mindful of the fact Dane was more than just my tormentor. He was the person who destroyed the family we once had. His glass clacked against the counter when he put it down.

"I know," he said.

"I never felt good enough for you. I thought maybe Dane was what I needed. If I could go back—" The truth stabbed at my insides. If only we could go back to our worst moments, erase their impact. We can't, and it's foolish to wish such things. "I'm sorry I was so selfish. You deserve happiness, Frank. And I hope you've found it."

He poured another glass and topped mine off. "I do have something to tell you." He waited again, the words paining him. "I asked Julie to marry me."

"Oh." Frank getting remarried meant he was truly gone. Our life before was officially over.

"I asked her last week. Her family is in town to celebrate and help pack up her place. She'll be moving in with me soon." I imagined Julie preparing meals with Frank, dressing Jake before school, sleeping in my old bedroom. I'd surrendered my right to say anything a long time ago, but the news still hurt. Frank could tell. "I was waiting for a good time to tell you. But it feels wrong talking about everything and not being upfront."

"Frank, no. I'm happy for you." The words sounded false and we both knew it. "You have to move on with your life, despite what's happening in mine."

"Julie being in the picture will change things. But I want you to know I'll always be here for you. You're Jake's mom, which means you'll always be family." He leaned over the counter, drawing me in.

My eyes watered again. "Of all people, you should have turned me away. Told me to handle my shit."

"I wouldn't do that to you, Olivia." Frank finished his drink before speaking again. "There's something else I need to say. You should know, I don't blame our divorce only on you. I'm also at fault."

"You did nothing wrong. I acted dumb and selfish and—"

"You were struggling. I knew it and I didn't do enough to help. I thought if we continued living our lives—working, loving, caring for Jake—your problems would go away. I ignored them, hoping they would disappear. Instead, it fueled them. And for that, I am sorry. I hurt when you left, but I was never angry with you. I never hated you. Deep down, I understood why you did what you did. *I* wasn't enough for you."

Everything he said, the way he described our relationship, it was as though we had lived through so much. Several lifetimes in a short amount of years. And yet, his face looked younger, full of light and promise. Like it did all those years ago, when he'd entered my life and vowed to make it better.

"You were enough, Frank," I said.

He moved closer. Our hands touched, and I could smell the wine on his breath.

"I worry about you," he said. "No matter what you say, it will always be my job to protect you."

My heart beat so happy it hurt. Was this a trap? Love always felt like a trap.

"I miss you." I leaned in until my thighs rubbed his. Waiting, in dread, for him to push me away and end our intimacy.

"We miss you, too." He struggled between what felt natural and what was right. He brushed loose hair from my face. "I miss you."

We shared a kiss, slow and cautious. As if we weren't real. As if the lights would flicker bright and we would be caught or wake up from this dream. Afraid it might end, I kissed him harder, pulling him close. I suddenly wanted him, all of him, more than anything on earth. As if this one moment could erase the years of absence in each other's lives.

We had sex in the kitchen, too lost in the moment to go any-where else. Afterward, we remained nude from the waist down, sweaty and panting. Not sure if we would regret what had been done. Not knowing the repercussions. Then we went upstairs and made love like civilized adults.

Within minutes of our second time, I drifted away. No dreams. No disturbances. The darkness of my old bedroom welcomed me home.

*

I woke up after midnight. I'd slept hard, and it pleased me to know I had several more hours remaining.

Frank wasn't beside me.

Checking on Jake as he slept was a habit I'd adopted since his infancy, despite the risk of waking him. I went downstairs—his new room had taken over my painting hideaway—and peeked in his door. He slept as peacefully as I had been minutes before.

Again, no Frank. He wasn't in the kitchen. Or the living area. And he didn't appear upstairs when I returned to the bedroom. His phone remained on the nightstand. I walked to the window which overlooked our backyard. Outside was dark except for the weak flames flickering in the fire pit. *Frank must be outside contemplating his next step*, I thought as I crawled back into bed. I needed to leave him alone. Perhaps things would go back to the way they were. Perhaps Dane and Julie would fade away like drunken memories. Within minutes, I slept again.

Frank's alarm buzzed early; the nostalgic tick made me question the year.

"Morning," I said. I extended my arms and wiggled my feet.

"Morning." Frank, already awake, sat on the bed's edge. His back faced me.

"I'll sneak out before Jake wakes up," I said.

"No need to rush." He turned, and I could tell by the lines on his face he hadn't slept much.

"It's fine. I don't want Jake being confused."

No telling where our relationship would go from here. I rolled to the right, searched the carpet for Frank's sweatpants, and pulled them on.

"Where are you going?" he asked.

"I need to go home." I stretched his hoodie over my head. "I have to find my purse and some other belongings."

"Are you sure? Maybe you shouldn't go alone," he said.

"Dane's probably still passed out. I'll leave for the rental house straight away. Besides, Jake needs to get to daycare, and you need to go to work."

"Last night you were afraid—"

"I'll be fine. I feel better about things now." I kissed his shoulder, thinking again about everything that had happened yesterday. The ugly and the beautiful. I only needed my essentials, then Dane would be out of my life for good.

The events from last night had given me hope, but left Frank conflicted. I knew he was wrestling with his conscience. He rarely made choices that might disappoint someone. Further decisions needed to be made, but I couldn't sit around for the deliberations.

"Let me know when you're ready to talk," I said.

"Olivia." Frank turned, stared at me like he was seeing a ghost. "Call me if you need me. And be careful."

I nodded.

Only three emergency pills remained in my car. I took one before departing Frank's driveway, hoping I'd be able to find more at the condo. I needed to be numb. Outside, the sun and moon worked in unison to cast a haze over the suburb while the protective mountains stood dark in the distance.

CHAPTER 29

After

Eddy drove me to my car, still at the hotel. Caution tape lined the hallway leading to Brock's room, and uniformed officers paced the sidewalk. I hurried to the condo and retrieved my pills. Terror flashed when I realized, given recent events, Farrah could no longer supply me. I'd need to find an alternative, but I had bigger obstacles to overcome. Time was running out. My life, like Brock's, could be in danger. If not my life, then at least my freedom. I could no longer handle the darkness and uncertainty on my own.

Julie appeared agitated when she met me at the front door of the Smithwood house. I'd only seen her once since the party, and we hadn't spoken. She recovered, offering a smile and a greeting.

"Evening, Olivia. We weren't expecting you," she said.

"I'm sorry to drop by unannounced." Again, I was at the mercy of Julie, a person I'd recently wronged. "There's… a lot going on. I'd like to visit with Jake, if that's all right."

We rarely did this type of thing anymore. My time vs. Frank's time was always predetermined, but I needed this one night. A shadow danced behind her. Jake came closer, his snaggletooth grin enlarging as he approached.

"Hey, Mamma," he said.

"Hi, baby." I looked back at Julie. It was obvious she did not want me inside, however, Jake's goofy beam softened her resistance. She pulled the door wide and I walked through.

"Watcha doin' here?" asked Jake, his hair rubbing against my sweater. The static grabbed at his ends and made them levitate.

"I needed a visit, is all. I won't stay long. I know you have school tomorrow." I gave his bony body a tight squeeze.

"It's almost Christmas," he cheered, randomly.

"I know. I can't wait," I said.

Indeed, Frank's house already mirrored one of those holiday stores open year-round. A tree blocking the living room window, stockings—only three—dangled above the fireplace. I had yet to put up any decorations and wasn't sure I'd be granted the opportunity. "Where's your Dad?" I asked him.

"He's running errands," Julie answered. "Should be back any minute."

"Yeah, he got a phone call," said Jake. "Got all sore."

"Oh, really?" My eyes found Julie's staring back. A classic *we need to talk, but not now* scowl.

Jake watched the last half of a Christmas cartoon. I joined him on the sofa while Julie fumbled around the kitchen, keeping an eye on us. For obvious reason, she didn't trust me around Frank. Was she apprehensive about Jake, too?

"You take a bath already?" I asked him.

"Yep," he said, grinning.

"And brushed your teeth?"

"Uh-huh."

"J-ay-ke," Julie called from the kitchen.

"I sorta brushed them," he amended. His eyes squinted up and he smiled as he always did when he hoped cuteness would outweigh punishment.

"Listen to Julie," I said. "Go brush your teeth."

As I tucked him into bed, he told me his Santa list. I wondered how many more years Santa would be a thing. I stroked his hair as he faded into sleep. Prayed, for the first time in too long, we'd share more nights together. Prayed I wouldn't be forced away from him. Prayed Brock would survive, both for himself and for me.

When I crept out, Julie had started a film in the living room.

"Asleep?" she whispered, just in case.

"Out like a light. Thanks for letting me hang tonight." Julie would never know, nor would I really want her to know, how much this night had meant to me. No matter how dark the situation, a few moments with Jake always made life seem a bit brighter.

"Sure." She paused the television, followed me into the kitchen as I gathered my belongings. "Look, Olivia. I've been wanting to talk with you about the party."

I'd been dreading this conversation, but knew it needed to happen. "Julie, I'm so sorry. I should never—"

"No, I need to apologize." She stopped me, raising her palms. "I do. I never should have hit you."

"Thank you, Julie. But I can't say I blame you. What I said was despicable. I—"

She stopped me again. "We have both said and done things over the years we regret. I'm trying to say I'm sorry. For all of it. And I hope we can move forward. For Jake. And Frank."

I hated her maturity and levelheadedness, although I respected it. She loved Frank, which stung. But she also loved Jake. And that mattered more than our petty past.

"I'm sorry, too. Moving on sounds great," I said. I placed my hand over hers and squeezed. "Frank not back?"

"No. I tried calling him a half dozen times. When I got home, he was on the phone with his lawyer. Do you have any idea what's going on?"

"Has Frank told you about my friend Brock? The writer?"

I gave her a summary of events, minus my confrontation with Farrah. On cue, Julie covered her mouth with a hand or flattened a palm over her heart. *Hotel rooms and 911 calls and police stations, oh my!* The more I revealed, the more I wondered how bizarre it must be to marry into such drama.

"How is your friend?" she asked.

"I know he's in surgery, which is promising. He lost a large amount of blood."

"What will you do now?" she asked.

"I'll head back to the condo and wait." I'd been many places and spoken with many people in recent hours. I should have rejoiced at the opportunity to be alone, and yet I resented it. After spending time with Jake in the coziness of my old home, the thought of leaving made me even lonelier than normal.

My phone vibrated, casting annoying rumbles across the quartz. Eddy. "Let me get this," I said to Julie.

"Olivia. Where are you?" he puffed out.

"I stopped by Frank's," I spoke into the phone.

"Of course you did," he said, followed by an irritated grumble.

"You told me to spend time with family." My voice was louder than it needed to be. No matter what I did, it was never the right thing.

"Yeah, yeah. I did." He couldn't push his words out fast enough. "Look, Frank's at the police station."

"Police station?" I screeched.

"They're questioning him about Brock's shooting."

"Why would they question him about Brock?" I asked.

Julie was listening intently, had been ever since the words *police station*.

"They claim his truck is visible on camera at the hotel. They ran plates and they recognized his name immediately."

"They have Frank on film?" I looked at Julie, who was still devouring my end of the conversation.

"No, not him. One of his company vehicles. Ridgeway Inn isn't big on security. The gas station across the street has a camera angled to show cars entering and exiting the motel parking lot, although no other details are visible," he explained.

"Is he under arrest?" I asked. Julie looked at me, morphed her mouth into a perfect little *O*.

"No. They don't have near enough evidence yet." I shook my head to Julie, and she wilted in relief.

"Why the hell is he down there?" It didn't make sense, unless he didn't have a choice. "Frank knows better than to talk to police."

"He'll probably be out within a few hours. His lawyer is with him."

I pulled the phone away from my mouth. "He might be a while, but he'll be home tonight," I whispered. Julie nodded, then paced the kitchen.

"Also," Eddy started up again. "I've got positive news about your friend, Brock. Appears he's going to pull through."

"Thank God," I said. "Is he awake?" Julie listened. I mouthed *Brock*.

"Doctor said surgery went well, but he won't be conscious for another day at least. The bullet was too close to his vital organs, and he's in an induced coma. He needs as much time to heal as possible," he said.

"Will he be able to tell us who shot him?" I asked, hopefully. I wanted to know who had hurt him. I wanted to know if that person also killed Dane.

"Odds are increasing," Eddy said. "Don't get your hopes too high. Anything could happen."

"Brock will pull through, I know it. He'll pull through and provide a name." The bragging rights of his involvement alone would be enough to keep him going.

"Can Julie hear me?" asked Eddy, his voice subdued.

Julie had expanded her wandering route, headed from the kitchen to the living room to the garage and repeated the circle.

"No, she walked out," I said, lowering my voice and turning around.

"You have any idea why Frank would have been at the hotel?" he asked.

"Not a clue. Unless… maybe Brock arranged an interview." Even though I knew, from both Frank and Brock, that was unlikely. Frank wouldn't associate with anyone in that area. His biggest connection to the outskirts was me. If he was in that parking lot, it was for a reason.

"Wouldn't Brock have told you?" Eddy asked.

"Our working relationship could be one-sided. He admitted there were details he couldn't tell me about yet." Brock's refusal to be transparent with me likely contributed to his attack, although he'd be too stubborn to admit it.

"How come?" he asked.

I sighed. "He described me as a loose cannon, at times. Didn't want me overreacting."

"I'm liking him more already," Eddy scoffed, snickering into the phone.

"Hush."

"I want you to think long and hard about Frank." The humor in his voice disappeared. He was stern, wanting to be heard. "He had no purpose in being at the hotel."

"You're not accusing—"

"I'm your lawyer, Olivia. I watch out for you. Be smart."

We got off the phone. I peered around the corner. Julie was in the garage, the door leading to the interior house open.

When I first woke up on the night Dane died, I never told anyone Frank wasn't beside me. Not the police or Farrah or Brock. Admitting his absence would harm both of us. I never checked to see if his car was in the driveway. I never saw him outside. But I did see the flames in the fire pit. I chose to believe he was there, because that's where he often went during times of stress.

Coincidences happen, even in murder investigations. Dane and I fought in the hours before he died, leaving our bodies equally and suspiciously bruised. Frank sat outside alone by the fire. An ordinary event when examined outside the context. But now? Could he have done it? Could he have been so desperate to protect me that he went to the condo to confront Dane, which resulted in his accidently killing him? Purposely killing him?

Surely, Frank would tell me. He would not remain a bystander while I received escalating police suspicion. He would not allow an innocent man to sit in prison, possibly forever, when he knew he was the one to blame. Frank was a decent person.

But so was Brock. As unbelievable as the idea of Frank shooting Brock was, I couldn't think of a logical reason why one of Frank's vehicles would be at Ridgeway Inn. None of his employees would have had a reason to be there. Only Frank. Had Brock's suspicions about Frank been right? Would Frank really risk hurting an innocent person to cover his tracks? Frank's absence on the night Dane died combined with his presence at Ridgeway Inn presented a startling conclusion: it must have been him. There was no other person—not Maura or Farrah or Eastwood—who was closely connected to both crimes. Other people wanted Dane dead for material reasons, but Frank's issues with him were personal. And the heart has a way of conjuring deadly reactions.

Julie re-entered the kitchen. I could tell she had been crying. Worried sick over Frank, a man we both loved, despite his secrets. For the first time, I felt sorry for her. Julie's annoying habits aside, she was loyal to Frank. He'd betrayed her once, with me. Was it possible he had been duping us both this whole time?

I didn't want it to be true. He had motive and opportunity and was now being questioned about an assault. A monstrous image of Frank formed in my mind. And if I had to come to terms with this possibility, so did Julie. She deserved full disclosure for once, and an opportunity to process.

"Julie, there is something you need to know about the night Dane died," I started. "It has to do with Frank…"

I stopped talking. Thoughts flew away like birds after a blast. My focus shifted to the gun Julie held in her hands. A gun I'd only seen once before on the night Dane threatened me.

Before I left. Before he died. Before the weapon disappeared.

CHAPTER 30

Before

I walked up the steps leading to the condo, thrust my key into the lock. There was no give when I turned it. Unlocked. That gave me some ease. Maybe Dane had passed out and I could grab my possessions and leave without incident.

The curtains were closed just enough for the rising sun to cast shadows around the room. Two barstools were overturned. Glass littered the counters. The room was a visual representation of what our marriage had become: hazardous and broken.

The stereo roared, but I still heard the silence. The sound of nothingness loomed. My purse lay on the floor, its contents scattered about. I bent down to gather them and caught sight of Dane's boot peeping out from behind the furniture.

Look.

I needed to leave. I was lucky he was asleep.

Look.

I crept toward him, feared disturbing his hibernation, reawakening his beast.

Look.

Dane slumped over the couch in an awkward position, even for a blackout. One boot on the ground, the other on the sofa. His chest and shoulders were on the seat, his face turned away.

A darkness covered his torso. Liquid. Wine or bourbon. No, heavier. Like paint.

Maternal instincts kicked in. I wanted to shift him, let him recover in a comfortable state.

Look.

I touched his back. Tepid and clotted. I looked at my palms, stained and dark.

"Dane," I said, trying to turn him. My exertion resulted in his thudding to the floor. And now I recognized darkness on the cushions, too. And his front. And the rug all around him.

I saw his face. Eyes open. The darkness—blood, it must be—dried against one side of his mouth.

"Dane, you're scaring me." As if he would respond. "Dane?"

Nothing. No more anger or ambition or hiding. All feeling replaced with the frozen expression of a man who had ceased to exist. A man I might have loved. A man I certainly feared.

All the confusion and grief exited my body at once, years of regret pouring out in minutes. Dane's eyes stared back at me, the charm and cruelty gone.

Look.

Logic arrived, and I called 911. The conversation can be heard partially on the Vanessa Hardgrave interview, in full by the likes of Wooley and others at the police department.

I hung up, even though they told me to remain on the line. My life had drifted away from protocol and procedure. I switched off the music. Sat with my knees up, by his body. Nothing would ever be as before. Nothing would ever be as I'd planned it. All this became clear in the minutes alone with Dane's corpse.

But for the briefest moment, before the officers arrived with their stretchers and tape and gunpowder kits, I felt solace. Relief illuminated the horror, because I thought, in that naïve moment, my life would never be harder than this. I knew all the threat and danger would be gone. I knew in time, I would have a chance at normalcy. Through Dane's death, I had recaptured my own life. I vowed to be better.

If only it could have been true.

CHAPTER 31

After

Nothing could have been more bizarre than the sight of Julie standing in my familiar kitchen, a piney garland lining the white cabinets, an assortment of Santa cookie jars on the far wall, with Dane's gun—I knew it was, had to be—in her hands.

"Julie, what are you doing?" I asked.

"I watched you that night," Julie said. "Through the window."

My eyes darted to the counter and I remembered Frank on top of me, pushing me harder and harder into the stone. We had been so selfishly lost in our own passion.

"The ring had been on my finger less than a week. My family came to Whitaker when I told them the news. Frank told me to take a few days and celebrate with them. But I missed him, so I snuck out," she said. She smiled all mean. "I came over to surprise my new fiancé and found him having sex with his ex-wife."

"I'm sorry you saw us, Julie. I didn't want you to find out—" She lifted the gun, my words spurring her into action.

"There is no good way to find out," she said.

"You're right." I raised my hands. "I'm sorry."

My apology prompted her to lower the weapon.

"I put everything I had into Frank. Dating is hard enough." Julie lost control as tears took over. She swiped her wet cheeks, smearing what makeup remained. "Frank was different. He was ready for a family. Lord knows Jake needed a mother."

Fear outweighed the comment's sting. "Frank and Jake are lucky to have you."

As if I'd solved a rudimentary equation, she said, "Plenty of men were lucky to have me. That didn't stop them from leaving me behind." She leaned forward against the countertop, abruptly drained. "All I ever wanted was what you had. A husband and a child. It's natural to want those things. You wasted your opportunities, and then returned to mess with mine."

Why was she telling me now? With Jake asleep in the other room, and Frank at the police station? Had he known Julie saw us that night?

"I should have confronted you. I should have defended myself. But I was too afraid. I was afraid of losing Frank," she continued, although she sounded as if she were lecturing herself, not me. Another bundle of tears broke through. "I needed to expose you. That's why I drove to the condo."

"You saw Dane that night?" I tried to understand what she was saying, why she was saying it, but the pieces were scattered, and a clear image refused to emerge.

"I thought Dane was my friend. We'd spent enough time around each other that summer; I thought I was doing him a favor by telling him what I saw." She shook her head, and I could tell she was confronting memories she'd buried a long time ago. "I smelled booze the moment he opened the door. He was a bigger mess than I was. Seemed frazzled—afraid, even. I'd never seen him like that."

Of course she hadn't. Dane, like me, always wore his best face in front of others. I was the only witness to his ugly unpredictability.

"I told him about you and Frank," she said. "I expected him to feel a little bit of the heartache I was experiencing. I thought he might even comfort me."

"What did he say?"

"He laughed." She shrugged and dropped her hands. After all this time, she still couldn't understand. "The whole time I was inside the damned condo he laughed and raved like a complete madman. Said you and fuckboy Frank were the least of his worries."

"Dane had other problems," I said.

She sniggered before her face tensed. She stared ahead, beyond me and through time, the scene from last year flashing before her. "He said we should get even and tried to kiss me. It was repulsive." She pawed her mouth as though wiping away the taste. "There I was, my future ruined. I wanted him to understand. I wanted someone to share in my loss. Dane just wanted an excuse to get off. I told him it wasn't going to happen, pushed him. I'd get away and he'd pull me back."

I imagined Dane and Julie dancing a twisted do-si-do through our living room, Julie dumbfounded by Dane's drunken desperation and trying to escape. "Did he—"

"Assault me? No, he eventually gave up and said if I wouldn't play nice, he'd play dirty, or something along those lines. He asked if I had any money, which made no sense. Then he started rambling about getting money from Frank, said he was going to call him." She looked down at the gun in her hands. "All I wanted was more time. Dane was only making things worse. I tried to take the phone from him. He wrestled it away from me, laughing the entire time. He said that you and Frank had never stopped loving each other, and that I was *too stupid* to see. I told him he was wrong. Frank *loved* me. Out of nowhere, I saw the gun. It was just sitting there. I picked it up, thinking he might finally give me the space I needed to leave. He called me a *stupid bitch*, walked away like I wasn't even a threat. Even with a gun in my hands, I was a joke. I'm always a joke.

"So I shot him. And then I shot again. He remained standing… I didn't know if it was real. Then he fell over and I saw the blood and…" Sobs took over, her hands shaking until her jewelry jangled. She panted, "I didn't even realize what I had done."

I imagined the entire scenario as she spoke. Julie unaware of how cold and calculating Dane could truly be. Dane lacking the sobriety or compassion to see Julie's fragility. Her anger brewing as he mocked her and the relief she must have felt, trailed by the realization of what she'd done.

"Julie, if Dane pushed himself on you—"

"I already told you that didn't happen."

"He intimidated you. You were scared." I tried my best to calm her. If anyone understood her fear and desperation, it was me. "I can help you. The police will understand what you did."

"Your word is shit with the police," she barked back.

"Frank knows about Dane being violent," I told her. "He'll back up what I say. He will protect us."

"Not *us*." The meanness returned to her voice. "Me. I want you out of our lives!"

"I'll go." My eyes stared at the gun, newly aware of how easy it would be for Julie to pull the trigger. "I'll leave."

"When the police started focusing on you, I couldn't have imagined a better scenario. Rowe confessing was a close second. I supposed it really was a dream. Maybe I hadn't killed him. Maybe I could finally live the life I deserved."

"You still can. We can make the police understand what happened."

In all the time I'd spent considering suspects—who would want Dane dead, and why—Julie never crossed my mind. She wasn't personally invested in Dane. She had more reason to dislike me than him. If she shot him that night, it was because of how he'd treated her. He'd pushed her, not realizing the danger. All the police had to do was compare Julie's temperament to Dane's, and they'd be able to see what happened.

"They won't understand about Brock," she said. Her words gutted my already flayed emotions. I pictured Brock lying on the hotel room floor, blood spilling out. Dane might have provoked his doom, but Brock didn't.

"You hurt Brock?" I asked.

"Didn't plan on it. Funny how a person can stumble upon two murders in one lifetime, huh?" Her creepy, high-pitched laugh made me shiver. The scared woman who'd shot Dane had been replaced with a menace trying to cover her tracks. "Except the second one didn't take. If he wakes up, he'll be able to name me as the shooter. Then everything will be found out."

"Why Brock? He barely mentioned you."

"He hounded us for an interview. I said no. Frank said no. Somehow he figured out I'd been leaving comments on his stupid website under an anonymous name."

"You read Brock's website?" I recalled all the comments bashing me, telling lies. Julie must have loved reading the awful words people wrote about me. The awful words *she* wrote about me. Brock and I discussed the negative remarks, but he'd never divulged Julie was a commenter.

"It only made sense to follow the case, didn't it?" She wiped her face again. "When we picked up Jake from your place last night, Brock confronted me. He said he wouldn't expose me if I'd be willing to answer some questions for his book."

Sounded exactly like Brock. Using people's baggage as leverage. Unaware of the dangers in doing so.

"What did you say?" I asked.

"Frank would have been upset with me. I agreed to meet with Brock as soon as I got off work. Frank didn't know." She shook her head, struggling to recall what had taken place hours before. "I'm not sure where I slipped up. Somehow Brock knew I was lying about Dane… I could tell he knew."

Listening to her narcissistic retelling was nauseating. The delusion that everything was done against her, and she was justified. I couldn't let her excuses slide.

"You brought a gun with you, Julie," I said. "And you drove Frank's work car instead of your own. You had a plan." The word *plan* jolted her back to the present, and she lifted the weapon again.

"I had no intention of hurting Dane or Brock," she claimed. "And none of this would have happened if it weren't for you."

A creaking door startled us both. Jake poked his head around the corner, using his bedroom wall as a shield.

"Mamma?" he said.

"Jake." Julie responded before I did. She slung the gun behind her back.

"Where's Daddy?" he asked.

"Honey, go back in your room," I said.

My eyes sprinted between Julie and Jake trying to assess her level of instability. Julie smiled, despite the black rivers streaming down her red cheeks.

"Jake, come with me. We're going to find Daddy," Julie said.

"Jake, no," I told him. "Go back in your room. Lock the door."

"I'm scared," he said. The quiver in his voice clawed my heart. I needed to tell him everything would be okay, but I wasn't sure I could. Not with Julie controlling the gun.

"Don't be scared," Julie cooed. "Mamma and I are only talking. We need to find your Daddy."

"Jake, do as I say," I said. This time I was firm. Even if it frightened him, he needed to listen. "Now."

His door slammed, and the lock clicked.

"Damn it," Julie screamed. She turned to me. "You need to stop ruining everything."

"There is no reason to involve Jake," I said.

"I am protecting him from you!" she screamed.

"Are you listening to yourself? You shot Brock. You killed Dane. Jake doesn't need protection from *me*."

The sympathy I'd built for Julie dissipated as quickly as it appeared. I no longer considered her an unfortunate girl in an unthinkable situation. She was a threat, to everyone, including Jake.

"Nothing would have happened if you had stayed out of our lives," she yelled. Each word's pitch increased by an octave. She strummed a hand through her hair, trying to concoct a plan amid her frenzied thoughts.

My mind, too, whirled. Regardless of her crazed state, I couldn't imagine Julie hurting Jake. She loved him. Or, she loved having a stepson she could manipulate into her own child. I couldn't abandon him to her storm of irrationality and revenge.

Julie looked at me, her eyes bright. She reached above the refrigerator and brought down a bourbon bottle. Grabbed two glasses from the cupboard. She poured an inch of liquid into one, then downed it. She repeated the process. Shivered off the icky taste.

"Where are your pills?" she asked.

"What?" I asked.

"Where are the pills, bitch?"

I reached in my bag, pulled out the bottle.

"How many do you have?" she asked, her tone low.

"Fifteen," I said. I didn't even need to count.

"Give 'em." She emptied them on the counter. Using the bottle's heavy bottom, she crushed them.

"What are you doing?" I asked.

"It's time you finally do what's right," she said. "You must do what is right for Jake."

"I don't understand."

She continued to press until the pills were a thin powder. Grabbing a spare piece of mail, she shifted the pile from the counter into the bourbon.

"Drink," she said.

"No way."

"Drink." She lifted the gun again. She didn't lower the weapon until I took a sip. The taste was expectedly bitter, and I coughed. She searched a nearby junk drawer for writing materials. She wiped the pen clean with a potholder before handing it over.

"Now write your confession," she said.

"What do you want me to say?" I had no idea what she wanted me to write. It couldn't be real, any of it.

"Admit to killing Dane," she said. "Admit to shooting Brock."

"This is pointless, Julie. When Brock wakes up, he's going to tell them you shot him."

"I have time to deal with Brock. I'm a nurse, remember? I can reach him before he wakes up. Right now, let's focus on you." She had created more plans than I realized, regardless of their plausibility. "Take another sip."

I obeyed.

"Write," she said, the gun wedged against my neck. I imagined Jake in the next room. Was he afraid? Could he sense something sinister on the other side of the wall? Hopefully he went back to sleep. No longer angry or frightened. He had been startled by nothing more than a bad dream.

I killed Dane, I scribbled, unsure how to convincingly admit to crimes I did not commit.

"Make it real," she said, the steel burning my skin.

I killed Dane. If it wasn't for me, he would be alive. I am sorry. He was a mean person with an ugly heart. He scared me, at times. He smothered me once. I thought he was dangerous and I wanted him gone. But he didn't deserve to die the way he did, and maybe his life would have been better if I'd never come along.

Julie nodded for me to continue. I took another sip.

I shot Brock, my friend. He was on a mission to find out the truth, but he got too close. He almost figured out what really happened. I had to protect myself. I'm sorry and I hope he survives.

The paper turned to tissue in spots due to my falling tears.

Frank, I am sorry for leaving you. All I ever wanted was to feel good enough for you, and I never did. I was foolish. I would give anything to go back to our boring life. I never stopped loving you.

Jake, baby. I love you so much. Know that the mother you knew was the real person. Not the woman people may tell you about in years to come. I wish you nothing but sunshine and happiness and smiles. I'm sorry I won't be there with you. Remember I love you. Always remember.

I cried heavily now. Julie read the words over my shoulder, unamused.

"I should take the last parts out," she said. "Guess it's more believable if I leave it in."

I finished the last swig. My head dizzied. Either medicine or lethargy had kicked in. I knew the eternal struggle would be over soon.

"Now what?" I asked.

"We wait," she said. Her eyes were filled with something, but it wasn't remorse. "Move to the couch."

I did. With my head on the armrest, my feet on the cushions, I cradled myself. My body as tranquil as the streets after a heavy rain.

"I will look after Jake," she said, her solitary condolence. "Life will be better for him this way. Maybe you can see that now."

Christmas lights, gold and red and teal, twinkled from the tree's decorated branches. What a beautiful combination. We placed the tree next to the fireplace when this was my home. Julie situated the fir by the living room window, merriment visible from the sidewalk, blocking the view. If a person looked, they wouldn't see me. They wouldn't see Julie. And that's how it would go forever and always. No one would see. No one would know. Jake would grow up with the memory of his mother dying a week before Christmas. What a tragedy.

I closed my eyes. Imagined Julie using her smile and scrubs to sneak past hospital security, find Brock's room. She'd unplug his breathing tube or stick a poisoned needle in his IV. *His gunshot wounds were too much*, they'd say. Frank would come home, who knew when, to find me dead on the sofa. The way I found Dane, but he'd think I died on purpose. *She was scared and needed a place to spend the night*, Julie would say. *I couldn't have known.* She'd cry and carry on. He'd hold her. Wooley would find my letter. Read his favorite parts to the younger deputies, saying, *I always knew it was her. I always knew.*

And I imagined Jake, growing up without me. Ultimately, he'd stop saying Julie, easier to say Mom. It would make him less weird to the other kids. Maybe Frank and Julie would have a baby, a sister or brother he could love. And his heart and mind would fill with so many memories, I would be forgotten. He'd pick up a picture at college graduation or on his wedding day to remember the lines in my face.

My life had caused insurmountable hurt for others. Frank and Dane and Brock. Maybe I could spare Jake from pain. If Julie's plan didn't work, if she couldn't reach Brock before he woke up, at least Jake wouldn't risk ruin by my hands.

Seconds passed like hours. The world around me blurred from the outside, inward. Julie sat in front of me. The gun beside her on the end table, her hand occasionally patting it like a parlor dog.

My eyes closed for a long while. The cloud unfurled all around me. Maybe this was my destiny. My face remained motionless; my heart smiled.

"Honey," Julie's voice cried out. "Honey, where are you?"

I felt her breeze as she rushed past me. I didn't move. What did it matter where she went? My breath weakened with each passing second. I heard her feet rumble up the stairs. "Jake," she yelled again.

His name adrenalized me. I opened my eyes, my vision in HD. Julie was gone. But the gun remained. *She believes I'm already dead,* whispered a voice inside. My legs debated whether to cooperate as I struggled to a standing position. I picked up the gun, stumbled under its weight.

I lumbered to Jake's bedroom. Empty. The December wind pouring in from the open window provided another rush of energy. Where was he? Surely, someplace safer than home. I leaned against the door frame, weaker by the step. *Hold on*, I thought. *Hold on for Jake.*

Julie's stomping returned to the main level.

"Jake?" she shouted.

I heard keys jingling as she prepared to chase after him. I'm not sure what alarmed her first. My absence from the couch or the gun's disappearance from the table.

"Olivia?" she yelled. She paused a moment, scanning the room.

I steadied the gun and waited for her to turn the corner, prayed for enough strength to pull the trigger. Otherwise, she would take back control and finish me.

She stepped off the bottom step. I caught sight of her and shot. The kickback tilted my body and I stumbled to my knees.

I stood again, moved closer to Julie. Too late. Blood covered her shoulder, streaming from a wound in her neck. Her eyes raged rabid and wide. With her right hand, she reached for the heaviest object she could find. A bronze reindeer sculpture. Before she had the chance to fully clutch it, I pushed it away. Her arm stretched after it, while her other hand covered her gaping neck. She was too weak do anything else. Within seconds, her body was still.

I slid to my knees, crawled to the couch, and put my head on the cushioned seat. I skidded the gun underneath, preventative measures should Jake return. I hoped he wouldn't. He didn't need to remember me this way. He didn't need to find Julie. Maybe Frank would get home first. I closed my eyes again. Made friends with the dark.

*

I jolted back to life.

"We need an ambulance. One's breathing," shouted an unknown voice. "Do you know your name?"

"Olivia," I wheezed.

"Are you hurt?" asked the voice, a man's voice.

I nodded.

"Where are you hurt?"

"Pills," I whispered.

He raised my arms around his neck and carried me from the house. The red-and-blue flashing pained my eyes. I scanned for a familiar face.

"Let me through," Frank's voice boomed. I saw him pushing past people to get closer. "Jake is all right, Olivia. Hold on for him."

A final comfort before fading to black.

CHAPTER 32

After

I ended up by myself in the hospital. No Frank or Jake. Also, no handcuffs linking me to the bedrail. Not a doctor or nurse in sight. Maybe Julie's plan succeeded. I was dead and alone for all eternity.

When I woke the second time, I knew I had landed in Hell.

"Welcome back," said Wooley.

He bent down to inspect my eyes. His familiar stench of coffee mixed with liquor clouded my nostrils, making me want to puke.

"Go away," I said.

"Now, now. Hear me out." He moved closer to the bed.

"Where is Jake?" I had earned the right to ask him questions, I believed. And there was still a lot of confusion as I crept closer to full consciousness. "Where is Frank?"

"Both fine," he said. His tone was almost kind. "We're keeping Frank busy. He'll be here as soon as he can."

"Tell me what is going on," I demanded.

"What do you remember?"

I shared my hazy recollections. I had to stop every few words, wrestling to determine if everything had occurred as I remembered. I wasn't sure of anything, only that I had somehow made it through.

"Everything checks out," he said, thumbing his chin and rereading his notes.

"Is Julie—"

"She was pronounced dead at the scene." He looked away from me and down at his hands. I'd killed Julie. Even though she had threatened me, it still didn't feel right. To take a life.

"Does anyone believe me?" I asked.

"Well, there was a letter found in your handwriting confessing to shooting both Dane and Brock." He paused, as did my heart. "Luckily, Brock pulled through. He also kept meticulous recordings of every person he interviewed, including Julie. We found his phone at the Smithwood house; it contained audio of the entire interaction."

I leaned back in relief. In all the recent madness, I'd almost forgotten about Brock. He had been fighting to survive, too. Warm tears filled my eyes at the realization he had. Then I laughed. Brock's investigative skills finally pulled through.

"What about me?" I asked.

"You ingested a fatal amount of medicine. You are lucky to be alive."

"How did the police know to come?" I asked. There hadn't been an opportunity to call 911, and I didn't recall seeing Frank until already outside.

"Your boy. Jake," Wooley said. "He said he woke up to arguing and you told him to lock himself in his room. After a while, he got scared. He snuck out and knocked on your neighbor's door, Maura Murphy. He couldn't provide many details, but said his mom and stepmom were fighting. She decided to phone the police. We probably wouldn't be speaking otherwise."

"Did Jake find Julie?" I pictured her laying on the floor, neck and eyes open. I braced for his response.

"No, no," he reassured. "Maura kept him until police arrived. He never re-entered the house."

I released a heavy sigh of relief. Julie had been in Jake's life for a long time. Even though he was too young to fully grasp the events,

I knew he would mourn her loss. And he didn't need that image of her seared into his brain, as it now was in mine.

"Julie told me she killed Dane," I said, wanting Wooley to understand that this horrendous case was now over.

"When you are feeling able, I'll need you to come to the station and provide a complete statement." He folded up his notepad and stood. "Until then, rest."

"Do you believe she did it?" I asked.

"The gun found with you on the scene appears to be Dane's," he said. "She must have held onto it, probably dumped the wallet somewhere near the mall, like Rowe originally said. We're trying to establish a timeline using phone and video records, which requires a lot of digging."

"Do you believe Julie killed Dane?" I asked again. After a year and a half of suspicion, coming from him especially, I needed to hear him say the words.

"I do." He tilted his head to the side. "The more we look into her, the more suspicious she becomes. Funny how that happens in an investigation."

"Is that an apology?" I asked.

He stopped in the doorway, spoke over his shoulder. "As close as you're going to get to one."

*

Frank checked me out of the hospital the following day. Between caring for Jake and appeasing police officers, he didn't find time to visit. Investigators tore through his house, cars, phone bills and bank statements, uncovering and recovering all aspects of Julie's life. Given their formal demands, you'd figure he was applying for a second mortgage, not identifying his deceased wife as a murderer.

When we met at the discharge desk, we hugged hard and tight. Much needed saying, but we lacked the words. After a painful pause, he spoke.

"Olivia, I am sorry." There was a layer of shame attached. For the past eighteen months, he'd treated me as a complication to his new life. He didn't realize my problems weren't the biggest threat.

"It's not your fault, Frank," I said.

"I knew something was off when my lawyer called and said my vehicle was spotted at the motel. I knew I hadn't been there, and Julie was the only other person who would have had reason to drive my car." He rubbed his temples. He couldn't make sense of it any better than I could. "I didn't say anything to the police. I wanted to talk to her first. Figure out what was going on. I never got the chance."

Frank didn't owe me any explanations. No one could have predicted Julie hurt Brock, let alone Dane. I felt sorry for Frank. His last moments with Julie were normal, happy probably. The next time he saw her, she was dead and being called a murderer. I couldn't imagine the conflicted feelings Frank was battling.

"Frank," I said, aware he was more fragile than I was. "You didn't do anything wrong. You can't blame yourself."

"She was around Jake. How could I let someone so damaged enter our lives?" His eyes filled with tears. He never recognized the raw side of Julie. She fooled him, as Dane fooled me.

"Look, you can't beat yourself up." I had been punishing myself for years, and it took all this suffering to realize how useless that was. "What matters is we are safe. We'll tackle the rest later."

"Okay," he whispered, his tall frame looming over mine. I was recovering physically, but he'd suffered an emotional loss that would need time to heal.

I bit my lip, afraid to hear the answer to my next question. "Does Jake know? About Julie?"

"Not exactly." He shook his head, laced his fingers around the back of his neck. "He thinks she's hurt. I haven't managed to tell him anything else."

"We'll figure out a way," I said.

"I'm happy he was smart enough to leave and find help. If not, you might have died. I might have stayed married to—"

I pulled him close before he could finish the sentence, hugged him. I'd spent years playing *What If* games. The time had come to focus on reality instead of possibility.

"Where is Jake?" I asked.

"He's in the car. I wanted to make sure you were well enough to see him."

"I've never wanted anything more in my life," I said.

He wrapped his arm around my body and walked me back into the world.

*

I returned to the hospital on Sunday, although not for myself. I had meant to visit Brock sooner, but Frank and Jake's temporary stay at the condo occupied my time.

"Merry Christmas," I said, peeking my head inside the door.

He sat up. A giddy smile covered his face when he recognized me. "We have a couple days, don't we?"

"We do," I said. "Will you be out by then?"

"Gah, I hope so. Getting shot is for the gulls." I hovered over his bed and provided a partial hug. He squeezed my shoulder as I leaned back. "Olivia, you are practically beaming."

"I'm relieved, but I feel guilty about you," I said.

"Don't," he said, propping up in the bed. "Can you imagine how amazingly successful my book will be now that I can say I got shot?"

"Good for you," I said. As always with Brock, everything went back to either the book or the blog. "I'm happy you almost died."

"How was your conversation with Farrah?" he asked, a familiar curiosity in his eyes.

"Picking up where we left off?"

"Good a place as any."

I filled him in on the confrontation in Calhoun Park, an encounter which seemed to have taken place a lifetime ago now. He began taking notes about halfway through my story.

"You told the police?" he asked.

"Eddy knows." He'd been extremely busy the past few days, trying to keep up with all the new information coming his way. "We've yet to decide a course of action."

"Talked to her since?"

"Nope."

"Plan on it?"

"Not sure." I'd not had enough space to determine what role other people deserved in my life. Was Farrah ever a friend to me, or was she covering her tracks? Only time would tell.

Brock grinned. "Explains the female blood found at the scene. It's a costly coincidence stumbling upon the dead body of someone who had wronged you."

"Doesn't appear as damning given the circumstances." I fumbled with my fingers. "Clearly they weren't the ones who killed him."

"Right," he said, lowering his eyes.

I told him, with much more detail than I told Wooley, about Julie's confession and the chaos which ensued. He had earned the inside scoop.

"Tell me," I paused midway. "Julie mentioned leaving comments on the blog. What did you have on her?"

"This one profile started posting more and more in the days following Rowe's release," Brock said. "Some of what it said was pretty outrageous, but also accurate. Like the fact Jake had stayed with Frank the entire week before the murder. Stuff even an avid follower of the case wouldn't know.

"Turns out, the email was connected to the hospital where she worked. It looks like that's where she did a lot of posting. Every time I reached out to Frank, he was adamant about wanting nothing to do with the case. So I thought it was strange Julie went out of her way to not only read the blog, but comment, too. When I saw her outside the condo that day, I told her I'd traced the account back to her. She agreed to meet, as long as I promised not to say anything to Frank."

"Doesn't explain why she chose to shoot you," I said.

"When she showed up at the hotel, she admitted to writing the comments. Claimed it was only because she had a complicated history with you. She understood I was writing a book and didn't want a negative portrayal."

"Of course." I rolled my eyes.

"I asked her about Dane. How well she knew him, who did she think killed him… basic stuff. No different than questions I asked every person associated with the case. She stammered and stuttered. I assumed she was annoyed. I'm used to getting that reaction."

He smiled, as did I.

"As you would call it," he continued, "my *shitty investigative skills* took over. I could tell she was holding back. She reacted the same way you did when I asked if Frank was with you the entire night." His eyes narrowed.

"You didn't believe me?" I asked.

"Never."

I looked around the room.

"Yeah, he left for a little while."

"Where'd he go?"

"He was outside in the backyard. A regular occurrence, but because it was on the same night Dane died—"

"It was a costly coincidence," he answered.

"I didn't want to incriminate him when he'd have no means to prove where he was."

"Wise. I wouldn't mention it to the police," Brock suggested.

"Not going to."

"Thanks for telling me, though." He shifted in his seat. "Anyway, we're in the room, she's a bag full of nerves. I decided to push her by reexamining her actions the night he died, even though I had access to the information already. She spouted off answers like a kid reciting the Gettysburg Address. All memorization, no thought. So, I bluffed her. Told her new evidence had been discovered linking a female to the attack."

"As we discussed."

"See, it wasn't a total lie. Of course, we were assuming Farrah. She thought I was chasing her. One minute I'm reaching for my pen, the next I'm on the ground. She shot me twice. Said she was sorry on her way out the door."

I couldn't imagine the fear he must have felt. He went from a civil conversation to fighting for his life. Although he'd never admit it, this case provided more than he'd bargained for.

"I found you, you know," I said.

"I do and I'm eternally grateful," he said.

"No suspicion for over a year, suddenly she's shooting you and trying to kill me." I still struggled to understand how Julie could have deceived so many people.

He shook his head. "She wanted what she wanted at any cost. Unlucky for you, she decided she wanted your life. Frank fell for it."

"He was desperate, too, at the time. Desperate to have the family I destroyed." I was quick to his defense. Frank would deal with enough backlash in the years to come. "Still, I am surprised he didn't see through her."

"We see what we want to see," Brock said. "Julie appeared charming. When her flaws surfaced, they did so in disastrous form. I'm sure she felt remorse, at first. Enough time passed, she probably felt justified. Reasoned with herself that what she did was right, therefore whatever she had to do to cover it up was also acceptable. Life carried on for her. When the investigation reopened, her life frayed. People can't handle living under suspicion."

"You can kiss your blogging days goodbye," I said. "You've got the fixings for a bestseller on your hands, and the bullet holes to prove it."

"Book or no book, *The Vindictive Type* is here to stay. The website provided my first loyal readership." He looked out the window, which provided a dismal view of downtown Whitaker. "Investigators are finding more evidence on Julie by the hour. Imagine the time saved if they'd been thorough the first time around."

"How do you know they are uncovering evidence?" I asked.

"I'm confined to a hospital bed, but I still have sources." He winked.

"Will you tell me who they are?"

"Never."

I smiled. With the case behind us, I wasn't sure what else we had to talk about.

"Any Christmas plans?" I asked.

"Docs say I'll be out in time. As soon as I'm allowed, I'll be heading back to Florida. I need a good dose of salt water. What are your plans?"

"Spending the holidays with Frank and Jake." I smiled. "We hope the house will be released in time."

"Nice. And after Christmas? You two going to patch things up now that your wicked step spouses are no longer with us?"

I punched his exposed arm. Brock's vulgar jokes had clearly made a full recovery.

"Reconciliation is the last thing on our minds. Frank's grieving, obviously. But we're headed in the right direction for Jake."

"Frank's improving. Jake's good. What about you?" Brock asked.

I sighed. A debate had been going on in my head whether I should tell him.

"After Christmas, I'm going to a treatment facility."

I stopped talking, but he waited, indicating there was more to be said.

"I'm high right now. Pills. If I can't take those, it's something else. I did better for a while, but reinvestigating Dane's case made me slip." I searched my lap, the confession harder when looking at another person face-to-face. "For a long time, I convinced myself it wasn't a problem. I realize now my dependency has clouded my choices. The affair with Dane and leaving Frank. The way I checked out of the whole investigation. The ways in which I neglected Jake. I believed I was fine as a screw-up. But I don't want to live like that anymore.

"I can't tell where my problems started. Maybe meeting Dane. Or the car accident. Hell, I might have suffered baby blues for the past five years. Regardless, I need change. I need change for Jake, but I also need it for me."

"I'm happy for you, Olivia." He reached over, held my hand. "How long will you be gone?"

"Thirty days, at least," I said, a part of me dreading being away for that long.

"You best make time for me when you return," he said. I smiled. Brock had brought equal parts frustration and insight into my life. He wasn't someone I wanted to just disappear.

"Of course. Considering hanging around Whitaker?" I asked.

"I'd miss the ocean too much, but I'll be back. We solved the case." He lifted his hands in the air. "Now I have to write the book."

"Can't wait to not read it."

We sat around talking until visiting hours ended. When I left, I figured I was parting from a true friend.

EPILOGUE

I confronted a multitude of demons while in treatment. Dane. Julie. The disappointments I caused others. The failures within myself.

Confronting those challenges sober was almost insurmountable. The remnants of withdrawal overtook my body with full force. The aches and sweats and illness. Sometimes, at night, Julie whispered to me. *Where are the pills, bitch?* She wanted to help me find them. She wanted to bring me back to the cloud.

Thirty days turned into sixty. In treatment, they talk about a different cloud. Not the heady, dark one I was used to. Those euphoric moments of new sobriety are likened to a pink cloud. A manic high masking a still present need to consume. If presented the opportunity, I'd gobble a handful of pills like Thanksgiving turkey. I learned strategies to help quiet my need, remembered what could be lost in the binge.

*

I sold the condo. It was nice living relatively rent-free, but it was time for a fresh start. A real fresh start. I realized, in all my attempts to start over before, I had allowed the past to dictate my future. I no longer wanted to lean on convenience.

I used the proceeds to cover remaining medical and legal costs, then put the rest in the bank. Buying property was too permanent a decision to make when my life was still in transition. Instead, I found an inexpensive rental downtown, and it wasn't one of Frank's, either. I had to break away from both Dane's memory and Frank's assistance. My new place wasn't as traditional as the Smithwood house or as hip as the condo, but it had the perfect amount of space for us. Jake and me.

Frank agreed to joint custody. I no longer had to wait over a week to spend time with Jake. He stayed with me for four or five days at a time, like he used to. It gave us time to reconnect, and it gave Frank time to heal.

I knew Julie's death still haunted Frank, understandably so. I'd been in a similar predicament with Dane: I discovered the ugly truth too late. And then he was gone. At least I fought with Dane about his demons; Frank never had the opportunity to confront Julie.

Part of Frank's next chapter would involve selling the Smithwood house. He bought a remodeled home on Tellit Mountain. I knew he'd eventually move there; we always return to the places we're from, one way or another. Frank postponed the move until the end of the school year; Jake already had too much upheaval in his life. He could finish his semester at his familiar preschool before entering kindergarten at the private academy.

*

Frank invited me to stay Easter weekend with them at the Smithwood house. It would be our last celebration as a family in our old home. We spent the Saturday before dying eggs. The shades ranged from pastel to bright to neon.

"Mamma, how do we put pictures on them?" Jake asked, repeatedly dipping an egg into orange liquid.

"Decoupage?" I answered.

"Yeah. Let's do that," he said, his eyes bright and smile wide.

"You're really into decorating this year," Frank said, rustling Jake's hair with his hand.

"Mamma and I always make stuff, Daddy." He giggled, glowed in the light of two parents smiling in the same room. Jake had been visiting a therapist for the past several months and seemed to be adjusting.

"You have old magazines lying around?" I asked Frank.

"Upstairs," he said. "Where I always keep them."

The Southern man's library: a basket in the bathroom.

"I'll grab the supplies. Take these outside and they'll dry faster," I said to Jake, handing him the carton of colored eggs.

I went upstairs and entered our bedroom for the first time in ages. I wanted to stretch out on the bed and be immersed in familiarity. Blink and Jake would be a baby again and Frank would lightly rub the balls of my feet.

I went into the bathroom, overrun with male neglect. I grabbed a handful of magazines, shuffled them into a tight stack on the bed. I picked up one, thumbed through the pages, until I found a cologne sample and inhaled. Just like when a new edition arrived each month. I was almost back there. At that happy place where our story started.

A rogue paper jutted from the middle of the book. I pulled it out to crumple and throw away. It had already been cut. My son and his flair for crafts. Made me proud.

A fabrics ad. The images remained, only a few letters absent. An S. Maybe a G. A chill crept up my spine. *Julie tells me everything*, Frank had said. I sat down on the bed thinking and rethinking everything I knew. Everything I had learned.

Many minutes passed before Frank joined me.

"It's about to storm," he said. "We better hide the eggs we've already finished."

"You knew, didn't you?" I asked, staring at this familiar man for what felt like the first time.

"What?" he asked, confused.

"You knew Julie killed Dane," I said.

He stood in the doorway, his eyes narrowed.

I lifted the magazine.

"*STOP SEARCHING*," I said. "You sent me the note."

Frank sighed and leaned against the wall. I could tell he was breathing rapidly, trying helplessly to remain calm. "Julie could have accessed my magazines."

"Well, did she?" I asked, staring at him. I already knew the answer.

"No," he said. "I did it."

"Which means you knew all this time she killed Dane. When the police investigated me. The media trashed me." My hands started shaking, my anger swelling. "You took custody of Jake! The whole time you knew."

"I tried to protect you both," he said, his voice wavering.

"You covered up for her."

He didn't say anything.

Suddenly Brock's voice echoed through my mind: *People can't keep this stuff in isolation.* Julie remained under the radar because she had Frank. He kept her stable while the world around me deteriorated.

"How long have you known?" I asked. Like a distorted game show where the answer is revealed on cue, I knew. "That's where you went the night Dane died, isn't it?"

"She called while you were asleep. She was hysterical. I couldn't even understand her at first. She saw us through the window and went to tell Dane. She couldn't explain how it happened, but she shot him, and he died. Nothing could be done about it." He lowered his head in shame. "By the time she called, she'd already left the condo. She took his wallet and keys and the gun with her to make the scene look like a robbery gone wrong. We met in a parking lot and I tried to calm her down."

"You should have called the police," I said.

"Dane was not a good person," he said, trying to justify his decision. "I didn't want to ruin Julie's life."

"She was a murderer!"

"She wasn't," he argued. "She was a normal, happy girl in a bad situation. Because of us."

"You can't equate our having sex with committing murder."

"If she hadn't seen us, if she hadn't gone over there… none of this would have happened. I owed her. So I helped. I told her to ditch Dane's belongings and return to her apartment. Her family never even knew she left. She never told me she kept the gun."

"I lied about your whereabouts for eighteen months," I said. "I protected you."

"*I* didn't murder Dane," he defended himself, as though he was an upstanding citizen for not pulling the trigger.

"You were an accomplice all this time. You allowed her around Jake. You kept her in our lives. Did you marry her out of guilt?" None of it made sense. Frank couldn't forgive me for my mistakes, but he could forgive Julie. He helped her evade detection, even when the blame was shifted in my direction. "She tried to kill me, Frank!"

"I didn't understand how warped she was until I found out about Brock. When they showed me the parking lot footage at the station, I knew she was the only person who would have driven my car there. I knew she had gone off the rails. I wasn't sure what I was going to do about it," he said, clenching his fists. The more he spoke, the angrier he became. "I only wanted to talk with her first. Hear her side of the story. I had no way of knowing you were over there."

Frank claimed he was doing what he thought best, but I don't think even he was confident about the decisions he'd made. "What if she had killed me, Frank? What would you have done then?"

"She didn't, thank God. What happened with Dane was an accident. You told me he could be violent, and I assumed she reacted out of fear." He raised his hands, pleading with me to understand. "Brock was different. And you. She was instigating the violence. I wouldn't have let her get away with it."

I wanted to believe him. But Frank consistently did what was easy over what was right. "What you did is wrong," I said.

"You don't think I've learned to live with shame? With hurt?" he roared, then gained composure. "We can't change anything now. Dane is gone. Julie is gone. We have to accept what's happened."

"I'm not sure I can," I said, tears flowing. We're all capable of doing wrong when pushed. Dane and Julie's actions proved that. I'd certainly made mistakes, allowing Dane and the pills to trick me. But now I saw that Frank had tricked me, too. He was never the stable rock I had envisioned him to be. He was an imposter.

We were interrupted by a scraping door and the sound of little feet thumping up the stairs.

"Come on, guys," Jake said. His cheeks shone red from the spring heat, radiating adoration and ignorance. "Mamma, you been crying?"

"I'm fine, honey," I said, wiping my face. I smiled. "We'll hide the eggs in a minute."

Jake returned to the main level. We heard the backyard door close. Frank stood motionless, trying to swallow whatever emotion had bubbled to the surface.

"Are we going to be okay?" he asked.

Some days, I still don't know.

A LETTER FROM MIRANDA

Dear Reader,

Thank you for taking the time to read *Some Days Are Dark*. If you liked it and would like information about upcoming releases, sign up with the following link. Your email address will never be shared, and you can unsubscribe at any time:

www.bookouture.com/miranda-smith

Writing this book was a deeply personal process and, at times, very lonely. In reading this book, you are now on this publishing journey with me, and I thank you!

While *Some Days Are Dark* centers around a specific crime, I think it also touches on ordinary instances of cruelty: how we label one another without knowing the full story, how we allow the past to negatively shape our present and how we are sometimes quick to judge but slow to forgive.

Olivia's story has always been one of redemption. It demonstrates that even from the depths of personal failure, a person can rebound and reclaim his or her life. Although some days are dark, tomorrow is always brighter.

If you'd like to further discuss the novel, I'd love to connect! You can find me on Instagram, Facebook or my website. If you enjoyed *Some Days Are Dark*, I would be thrilled for you to leave a review on either Amazon or Goodreads. It only takes a few minutes and does wonders in helping readers discover my books for the first time.

Thank you again for your support!

All very best,
Miranda Smith

        🖥 mirandasmithwriter.com

        ⬛ MirandaSmithAuthor

        📷 @mirandasmithwriter

ACKNOWLEDGMENTS

There are several people I'd like to thank for their contribution in getting *Some Days Are Dark* into the hands of readers:

To my editor, Ruth Tross: thank you for pulling my manuscript out of the submissions pile and giving it a chance. You've always championed Olivia's story. Your input has created a better book and made me a better writer.

To everyone else at Bookouture: thank you for providing such a supportive place for authors. I'm grateful to join this dedicated and knowledgeable team.

John A. Bell, Judge Retired: thank you for speaking with me about the crime details in the book. Any mistakes or inaccuracies are entirely my own.

Mindy McGinnis: thank you for critiquing my manuscript and providing invaluable advice on how to improve it.

Carol: thank you for your support and readiness to watch the kids.

Seth: thank you for the photographs and for making me Twitter famous.

Whitney, Jennifer and Allison: thank you for reading chapters, juggling baby duty and providing various forms of support throughout the years. And thanks for the laughter.

Mom and Dad: thank you for everything. Your love has been the foundation for my personal and professional successes.

Chris: thank you for your patience and willingness to support my ambitions.

And to Harrison, Lucy and Christopher: while you three are my biggest distraction, you're also my greatest motivation. Big dreams and hard work are a winning combination. I love you.

Printed in Great Britain
by Amazon